Praise for Thomas M. Disch's
On Wings of Song

"Extraordinarily compelling. . . . The novel is a version of *1984*, an anti-utopia of the 21st century. . . . The vision has an authentic note of nightmare, and the questions posed are serious ones. The book's intellectual daring and sophistication are reminders of what fantasy can, at its best, bring to the novel."

—*The New Statesman*

"Tragic and funny, biting and sensitive, this brilliant novel should appeal to readers of mainstream novels as well as science fiction, both as entertainment and art."

—*Publishers Weekly*

"A free-falling talent—full of startling invention, humor, distancing surmise and many, many immediate pleasures."

—*Kirkus Reviews*

"Impressive and entertaining. . . . His narrative line remains vital and he writes clear, distinctive prose. The novel is often funny, sometimes witty, and the ironies are well pointed. *On Wings of Song* provides hours of good reading."

—*Library Journal*

On Wings of Song

Thomas M. Disch

CARROLL & GRAF PUBLISHERS
NEW YORK

On Wings of Song

Carroll & Graf Publishers
An Imprint of Avalon Publishing Group Inc.
161 William Street, 16th Floor
New York, NY 10038

First Carroll & Graf trade paperback edition 2003
First Carroll & Graf mass market edition 1988

Library of Congress Cataloging-in-Publication Data is available.

ISBN: 0-7867-1122-1

Printed in the United States of America
Distributed by Publishers Group West

For Charles Naylor

PART I

I

WHEN HE WAS five Daniel Weinreb's mother disappeared. Though, like his father, he chose to regard this as a personal affront, he soon came to prefer the life they led without her. She'd been a weepy sort of girl, given to long disconnected speeches and spells of stifled hatred for Daniel's father, some of which always spilled over onto Daniel. She was sixteen when she'd married, twenty-one when she vanished with her two suitcases, the sound system, and the silver flatware in a service for eight that had been their wedding present from her husband's grandmother, Adah Weinreb.

After the bankruptcy proceedings were over—they'd been going on for a good while even before this—Daniel's father, Abraham Weinreb, D.D.S., took him a thousand miles away to live in the town of Amesville, Iowa, which needed a dentist because their last one had died. They lived in an apartment over the clinic, where Daniel had his own room, not just a couch that made up into a bed. There were backyards and streets to play in, trees to climb, and mountains of snow all winter long. Children seemed more important in Amesville, and there were more of them. Except for breakfast, he ate most of his meals in a big cafeteria downtown, and they were much better than his mother had cooked. In almost every way it was a better life.

Nevertheless when he was cross or bored or sick in bed with a cold he told himself that he missed her. It seemed monstrous that he, who was such a success ingratiating himself with the mothers of his friends, should not have a mother of his own. He felt set apart. But even this had its positive side: apart might be above. At times it seemed so. For his mother's absence was not the matter-of-fact missingness of death, but a mystery that Daniel was always pondering. There was an undeniable prestige in being the son of a mystery and associated with such high drama. The absent Milly Weinreb became Daniel's symbol of all the wider possibilities of the world beyond Amesville, which even at age six and then age seven seemed much diminished from the great city he'd lived in before.

He knew, vaguely, the reason she had gone away. At least the reason his father had given to Grandmother Weinreb over the phone on the day it happened. It was because she wanted to learn to fly. Flying was wrong, but a lot of people did it anyhow. Not Abraham Weinreb, though, and not any of the other people in Amesville either because out here in Iowa it was against the law and people were concerned about it as part of the country's general decline.

Wrong as it surely was, Daniel did like to imagine his mother, shrunk down to just the size of a grown-up finger, flying across the wide expanse of snowy fields that *he* had flown over in the plane: flying on tiny, golden, whirring wings (back in New York he'd seen what fairies looked like on tv, though of course that was an artist's conception), flying all the way to Iowa just to secretly visit him.

He would be playing, for instance with his Erector set, and then he'd get an impulse to turn off the fans in all three rooms, and open the flue of the chimney. He imagined his mother sitting on the sooty bricks up at the top, waiting for hours for him to let her in the house, and then at last coming down the opened flue and fluttering about. She would sit watching him while he played, proud and at the same time woebegone because there was no way she could talk to him or even let him know that she existed. Maybe she might bring her fairy friends to visit too . . . a little troupe of them, perched on the bookshelves and the hanging plants, or clustered like moths about an electric light bulb.

And maybe they *were* there. Maybe it wasn't all imagination, since fairies are invisible. But if they were, then what he was doing was wrong, since people shouldn't let fairies into their houses. So he decided it was just himself, making up the story in his mind.

When he was nine Daniel Weinreb's mother reappeared. She had the good sense to telephone first, and since it was a Saturday when the girl was off and Daniel was handling the switchboard, he was the first to talk to her.

He answered the phone the way he always did, with "Good morning, Amesville Medical Arts Group."

An operator said there was a collect call from New York for Abraham Weinreb.

"I'm sorry," Daniel recited, "but he can't come to the phone now. He's with a patient. Could I take a message?"

The operator conferred with another voice Daniel could barely make out, a voice like the voice on a record when the speakers are off and someone else is listening with earphones.

When the operator asked him who he was, somehow he knew it must be his mother who was phoning. He answered that he was Abraham Weinreb's son. Another shorter conference ensued, and the operator asked if *he* would accept the call.

He said he would.

"Danny? Danny, is that you, love?" said a whinier voice than the operator's.

He wanted to say that no one ever called him Danny, but that seemed unfriendly. He limited himself to an equivocal Uh.

"This is your mother, Danny."

"Oh. Mother. Hi." She still didn't say anything. It was up to him entirely. "How are you?"

She laughed and that seemed to deepen her voice. "Oh, I could be worse." She paused, and added, "But not a lot. Where is your father, Danny? Can I talk to him?"

"He's doing a filling."

"Does he know I'm calling?"

"No, not yet."

"Well, would you *tell* him? Tell him it's Milly calling from New York."

He weighed the name on his tongue: "Milly."

"Right. Milly. Short for . . . do you know?"

He thought. "Millicent?"

"God almighty no. Mildred—isn't that bad enough? Doesn't he *ever* talk about me?"

He wasn't trying to avoid her question. It was just that his own seemed so much more important: "Are you coming *here*?"

"I don't know. It depends for one thing on whether Abe sends me the money. Do *you* want me to?"

Even though he wasn't sure, it seemed required of him to say that yes he did. But he'd hesitated, noticeably, so most of the credit for saying the right thing was lost. She knew he was being polite.

"Danny, why don't you go *tell* him I'm on the phone?" Her voice was whiney again.

Daniel obeyed. As he'd known he would be, his father was annoyed when Daniel appeared in the doorway. For a while he just stood there. He didn't want to say who it was out loud in front of the patient in the chair, a fat farmwoman who was getting a crown put on a left upper canine. He said, "There's a phonecall from New York."

His father still looked daggers. Did he understand?

"A woman," Daniel added significantly. "She's calling collect."

"You know better than to interrupt me, Daniel. Tell her to wait."

He went back to the switchboard. Another call was coming in. He put it on Hold quickly, then said to his mother: "I told him. He said to wait. He really can't stop in the middle."

"Well then, I'll wait."

"There's another call. I have to put you on Hold."

She laughed again. It was a pleasant laugh. He foresaw, though not in so many words, the necessity of keeping her in a good humor. Assuming that she came to Amesville. So, almost deliberately, he added a fond P.S.: "Gee, Mom, I hope it works out so you can come and live with us." He put her on Hold before she could reply.

Because the plane had come from New York there was a long wait for the passengers and their luggage to be cleared through the State Police Inspection Station. Daniel thought that several of the women who came through the white formica doors might be his mother, but when she finally did appear, all frazzled and frayed, the very last passenger to be processed, there was no mistaking her. She wasn't the mother he'd imagined over the years, but she was undoubtedly the one he'd tried and never quite managed to forget.

She was pretty but in the direction of vulnerability rather

than of zest and health, with big tired brown eyes and a tangled mass of horsetail hair that hung down over her shoulders as if it were meant to be a decoration. Her clothes were plain and pleasant but not warm enough for Iowa in the middle of October. She was no taller than an average eighth-grader and, except for big, bra-ed-up breasts, no more fleshed-out than the people you saw in advertisements for religion on tv. She'd let her nails grow weirdly long and she fluttered her fingers when she talked so you were always noticing. One arm was covered with dozens of bracelets of metal and plastic and wood that clinked and jangled all the time. To Daniel she seemed as bizarre as an exotic breed of dog, the kind that no one ever owns and you only see in books. People in Amesville would stare at her. The other people in the airport restaurant already were.

She was eating her hamburger with a knife and fork. Maybe (Daniel theorized) her long fingernails prevented her from picking it up by the bun. The fingernails were truly amazing, a spectacle. Even while she ate she never stopped talking, though nothing that she said was very informative. Obviously she was trying to make a good impression, on Daniel as well as his father. Just as obviously she was pissed off with the inspection she'd gone through. The police had confiscated a transistor radio and four cartons of cigarettes she hadn't had the cash to pay the Iowa Stamp Tax on. Daniel's father was able to get the cigarettes back for her but not the radio since it received stations in the prohibited frequency ranges.

In the car on the way back to Amesville his mother smoked and chattered and made lots of nervous not very funny jokes. She admired everything she saw in a tone of syrupy earnestness, as though Daniel and his father were personally responsible and must be praised for the whole of Iowa: the stubble of cornstalks in the fields, the barns and siloes, the light and the air. Then she'd forget herself for a moment and you could tell she really didn't mean a word of it. She seemed afraid.

His father started smoking the cigarettes too, though it was something he never did otherwise. The rented car filled with smoke and Daniel began to feel sick. He focused his

13

attention on the odometer's steady whittling away of the distance left to go to get to Amesville.

Next morning was Saturday and Daniel had to be up at six a.m. to attend a Young Iowa Rally in Otto Hassler Park. By the time he was back home, at noon, Milly had been shaped up into a fair approximation of an Amesville house-wife. Except for her undersize stature she might have stepped right out of a ladies' clothing display in Burns and McCauley's window: a neat practical green blouse speckled with neat practical white daisies, a knee-length skirt with wavy three-inch horizontal bands of violet and lime, with matching heavy-duty hose. Her fingernails were clipped to an ordinary length and her hair was braided and wound around into a kind of cap like Daniel's fourth-grade teach-er's (he was in fifth grade now), Mrs Boismortier. She was wearing just one of yesterday's bracelets, a plastic one matching the green in her skirt.

"Well?" she asked him, striking a pose that made her look more than ever like a plaster mannikin.

He felt dismayed all over again. His hamstrings were trembly from the calisthenics in the park, and he collapsed on the sofa hoping to cover his reaction with a show of exhaustion.

"It's that bad?"

"No, I was only. . . ." He decided to be honest, and then decided against it. "I liked you the way you were." Which was half the truth.

"Aren't you the proper little gentleman!" She laughed.

"Really."

"It's sweet of you to say so, dear heart, but Abe made it quite clear that the old me just would not do. And he's right, it wouldn't. I can be realistic. So—" She struck another shop-window pose, arms lifted in a vaguely defensive gesture. "—What I want to know is: will the new me do?"

He laughed. "For sure, for sure."

"Seriously," she insisted, in a tone he could not believe was at all serious. It was as though just by doing any ord-inary thing she parodied it, whether she wanted to or not.

He tried to consider her freshly, as though he'd never seen

her the way she'd arrived. "As far as what you're wearing and all, you look just fine. But that won't make you . . ." He blushed. ". . . Invisible. I mean. . . ."

"Yes?" She crinkled her painted eyebrows.

"I mean, people are curious, especially about Easterners. Already this morning kids had heard and they were asking me."

"What about, exactly?"

"Oh, what you look like, how you talk. They see things on television and they think they're true."

"And what did you tell them?"

"I said they could wait and see for themselves."

"Well, don't worry, Danny—when they do see me I'll look so ordinary they'll lose all their faith in tv. I didn't come here without a good idea of what I'd be getting into. We've got tv in the East too, you know, and the Farm Belt gets its share of attention."

"They say we're very conformist, don't they?"

"Yes, that's certainly one thing they say."

"So why did you want to come here? I mean, aside from us."

"Why? I want a nice, comfortable, safe, prosperous life, and if conformity's the price I've got to pay, so be it. Wherever you are, you know, you're conforming to something."

She held out her hands in front of her, as though considering the pared-down nails. When she started talking again it was in a tone of unquestionable seriousness. "Last night I told your father I'd go out and get a job to help him take up his indenture a little faster. It would actually be a joy for me to work. But he said no, that wouldn't look right. That's my job, looking right. So I'll be a nice little homebody and crochet the world's largest potholder. Or *whatever* homebodies do here. I'll do it and by damn I'll look right!"

She plunked down in an armchair and lit a cigarette. Daniel wondered if she knew that most Amesville housewives didn't smoke, and especially not in public. And then he thought: being with him wasn't the same as being in public. He was her son!

"Mother . . . could I ask you a question?"

"Certainly, so long as I don't have to answer it."

"Can you fly?"

"No." She inhaled shallowly and let the smoke spill out of her open mouth. "No, I tried to but I never had the knack. Some people never do learn, no matter how hard they try."

"But you wanted to."

"Only a fool would deny wanting to. I *knew* people who flew, and from the way they talked about it. . . ." She rolled back her eyes and pouted her bright red lips, as if to say, *Pure heaven!*

"At school there was a special lecture in the gym last year, an authority from the government, and *he* said it's all in your head. You just *think* you're flying but it's a kind of dream."

"That's propaganda. *They* don't believe it. If they did they wouldn't be so afraid of fairies. There wouldn't be fans whirling everywhere you went."

"It's real then?"

"As real as the two of us sitting here. Does that answer your question?"

"Yeah. I guess so." He decided to wait till later on to ask what her friends had said it felt like.

"Good. Then remember this: you must never, never talk about this to anyone else. I don't even want you to talk about it again to me. Anything to do with flying, anything at all. Has your father explained to you about sex?"

Daniel nodded.

"About fucking?"

"Uh . . . here in Iowa . . . you don't ever. . . ."

"You don't talk about it, right?"

"Well, kids don't talk about it with grown-ups."

"Flying's just the same. We don't talk about it. Ever. Except to say that it's very very wrong, and that people wicked enough to do it deserve every terrible thing that happens to them."

"Is that what you believe?"

"Never mind 'believe'. What I'm *saying* now is the official Undergod truth. Flying is wrong. Say that."

"Flying is wrong."

She pushed herself up out of the armchair and came over

16

and kissed him on the cheek. "You and I," she said with a wink, "are two of a kind. And we're going to get along."

2

AT THE AGE of eleven Daniel developed a passion for ghosts; also vampires, werewolves, mutated insects, and alien invaders. At the same time and mostly because they shared an appetite for the monstrous, he fell in love with Eugene Mueller, the younger son of Roy Mueller, a farm equipment dealer who'd been the mayor of Amesville until just two years ago. The Muellers lived in the biggest and (they said) oldest house on Amesville's prestigious Linden Drive. A total of five of the town's mayors and police chiefs had lived in that house, and three of those five had been Muellers. In the attic of the Muellers' house, among many other forms of junk, were a great many boxes of old books, mostly unreadable relics of the irrelevant past—books about dieting and being successful, the multi-volume memoirs of a dead president, textbooks for French, home ec., accounting, and yard upon yard of *Reader's Digest* Condensed Books. Buried, however, in the deepest level of these cast-off ideas, Eugene Mueller had discovered an entire carton filled with paperback collections of supernatural tales, tales of an artfulness and awfulness surpassing any known to him from the oral traditions of summer camp and the *Register* delivery office.

Eugene would sneak single volumes down to his room hidden in his underwear and read them there by candlelight late at night. The books were like ghosts themselves, their margins crumbling to dust at his fingers' touch. He'd read each story once quickly and, if it was one he liked, a second time, lingeringly. Then, with its topoi fresh in his memory, he would retell the story to the news-carriers at the *Register* office while they waited for the truck to arrive with the papers. Sometimes he would draw it out over several days to increase the suspense.

Daniel also had a paper route, though not as lucrative a one as the ex-Mayor's son. He listened to Eugene Mueller's

18

stories with the ravished reverence of a disciple. They—and their presumed author—became an emotional necessity to him. Months ago he'd exhausted the school library's meager resources—a ragged copy of thirteen tales by Poe and bowdlerized editions of *Frankenstein* and *The War of the Worlds*. Once he'd bicycled to Fort Dodge and back, forty miles each way, to see a double feature of old black-and-white horror movies. It was terrible loving something so inaccessible, and all the more wonderful, therefore, when the long drought came to an end. Even when Eugene confessed, privately, to having practised on his friend's credulity and had shown him his store of treasures, even then Daniel went on thinking of him as a superior person, set apart from other seventh and eighth graders, possibly even a genius.

Daniel became a frequent overnight guest at the Mueller home. He ate with Eugene's family at their dinner table, even times when his father was there. With all of them Daniel was charming, but he only came alive when he was alone with Eugene—either in the attic, reading and creating their own artless Grand Guignol, or in Eugene's room, playing with the great arsenal of his toys and games.

In his own way he was as bad—that is, as good—a social climber as his mother.

Three days before he got his certificate for passing seventh grade, Daniel received third prize in a statewide contest sponsored by the Kiwanis (a pair of front row seats at a Hawkeye game of his choosing) for his essay on the topic, 'Good Sports Makes Good Citizens'. He read the essay aloud at a school assembly and everyone had to clap until Mr Cameron, the Principal, held up his hand. Then Mr Cameron gave him a book of speeches by Herbert Hoover, who was born in West Branch. Mr Cameron said that some day, when the country got back on its feet again, he wouldn't be surprised to see another Iowan occupying the White House. Daniel supposed that Mr Cameron was referring to him and felt a brief intense ache of gratitude.

On that same day the Weinrebs moved to their new home on Chickasaw Avenue, which was reckoned (by those who lived there) to be nearly as nice a neighborhood as Linden Drive. It was a smallish gray clapboard ranch-style house with two bedrooms. Inevitably the second bedroom fell to the twins, Aurelia and Cecelia, and Daniel was relegated to the room in the basement. Despite its gloom and the damp cinder-block walls he decided it was to be preferred to the twins' room, being larger and so private that it could boast its own entrance onto the driveway.

The last owner of the house had tried to make ends meet (and failed, apparently) by renting the basement room to a family of Italian refugees. Think of it: four people living in this one room, with two basement windows for light, and a sink with only a cold water tap!

Daniel kept the laminated nameplate with their name on it: Bosola. Often late at night, alone in his room, he tried to imagine the sort of life the Bosolas had led hemmed in by these four gray walls. His mother said they'd probably been happier, which was her way of ignoring any otherwise incontrovertible misery. No one in the neighborhood knew what had become of them. Maybe they were still in Amesville. A lot of Italians lived in trailer courts on the outskirts of town and worked for Ralston-Purina.

Daniel's father was a refugee too, though his case was different from most. His mother had been American, his father a native-born Israeli. He'd grown up on a kibbutz four miles from the Syrian border, and gone to the University in Tel Aviv, majoring in chemistry. When he was twenty his maternal grandparents offered to put him through dental school if he would come and live with them in Queens. A providential kindness, for two weeks after he left for the States the rockets which destroyed most of Tel Aviv were launched. On his twenty-first birthday he had the choice of which country's citizen he wanted to be. At that point it couldn't really be called a choice. He pledged his allegiance to the United States of America and to the Republic for which it stood, and changed his name from Shazar to Weinreb in deference to his grandfather and the bill he was footing at N.Y.U. He got through dental school and joined the elder Weinreb's faltering practice in Elmhurst, which went on faltering for twelve more years. The one action in his whole life he had seemed to undertake of his own spontaneous and uncoerced will was at age thirty-nine to marry sixteen-year-old Milly Baer, who had come to him with an impacted wisdom tooth. As Milly would often later insist, in her fits of reminiscence, even that choice had not been, in the final analysis, his.

Daniel was never able to account satisfactorily for the fact that he didn't like his father. Because he wasn't as important or as well-to-do as Roy Mueller? No, for Daniel's feeling, or lack of it, went back before the time he'd become aware of his father's limitations in these respects. Because he was a refugee? Specifically, a Jewish refugee? No, for if anything he wasn't sufficiently a Jewish refugee. Daniel was still young enough to take a romantic view of hardship, and to his way of thinking the Bosolas (as he imagined them) were a much better, more heroic sort than any Weinrebs whatsoever. Then why?

Because—and this possibly was the real reason, or one of of them—he sensed that his father, like every other father, expected him and, what was worse, wanted him to follow the same career that he'd been sinking in throughout his life. He wanted Daniel to become a dentist.

It wasn't enough for Daniel to insist that *he* didn't want to be one. He had to find something he *did* want to be. And he couldn't. Not that it made a great deal of difference, yet. He was young, he had time. But even so—he didn't like thinking about it.

The house of Mrs Boismortier, his old fourth-grade teacher, was the very last stop on Daniel's route. She was an older woman, forty or fifty years old, and fat, like a lot of other women her age in Amesville. Her name was pronounced Boys-More-Teer. No one that Daniel had ever talked to could remember a time when there had been a Mr Boismortier, but there must have been one once in order for her to be a Mrs.

Daniel remembered her as a careful rather than an inspired teacher, content to return eternally to the verities of spelling, grammar, and long division rather than to call down the lightning of a new idea. She would never read them stories, for instance, or talk about things from her own life. Her only livelier moments were on Fridays when for an hour at the end of the day she led her class in singing. They always started with the National Anthem and ended with 'Song of

Iowa'. Daniel's three favorite songs in their songbook had been 'Santa Lucia', 'Old Black Joe', and 'Anchors Aweigh'. Most teachers shied away from teaching music in the Friday free periods because it was controversial, but whenever the subject came up, either at a P.T.A. meeting or in class discussions, Mrs Boismortier simply declared that any country whose schoolchildren could not do justice to their own National Anthem was a country in deep trouble, and how could you argue with that? But for all her talk of God and Country, it was obvious to the children in her classes that she taught them singing because she enjoyed it herself. In every song her voice was loudest and loveliest, and no matter what kind of singer you might be yourself it was a pleasure to sing along because it was her voice you heard, not your own.

Nevertheless, over the years Mrs Boismortier had made enemies by insisting on teaching music, especially among Undergoders, who were very strong in this part of Iowa, and very outspoken and sure of themselves. If you could believe the *Register*, they practically ran Iowa, and they'd been even more powerful in the days just after the defeat of the national Anti-Flight Amendment, when they were able to get the State Legislature to pass a law prohibiting all secular musical performances, live or recorded. Three days after Governor Brewster vetoed this law his only daughter was shot at and though it was never proven that her would-be killer had been an Undergoder the crime did turn a lot of sympathizers away. Those days were over, and the worst that Mrs Boismortier had to worry about now was the occasional broken window or dead cat strung up on her front porch. Once when Daniel was delivering her paper he found a two-inch hole drilled into the middle of the front door. At first he supposed it was for the paper, and then he realized it was meant to be a fairy-hole. As a sign of his solidarity Daniel made a tight cylinder of the paper and forced it into the hole, as if that is what it was there for. At school the next day Mrs Boismortier went out of her way to thank him, and instead of repairing the hole she enlarged it and covered it with a metal plate that could be slipped to the side, thereby making it officially a slot for the *Register*.

That had been the beginning of the special relationship

between Daniel and Mrs Boismortier. Often on the coldest winter nights she would waylay him when he brought the paper and have him come into her living room for a hot cup of something she made from corn starch. "Embargo cocoa", she called it. There were either books or pictures on all the walls, including a very careful watercolor of the First Baptist Church and a store next to it (where there wasn't any now) called A. & P. Also, right in plain sight, with shelves of records above it up to the ceiling, was a stereo phonograph. There wasn't anything illegal about that, strictly speaking, but most people who had records—the Muellers, for instance—kept them out of sight and, usually, locked up. It seemed very gutsy, considering the way she was harassed in general.

As his fingers and ears grew warmer and started tingling, Mrs Boismortier would ask him questions. Somehow she'd learned that he liked ghost stories, and she would recommend titles that he could ask his mother to take out for him from the adult section of the library. Sometimes these were a little too plodding and high-toned for his taste but twice at least she hit the nail on the head. She almost never talked about herself, which seemed unusual in someone basically so talkative.

Gradually, as he began to realize that despite her reticence and her fat incapable body Mrs Boismortier was a definite human being, Daniel began to grow curious. Mostly about the music. He knew that music was not something you talked about with other people, but it was hard not to think about, especially with those shelves of records looming down, like a microfilm library of all the sins in the world. Not that music was wrong, exactly. But where there's smoke, as they say. After all, it was music that helped people fly. Not listening to music, of course, but doing it. And anything associated with flying was irresistibly interesting.

And so, one snowy afternoon in November, after he'd accepted his cup of embargo cocoa, he screwed up his courage and asked if he might be allowed hear one of her records.

"Why surely, Daniel, what record would you like to hear?"

The only pieces of music he knew by name were the songs in the school's songbook. He was certain, just because they *were* in the songbook, that those weren't the kinds of music that people used to fly.

"I don't know," he admitted. "Something that *you* like."

"Well, here's something I listened to last night, and it seemed quite splendid, though it may not appeal to you at all. A string quartet, by Mozart." Ever so tenderly, as if the record were a living thing, she slipped it from its cardboard sleeve and placed it on the turntable.

He braced his mind against some unimaginable shock, but the sounds that issued from the speakers were dull and innocuous—wheezings and whinings, groanings and grindings that continued interminably without getting anywhere. Once or twice out of the murk he could hear melodies begin to get started but then they'd sink back into the basic diddle-diddle-diddle of the thing before you could start to enjoy them. On and on and on, sometimes faster, sometimes slower, but all of a dullness and drabness uniform as housepaint. Even so, you couldn't just say thank you, that was enough, not while Mrs Boismortier was swaying her head back and forth and smiling in a faraway way, as if this really were some incredible mystic revelation. So he stared at the record revolving on the turntable and sweated it out to the end. Then he thanked Mrs Boismortier and trudged home through the snow feeling betrayed, disillusioned and amazed.

That *couldn't* be all there was to it. It just could not. She was hiding something. There was a secret.

That winter, in the first week of the new year, there was a national crisis. Of course if you could believe the *Register* the nation was always having crises, but they seldom impinged on Iowa. There had been a small uproar once when the Federal Government threatened to send in agents to collect the twelve per cent luxury tax on meat, but before a real confrontation could develop the Supreme Court declared Iowa to have been right all along in maintaining that meats, except for ham and sausages, were 'unprocessed' and so not taxable, at least in Iowa. Another time there had been a riot in Davenport concerning which Daniel only remembered that the *Register* printed an unusual number of photos, all showing the State Police in firm control. With these two exceptions life had gone along from day to day

24

without being affected by the news. What happened in January was that unidentified terrorists blew up the Alaska pipeline. Despite precautions this had happened many times before, and there was supposed to be a foolproof system for shutting down the flow, patching up the damage, and getting back to normal before there were major repercussions. This time, though, several miles of line were taken out by bombs that went off at neat six hundred yard intervals. According to the *Register* this meant that the bombs must have traveled *inside* the giant pipes, with the oil, and there were diagrams showing why this was impossible. Fairies were blamed, but so were, variously, Iran, Panama, several sorts of terrorists, and the League of Women Voters.

How this affected Iowa was very simple: there was no fuel. Every conceivable form of leverage and legal blackmail was used to wangle concessions for the Farm Belt states, but the fuel really wasn't there. Now they were going to have a taste of what winter rationing was like for the unfortunates who lived in less affluent parts of the country.

The taste was bitter. The winter's cold crept into stores and schools and houses, into the food you ate and the water you bathed in, into your every bone and thought. The Weinrebs camped in their own living room and kitchen to squeeze as much warmth as possible from the remaining liters of fuel in the tank. After eight p.m. there was no electricity so you couldn't even read or watch tv to make the freezing hours pass a little faster. Daniel would sit with his parents in the dark and silent room, unmoving, unable to sleep, hoarding the warmth of his sweaters and blankets. The boredom became a worse torment than the cold. Nine-thirty was bedtime. He slept between his two sisters and began to smell of their piss.

Sometimes he would be allowed to visit Eugene and if he were lucky he might be asked to spend the night. The Muellers' house was noticeably warmer. For one thing, they had a fireplace and through the early evening there would always be a fire going. They used the books in the attic as fuel (with Daniel's help Eugene was able to spirit away their horror stories), as well as unwanted sticks of furniture. Mr Mueller also had a source (Daniel suspected) of bootleg fuel.

The *Register* had temporarily suspended publication for

the duration of the crisis, so that at least he didn't have to freeze his ass off delivering papers. The world seemed different without news. Daniel hadn't supposed, till now, that he was interested in the official world represented by the *Register*, the world of strikes and settlements, debates and issues, Republicans and Democrats. He would have been hard-pressed to say what most of the headlines he'd looked at were about, but now that there weren't any it was as though civilization had ground to a halt, like some old Chevy that no one could get started, as though winter had overtaken not only nature but history as well.

In March, with life beginning to look almost ordinary again, Daniel's father came down with pneumonia. The Iowa winters had always been hard for him. He got through them by pumping himself full of antihistamines. Finally, like a tooth that's been drilled and filled until there's nothing left of it, his health collapsed. He'd gone into the office feverish and had to let his nurse finish the draining of a root-canal when he couldn't keep his hands from shaking. Against her employer's protests the nurse called in Dr Caskey from down the hall. Caskey, after examining his colleague, wrote out an admission order to the hospital in Fort Dodge.

Through the whole crisis hospitals were the one place you could be warm, and Milly, Daniel and the twins would have basked at Abraham's bedside every day from the start of visiting hours till the nurses threw them out—if only Fort Dodge hadn't been so far away. As it was, they wouldn't have seen him at all if it hadn't been for Roy Mueller, who drove in to Fort Dodge in his pick-up two or three times a week and always had room for either Daniel or Milly, though not for both at once.

There wasn't a great deal of communication at the best of times between Daniel and his father. Abraham Weinreb was fifty-two now and he looked, with his fringe of gray hair and the loose flesh wrinkling on his face, like someone living on Social Security. Since coming to the hospital he had developed a strain of lachrymose seriousness that made Daniel more than usually uneasy when they were together. One windy Saturday during the first real thaw of the year Abraham took a New Testament from the metal night-table by his bed and asked Daniel to read aloud to him from the beginning of John. All the while he read Daniel kept worrying whether his father were developing into some kind of religious fanatic, and when he told Milly about it that night she was even more alarmed. They were both certain he was dying.

The Weinrebs were church-goers as a matter of course. No one who earned more than a certain amount of money in Amesville was so impolitic as not to be. But they went to the Congregationalist Church, which was generally recognized as the most lukewarm and temporizing of the town's churches. The Congregationalist God was the God commemorated on the coins and dollar bills that went into the collection baskets, a God who made no other demands of his worshippers than that they waste a certain amount of cash and time each Sunday on his behalf. One could have met a better class of people by being Episcopalian but then one stood the risk of being snubbed. The real aristocracy of Iowa, the farmers, were Undergoders—Lutherans, Baptists, Methodists—but it was impossible to *pretend* to be an Undergoder since it involved giving up almost anything you might enjoy—not just music, but tv and most books and even talking with anyone who wasn't another Undergoder. Besides, the farmers lumped all the townspeople together with the great unregenerate mass of agitators, middlemen, and the unemployed that comprised the rest of the country, so it didn't do much good even for those who tried to pretend.

Milly and Daniel needn't have worried. Abraham did not became an Undergoder, and after a few failed dialogues he didn't even try to talk about whatever it was that had got him going on the subject of Jesus. The only difference in his behavior after he came back from Fort Dodge was that he seemed to have lost some of his old confidence and appetite for the jokes and trivia of day-to-day life that had kept conversation alive at the dinner table. It was as though his recent brush with death had made every ordinary food taste rotten to him.

Daniel avoided him more than ever. His father seemed either not to notice or not to mind.

The *Register* never did go back into business, even after

the pipeline was functional and the President had assured the whole country that the emergency was over. Its circulation had been dwindling for a long time, advertising revenues were down to a record low, and even at the current newstand price of one buck ($5.50 a week for subscribers) it could no longer survive. Furthermore, it had become increasingly easy anywhere in Iowa to get copies of the *Star-Tribune*. Though its editorials were outspokenly against flying *per se*, the *Star-Tribune* ran ads for flight apparatus and its news stories often shed a well-nigh roseate light on various self-confessed fairies, especially in the media. The ads by themselves were enough to make the Minneapolis paper illegal in Iowa, but the police didn't seem to be interested in cracking down on the two taverns that sold smuggled-in copies, despite recurrent anonymous denunciations (phoned in by *Register* delivery boys) to the Amesville Sheriff's office and the State Police as well. Apparently the paper's seventy-cent cover price included a percentage for pay-offs.

The demise of the *Register* came at a bad time for Daniel. Over and above his father's theoretical objections to allowances for teenagers (which Daniel had lately become) the money just wasn't there. Though he had at last taken up his indentures and was no longer in debt to the county, Abraham Weinreb did have to meet stiff monthly payments on the house, and now there was the hospital's bills to settle. What's more, he was under strict orders to cut back on his work-load, so there was significantly less money coming in.

Daniel stewed over the dilemma for the better part of a month, while the daily demands of friendship and ostentation ate up the little money he'd saved against the day, next July, when Young Iowa was to go camping in the Black Hills of South Dakota. Then he took the initiative and went to speak to Heinie Youngermann at the Sportsman's Rendezvous, one of the taverns that sold the *Star-Tribune*. Not only was Daniel able to secure a route for himself, but he was put in charge of the entire delivery operation (with a two per cent rake-off). Admittedly, there weren't as many subscribers as there had been for the above-board *Register*, but the per-copy profit was as good, and by making each route a little larger each of the boys stood to earn as much as he used to, while Daniel, with that beautiful two per cent, was pulling down a weekly income of nearly fifty dollars, which was as much as a lot of grown-ups got at full-time jobs. His friend Eugene Mueller continued to deliver in the Linden Drive section of town, virtually guaranteeing that the police would not interfere.

Besides the basic good news of being flush, it was spring. Lawns were turning green before the rains had washed away the last impacted traces of the snow. The main street was alive with pushcarts and bicycles. Suddenly it was Central Daylight Time and the sun stayed up till seven-thirty. Milly's face went from sallow to rosy to tan from her stints of backyard gardening. She acted happier than he could ever remember. Even the twins seemed interesting and agreeable now that he no longer had to be their bed-warmer. They'd learned to talk. In (as Daniel had quipped) a manner of speaking. Buds swelled on branches, clouds scudded through the sky, robins appeared out of nowhere. It truly was spring.

One Sunday for the sheer hell of it Daniel decided to ride his bicycle out along County Road B to where a schoolfriend of his lived, Geraldine McCarthy, in the village of Unity, a round trip of fourteen miles. In the fields on either side of the road the new cornplants were springing up through the black Iowa soil. The cool air rippled through his cotton shirt as if on purpose to share its growing excitement.

Halfway to Unity he stopped pedaling, overcome with a sense that he was an incredibly important person. The future, which usually he never gave much thought to, became as intensely real as the sky overhead, which was sliced in two neat pieces by the vapor trail of a jet. The feeling became so powerful it almost got frightening. He knew, with an absoluteness of knowing that he would never doubt for many years, that someday the whole world would know who he was and honor him. How and why remained a mystery.

After the vision had departed he lay down in the young weeds by the side of the road and watched the clouds massing at the horizon. How strange, how fortunate, and how unlikely to be Daniel Weinreb, in this small town in Iowa, and to have such splendors in store.

3

GENERAL ROBERTA DONNELLY, the Republican candidate for President, was going to be giving a major speech at a Fight Against Flight Rally in Minneapolis, according to the *Star-Tribune*, and Daniel and Eugene decided to go and hear her and even get her autograph if they could. They'd have a real adventure for a change instead of just going off into the Muellers' attic or the Weinrebs' basement and acting one out. In any case they were getting too old for that sort of thing. Eugene was fifteen, Daniel fourteen (though of the two he seemed the older, being so much hairier everywhere it counted).

There was no way they could let their parents know what they were planning. Setting off for Des Moines on their own would have been gently discouraged and maybe eventually allowed, but Minneapolis was as unthinkable a destination as Peking or Las Vegas. Never mind that the reason for their going there was to see General Donnelly, as true-blue and red-blooded a motive as any Undergoder could have asked for. For all right-thinking Iowans the Twin Cities were Sodom and Gomorrah. (On the other hand, as right-thinking Minnesotans liked to point out, what had happened there would have happened in Iowa too, if only six per cent more voters had swung the other way.) It was scary—but also, for that very reason, exciting—to think of going across the border, and there comes a time in your life when you have to do something that is scary in this particular way. No one else would ever need to know about it, except Jerry Larsen, who had agreed to take over both their routes for the two afternoons they meant to be away.

Having told their parents they were going camping and skillfully avoided saying where, they rode their bikes north as far as U.S.18, where they folded them up and hid them inside a storm culvert under the road. They struck luck

with their very first ride, an empty semi returning to Albert
Lea. It smelled of pigshit, even up in the cab with the
driver, but that simply became the special smell of their
adventure. They got so friendly talking with the driver that
they considered asking him to say that they were all together, but that seemed an unnecessary complication to the
plan they'd already made. When they reached the border
Eugene only had to mention his father's name to the Cus-
toms Inspector and they were across.

The unspoken understanding was that they were on
their way to see the latest double-feature at the Star-Lite
Drive-In outside of Albert Lea. Flying was far from being
the only forbidden fruit available in Minnesota. Pornography was also an attraction, and—in the eyes of most
Iowans—a much more real one. (It was chiefly on account
of its ads for border drive-ins that the *Star-Tribune* was
banned in neighboring Farm Belt states.) Eugene and
Daniel were doubtless a little young to be sneaking across
the border to the Star-Lite, but no one was about to make
a fuss over Roy Mueller's son, since both Roy himself and
his older son Carl were both such frequent visitors at this
particular checkpoint. Sexual precocity has always been
one of the prerogatives—if not indeed a solemn duty—of
the ruling class.

From Albert Lea it was eighty miles due north to Minneapolis. They went in a Greyhound bus without even bothering to try and hitch. The fields you could see from the
bus window seemed no different from equivalent fields in
Iowa, and even when they hit the outskirts of the city it
was distressingly like the outskirts of Des Moines—patches
of ramshackle slums alternating with smaller well-secured
stretches of suburban affluence, with the occasional shopping mall and service station proclaiming their triumph with
the giant letters of their names revolving on high poles.
There was possibly a little more traffic than there would
have been outside Des Moines, but that may have been on
account of the Rally. Everywhere you went—on lawns, in
store windows, stuck to the sides of buildings—were posters
announcing the Rally and urging the enactment of the
Twenty-Eighth Amendment. It was hard to believe, when
there were obviously so many million people behind it, that

31

the Amendment could ever be defeated but it had been, twice.

Downtown Minneapolis was an amazement of urbanity: its colossal buildings, its sumptuous stores, its swarming streets, the sheer noise, and then, beyond these ascertainable realities, the existence, surmised but wholly probable, of fairies swooping and darting through the glass-and-stone canyons, flitting above the trafficked streets, lighting in flocks on the carved façades of monolithic banks, then spiraling larklike into the azures of mid-afternoon, like a vastation of bright invisible locusts that fed not on the leaves of trees or on the potted flowers decorating the Mall but on the thoughts, the minds, the souls of all these calm pedestrians. If indeed they did. If indeed they were there at all.

The Rally was to be at eight o'clock, which gave them another good five hours to kill. Eugene suggested that they see a movie. Daniel was amenable but he didn't want to be the one to suggest which one, since they both knew, from the ads that had been appearing for months in the *Star-Tribune*, what it would have to be. They asked the way to Hennepin Avenue, along which all the movie-houses clustered, and there on the marquee of the World, spelled out in electric letters big as table lamps, was the unacknowledged golden fleece of their questing: *not* General Donnelly, not for a moment, but the last legendary musical of the great Betti Bailey, *Gold-Diggers of 1984.*

The movie had a considerable effect on Daniel, then and thereafter. Even if the movie hadn't, the World would have, being so grand and grave, a temple fit for the most solemn initiations. They found seats at the front of the theater and waited while wild sourceless music swelled about them.

This, then, was what it was all about. This, when it issued from within you, was the liberating power that all other powers feared and wished to extirpate: song. It seemed to Daniel that he could feel the music in the most secret recesses of his body, an ethereal surgeon that would rip his soul free from its crippling flesh. He wanted to surrender himself to it utterly, to become a mere magnificence of resonating air. Yet at the same time he wanted to rush back to the usher with the handsome gold braid hat and ask him what this music was called so he could buy the cassette for himself and possess it forever. How terrible that each new rapture should be a farewell! That it could only exist by being taken from him!

Then the lights dimmed, motors parted the shimmering curtains on the stage, and the movie began. The very first sight of Betti Bailey extinguished every thought of the music's ravishments. She was the spitting image of his mother—not as she was now but as he first had seen her: the fingernails, the bra-ed-up breasts and mane of hair, the crisp ellipses drawn above the eyes, the lips that seemed to have been freshly dipped in blood. He had forgotten the impact of that meeting, the embarrassment. The horror. He wished Eugene weren't sitting by him, seeing this.

And yet you had to admit that she—Betti Bailey—was beautiful. In even, strangest of all, an ordinary way.

In the story she was a prostitute who worked in a brothel in St Louis that was only for policemen. She didn't like being a prostitute though and dreamed of being a great singer. In her dreams she *was* a great singer, the kind that made the whole audience in the movie theater forget she was only a shadow moving on a screen and applaud her along with the audiences of the dream. But in real life, in the brothel's big red bathtub, for instance, or the one time she went walking through the ruins of a Botanical Garden with the interesting stranger (played by Jackson Florentine), her voice was all wobbly and rasping. People who listened couldn't help cringing, even Jackson Florentine, who (it turned out) was a sex maniac being hunted by the police. By the time you found that out he was already working at the brothel, since it was one of the few places people weren't bothered about their ID. He did a comic tap dance in black face with a chorus line of real life black cops, which led into the big production number of the show, 'March of the Businessmen'. At the end of the movie the two lovers hooked into a flight apparatus and took off from their bodies for an even bigger production number, an aerial ballet representing their flight north to the icebergs of Baffin Island. The special effects were so good you couldn't help but believe the dancers weren't verily fairies, especially Betti Bailey, and it certainly added to one's sense of its gospel truth to know that shortly after making *Gold-Diggers* Betti Bailey had done the same thing herself—hooked in and taken off, never to return. Her body was still curled up in a foetal ball in some L.A. hospital and God only knew where the rest of her was—burning up inside the sun or whirling around the rings of Saturn, anything was possible. It did seem a pity that she had never come back just long enough to make another movie like *Gold-Diggers*, at the end of which the police found the bodies of the lovers hooked up into the apparatus and machine-gunned them with the most vivid and painstaking cinematic detail. There wasn't a dry eye in the theater when the lights came on again.

Daniel wanted to stay and hear the music that was starting up again. Eugene needed to go to the toilet. They agreed to meet in the lobby when the music was over. There was still plenty of time to get to the Donnelly Rally.

Coming on top of the movie the music no longer seemed so impressive, and Daniel decided that his time in Minneapolis was too precious to bother repeating any experience, however sublime. Eugene wasn't in the lobby, so he went downstairs to the Men's Room. Eugene wasn't there either, unless he was inside the one locked stall. Daniel bent down to look under the door and saw not one pair but two pairs of shoes. He was shocked silly but at the same time a little gratified, as though he'd just scored a point for having seen another major sight of the big city. In Iowa people did not do such things, or if they did and were found out, they were sent away to prison. And rightly so, Daniel thought, making a hasty exit from the Men's Room.

He wondered whether the same thing had been going on when Eugene had been down here. And if so, what he'd thought of it. And whether he dared to ask.

The problem never arose. Daniel waited five, ten, fifteen minutes in the lobby and still no sign of Eugene. He went up to the front of the theater as the credits for *Gold-Diggers* came on and stood in the flickering dark scanning the faces in the audience. Eugene was not there.

He didn't know if something awful and typically urban had happened to his friend—a mugging, a rape—or if

34

some whim had taken him and he'd gone off on his own. To do what? In any case there seemed no point in waiting around the World, where the usher was obviously becoming impatient with him.

On the theory that whatever had happened to Eugene he'd be sure to try and meet up with Daniel at the Rally, he started walking to Gopher Stadium on the University of Minnesota campus, where it was to be held. For a block before he got to the pedestrian bridge across the Mississippi there were squadrons of students and older sorts handing out leaflets to whoever would take them. Some leaflets declared that a vote for Roberta Donnelly was a vote against the forces that were destroying America and told you how to get to the Rally. Other leaflets said that people had every right to do what they wanted, even if that meant killing themselves, and still others were downright peculiar, simple headlines without text that could be interpreted as neither for nor against any issue. As, for instance: I DON'T CARE IF THE SUN DON'T SHINE. Or: GIVE US FIVE MINUTES MORE. Just by looking at their faces as you approached them wouldn't tell you which were Undergoders and which weren't. Apparently there were sweet types and sour types on both sides.

The Mississippi was everything people said, a beautiful flat vastness that seemed to have swallowed the sky, with the city even more immense on either shore. Daniel stopped in the middle of the bridge and let his collection of colored leaflets flutter down one by one through that unthinkable space that was neither height nor depth. Houseboats and shops were moored on both sides of the river, and on three or four of them were naked people, men as well as women, tanning in the sun. Daniel was stirred, and disturbed. You could never fully understand any city of such extent and such variety: you could only look at it and be amazed, and look again and be terrified.

He was terrified now. For he knew that Eugene would not be at the Rally. Eugene had made his break for it. Maybe that had been his intention from their starting out or maybe it was the movie that convinced him, since the moral of it (if you could call it a moral) was: 'Give Me Liberty— Or Else!' Long ago Eugene had confided that *some day* he

35

meant to leave Iowa and learn to fly. Daniel had envied him his bravado without for a moment suspecting he could be so dumb as to go and do it like this. And so treacherous! Is that what a best friend was for—to betray?

The son of a bitch!

The sneaky little shit!

And yet. And even so. Hadn't it been and wouldn't it always be worth it—for just this one sight of the river and the memory of that song?

The answer pretty definitely was no, but it was hard to face the fact that he'd been so thoroughly and so needlessly fucked over. There was no point now in seeing General Donnelly, even as an alibi. There was nothing to be done but scoot back to Amesville and hope. He'd have till tomorrow to come up with some halfway likely story to tell the Muellers.

When Eugene's mother stopped by, two evenings later, Daniel's story was plain and unhelpful. Yes, they had camped out in the State Park, and no, he couldn't imagine where Eugene could have gone to if he hadn't come home. Daniel had ridden back to Amesville ahead of Eugene (for no very cogent reason) and that was the last he knew about him. She didn't ask half the questions he'd been expecting, and she never called back. Two days later it became generally known that Eugene Mueller was missing. His bicycle was discovered in the culvert, where Daniel had left it. There were two schools of thought as to what had happened: one, that he was the victim of foul play; the other, that he'd run away. Both were common enough occurrences. Everyone wanted to know Daniel's opinion, since he was the last person to have seen him. Daniel said that he *hoped* that he'd run away, violence being such a horrible alternative, though he couldn't believe Eugene would have done something so momentous without dropping a hint. In a way his speculations were entirely sincere.

No one seemed at all suspicious, except possibly Milly, who gave him odd looks now and then and wouldn't stop pestering him with questions that became increasingly personal and hard to answer, such as where, if Eugene had run away, would he have gone to? More and more Daniel felt as though he'd murdered his friend and concealed the body. He could understand what a convenience it was for Catholics to be able to go to confession.

Despite such feelings things soon went back to normal. Jerry Larsen took over Eugene's paper route permanently, and Daniel developed an enthusiasm for baseball that gave him an excuse for being out of the house almost as much as his father.

In July there was a tornado that demolished a trailer court a mile outside of town. That same night, when the storm was over, the county sheriff appeared at the Weinrebs' front door with a warrant for Daniel's arrest. Milly became hysterical and tried to phone Roy Mueller, but couldn't get past his answering device. The sheriff insisted stonily that this had nothing to do with anyone but Daniel. He was being arrested for the sale and possession of obscene and seditious materials, which was a Class D felony. For misdemeanors there was a juvenile court, but for felonies Daniel was an adult in the eyes of the law.

He was taken to the police station, fingerprinted, photographed, and put in a cell. The whole process seemed quite natural and ordinary, as if all his life he'd been heading towards this moment. It was a large moment, certainly, and rather solemn, like graduating from high school, but it didn't come as a surprise.

Daniel was as sure as his mother that Roy Mueller was behind his being arrested, but he also knew that he'd been caught dead to rights and that there'd be no wriggling out of it. He'd done what he'd been booked for. Of course, so had about ten other people, not even counting the customers. And what about Heinie Youngermann—were all his pay-offs down the drain? How could they try Daniel and not him?

He found out a week later when the trial was held. Every time the Weinrebs' lawyer would ask Daniel, on the witness stand, where his copies of the *Star-Tribune* had come from, or who else had delivered them, anything that would have involved naming other names, the opposing lawyer raised an objection, which the judge, Judge Cofflin, sustained. Simple as that. The jury found him guilty as charged and he was sentenced to eight months in the State Correction Facility at Spirit Lake. He could have got as much as five years, so their lawyer advised them against entering an appeal, since it was up to the same judge whether Daniel would be let off on probation when school started in the fall. They'd have been certain to lose the appeal in any case. Iowa and the rest of the Farm Belt weren't called police states for nothing.

Sitting in the cell day after day and night after night with no one to talk to and nothing to read, Daniel had had a thousand imaginary conversations with Roy Mueller. By the time, late on the night before he was to be sent off to Spirit Lake, that Roy Mueller finally did get around to seeing him, he'd been through every possible combination of anger, anguish, dread, and mutual mistrust, and the actual confrontation was a little like the trial, something he had to go through and get over with.

Mueller stayed outside the locked cell. He was a sub-stantial-looking man with a paunch, thick muscles and a friendly manner, even when he was being mean. With his own children he liked to think of himself as a kind of Solomon, stern but munificent, but his children (Daniel knew from Eugene) all lived in terror of him although they acted out their roles as his spoiled darlings.

"Well, Daniel, you've got yourself in a fair fix, haven't you?"

Daniel nodded.

"It's too bad, your being sent away like this, but maybe it will do you good. Build some moral fiber. Eh?"

Their eyes met. Mueller's were beaming with pleasure, which he passed off as benevolence.

"I thought there might be something you'd want to tell me before you go. Your mother has been on the phone with me at least once a day since you got in trouble. I thought the least I could do for the poor woman was to come and talk to you."

Daniel said what he'd made his mind up to say: he was guilty of selling the *Star-Tribune* and very sorry for it.

"I'm glad to hear you're taking your medicine in the right spirit, Daniel, but that wasn't exactly what I had in mind for us to talk about. I want to know where my son is, and you're the one who can tell me. Right, Daniel?"

"Honestly, Mr Mueller, I don't know where he is. If I knew I'd tell you. Believe me."

"No hunches or theories?"

"He might—" Daniel had to clear his throat, which was dry and sticky with fear. "He might have gone to Minneapolis."

"Why Minneapolis?"

"We . . . used to read about it. When we were delivering the *Star-Tribune*."

Mueller brushed aside the implications of this—that his son had shared Daniel's so-called crime, and that he'd known about it all along—with another toothy smile and a lifting and settling of his paunch.

"And it seemed like an exciting place to go, is that it?"

"Yes. But not. . . . I mean, we never talked about leaving Amesville permanently. We just wanted to see it."

"Well, what did you think when you saw it? Did it live up to your expectations?"

"I didn't say—"

But there seemed no point in sparring just for the sake of delaying the inevitable. Daniel could see it went beyond suspicions: Mueller knew.

"We did go there, Mr Mueller, but believe me, I didn't have any idea that Eugene didn't mean to come back with me. We went there to see Roberta Donnelly. She was giving a speech at Gopher Stadium. After we saw her we were heading right back here. Both of us."

"You admit going there, that's some progress. But I didn't need you to tell me that, Daniel. I knew the night you set off from Lloyd Wagner, who let the two of you across the border, which is a mistake that Lloyd has had reason to regret. But that's another story. When there was no sight of you coming back after the Star-Lite's last show, Lloyd realized he'd made a mistake and called me. It was a simple thing, from there, to have the Albert Lea police check out the bus station and the drivers. So you see, my lad, I need a little more information than just—" He parodied Daniel, making his eyes wide with false candor, and whispering: "—Minneapolis."

39

"Truly, Mr Mueller, I've told you all I know. We went to a movie together and at the end of it Eugene said he had to go to the bathroom. That was the last I saw of him."

"What movie?"

"*Gold-Diggers of 1984*. At the World Theater. The tickets cost four dollars."

"He disappeared and that was it? You didn't look for him?"

"I waited around. And then, after a while, I went to the Rally, hoping to see him there. What else *could* I do? Minneapolis is huge. And also. . . ."

"Yes?"

"Well, I figured he probably *meant* to get away from me. So he was probably deliberately hiding from me. But what I couldn't understand then, and I still can't, is why, if he *knew* he wasn't coming back, why he had to involve me in it. I mean, I'm his best friend."

"It's not very logical, is it?"

"It's not. So my theory—and I've had a lot of time to think about this—my theory is that the idea came to him while he was there, probably right during the movie. It was a movie that could have done that."

"There's only one thing wrong with your theory, Daniel."

"Mr Mueller, I'm telling you everything I know. Everything."

"There's one good reason why I don't believe you."

Daniel looked down at the toes of his shoes. None of his imaginary conversations with Mr Mueller had gone as badly as this. He had made his confession but it had done him no good. He'd run out of possible things to say.

"Don't you want to know what that reason is?"

"What."

"Because my son had the foresight to steal $845 from my desk before he went away. That doesn't sound like a spur-of-the-moment decision, does it?"

"No." Daniel shook his head vigorously. "Eugene wouldn't do that. He just wouldn't."

"Well, he did. The money's gone, and I scarcely think it

was a coincidence that Eugene should decide to run away at the exact same time."

Daniel didn't know what to think. His expression of disbelief had been no more than the last remnant of his loyalty. Friends don't involve their friends in crimes. Except, apparently, they do.

"Do you have any other suggestions, Daniel, as to where I can tell the police to look for my son?"

"No, Mr Mueller. Honestly."

"If any idea should come to you, you have only to ask to talk to Warden Shiel at Spirit Lake. Of course, you understand that if you are able to help us find Eugene you'll be doing yourself a considerable favor when it comes time to discuss your parole. Judge Cofflin knows about this situation, and it was only at my repeated insistence that you weren't indicted for first degree robbery as well."

"Mr Mueller, believe me, if I knew anything else at all, I'd tell you."

Mueller looked at him with a look of leisurely, contented malice and turned to leave.

"Really!" Daniel insisted.

Mueller turned back to look at him a last time. From the way he stood there, smiling, Daniel knew that he believed him—but that he didn't care. He'd got what he was after, a new victim, an adopted son.

4

H IS FIRST NIGHT in the compound at Spirit Lake,
sleeping out of doors on sparse, trampled crabgrass, Daniel
had a nightmare. It began with music, or sounds like but
less ordered than music, long notes of some unknown
timbre, neither voice nor violin, each one sustained beyond
thought's reach, yet lacing together into a structure large
and labyrinthine. At first he thought he was inside a church,
but it was too plain for that, the space too open.

A bridge. The covered bridge above the Mississippi. He
stood on it, suspended above the moving waters, an intolerable expanse of blackness scored with the wavering lights
of boats that seemed as far away and as unapproachable as
stars. And then, causelessly, awfully, this scene was ro-
tated through ninety degrees and the flowing river became
a wall still whirling upwards. It towered to an immense
unthinkable height and hung there, threatening to collapse.
No, its flowing and its collapse were a single, infinitely slow
event, and he fled from it over the windows of the inner
bridge. Sometimes the long sheets of glass would fracture
under his weight, like the winter's earliest ice. He felt as
though he were being hunted by some sluggish, shapeless
god that would—let him flee where he might—surely crush
him and roll him flat beneath his supreme inexorable immensity. All this, as the music lifted, note by note, into a
whistling louder and more fierce than any factory's to become at last the P/A system's tape of reveille.

His stomach still hurt, though not so acutely as in the
first hours after he'd forced down the P-W lozenge. He'd
been afraid then that despite all the water he was drinking it
would lodge in his throat instead of his stomach. It was that
big. The first set of its time-release enzymes burned out a
small ulcer in the lining of the stomach, which the second
set (the ones working now) proceeded to heal, sealing the
lozenge itself into the scar tissue of the wound it had

created. The whole process took less than a day, but even so Daniel and the seven other newly-admitted prisoners had nothing to do but let their situation sink in while the lozenges wove themselves into the ruptured tissues.

Daniel had supposed he'd be the youngest prisoner, but it turned out that a good percentage of the people he could see being assembled and sent out in work crews were his own age, and many of these, if not probably younger, were a lot scrawnier. The moral of this observation being the basically happy one that if they could survive at Spirit Lake, then so could he.

It seemed to be the case that a majority of the others, even those his age, had been in prison before. That, anyhow, was the subject that united five of the seven others once the compound had been emptied by the morning's call-up. For a while he sat on the sidelines taking it in, but their very equanimity and easy humor began to get at him. Here they were, many of them sentenced to five years or more of what they already knew was going to be sheer misery, and they were acting like it was a family reunion. Insane.

By comparison the poultry farmer from Humboldt County, who'd been sent up for child abuse seemed, for all his belly-aching, or maybe because of it, normal and reasonable, a man with a grievance who wanted you to know just how all-out miserable he was. Daniel tried talking to him, or rather listening, to help him get his mind more settled, but after a very short time the man developed a loop, saying the same things over in almost the identical words as the first and then the second time through—how sorry he was for what he'd done, how he hadn't *meant* to harm the child, though she had baited him and *knew* she was at fault, how the insurance might pay for the chickens but not for all the work, not for the time, how children *need* their parents and the authority they represent; and then, again, how sorry he was for what he'd done. Which was (as Daniel later found out) to beat his daughter unconscious and almost to death with the carcass of a hen.

To get away from him Daniel wandered about the compound, facing up to his bad news item by item—the stink of the open latrines, the not much nicer stink inside the dormitories, where a few of the feeblest prisoners were laid out on the floor, sleeping or watching the sunlight inch along the grimy sheets of plywood. One of them asked him for a glass of water, which he went and drew at the tap outside, not in a glass, since there were none to be found, but in a paper cup from McDonald's so old and crunched out of shape it barely served to hold the water till he got back inside.

The strangest thing about Spirit Lake was the absence of bars, barbed wire, or other signs of their true condition. There weren't even guards. The prisoners ran their own prison democratically which meant, as it did in the bigger democracy outside, that almost everyone was cheated, held to ransom, and victimized except for the little self-appointed army that ran the place. This was not a lesson that Daniel learned at once. It took many days and as many skimped dinners before the message got across that unless he reached some kind of accommodation with the powers-that-be he wasn't going to survive even as long as to September, when he expected to be paroled back to school. It was possible, actually, to starve to death. That, in fact, was what was happening to the people in the dormitory. If you didn't work, the prison didn't feed you, and if you didn't have money, or know someone who did, that was it.

What he did learn that first morning, and unforgettably, was that the P-W lozenge sealed in his innards was the authentic and bonafide sting of death.

Some time around noon there was a commotion among the other convalescent prisoners. They were shouting at the poultry farmer Daniel had talked to earlier, who was running full tilt down the gravel road going to the highway. When he'd gone a hundred yards and was about the same distance from the fieldstone posts that marked the entrance to the compound a whistle started blowing. A few yards farther on the farmer doubled over: radio signals broadcast by the P-W security system as he passed through the second perimeter had detonated the plastic explosive in the lozenge in his stomach.

In a while the Warden's pick-up appeared far off down the highway, hooting and flashing its lights.

"You know," said one of the black prisoners, in a reflective, ingratiating tone, like an announcer's, "I could see that coming a mile away, a mile away. It's always that kind that lets go first."

"Dumb shit," said a girl who had something wrong with her legs. "That's all he was, a dumb shit."

"Oh, I'm not so sure," said the black. "Anyone can get an attack of conscience. Usually it takes a bit more abuse, not just the idea."

"Do many people . . . uh . . . ?" It was the first Daniel had spoken, except to fend off questions.

"Let go? A camp this size, about one a week, I'd say. Less in summer, more in winter, but that's the average."

Others agreed. Some disagreed. Soon they were comparing notes again. The farmer's body, meanwhile, had been loaded into the rear of the pick-up. Before he got back into the cab, the guard waved at the watching prisoners. They did not wave back. The truck did a u-turn and returned, squealing, back to the green horizon from which it had appeared.

Originally the P-W security system (the initials commemorated the Welsh physicians who developed it, Drs Pole and Williams) had employed less drastic means of reforming character than instant death. When triggered, the earlier lozenges released only enough toxins to cause momentary yet acute nausea and colonic spasms. In this form the P-W system had been hailed as the model-T of behavioral engineering. Within a decade of its commercial availability there was scarcely a prison anywhere in the world that hadn't converted to its use. Though the motive for reform may have been economic, the result invariably was a more humane prison environment, simply because there was no longer a need for the same close scrutiny and precautions. It was for this reason that Drs Pole and Williams were awarded the Nobel Peace Prize in 1991.

Only gradually, and never in the United States, was its use extended to so-called "hostage populations" of potentially dissident civilians—the Basques in Spain, Jews in Russia, the Irish in England, and so on. It was in these countries that explosives began to replace toxins and where, too, systems of decimation and mass reprisal were developed, whereby a central broadcasting system could transmit coded signals that could put to death any implanted individual, any group or a given proportion of that group, or, conceivably, an entire population. The largest achieved kill-ratio was the decimation of Palestinians living in the Gaza strip, and this was not the consequence of a human decision but of computer error. Usually the mere presence of the P-W system was sufficient to preclude its use except in individual cases.

At the Spirit Lake Correction Facility it was possible to send out work crews to farms and industries within a radius of fifty miles (the range of the system's central radio tower) with no other supervision than the black box by which the prisoners, singly or as a group, could be directed, controlled, and, if need be, extirpated. The result was a work-force of singular effectiveness that brought the State of Iowa revenues far in excess of the cost of administration. However, the system was just as successful in reducing crime, and so there was never enough convict labor to meet the demands of the area's farms and factories, which had to resort to the more troublesome (if somewhat less costly) migrant workers, recruited in the bankrupt cities of the eastern seaboard.

It was such urban migrants who, falling afoul of the law, constituted by far the better part of the prison population at Spirit Lake. Daniel had never in his life known such various, interesting people, and it wasn't just Daniel who was impressed. They all seemed to take an inflated view of their collective identity, as though they were an exiled aristocracy, being larger and more honorable than the dogged trolls and dwarfs of day-to-day life. Which is not to say that they were nice to each other (or to Daniel): they weren't. The resentment they felt for the world at large, their sense of having been marked, almost literally, for the slaughter, was too great to be contained. It could lead even the mildest of them at times to betray this theoretical sodality for the sake of a hamburger or a laugh or the rush that accompanied the smash of your own fist into any available face. But the bad moments were like firecrackers—they exploded and a smell lingered for a few hours and then even that was gone—while the good moments were like sunlight, a fact so basic you almost never considered it was there.

46

Of course it was summer, and that helped. They worked longer hours, but they worked at pleasant jobs, out of doors, for farmers who had a rational regard for what was possible. (The factories were said to be much worse, but they wouldn't re-open till late in October.) Often there would be extra food, and when your life centers around getting enough to eat (the rations at Spirit Lake were, deliberately, *not* enough) this was an important consideration.

It was the times in between that were so weirdly wonderful, times of an idleness as plain and pure as the shaking of leaves in a tree. Times between reveille and being hustled into the trucks, or times you waited for a truck to come and take you back. Times that a sudden storm would cancel out the day's appointed baling and you could wait among the silences of the ceasing rain, in the glow of the late, returning light.

At such times consciousness became something more than just a haphazard string of thoughts about this, that, and the other. You knew yourself to be alive with a vividness so real and personal it was like God's gloved hand wrapping itself about your spine and squeezing. Alive and human: he, Daniel Weinreb, was a human being! It was something he'd never even considered up till now.

There was a part of the compound set aside for visitors, with pine trees, picnic tables, and a row of swings. Since visitors were only allowed on Sundays, and since few of the prisoners were ever visited in any case, the place looked unnaturally nice compared to the weedy fields and bare dirt of the compound proper, though for the visitors, coming to it from the outside world, it probably seemed plain enough, a park such as you would have found in any neighboring town.

Hearing the squeals of his sisters before they became visible behind the screen of pines, Daniel stopped to get hold of himself. He seemed quite steady and far from tears. Approaching nearer, he could see them through the branches. Aurelia was on one of the swings and Cecelia was pushing her. He felt like a ghost in a story, hovering about his living past. There beyond the twins was his father, in the front seat of a Hertz, smoking his pipe. Milly was nowhere to be

47

seen. Daniel had thought she wouldn't come but even so it was a disappointment.

To his credit he didn't let that show when at last he emerged from behind the trees. He was all hugs and kisses for the twins, and by the time his father reached the swings, Daniel's arms were full.

"How are you, Daniel?" Abraham asked.

Daniel said, "I'm fine." And then, to nail it down, "In fact I really am." He smiled—a smile as plausible as this little park.

He set the twins down on the grass and shook hands with his father.

"Your mother meant to come but at the last minute she didn't feel up to it. We agreed it probably wouldn't do your morale any good to see her in one of her . . . uh. . . ."

"Probably," Daniel agreed.

"And it probably wouldn't be that good for *her* morale, either. Though, I must say, this place," pointing at the trees with his pipestem, "is a bit, uh, nicer than I was expecting."

Daniel nodded.

"Are you hungry? We brought a picnic."

"Me? I'm always hungry." Which was truer than he would have cared to be known.

While they spread out the food on the table, another car arrived with other visitors. Having them as an audience made it easier. There was a roast chicken, which Daniel got the better part of, and a bowl of potato salad with what seemed a pound of bacon crumbled in it. Abraham apologized for there being only a quart of milk for everyone to share. The beer he'd brought had been confiscated at the checkpoint on the highway.

While they ate, his father explained all that was being done to have Daniel released. A lot of people, apparently, were incensed about his being sent to Spirit Lake, but they were none of them the right people. A petition had been sent to Mayor MacLean, who returned it saying the whole thing was out of his hands. His father showed him a typed list of the names on the petition. A lot of them had been customers on his route, others he recognized as his father's patients, but the surprising thing was how many of them he'd never heard of. He had become a cause.

For all that it was the food that registered. Daniel had got so used to the process food at Spirit Lake he'd forgotten what an enormous difference there could be between that and the real thing. After the chicken and potato salad, Abraham unwrapped a carrot cake. It was the closest Daniel came to breaking down during the whole visit.

When the food was gone Daniel became conscious of the usual obscuring awkwardness rising up again between him and his father. He sat there staring at the weathered boards of the table, trying to think of what to say, but when he did come up with something it never precipitated a real conversation. The excitement at the other picnic table, where they were talking Spanish, seemed a reproach to their own lengthening silences.

Cecelia, who had already been carsick on the ride to Spirit Lake, rescued them by tossing up her lunch. After her dress had been sponged clean, Daniel played hide-and-seek with the twins. They had finally got the idea that there wasn't just a single hiding place to hide in, but a whole world. Twice Aurelia went beyond the fieldstone posts marking the perimeter to find a place to hide, and each time it was like a knife right through his stomach. Theoretically you weren't supposed to be able to feel the lozenge, but no one who'd ever been implanted believed that.

Eventually it was time for them to go. Since he hadn't found a way to lead round to it by degrees, Daniel was forced to come right out with the subject of McDonald's. He waited till the twins were strapped into their seatbelts, and then asked his father for a word in private.

"It's about the food here," he began when they were by themselves.

As he'd feared, his father became indignant when he'd explained about the rations being deliberately less than the minimum for subsistence. He started going on about the petition again.

Daniel managed to be urgent without being swept along: "It's no use complaining, Dad. People have tried and it doesn't do any good. It's the policy. What you can do is pay what they call the supplement. Then they bring in extra food from McDonald's. It doesn't make such a big difference now, 'cause most of the farmers, when we go out and work for them, usually scrape up something extra for us. But later on, in winter, it can be nasty. That's what they say."

"Of course, Daniel, we'll do all we possibly can. But you certainly will be home before winter. As soon as school starts again they'll have to put you on probation."

"Right. But meanwhile I need whatever you can let me have. The supplement costs thirty-five dollars a week, which is a lot to pay for a Big Mac and french fries, but what can I say? They've got us over a barrel."

"My God, Daniel, it's not the money—it's the idea of what they're doing here. It's extortion! I can't believe—"

"Please, Dad—*whatever* you do, don't complain."

"Not till you're out of here, certainly. Who do I pay?"

"Ask for Sergeant Di Franco when they stop you at the checkpoint on the way back. He'll tell you an address to send the money to. I'll pay it all back, I promise."

Abraham took his appointment book out of the breast pocket of his suit and wrote down the name. His hand was shaking. "Di Franco," he repeated. "That reminds me. I think that was the fellow who made me leave your book with him. Your old friend Mrs Boismortier has been by the house several times, asking after you, and the last time she brought a present for me to bring you. A book. You may get it eventually, once they've made sure it's not subversive."

"I don't know. They don't let many books through. Just bibles and like that. But tell her thank you for me anyhow."

The last formalities went off without a hitch, and the Hertz drove away into the brightness of the inaccessible world outside. Daniel stayed in the visiting area, rocking gently in one of the swings until the whistle blew, summoning him to the six o'clock roll-call. He kept thinking of the mixing bowl that the potato salad had come in. Something about its shape or its color seemed to sum up everything he'd ever loved. And lost forever.

Forever, fortunately, isn't a notion that can do you lasting harm at the flexible age of fourteen. True enough, there was something Daniel *had* lost forever by coming here to Spirit Lake. Call it faith in the system—the faith that had allowed him to write his third-prize essay way back when— or maybe just an ability to look the other way while the

50

losers were being trounced by the winners in the fixed game of life. But whatever you call it, it was something he'd have had to lose eventually anyhow. This was just a rougher form of farewell—a kick in the stomach rather than a wave of the hand.

It didn't even take a night's sleep with its standard nightmare to put Daniel into a fitter frame of mind. By lights-out he was already looking at the little horrors and afflictions of his prison in the perspective of practical sanity, the perspective by which one's immediate surroundings, whatever they are, are seen simply as what is.

He had played a game of chess with his friend Bob Lundgren, not an especially good game but no worse than usual. Then he had wormed his way into a conversation between Barbara Steiner and some of the other older prisoners on the subject of politics. Their talk was in its own way as much over his head as Bob Lundgren's chess, at least as far as his being able to contribute to it. They made hash of his most basic assumptions, but it was delicious hash, and Barbara Steiner, who was the clearest-headed and sharpest-tongued of the lot of them, seemed to know the effect she was having on Daniel and to enjoy leading him from one unspeakable heresy to the next. Daniel didn't consider whether he actually agreed with any of this. He was just caught up in the excitement of being a spectator to it, the way he enjoyed watching a fight or listening to a story. It was a sport and he was its fan.

But it was the music that had the largest (if least understandable) effect on him. Night after night there was music. Not music such as he'd ever conceived of before, not music that could be named, the way, when it was your turn to ask for your favorite song in Mrs Boismortier's class, you could ask for 'Santa Lucia' or 'Old Black Joe' and the class would sing it and it would be there, recognizably the same, fixed always in that certain shape. Here there were tunes usually, yes, but they were always shifting round, disintegrating into mere raw rows of notes that still somehow managed to be music. The way they did it was beyond him, and at times the why of it as well. Especially, it seemed, when the three prisoners who were generally accounted the best musicians got together to play. Then, though he might be swept off his feet at the start, inevitably their music would move off somewhere he couldn't follow. It was like being a three-year-old and trying to pay attention to grown-up talk. But there seemed to be this difference between the language of music and the language of words: it didn't seem possible, in the language of music, to lie.

Days later, after he'd dismissed the possibility of ever seeing it, the book Mrs Boismortier had sent Daniel via his father arrived. It had got past the censor relatively intact, with only a few pages snipped out towards the end. The front cover showed an ingratiating Jesus crowned with thorns, holding out a hamburger. Drops of blood from Jesus and drops of catsup from the burger mingled in a crimson pool from which the words of the title rose up like little lime-green islands: *The Product is God* by Jack Van Dyke. It came with testimonials from a number of unfamiliar show business celebrities and from the *Wall Street Journal*, which called Reverend Van Dyke "the sinister minister" and declared his theology to be "the newest wrinkle in eternal truth. A real bombshell." He was the head of Marble Collegiate Church in New York City.

Though it was about religion, an area Daniel had never supposed he could take an interest in, he was glad to get it. In the congested dorms of Spirit Lake, a book, any book, was a refuge, the nearest possible approach to privacy. Besides, Mrs Boismortier's earlier batting average had been pretty good, so maybe *The Product of God* would be truly interesting. The cover was lurid enough. Anyhow what was the competition? A couple of scruffy bibles and a stack of unread (because unreadable) Undergod tracts about iniquity, repentance, and how suffering was a matter for rejoicing once you found Christ. Only prisoners with desperately long terms, fifteen or twenty years, ever pretended to take any of that seriously. There was theoretically a better chance to get paroled if you could convince the authorities you were a true believer. Needless to say, it never helped: the hope was part of the punishment.

It was clear right from page one that Van Dyke was no Undergoder, though just what he was Daniel couldn't quite tell. An atheist it almost seemed, from some of the things he said. Like this, from the 'Prefatory Postscript', before he even got warmed up: "Often it has been objected, by this book's admirers and its detractors alike, that I speak of Almighty God as though He were no more than some exceptionally clever idea I'd got hold of, like a new theorem in geometry, or a scenario for an original ballet. In large part I must allow that this is so, but it doesn't bother me, and I'm sure it doesn't bother God. However He may concern Himself with human fate, He is surely indifferent to human controversy." Or this, from the same Postscript: "The Most High is perfectly willing to be understood as an illusion since our doubts only make our trust in Him that much more savory on His tongue. He is, we must remember, the King of Kings, and shares the general kinky taste of kings for displays of their subjects' abasement. Doubt Him, by all means, say I, when I speak to doubters, but don't on that account neglect to worship Him."

This was religion? It seemed almost the opposite, a burlesque, but Mrs Boismortier (a good Episcopalian) had sent the book to him, and someone in the hierarchy of the prison, possibly even Warden Shiel, had passed it on, and millions of people, according to the cover, were able to take Reverend Van Dyke seriously.

Seriousness aside, Daniel was enthralled by the book. After a long dusty day of detasseling corn he would return to its paradoxes and mental loop-the-loops with a feeling of immersing himself in seltzer water. Just a few paragraphs and his mind was all tingly and able to think again, at which point he would return the book to its home in his mattress of huskings and straw.

Chapter One was an explanation, more or less, of the book's garish cover, and of its title too. It was about a bunch of people who start a chain of fast-food restaurants, called Super-King. The chain is run not for profit but to give everybody something really good—Super-King Hamburgers and Super-King Cola, which, according to the chain's big ad campaign, are supposed to make you live forever and always be happy, if you eat enough of them. No one is actually expected to *believe* the ads, but the chain is an enormous success anyhow. There were graphs and sales figures to illustrate its growth across the whole country and around the world. Of course the actual product the Super-King people were selling wasn't hamburgers and such, it was an idea—the idea of Jesus, the Super-King. All products, Van Dyke insisted, were only ideas, and the most mind-boggling idea was the idea of Jesus, who was both God and an ordinary man and therefore a complete impossibility. *Therefore*, since He represented the best possible bargain, everybody should buy that product, which was basically what had happened over the last two thousand years—the rise of Christianity being the same as the success of the Super-King chain.

Chapter Two was about the difficulty of believing in things—not just in religion, but in advertising, in sex, in your own daily life. Van Dyke argued that even when we know that companies aren't telling the complete truth about their products, we should buy them anyhow (as long as they aren't actually harmful) because the country and the economy would collapse if we didn't. "By the same token," Van Dyke wrote, "lies about God, such as we find in Holy Scripture, help us keep our psychic economy running. If we can believe, for instance, that the world was all knocked together in six days rather than in however many billions of years, we've come a long way toward self-mastery." The rest of the chapter was a kind of advertisement for God and all the things He would do for you once you "bought" Him, such as keeping you from ever being depressed or bitter or from coming down with colds.

Chapter Three was titled 'Wash Your Own Brain' and was about techniques you could use in order to start believing in God. Most of the techniques were based on methods of acting. Van Dyke explained that long ago religious-type people had been against plays and actors because by watching them people learned to think of all their feelings and ideas as arbitrary and interchangeable. An actor's identity was nothing more than a hat he put on or took off at will, and what was true for actors was true for us all. The world was a stage.

"What our Puritan forebears failed to recognize," Van Dyke wrote, "is the evangelical application of these insights. For if we become the kind of people we are by pretending, then the way to become good, devout, and faithful Chris-

54

tians (which, admit it, is a well-nigh impossible undertaking) is to *pretend* to be good, devout, and faithful. Study the role and rehearse it energetically. You must *seem* to love your neighbor no matter how much you hate his guts. You must *seem* to accept sufferings, even if you're drafting your suicide note. You must say that you *know* that your Redeemer liveth, even though you know no such thing. Eventually, saying makes it so."

He went on to relate the story of one of his parishioners, the actor Jackson Florentine (the same Jackson Florentine who'd co-starred in *Gold-Diggers of 1984*!), who had been unable to believe in Jesus with a fervent and heartfelt belief until Reverend Van Dyke had made him pretend to believe in the Easter Bunny, a major idol in Florentine's childhood pantheon. The doubting actor prayed before holographic pictures of the Easter Bunny, wrote long confessional letters to him, and meditated on the various mysteries of his existence or non-existence, as the case might be, until at last on Easter morning he found no less than 144 brightly dyed Easter eggs hidden all over the grounds of his East Hampton estate. Having revived this "splinter of the Godhead" as Van Dyke termed it, it was a simple matter to take the next step and be washed in the blood of the Lamb and dried with its soft white fleece.

Before Daniel got to Chapter Four—'A Salute to Hypocrisy'—the book was missing from his mattress. For a moment, finding it gone, he felt berserk with loss. Wave after wave of desolation swept through him and kept him from sleep. Why should it mean so much? Why should it mean anything? It was a ridiculous book that he'd never have bothered with if there had been anything else to hand.

But the feeling couldn't be argued away. He wanted it back. He ached to be reading it again, to be outraged by its dumb ideas. It was as though part of his brain had been stolen.

Over and above this simple hurt and hunger was the frustration of having no one to complain to. The theft of a book was a trifling injustice in a world where justice did not obtain and no one expected it to.

Late in September the word came through, in a letter from

his lawyer in Amesville that his sentence was *not* to be reduced or suspended. It didn't come as a surprise. He'd tried to believe he'd be paroled but never really believed he'd believed it. He didn't believe anything. It amazed him how cynical he'd become in just a couple of months.

Even so there were times when he felt such a passionate self-pity he had to go off by himself and cry, and other times worse than that when a depression would settle over him so black and absolute that there was no way to fight against it or argue his way out of it. It was like a physical disease.

He would tell himself, though not out loud, that he *refused* to be broken, that it was just a matter of holding out one day at a time. But this was whistling in the dark. He knew if they wanted to break him they would. In fact, they probably weren't going to bother. It was enough that he should be made to appreciate that their power, so far as it affected him, was limitless.

Until March 14.

What he hadn't been prepared for was the effect this news had on the attitude of the other prisoners. All through the summer Daniel had felt himself ignored, avoided, belittled. Even the friendliest of his fellow prisoners seemed to take the attitude that this was his summer vacation, while the unfriendliest were openly mocking. Once he'd had to fight to establish his territorial rights in the dorm, and thereafter no one had overstepped the bounds of a permitted formal sarcasm. But now, surely, the fact (so clear to Daniel) that *he* was as much a victim as they were should have begun to be clear to them too. But it wasn't. There were no more jokes about summer camp, since summer was definitely over, but otherwise he remained an outsider, tolerated at the edge of other people's conversations but not welcomed into them.

This is not to say that he was lonely. There were many other outsiders at Spirit Lake—native Iowans who'd been sent up for embezzlement or rape and who still considered themselves to be uniquely and privately guilty (or not guilty, for what difference that made) rather than members of a community. They still believed in the possibility of good and evil, right and wrong, whereas the general run of prisoners seemed genuinely impatient with such ideas. Besides the Iowa contingent there was another large group of prisoners who were outsiders—the ones who were crazy. There were perhaps twenty concerning whom there was no question. They weren't resented the way Iowans were, but they were avoided, not just because they were liable to fly off the handle but because craziness was thought to be catching.

Daniel's friend Bob Lundgren was both an Iowan and crazy, in a mildly dangerous but amiable way. Bob, who was twenty-three and the youngest son of an Undergod farmer in Dickson County, was serving a year for drunk driving, though that was only a pretext. In fact he'd tried to kill his older brother, but a jury had found him not guilty, since there'd been no one's word for it but the brother's, who was an unpleasant, untrustworthy individual. Bob told Daniel that he had indeed tried to kill his brother and that as soon as he was out of Spirit Lake he was going to finish the job. It was hard not to believe him. When he talked about his family his face lighted up with a kind of berserk poetic hatred, a look that Daniel, who never felt such passionate angers, would watch entranced as if it were a log burning in a fireplace.

Bob wasn't a big talker. Mostly they just played slow, thinking games of chess when they got together. Strategically, Bob was always way ahead. There was never any chance of Daniel's winning, any more than he could have won against Bob at arm-wrestling, but there was a kind of honor in losing by a slow attrition rather than being wiped out by a completely unexpected coup. After a while there was a strange satisfaction that had nothing to do with winning or losing, a fascination with the patterns of play that developed on the board, patterns like the loops of magnetic force that iron filings will form on a sheet of paper, only much more complicated. Such a blessed self-forgetfulness came over them then, as they sat there contemplating the microcosm of the chessboard, as if they were escaping from Spirit Lake; as if the complex spaces of the board were truly another world, created by thought but as real as electrons. Even so, it would have been nice to win just one game. Or to play to a draw, at least.

He always lost to Barbara Steiner too, but there seemed less disgrace in that, since their contests were only verbal and there were no hard-and-fast rules. Logomachies. Winning was anything from a look in the other person's eye to downright belly laughter. Losing was simply the failure to score as many points, though you could also lose more spectacularly by being a bore. Barbara had very definite opinions as to who was and wasn't a bore. People who told jokes, even very good jokes, were automatically set down as bores, as well as people who described the plots of old movies or argued about the best make of automobile. Daniel she accounted a hick, but not a bore, and she would listen contentedly to his descriptions of various typical Amesville types, such as his last year's homeroom teacher, Mrs Norberg, who was a social studies teacher and had not read a newspaper in over five years because she thought they were seditious. Sometimes she let him run on for what seemed hours, but usually they took turns, one anecdote leading to another. Her range was enormous. She'd been everywhere, done everything, and seemed to remember it all. Now she was serving three years, half of it behind her, for performing abortions in Waterloo. But that, as she liked to say, was just the tip of the iceberg. Every new anecdote seemed to have her in a different state working at another kind of job. Sometimes Daniel wondered if she wasn't making at least a part of it up.

People had different opinions as to whether Barbara was homely or only plain. Her two most noticeable defects were her wide, meaty-looking lips and her stringy black hair that was always dotted with enormous flakes of dandruff. Perhaps with good clothes and beauty parlors she might have passed muster, but lacking such assists there wasn't much she could do. Also, it didn't help that she was six months pregnant. None of which stood in the way of her having as much sex as she liked. Sex at Spirit Lake was a seller's market.

Officially the prisoners weren't supposed to have sex at all, except when spouses came to visit, but the monitors who watched them over the closed-circuit tv would usually let it pass, so long as it didn't look like a rape. There was even a corner in one of the dorms screened off with newspapers, like a Japanese house, where you could go to fuck in relative privacy. Most women charged two Big Macs or the equivalent, though there was one black girl, a cripple, who gave blow jobs for free. Daniel watched the couples going in back of the paper screen and listened to them with a kind of haunted feeling in his chest. He thought about it more than he wanted to, but he abstained. Partly from prudential reasons, since a lot of the prisoners, men and women both, had a kind of venereal warts for which there didn't seem to be a cure, but also partly (as he explained to Barbara) because he wanted to wait till he was in love. Barbara was quite cynical on the subject of love, having suffered more than her share in that area, but Daniel liked to think she secretly approved of his idealism.

She wasn't cynical about everything. At times, indeed, she could outdo Daniel in the matter of principles, the most amazing of which was her latest idea that everyone *always* got exactly what he or she deserved. At Spirit Lake this was on a par with praising steak to vegetarians, since just about everyone, including Daniel, felt he'd been railroaded. They might or might not believe in justice in an abstract sense, but they certainly didn't think justice had anything to do with the legal system of the State of Iowa.

"I mean," Daniel insisted earnestly, "what about *my* being here? Where is the justice in that?"

Only a few days before, he'd told her the complete story of how, and why, he'd been sent up (hoping all the while that the monitors, off in their offices, were tuned in), and Barbara had agreed then it was a travesty. She'd even offered a theory that the world was arranged so that simply to exist you had to be violating some law or other. That way the higher-ups always had some pretext for pouncing when they wanted you.

"The justice of your being here isn't for what you *did*, dumbbell. It's for what you didn't do. You didn't follow your own inner promptings. That was your big mistake. *That's* what you're here for."

"Bullshit."

"Bull-*shit*," she replied coolly, turning the inflection around against him. "Purity of heart is to will one thing. You ever heard that saying?"

"A stitch in time saves nine. Won't that do as well?"

"Think about it. When you went to Minneapolis with that friend of yours, *then* you were doing the right thing, following the spirit where it led. But when you came back you did the wrong thing."

"For Christ's sake, I was fourteen."

"Your friend didn't go back to Iowa. How old was he?"

"Fifteen."

"In any case, Daniel, age has nothing to do with anything. It's the excuse people use till they're old enough to acquire better excuses—a wife, or children, or a job. There are always going to be excuses if you look for them."

"Then what's yours?"

"The commonest in the world. I got greedy. I was pulling in money hand over fist, and so I stayed on in a hick town long after I should have left. I didn't like it there, and *it* didn't like me."

"You think it's fair you should be sent to prison for that, for going after the money? 'Cause you did say, the other day, that you didn't think doing the abortions was in any way wrong."

"It was the first time I ever sinned against my own deepest feelings, and also the first time I've been to prison."

"So? It could be a coincidence, couldn't it? I mean, if there were a tornado tomorrow, or you were struck by lightning, would that also be something you *deserved*?"

"No. And that's how I know there won't be a tornado. Or the other thing."

"You're impossible."

"You're sweet," she said, and smiled. Because of her pregnancy her teeth were in terrible condition. She got supplements, but apparently not enough. If she wasn't careful, she was going to lose all of them. At twenty-seven years of age. It didn't seem fair.

There were a couple weeks in the middle of October when the pace slackened. There wasn't enough work left on the farms to make it worth the gasoline to drive to Spirit Lake and get a crew. Daniel wondered if the prisoners were really as glad to be lazing about the compound as they said. Without work the days stretched out into Saharas of emptiness, with the certainty of something much worse waiting up ahead.

When the new winter rosters were made up, Daniel found himself assigned to Consolidated Food Systems' nearby 'Experimental Station 78', which was not, in fact, all that experimental, having been in production steadily for twenty years. The company's P.R. department had simply never found a more attractive way to describe this side of the business, which was the breeding of a specially mutated form of termite that was used as a supplement in various extended meat and cheese products. The bugs bred at Station 78, in all their billions, were almost as economical a source of protein as soybeans, since they could be grown in the labyrinthine underground bunkers to quite remarkable sizes with no other food source than a black sludge-like paste produced for next to nothing by various urban sanitation departments. The termites' ordinary life-cycle had been simplified and adapted to assembly-line techniques, which were automated so that, unless there was a breakdown, workers weren't obliged to go into the actual tunnels. Daniel's job at the station was to tend a row of four-kiloliter vats in which the bugs were cooked and mixed with various chemicals, in the course of which they changed from a lumpy dark-gray mulch to a smooth batter the color of orange juice. In either condition it was still toxic, so as to protein there was no dividend working here. However, the job was considered something of a plum, since it involved very little real work and the temperature down in the station was an invariable 83°F. For eight hours a day you were guaranteed a level of warmth and well-being that was actually illegal in some parts of the country.

Even so, Daniel wished he'd been posted to any other job. He'd never had any qualms before about extended foods, and there was little resemblance between what he could imagine back in the tunnels and what he could see in the vats, but despite that he couldn't get over a constant queasiness. Sometimes a live termite, or a whole little swarm of them, would manage to make it past the mashers and into the area where Daniel worked, and each time it was as though a switch had been thrown that turned reality into nightmare. None of the other prisoners were so squeamish, it was irrational, but he couldn't help it. He would have to go after the loose bugs, to keep them from getting into the batter in the vats. They were blind and their wings were not suited to sustained flight, which made them easy to swat but also more sinister somehow, the way they caromed and collided into things. There was nothing they could do and nowhere they could go, since they couldn't reproduce sexually and there was nothing outside the station's tunnels they could digest. Their only purpose in life was to grow to a certain size and then be pulped—and they'd evaded that purpose. To Daniel it seemed that the same thing had happened to him.

With the coming of winter things got steadily worse, week by week. Working down in the station, Daniel saw less and less of actual daylight, but that wasn't so different from going to school during the darkest months of the year. The worst of it was the cold. The dorms leaked so badly that from the middle of November on it was hard to sleep, the cold was that intense. Daniel slept with two older men who worked the same shift at Station 78, since people in general objected to the smell of the bugs they all swore they could smell on them. One of the men had a problem with his bladder and wet the bed sometimes while he was asleep. It was strange having the same thing happen here with grown men that had happened during the pipeline crisis with the twins.

He began having trouble with his digestion. Even though he was hungry all the time, something had happened to his stomach acids so that he constantly felt on the verge of throwing up. Other people had the same problem, and blamed it on the Big Macs which the guards delivered to the dorm half-frozen. Daniel himself believed it was psychological and had to do with his job at the station. Whatever the reason, the result was that he was always at odds with his body, which was cold and weak and nauseous and would fumble the simplest task, turning a doorknob or blowing his nose. And it stank, not just at the crotch and the armpits, but through and through. He began to hate himself. To hate, that is, the body he was attached to. He hated the other prisoners just as much, for they were all in more or less the same falling-to-pieces condition. He hated the dorms, and the station, and the frozen ground of the compound, and the clouds that hung low in the sky with the weight of the winter within them, waiting to fall.

Every night there were fights, most of them inside the dorms. The monitors, if they were watching, seldom tried to intervene. They probably enjoyed it the way the prisoners did, as sport, a break in the monotony, a sign of life.

Time was the problem, how to get through the bleak hours at work, the bleaker hours at the dorm. Never mind the days and weeks. It was the clock, not the calendar, that was crushing him. What to think of in those hours? Where to turn? Barbara Steiner said the only resources are inner resources, and that so long as you were free to think your own thoughts you had as much freedom as there is. Even if Daniel could have believed that, it wouldn't have done him much good. Thoughts have got to be about something, they've got to go somewhere. His thoughts were just loops of tape, vain repetitions. He tried deliberately daydreaming about the past, since a lot of the prisoners swore that your memory was a regular Disneyland where you could spend days wandering from one show to another. Not for Daniel: his memory was like a box of someone else's snapshots. He would stare at each frozen moment in its turn, but none of them came alive to lead the way into a living past.

The future was no better. For the future to be interesting your desires, or your fears, must have a home there. Any future Daniel could foresee back in Amesville seemed only a more comfortable form of prison, which he could neither wish for nor dread. The problem of what he would do with his life had been with him for as many years as he could remember, but there'd never been any urgency about it. Quite the opposite: he'd always felt contempt for those of his school-fellows who were already hot on the scent of a 'career'. Even now the word, or the idea behind it, seemed blackly ridiculous. Daniel knew he didn't want anything that could be called a career, but that seemed perilously near to not wanting a future. And when people stopped having an idea of their future after Spirit Lake, they were liable to let go. Daniel didn't want to let go, but he didn't know what to hang on to.

This was his frame of mind when he began reading the bible. It served the essential purpose of passing time, but beyond that it was a disappointment. The stories were seldom a match for the average ghost story, and the language they were told in, though poetic in patches, was usually just antiquated and obscure. Long stretches of it made no sense at all. The epistles of St Paul were particularly annoying that way. What was he to make of: "Beware of dogs, beware of evil workers, beware of the concision, for we are the circumcision, which worship God in the spirit, and rejoice in Christ Jesus, and have no confidence in the flesh, though I might also have confidence in the flesh." Gobbledegook! Even when the language was clearer, the ideas were murky, and when the ideas were clear they were usually dumb, like the dumb ideas of Reverend Van Dyke but without his sense of humor. Why did serious people ever take it seriously? Unless the whole thing was a kind of secret code (this was Bob Lundgren's theory) which made completely good sense when you translated it from the language of two thousand years ago to the language that people spoke today. On the other hand (this was Daniel's theory) what if St Paul was talking about experiences that *nobody* had any more, or only people crazy enough to believe that black was white, and suffering some kind of medicine, and death the beginning of a better kind of life? Even then it was doubtful if believers believed in all they said they did. More likely they'd taken Van Dyke's advice and were brainwashing themselves, saying they believed such stuff so that some day they actually might.

But *he* didn't believe it, and he wouldn't pretend that he did. He only kept reading it because there was nothing else to read. He only kept thinking about it because there was nothing else to think about.

By the first snowfall, in mid-November, Barbara Steiner was very pregnant and very depressed. People began avoiding her, including the men she'd been having sex with. Not having sex meant she wasn't getting as many Big Macs as usual, so Daniel, who'd been having stomach trouble, would often let her share his, or even give her the whole thing. She ate like a dog, quickly and without any sign of pleasure.

All the talk had gone out of her. They would sit cross-

64

legged on her rolled-up bedding and listen to the wind slam against the windowpanes and rattle the doors. The first full-scale blizzard of the year slowly buttressed the leaky walls with snowdrifts, and the dorm, so sealed, became warmer and more bearable.

There was such a feeling of finality somehow, as though they were all inside some ancient wooden ship that was locked into the ice, eking out rations and fuel and quietly waiting to die. Cardplayers went on playing cards as long as the lights were on, and knitters would knit with the wool they had knit and unraveled a hundred times before, but no one spoke. Barbara, who had already been through two winters at Spirit Lake, assured Daniel that this was just a phase, that by Christmas at the latest things would get back to normal.

Before they did, though, something quite extraordinary happened, an event that was to shape the rest of Daniel's life—and Barbara's as well, though in a far more terrible way. A man sang.

There had been less and less music of any sort lately. One of the best musicians at Spirit Lake, a man who could play just about any musical instrument there was, had been released in October. A short time after that a very good tenor who was serving twelve years for manslaughter had let go, walking out beyond the perimeter early one Sunday morning to detonate the lozenge in his stomach. No one had had the heart, after that, to violate the deepening silence of the dorms with songs unworthy of those whom they could all still clearly call to mind. The only exception was a feeble-minded migrant woman who liked to drum her fingers on the pipes of the Franklyn stove, drumming with a stolid, steady, rather cheerful lack of invention until someone would get fed up and drag her back to her mattress at the far end of the dorm.

Then on the evening in question, a windless Tuesday and bitterly cold, that single voice rose from their assembled silence like a moon rising over endless fields of snow. For the briefest moment, for the length of a phrase, it seemed to Daniel that the song could not be real, that it sprang from inside himself, so perfect it was, so beyond possibility, so willing to confess what must always remain inexpressible, a despair flowering now like a costly fragrance in the dorm's fetid air.

It took hold of each soul so, leveling them all to ashes with a single breath, like the breath of atomic disintegration, joining them in the communion of an intolerable and lovely knowledge, which *was* the song and could not be told of apart from the song, so that they listened for each further swelling and subsiding as if it issued from the chorus of their mortal hearts, which the song had made articulate. Listening, they perished.

Then it stopped.

For another moment the silence sought to extend the song, and then even that vestige was gone. Daniel breathed, and the plumes of his breath were his own. He was alone inside his body in a cold room.

"Christ," Barbara said softly.

There was a sound of cards being shuffled and dealt.

"Christ," she repeated. "Couldn't you just curl up and die?" Seeing Daniel look puzzled, she translated: "I mean, it's just so fucking beautiful."

He nodded.

She lifted her jacket off the nail on which it hung. "Let's go outside. I don't care if I freeze to death—I want some fresh air."

Despite the cold, it did come as a relief to be out of the dorm, in the seeming freedom of the snow. They went where no feet had trampled it to stand beside one of the square stone posts that marked the camp's perimeter. If it hadn't been for the glare of the lights on the snow they might have been standing in any empty field. Even the lights, high on their metal poles, didn't seem so pitiless tonight, with the stars so real above them in the spaces of the sky.

Barbara, too, was considering the stars. "They go there, you know. Some of them."

"To the stars?"

"Well, to the planets, anyhow. But to the stars too, for all that anybody knows. Wouldn't you, if you could?"

"If they do, they must never come back. It would take such a long time. I can't imagine it."

"I can."

She left it at that. Neither of them spoke again for a long while. Far off in the night a tree creaked, but there was no wind.

"Did you know," she said, "that when you fly the music doesn't stop? You're singing and at a certain point you kind of lose track that it's you who's singing, and that's when it happens. And you're never *aware* that the music stops. The song is always going on somewhere. Everywhere! Isn't that incredible?"

"Yeah, I read that too. Some celebrity in the Minneapolis paper said the first time you fly it's like being a blind man who has an operation and can see things for the first time. But then, after the shock is over, after you've been flying regularly, you start taking it all for granted, the same as the people do who've never been blind."

"I didn't *read* it," Barbara said, miffed. "I heard it."

"You mean you flew?"

"Yes."

"No kidding!"

"Just once when I was fifteen."

"Jesus. You've actually *done* it. I've never known anyone who has."

"Well, now you know two of us."

"You mean the guy who sang in there tonight? You think he can fly?"

"It's pretty obvious."

"I did wonder. It wasn't like anyone else's singing I'd ever heard. There was something . . . uncanny about it. But Jesus, Barbara, you've done it! Why didn't you ever say so before? I mean, Christ Almighty, it's like finding out you shook hands with God."

"I don't talk about it because I only did it that one time. I'm not naturally musical. It just isn't in me. When it happened I was very young, and very stoned, and I just took off."

"Where were you? Where did you go? Tell me about it!"

"I was at my cousin's house in West Orange, New Jersey. They had a hook-up in the basement, but no one had ever got off on it. People would buy an apparatus then the way they'd buy a grand piano, as a status symbol. So when I hooked up I didn't really expect anything to happen. I started singing, and something happened inside my head, like when you're falling asleep and you begin to lose your sense of what size you are, if you've ever had that feeling. I didn't pay any attention to it, though, and went right on singing. And then the next thing I knew I was outside my body. At first I thought my ears had popped, it was as simple as that."

"What did you sing?"

"I was never able to remember. You lose touch with your ego in an ordinary way. If you're totally focused on what you're singing, any song can get you off, supposedly. It must have been something from the top twenty, since I wouldn't have known much else in those days. But what counts isn't the song. It's the way you sing it. The commitment you can give."

"Like tonight?"

"Right."

"Uh-huh. So then what happened?"

"I was alone in the house. My cousin had gone off with her boyfriend, and her parents were away somewhere. I was nervous and a bit afraid, I guess. For a while I just floated where I was."

"Where was that?"

"About two inches above the tip of my nose. It felt peculiar."

"I'll bet."

"Then I began flying from one part of the basement to the other."

"You had wings? I mean, *real* wings?"

"I couldn't see myself, but it felt like real wings. It felt like a great charge of power in the middle of my spine. *Will* power, in the most literal sense. I had this sense of being totally focused on what I was doing, and where I was going—and that's what the flying *was*. It was as though you could drive a car by just looking at the road ahead of you."

Daniel closed his eyes to savor the idea of a freedom so perfect and entire.

"I flew around the basement for what seemed like hours. I'd closed the basement door behind me, like a dummy, and the windows were all sealed tight, so there was no way to get out of the basement. People don't consider making fairy-holes until they've actually got off the ground. It didn't matter though. I was so small that the basement seemed as big as a cathedral. And almost that beautiful. *More* than almost—it was incredible."

"Just flying around?"

"And being aware. There was a shelf of canned goods. I can still remember the light that came out of the jars of jam and tomatoes. Not really a light though. It was more as though you could see the life still left in them, the energy they'd stored up while they were growing."

"You must have been hungry."

She laughed. "Probably."

"What else?" he insisted. It was Daniel who was hungry, who was insatiable.

"At a certain point I got afraid. My body—my *physical* body that was lying there in the hook-up—didn't seem real to me. No, I suppose it seemed real enough, maybe even too much so. But it didn't seem mine. Have you ever been to a zoo?

Daniel shook his head.

"Well then I can't explain."

Barbara was quiet for a while. Daniel looked at her body, swollen with pregnancy, and tried to imagine the feeling she couldn't explain. Except in gym class he didn't pay much attention to his own body. Or to other people's, for that matter.

"There was a freezer in the basement. I hadn't noticed it till at one point the motor started up. You know how there's a shudder first, and then a steady hum. Well, for me, then, it was like a symphony orchestra starting up. I was aware, without seeing it, of the part of the engine that was spinning around. I didn't go near it, of course. I knew that any kind of rotary motor is supposed to be dangerous, like quicksand, but it was so . . . intoxicating. Like dance music that you can't possibly resist. I began spinning around where I was, very slowly at first, but there was nothing to keep me from going faster. It was still pure will power. The faster I let myself spin the more exciting, and inviting, the motor seemed. Without realizing it, I'd drifted over to the freezer and I was spinning along the same axis as the motor. I lost all sense of everything but that single motion. I felt like . . . a planet! It could have gone on forever and I wouldn't have cared. But it stopped. The freezer shut itself off, and as the motor slowed down, so did I. Even that part was wonderful. But when it had stopped completely, I was scared shitless. I realized what had happened, and I'd heard that that was how a lot of people had just disappeared. *I* would have. Gladly. I would to this day. When I remember."

"What *did* you do then?"

"I went back to the hook-up. Back to my body. There's a kind of crystal you touch, and the moment you touch it, zip, you're back inside yourself."

"And the whole thing was real? You didn't just imagine it?"

"As real as the two of us talking. As real as the snow on the ground."

"And you never flew again after that?"

"It wasn't for want of trying, believe me. I've spent a small fortune on voice lessons, on drugs, on every kind of therapy there is. But I could never reach escape velocity no matter how I tried. A part of my mind wouldn't join in, wouldn't let go. Maybe it was fear of getting trapped inside some dumb engine. Maybe, like I said before, I just don't have a gift for singing. Anyhow, nothing helped. Finally I stopped trying. And that's the story of my life. And all I can say is, piss on it."

Daniel had the good sense not to try and argue against her bitterness. There even seemed something noble and elevated about it. Compared to Barbara Steiner's, his own little miseries seemed pretty insignificant.

There was still a chance, after all, that *he* could fly.

And he would! Oh, he would! He knew that now. It was the purpose of his life. He'd found it at last! He would fly! He would learn how to fly!

Daniel didn't know how long they'd been standing there in the snow. Gradually, as his euphoria sailed away, he realized that he was cold, that he was aching with the cold, and that they'd better head back to the dorm.

"Hey, Barbara," he said, catching the sleeve of her coat in his numb fingers and giving it a reminding yank. "Hey."

"Right," she agreed sadly, but without stirring.

"We'd better head back to the dorm."

"Right."

"It's cold."

"Very. Yes." She still stood there. "Would you do me a favor first?"

"What?"

"Kiss me."

Usually he would have been flustered by such a suggestion but there was something in the tone of her voice that reassured him. He said, "Okay."

With her eyes looking straight into his, she slid her fingers under the collar of his jacket and then back around his neck. She pulled him close until their faces touched. Hers was as cold as his, and probably as numb. Her mouth opened and she pressed her tongue against his lips, gently urging them apart.

He closed his eyes and tried to let the kiss be real. He'd kissed a girl once before, at a party, and thought the whole process a bit unnatural, if also, at last, rather nice. But he couldn't stop thinking of Barbara's bad teeth, and by the time he'd braced himself to the idea of pushing his tongue around inside her mouth, she'd had enough.

He felt guilty for not having done more, but she seemed not to care. At least Daniel supposed that her faraway look meant she'd got what she wanted, though he didn't really know what that might have been. Even so, he felt guilty. Or at the very least confused.

"Thank you," she said. "That was sweet."

With automatic politeness Daniel answered, "You're welcome." Oddly that was not the wrong thing to say.

Of the man whose song had so wrought upon him, Daniel knew little, not even his real name. In the camp he was known as Gus, having inherited a work shirt across the back of which a former prisoner had stenciled that name. He was a tall, lean, red-faced, ravaged-looking man, somewhere in his forties, who had arrived two weeks ago with a nasty cut over his left eye that was now a puckered scarlet scar. People speculated that he'd been sent up for the fight that had got him the scar, which would have been congruent with his sentence; a bare ninety days. Likely, he'd started the

71

fight on purpose to get that sentence, since a winter at Spirit Lake was more survivable than a jobless and houseless winter in Des Moines, where he came from, and where vagrants, which is what he seemed to be, often died en masse during the worst cold spells.

An ugly customer, without a doubt, but that did not prevent Daniel, as he lay awake that night, from rehearsing, in rather abundant detail, their future relationship, beginning at the moment, tomorrow, that Daniel would approach him as supplicant and maybe, ultimately, as a friend, though the latter possibility was harder to envision in concrete terms, since, aside from his being such a sensational singer, Daniel couldn't yet see what there was to like in Gus, or whoever he was, though it had to be there—his song was the proof. With this faith then in Gus's essential goodness, despite appearances, Daniel (in his daydream) approached the older man (who was, at first, not friendly at all and used some extremely abusive language) and put this simple proposition to him— that Gus should teach Daniel to sing. In payment for his lessons Daniel agreed, after much haggling and more abuse, to give over to Gus each day his supplementary dinner from McDonald's. Gus was skeptical at first, then delighted at such generous and self-sacrificing terms. The lessons began (this part was rather sketchy, since Daniel had no very clear notion of what, besides scales, voice lessons might entail) and came to an end with a kind of graduation ceremony that took place on the evening before Daniel's release. Daniel, gaunt from his long fast, his eyes aglow with inspiration, took leave of his fellow prisoners with a song as piercing and authentic as the song Gus had sung tonight. Perhaps (being realistic) this was asking too much. Perhaps that level of mastery would take longer. But the essential part of the daydream seemed feasible, and in the morning, or at the latest after work, Daniel meant to set his plan in motion.

Daniel's life—the life of his own choosing—was about to begin! Meanwhile, once more, he let his wishes soar, like a little flock of birds, over the vistas of an achieved and merited delight, towards the rustling fields of sleep.

The next morning, several minutes before the usual five-thirty reveille, the whistle sounded. While people were still struggling out of their blankets, its shrill ululation stopped. They all realized that someone had let go, and by the simple process of counting off they found out it had been Barbara Steiner, at whose number, twenty-two, there was only a silence.

A man at the other end of the dorm remarked, in a tone of elegy, "Well, she's performed her last abortion."

Most of the prisoners curled back into their mattresses for the moments of warmth still due them, but three of them, including Daniel, got dressed and went outside in time to see the Warden's pick-up come and cart her body away. She'd gone through the perimeter at just the point where they had talked together the night before.

All the rest of the day, as he tended the vats in the steamy false summer of the station, Daniel tried to reconcile his grief at Barbara's suicide, which was quite genuine, with a euphoria that no other consideration could deplete or noticeably modify. His new-fledged ambition was like a pair of water-wings that bore him up to the sunlit surface of the water with a buoyancy stronger than every contrary effort towards a decent, respectful sorrow. Sometimes, indeed, he would feel himself drifting toward tears, but with a sense rather of comfort than of pain. He wondered if there hadn't been more of comfort than of pain for Barbara in the thought of death. Wasn't it possible that that was what their kiss had meant? A kind of farewell, not just to Daniel but to hopefulness in general?

Of course, the thought of death and the fact of it are two different things, and Daniel couldn't finally agree that the fact is ever anything but bad news. Unless you believed in some kind of afterlife or other. Unless you thought that a spark of yourself could survive the ruin of your body. After all, if fairies could slip loose from the knot of the flesh, why not souls? (That had been Daniel's father's view of the matter, the one time they'd discussed it, long ago.)

There was, however, one major stumbling-block to believing in the old-fashioned, Christian type of soul. Namely, that while fairies were aware of fairies in exactly the way that people are aware of each other, by the senses of sight

73

and hearing and touch, no fairy had ever seen a soul. Often (Daniel had read) a group of them would gather at the bedside of someone who was dying, to await the moment, wished for or believed in, of the soul's release. But what they always had witnessed, instead, was simply a death—not a release but a disappearance, a fading-out, an end. If there were souls, they were not made of the same apprehensible substance as fairies, and all the theories about the soul that had been concocted over the centuries were probably based on the experiences of the rare, fortunate individuals who'd found their way to flight without the help of a hook-up, like the saints who had floated while they prayed, and the yogis of India, etc. Such was the theory of people who had flown, and their outspokenness was one of the reasons that flying and everything to do with it were the focus of such distress and downright hatred among the Undergoders, who *had* to believe in the soul and all the rest of that, since what else was there for them to look forward to *except* their hereafter? The poor, benighted sons-of-bitches.

For that matter, what had *he* had to believe in up till now? Not a thing. But now! Now belief had come to him and burned inside him. By the light of its fire all things were bright and fair, and the darkness beyond the range of his vision was of no concern.

His faith was simple. All faiths are. He would fly. He would learn to sing, and by singing he would fly. It was possible. Millions of others had done it, and like them, so would he. He would fly. It was only necessary to hang on to that one idea. As long as he did, nothing else mattered—not the horror of these vats, not the rigors or desolations of Spirit Lake, not Barbara's death, nor the life he'd go back to in Amesville. Nothing in the world mattered except the moment, dim but certain in the blackness of the years ahead, when he would feel wings spring from his immaterial will and he would fly.

Daniel got back to the dorm just as the auction of Barbara Steiner's personal effects was getting under way. They were spread out for inspection, and people were filing past the table with the same skittish curiosity mourners would pay to a dead body. Daniel took his place in the line, but when he got near enough to the table to recognize the single largest item being offered up (besides the ticking and stuffing of her mattress), he let out a whoop of pure, unthinking indignation, pushed his way to the table, and re-appropriated his long-lost copy of *The Product is God*.

"Put that back, Weinreb," said the trustee in charge of the auction, a Mrs Gruber, who was also, by virtue of her seniority at Spirit Lake, the chief cook and head janitor. "You can bid for that the same as anyone else."

"This book isn't up for auction," he said with the belligerence of righteousness. "It's already mine. It was stolen out of my mattress weeks ago and I never knew who by."

"Well, now you know," said Mrs Gruber complacently. "So put it the fuck back on the table."

"God damn it, Mrs Gruber, this book *belongs* to me!"

"It was inside Steiner's mattress with the rest of her crap, and it is going to be auctioned."

"If that's where it was, it's because she stole it."

"Begged, borrowed, stole—makes no difference to me. Shame on you anyhow for talking that way about your own friend. God only knows what she had to do to get that book."

There was laughter, and one voice in the crowd, and then another, elaborated Mrs Gruber's implication with specific suggestions. It was flustering, but Daniel stood by his rights.

"It *is* my book. Ask the guards. They had to cut pages out before I could have it. There's probably a record of that somewhere. It *is* mine."

"Well, that may be or it may not, but there's no way you can prove to us that Barbara didn't come by it fair and square. We've only got your word for it."

He could see that she had the majority behind her. There was nothing to be done. He gave her the book, and it was the first item to go to the block. (There weren't that many more.) Then some son-of-a-bitch had the nerve to bid against him, and he had to go up to five Big Macs, almost a full week's dinners, to get it back.

Only after the bidding was done did he realize that the voice he'd been bidding against belonged to Gus.

After the auction was the lottery. Everyone had the number he counted off by at reveille. Daniel was thirty-four, and it

75

came up, winning him back one of his McDonald's vouchers. But not the one for tonight's meal, so that when the guard brought round the dinners that night Daniel had to make do with a bowl of Mrs Gruber's watery soup and a single slice of white bread smeared with a dab of extended cheese.

For the first time in weeks he felt hungry. Usually dinner left him with a queasy sensation. It must have been the anger. He would have liked to drown old Mrs Gruber in a kettle of the slop she cooked. And that was just the first of his angers. Peel that away and there were more— against Barbara for stealing his book, against Gus for bidding for it, against the whole lousy prison and its guards, and all the world outside the prison, because they were the ones who had sent him here. There was no way to think about it without going crazy, and there was no way, once you started, to stop.

Clearly, this was not the right time to approach Gus and make his proposition. Instead he played chess with Bob Lundgren, and played so well that (although he didn't finally win) for the first time he put Lundgren on the defensive and even captured his queen.

While they played he was aware, at different times, that Gus, who had never (so far as he knew) paid any notice to him before, was looking at him with a far-off but unwavering attention. Why should that be? It seemed almost a kind of telepathy, as if Gus knew, without his saying anything, what Daniel had in mind.

The next day the truck conveying Daniel and the rest of the E.S.78 work crew back to the compound was delayed by a road block. This was an unusually thorough one. Everyone, including the guards, had to get out and be frisked, while another set of inspectors examined the truck from its broken headlights to its raggedy mudflaps.

They were an hour late clocking in at the dorm. Daniel had been meaning, very first thing, to go to Gus and get it over, but once again the moment wasn't right. Gus and Bob Lundgren were already deep in a game of chess, which Daniel was invited to watch, and which for a while he did. But they played slowly, and without a personal stake in the game it was impossible to pay attention.

Daniel decided to return to *The Product is God*. It was no longer the book he'd begun four months ago. Just the fact that Barbara Steiner had preceded him through its final chapters, leaving behind a spoor of scribbled marginalia, made it seem not quite the harmless trampoline for bright, beside-the-point ideas that it had seemed at first glance.

Dangerous ideas, however, are also, necessarily, more interesting ideas, and Daniel read the book this time with none of his former, lingering pleasure. He read greedily, as though it might be snatched away again before he'd discovered its secret. Again and again he found ideas that Barbara had lifted out of the book and used in her own arguments, such as the one about purity of heart being to will one thing, which turned out not even to be Van Dyke's idea, but somebody else's centuries ago.

What did seem to be Van Dyke's own idea (and which eventually connected up with the other) was his theory that people live in two completely unrelated worlds. The first was the world that comes in a set with the flesh and the devil—the world of desire, the world people think they can control. Over against this was God's world, which is larger and more beautiful, but crueller too, at least from the limited viewpoint of human beings. The example Van Dyke gave was Alaska. In God's world you just had to give up trying and trust to luck, and you would probably either freeze to death or die of starvation.

The other world, the human world, was more viable, more survivable, but it was also, unfortunately, completely corrupt, and the only way to get ahead in it was to take a hand in the corruption. Van Dyke called this "rendering unto Caesar". The basic problem for anyone wanting to lead a life that wasn't just dog-eat-dog was how to render unto God. Not, Van Dyke insisted, by trying to live *in* God's world, since that amounted to suicide, concerning which there was an entire chapter called 'The Saints Go Marchin' In!' (Here Barbara's underlinings became almost co-extensive with the text, and the margins flowered with breathless assents: "How true!" "Exactly!" "I agree." Rather than try to take heaven by storm Van Dyke suggested that you set yourself a single life-task and stick to it through hell or high water. ("Purity of heart", etc.). It made no difference *which* life-task, so long as it was of no material advantage. Van Dyke offered a number of silly possibilities and anecdotes about celebrities who'd found their way to God by such diverse paths as basket-weaving, breeding dachshunds, and translating *The Mill on the Floss* into a language that only computers could read.

Daniel, happy in the discovery of his own life-task, could follow the book easily up to this point, but not beyond. For the theory that all this seemed to be leading up to was that the world was coming to an end. Not God's world—that would always go rolling along—but the world of man, Caesar's world. Van Dyke, like some bearded prophet in a cartoon, was announcing the end of Western Civilization—or, as he styled it, "the Civilization of the Business Man". ("Biz Civ" for short.)

Van Dyke seemed to face this prospect with his usual cold-blooded equanimity. "How much better," he wrote, "to live at the end of such a civilization than at its heights. Now, with half the faulty mechanism in ruins and the other half grinding to a halt for want of lubrication, its power over our souls and our imaginations is so much less than it would have been if we'd lived a hundred or two hundred years ago, when the whole capitalist contraption was just getting its first head of steam. We see now, as our forebears never could, where this overweening enterprise was leading—to the ruin of humankind, or of as much of humankind, at least, as has cast its lot with Biz Civ. But a ruin, let us admit it, that is altogether fitting and proper, a thoroughly *merited* ruin, which we are obliged to inhabit as becomes decaying gentry. That is to say, with as much style as we can muster, with whatever pride we can still pretend to, and with, most importantly, a perfect nonchalance."

Daniel was not about to admit that *his* world was coming to an end, much less that it ought to. This particular corner of it was nothing to write home about, certainly, but it would be a hard thing for any lad freshly come to a sense of his own high purpose to be told that the firm is going out of business. Who was Reverend Van Dyke to be making such pronouncements? Just because he'd spent a few weeks traveling to such places as Cairo and Bombay for the National Council of Churches' Triage Committee didn't give him the authority to write off the whole damned world! Things might be as bad as he said in the places he'd been to, but he hadn't been everywhere. He hadn't, for one thing, been to Iowa. (Unless the pages the prison censor had torn from the back of the book were about the Farm Belt, which didn't seem likely from the title of the missing chapter that was printed on the contents page—'Where Peace Prevails.') Iowa, for all its faults, was not about to run into an iceberg and sink, like Van Dyke's favorite example of the fate of Biz Civ, the lost city of Brasilia.

It was an infuriating book. Daniel was glad to be done with it. If that was the way people thought in New York he could almost understand Undergoders wanting to send in the National Guard and take the city over. Almost but not quite.

The next day was Christmas Eve, and when Daniel got back from work a ratty old tree was going up in the dorm under Warden Shiel's personal supervision. Once the limbs were slotted into the trunk and the ornaments had been hung up and, for a final glory, a tinsely angel had been tied to the top, the prisoners were assembled around the tree (Daniel stood in the last row, with the tallest) and Warden Shiel took their picture, copies of which would later be mailed out to relevant relatives.

Then they sang carols. 'Silent Night' first, then 'O Little Town of Bethlehem', then 'Faith of Our Fathers', and finally 'Silent Night' again. Three or four clear strong voices rose above the muddy generality, but strangely Gus's was not among these. Daniel screwed up his courage—he'd never liked singing in public (or anywhere else, for that matter)—and sang. Really sang. The man directly in front of him turned his head round briefly to see who was suddenly making such a noise, and even Warden Shiel, sitting there on his folding chair, with his right hand resting benignly on the P-W module, seemed to take approving notice. It was embarrassing in the same way and to the same degree as getting undressed in front of other kids in a locker room. The worst of it was in the imagining. By the time you were doing it, so was everybody else.

After the carols, presents were distributed to the prison-

79

ers who had families and friends on the outside to be thinking of them, following which the Warden went on to the next dorm to repeat these holiday procedures. The presents, as many as were edible, were then further portioned out. Daniel bolted one slice of his mother's fruitcake and put aside another in his mattress. So long as you assumed some part of the burden towards the dorm's have-nots you could choose who you were nice to, and the next slice of the fruitcake went, as a matter of course, to Bob Lundgren. The Lundgrens had sent their son a packet of Polaroids taken at their last Thanksgiving dinner, which Bob was studying with baleful incredulity. The banked fires of his inner rage were glowing at such intensity it was all he could do to say thank you.

Gus was in the farthest corner of the room, doling out crumbled cookies from a large tin box. Somehow Daniel hadn't been expecting that. For some reason, perhaps the slow-healing scar, he'd imagined Gus as utterly bereft and friendless, unless Daniel himself were to become his friend. Daniel made his way over to Gus's corner and, with what diffidence he could summon up, offered him a piece of the cake.

Gus smiled. This close, Daniel, who had a developed judgement of dental work, could see that his perfect upper incisors were actually caps, and of the first quality at that. The lower incisors, as well. All in all, a couple thousand dollars worth of work, and that was only what showed when he smiled.

"The other night," Daniel said, taking the plunge, "when you sang . . . I really enjoyed that."

Gus nodded, swallowing. "Right," he said. And then, taking another bite, "This is terrific cake."

"My mother made it."

Daniel stood there, watching him eat, not knowing what else to say. Even as he ate, Gus went on smiling at him, a smile that encompassed the compliment to his singing, his pleasure in the food, and something else besides. A recognition, it seemed to Daniel, of some common bond.

"Here," Gus said, holding out the box of crumbs, "have some of mine, Danny-boy."

Danny-boy? That was several degrees worse than just

'Danny', and even that he'd always resisted as a nickname. Still, it showed that Gus—without their ever talking to each other before—was aware of him, was even curious about him perhaps.

He took a couple broken cookies and nodded his thanks. Then, with an uneasy sense of having done the wrong thing, he moved off, bearing the ever-diminishing cake.

Soon enough the goodies were gone and the party was over. The dorm became very quiet. Over intermittent blasts of wind you could hear the prisoners singing the same carols in the next dorm. Mrs Gruber, with her mattress wrapped around her where she sat in front of the Franklyn stove, began to croon along wordlessly, but when no one else showed any Christmas spirit, she gave up.

In the next dorm the caroling stopped, and a short while later there was the sound of the pick-up's motor turning over. As if he'd been waiting for this signal, Gus got up and went over to where the Christmas tree had been. Someone sounded a note on a harmonica, and Gus hummed the same note, rumblingly.

The hush of the room, from having been a hush of gloom, became the hush of fixed attention. Some people went and formed a ring around the singer, while others stayed where they were. But all of them listened as if the song were a newscast announcing a major worldwide disaster.

These were the words of the song Gus sang:

> O Bethlehem is burning down
>   And Santa Claus is dead
> But the world continues turning round
>   And so does my head!
>
> The Tannenbaum is bare as bone
>   And soon I will be too
> But who's that lady lying prone
>   On sheets of baby blue?
>
> O Christmas Eve is cold and scary
> Who could believe the Virgin Mary
>   Would ever discover
>   The likes of a lover
> Like you, my lad, or me?

81

Chorus:
Roll over Joe
I've sold my soul
For a fal doll diddle
And a jolly little O
For a fox and a fiddle
And a ho ho ho!

So
Then
We'll wang her and bang her
And rim her and trim her
And tell her the reason why

We'll toast her and roast her
And nail up a poster
To show her the set-up to buy

We'll poke her and stroke her
And spank her and thank her
For a beautiful piece of pie

We'll scourge her and urge her
To consider a merger
Between the earth and the sky!

Daniel couldn't tell for quite a while if this were a real song or one that Gus was making up then and there, but when people started to sing along at the part that started at 'Roll over Joe', he decided it had to be real. There were a lot of songs you never heard in Iowa, radio broadcasts being so strictly controlled.

They sang the song over and over, not just the chorus, which got louder and rowdier with each repetition, but the whole thing. It seemed, if you didn't fasten on the words, like the most exquisite and decorative of Christmas carols, a treasure from a dim and pretty past of sleigh rides, church bells, and maple syrup. Annette, the feeble-minded migrant woman who liked to drum on the stovepipes, got caught up in the excitement and started doing an impromptu strip dressed in the discarded Christmas wrappings, until Mrs Gruber, who was officially responsible for the collective good behavior of the dorm, put a stop to it. Prisoners from the next-door dorm came and insisted, against Mrs Gruber's protests, that the song be sung over from the beginning for them, and this time round Daniel was able to add his own few decibels to the general effect. People started dancing, and the ones who didn't dance held on to each other and swayed in time. Even Bob Lundgren forgot about murdering his brother and sang along.

The festivity lasted till at last the loudspeaker blared out: "All right, assholes, Christmas is over so shut the fuck up!" With no more warning than that the lights went out, and people had to scramble around in the dark locating their mattresses and spreading them out on the floor. But the song had already served its purpose. The foul taste of Christmas had been washed from every mind.

Everyone got to take off Christmas Day as a holiday except for the workers at E.S. 78, since there was no way to tell the termites, squirming forward through their black tunnels on their way to the waiting vats, to slow down because it was Christmas. It was just as well, Daniel told himself. It was easier to lead a rotten life than to lie back and think about it.

That night, when he got back to the dorm, Gus was lying in front of the lukewarm stove. His eyes were closed, but his fingers were moving in slow, fixed patterns across the zipper of his jacket. It was almost as though he were waiting for him. In any case, the moment couldn't be put off any longer. Daniel squatted beside him, nudged his shoulder, and asked him, when he opened his eyes, if they could go outside to talk. He didn't have to explain. There was supposed to be much less chance of the monitors tuning in on conversations if you were out of the dorms. In any case, Gus didn't seem surprised to be asked.

At the mid-point between dorm and latrine, Daniel delivered his message with telegraphic brevity. He'd been thinking of just how to say it for days. "The other night, last night, when I said how much I enjoyed your singing, I actually had something more in mind. You see, I've never heard much real singing before. Not like yours. And it really got to me. And I've decided. . . ." He lowered his voice. "I've decided that I want to learn to sing. I've decided that's what I'm going to do with my life."

"Just sing?" Gus asked, smiling in a superior way and shifting his weight from one leg to the other. "Nothing else?"

Daniel looked up, imploring. He didn't dare spell it out in more detail. The monitors might be listening. They might be recording everything he said. Surely Gus understood.

"You want to fly—isn't that it, really?"

Daniel nodded.

"Pardon?"

"Yes," he said. And then, since there was no reason now not to blurt out anything, he put his own rhetorical question to Gus: "Isn't that why *most* people learn to sing?"

"Some of us do just fall into it, but in the sense you mean, yes, I suppose that's so for most people. But this is Iowa, you know. Flying's not legal here."

"I know."

"And you don't care?"

"There's no law says I've got to live in Iowa the rest of my life."

"True enough."

"And there's no law against singing, even in Iowa. If I want to learn to sing, that's my own business."

"And that's true enough too."

"Will you teach me?"

"I was wondering where I came into this."

"I'll give you all my vouchers from here on in. I get the full supplement. It costs thirty-five dollars a week."

"I know. I get it too."

"If you don't want to eat that much you can trade my vouchers for something you do want. It's all I've got, Gus. If I had anything else, I'd offer that."

"But you do, Danny-boy," Gus said. "You've got something I find *much* more appealing."

"The book? You can have that too. If I'd known it was you who was bidding, I wouldn't have bid against you."

"Not the book. I only did that to get your goat."

"Then what *do* you want?"

"Not your hamburgers, Danny-boy. But I *could* go for the buns."

He didn't understand at first, and Gus offered no more by way of explanation than a strange relaxed sort of smile, with his mouth half open and his tongue passing slowly back and forth behind his capped teeth. When it finally dawned on him what Gus was after, he couldn't believe it. That, anyhow, was what he told himself: *I can't believe it!* He tried to pretend, even then, that he still hadn't got the message.

Gus knew better. "Well, Danny-boy?"

"You're not serious."

"Try me out and see."

"But—" His objection seemed so self-evident he didn't see any need to spell it out beyond that.

Gus shifted his weight again in a single over-all shrug. "That's the price of music lessons, kiddo. Take it or leave it."

Daniel had to clear his throat to be able to say that he would leave it. But he said it loud and clear, in case the monitors were taking any of it down.

Gus nodded. "You're probably doing the right thing."

Daniel's indignation finally bubbled over. "I don't need *you* to tell me that! Jesus!"

"Oh, I don't mean holding on to your cherry. You'll lose that one of these days. I mean it's just as well you don't try and become a singer."

"Who says I'm not going to?"

"You can try, true enough. No one can stop that."

"But I won't make it, is that what you mean? Sounds like sour grapes to me."

"Yes, partly. I wouldn't have offered my candid opinion if you'd decided to invest in lessons. But now there's no reason not to. And my candid opinion is that you are a punk singer. You could take voice lessons from here till doomsday and you'd never get *near* escape velocity. You're too tight. Too mental. Too much the Iowa type. It's a shame, really, that you got this idea into your head, 'cause it can only mess you up."

"You're saying that from spite. You've never heard me sing."

"Don't have to. It's enough to watch you walk across a room. But in fact I have heard you sing. Last night. That was quite enough. Anyone who can't handle 'Jingle Bells' is not cut out for a major career."

"We didn't sing 'Jingle Bells' last night."

"No? Could have fooled me."

"I know I need lessons. If I didn't, I wouldn't have asked."

"Lessons can only do so much. There has to be a basic capacity. A dog won't learn arithmetic, no matter who his teacher is. You want the particulars? Number one, you're tone-deaf. Two, you've got no more sense of rhythm than a road-grader. Beyond one and two, there is something still more essential missing, which we who have it call soul."

"Fuck you."

"That might be the beginning, yes."

With which Gus patted Daniel's cheeks smartly with the flat of both hands and smiled a still partly-friendly parting smile and left him to a desolation he had never imagined could be his, a foretaste of failure as black and bitter as a child's first taste of coffee. The thing he wanted most in life, the only thing, would never be. Never. The idea was a skull in his hand. He couldn't put it down. He couldn't look away.

A month went by. It was as though the worst single hour of his life, the absolutely blackest moment, was to be stretched out, like railroad tracks on a bed of cinders, to the horizon. Each day he woke, each night he went to bed, he faced the same unrelieved prospect, a bleakness by whose wintry light all other objects and events became a monotony of cardboard zeroes. There was no way to combat it, no way to ignore it. It was the destined shape of his life, as the trunk and branches of a pine are the shape of its life.

Gus's eyes seemed always to be following him. His smile seemed always to be at Daniel's expense. The worst torment of all was when he sang, which he'd begun to do more often since Christmas Eve. His songs were always about sex, and always beautiful. Daniel could neither resist their beauty nor yield to it. Like Ulysses he struggled against the bonds that tethered him to the mast, but they were the bonds of his own obdurate will and he could not break them. He could only twist and plead. No one noticed, no one knew.

He kept repeating, in his thoughts, the same lump of words, like an old woman saying prayers. "I wish I were dead. I wish I were dead." If he ever thought about it, he knew this was only a maudlin imposture. But yet in a way it was true. He did *wish* he were dead. Whether he ever mustered the courage to carry out such a wish was another matter. The means lay readily to hand. He had only, like Barbara Steiner, to step across the perimeter of the camp and a radio transmitter would take care of the rest. One step. But he was chickenshit, he couldn't do it. He would stand there, though, for hours, beside the fieldstone post that marked the possible end of his life, repeating the mindless lie that seemed so nearly true: "I wish I were dead. I wish I were dead. I wish I were dead."

Once, just once, he managed to go past the post, whereupon, as he had known it must, the warning whistle started to blow. The sound petrified him. It was only a few yards farther to his wish, but his legs had stopped obeying him. He stood fast in an enchantment of rage and shame, while people filed out of the dorms to see who'd let go. The whistle kept blowing till at last he tucked his tail between his legs and returned to the dorm. No one would talk to him, or even look at him. The next morning, after roll-call, a guard gave Daniel a bottle of tranks and watched while he swallowed the first capsule. The pills didn't stop his depression, but he was never so silly again.

In February, a month before he was due to be released, Gus was paroled. Before he left Spirit Lake he made a point of taking Daniel aside and telling him not to worry, that he could be a singer if he really wanted to and made a big enough effort.

"Thanks," Daniel said, without much conviction.

"It's not your vocal equipment that matters so much as the way you *feel* what you sing."

"Does not wanting to be screwed by some skid row derelict show that I don't have enough feeling? Is that my problem, huh?"

"You can't blame a guy for trying. Anyhow, Danny-boy, I didn't want to leave without telling you not to give up the ghost on my say-so."

"Good. I never intended to."

"If you work at it, you'll probably get there. In time."

"Your generosity is killing me."

Gus persisted. "So I've thought about it, and I've got a word of advice for you. My own last word on the subject of how to sing."

Gus waited. For all his resentment, Daniel couldn't keep from clutching at the talisman being dangled before him. He swallowed his pride and asked, "And what is that?"

"Make a mess of your life. The best singers always do."

Daniel forced a laugh. "I seem to have a good start at that."

"Precisely. That's why there's still hope for you." He pursed his lips and tilted his head to the side. Daniel backed away from him as though he'd been groped. Gus smiled. He touched a finger to the almost-vanished scar above his eye. "Then, you see, when the mess is made, the music pulls it all together. But remember, the mess has to come first."

"I'll remember. Anything else?"

"That's all." He offered his hand. "Friends?"

"Well, not enemies," Daniel allowed, with a smile of his own that was not more than fifty per cent sarcastic.

At the end of February, only a couple weeks before Daniel was due to be released, the Supreme Court ruled, in a six-to-three decision, that the measures taken by Iowa and other Farm Belt states to prohibit the distribution of newspapers and other printed material originating in other states was in violation of the First Amendment. Three days later, Daniel was released from Spirit Lake.

On the night before he was to leave the prison Daniel dreamed that he was back in Minneapolis, standing on the shore of the Mississippi at the point where it was spanned by the pedestrian bridge. But now instead of that remembered bridge there were only three inch-thick steel cables— a single cable to walk on and two higher up to hold on to. The girl with Daniel wanted him to cross the river on these simulated vines, but the span was too wide, the river too immensely far below. Going out even a little way seemed certain death. Then a policeman offered to handcuff one of his hands to a cable. With that safeguard Daniel agreed to try.

The cables bounced and swayed as he inched his way out over the river, and his insides frothed with barely controlled terror. But he kept going. He even forced himself to take real footsteps instead of sliding his feet along the cable.

At the midpoint of the bridge he stopped. The fear was gone. He looked down at the river where its storybook blue reflected a single sunlit cloud. He sang. It was a song he'd learned in the fourth grade from Mrs Boismortier.

"I am the Captain of the Pinafore," Daniel sang, "and a right good captain too. I'm very very good, and be it understood, I command a right good crew."

From either shore choruses of admiring spectators replied, like the faintest of echoes.

He didn't know the rest of the song, so he stopped. He looked at the sky. He was feeling terrific. If it hadn't been for the damned handcuffs he could have flown. The air that had accepted his song would have accepted his body with no greater difficulty. He was as sure of this as he was that he was alive and his name was Daniel Weinreb.

PART II

5

THE CLOUDS OVER Switzerland were pink puffy lobes of brain with, at intervals, great splintered bones of granite thrusting up through them. She loved the Alps, but only when she was above them. She loved France too, all purposeful and rectilinear in solemn shades of dun and olive-tinged viridian. She loved the whole round world, which seemed, at this moment, to be present to view in all its revolving glory, as the Concorde rose still higher.

On the console before her she jabbed the numbers of her wish, and in an instant the beneficent mechanism beside her seat ejected yet another pink lady, her third. Apparently it made no difference, at this altitude, that she was only seventeen. It was all so lawless and lovely, and she loved it all, the pink ladies, the almonds, the off-blue Atlantic whizzing by below. She loved most of all to be returning home at long, long last and to be saying farewell and fuck you to the gray walls, gray skies, and gray smocks of Ste Ursule.

Boadicea Whiting was an enthusiast. She could, with the same heartfelt if fleeting passion of appreciation, applaud the world's least raindrop or its most lavish hurricane. But she was no scatterbrain. She had other passions more abiding, and the chief of these was for her father, Mr Grandison Whiting. She had not seen him for nearly two years, not even on cassettes, since he was fastidious about his personal correspondence and would send only hand-written letters. Though he'd written quite regularly, and though he was quite right (in matters of taste he was infallible), she had missed him terribly, missed the warmth and light of his presence, like a plant kept from the sun, like a nun. What a life it is, the life of repentance—or rather, what a life it isn't! But (as he'd written in one of his weekly letters) the only way to learn the price of something is to pay it. And, she'd replied (though the letter was never sent), pay it and pay it.

The seatbelt sign winked off, and Boadicea unstrapped herself and climbed the short windy staircase to the lounge. One other passenger had beat her to the bar, a heavy, red-faced man in a really ugly red blazer. Synthetic, she thought—a judgement against which there could be no appeal. A sin (Grandison was wont to say) may be forgiven, but not a synthetic. The man in the blazer was complaining, nasally, to the steward at the bar that every time he'd ordered a drink during takeoff the god-damn idiot machine had flashed a god-damn sign at him to say sorry, he wasn't old enough, and god-damn it, he was thirty-two! With each god-damn, he would glance at Boadicea to see if she were scandalized. She couldn't keep from beaming at the steward's explanation—that the computer had got the man's passport or seat number mixed up with someone else's. The man mistook the meaning of her smile. With the miraculous self-regard of his kind, he came over and offered her a drink. She said she would like a pink lady.

Would four be a mistake, she wondered? Would it prevent her, when she arrived, from shining? It would scarcely do to leave in disgrace and return, two years later, drunk. So far, however, she felt in command of herself, if maybe slightly more susceptible than usual.

"Aren't the clouds beautiful?" she said, when he'd returned with the drink and they had settled down before their first class view of heaven.

Dismissing the question with a sociable smile, he asked if this were her first trip to America. Evidently, Ste Ursule had done its work. She said no, it had been her first trip to Europe and now she was coming back.

He asked her what she had seen. She said she'd seen art museums and churches mostly. "And you?" she asked.

"Oh, I didn't have time to go in for that kind of thing. It was a business trip."

"Oh. What business are you in?" She felt a guttersnipe delight in asking that most American of questions.

"I'm a representative for Consolidated Food Systems."

"Really? My uncle is a representative too, though not for C.F.S. He has some connection with them, though."

"Well, C.F.S. is the biggest company in Des Moines, so it's not surprising."

"Is that where you live?"

"I live just about anywhere C.F.S. cares to send me, and at this point they've sent me just about anywhere." He had that down pat. She wondered if it were something he'd made up himself at one time, or if all the C.F.S. salesmen learned it when they were being trained. Then he took her by surprise. "Do you know," he said, in a tone of completely believable regret, and even thoughtfulness, "I do have an apartment in Omaha, but I haven't seen the inside of it for over a year."

At once she felt guilty for baiting him. And why? Because he had a paunch and didn't know how to dress? Because his voice was the whining, forlorn voice of the prairie? Because he had wanted the few minutes of their passage across the ocean to bear the stamp of an actual human encounter? Didn't *she*, after all?

"Are you all right?" he asked.

"I think I may be drunk," she said. "I'm not used to airplanes."

The clouds were now so far below they looked like a formica tabletop, opaque white sworled with a dismal grayish blue. In fact, the ledge on which she'd placed her drink was made of just such lamentable formica.

"But I like," she added, a little desperately, as he continued simply staring, "to fly. I think I could spend my whole life on the wing, just whizzing about like this. Whiz, whiz."

He looked at his watch so as not to have to look before him at the blue beyond the glass. Even here, she realized, even at twenty-five thousand feet, it was bad form to praise the act and power of flight. America!

"And where do *you* live?" he asked.

"In Iowa, on a farm."

"Is that so? A farmer's daughter." He fairly underlined his innuendo with a grin of masculine condescension.

She could *not* keep hold of a sense of fairness. Everything about the man was an offense to decency—his flat, uninflected speech, his complacence, his stupidity. He seemed thoroughly to deserve his wretched life, and she wanted, meanly, to make him see the actual squalid shape of it.

"Yes, that's me. Though if one has to be any particular

kind of daughter these days, that's the kind to be. Don't you agree?"

He agreed, with a sufficient sense of having been deflated. He knew what she meant. She meant she had money and he did not, and that this was a superior advantage to being of the advantaged sex.

"My name is Boadicea," she informed him, seeming to offer, briefly, her hand, but then, before he could respond, reaching for her drink.

"Boadicea," he repeated, changing every vowel.

"My friends call me Bo, or sometimes Boa."

Among a certain class this would have been enough. But he was certainly not of that class, nor ever would be, though it was clear from the way his eyes were fixed on her now, that the wish lingered on.

"And my *father* calls me Bobo." She sighed theatrically. "It is hard to go through life with such a peculiar name, but my father is a fanatical Anglophile, as was his father before him. Both Rhodes scholars! I'm fairly sure my brother won't be though. *His* name is Serjeant, and my sister's is Alethea. I'm lucky, I suppose, that I wasn't christened Britannia. Though as to nicknames, then I'd have had a choice between Brit and Tania. Do *you* like England?"

"I've been there, but only on business."

"Does business lift you up so far, then, that liking simply doesn't enter in?"

"Well, it rained most of the time I was there, and the hotel I stayed in was so cold I had to wear my clothes to bed, and there was food rationing then, which is why I was sent there to begin with. But aside from that I guess I liked it well enough. The people were friendly, the ones I had to deal with."

She looked at him with a blank smile, and sipped the pink lady, which had begun to seem cloying. From marveling at the elegance and bitchery of what she'd just said she hadn't taken in a word of his.

"I find," he said resolutely, "that people usually are, if you let 'em."

"Oh, people . . . yes. I think so too. People are wonderful. You're wonderful, I'm wonderful, and the steward has wonderful red hair, though not as wonderful by half as my father's. I have a theory about red hair."

"What's that?"

"I believe it's a sign of spiritual distinction. Swinburne had intensely red hair."

"Who was Swinburne?"

"The greatest poet of Victorian England."

He nodded. "There's Dolly Parsons too. Her hair's pretty red."

"Who's Dolly Parsons?"

"The faith-healer. On tv."

"Oh. Well, it's only a theory."

"Some of the things she does are pretty incredible too. A lot of people really believe in her. I've never heard anyone else say it was her hair though. I've got a cousin out in Arizona—he's got red hair and says he hates it. He says people are always ribbing him about it, give him funny looks."

She felt, as she sat listening to the steady unreeling of his speech, as if she had mounted a carousel, which was now revolving too fast for her to get off. The plane had canted several degrees to the left. The sun had moved noticeably *higher* in the west, so that its light made vast semaphores on the heaving waves, from which the clouds had all been wiped away.

"You must excuse me," she said, and hastily left the lounge.

In the washroom a dim green light seemed to spill from the mirrors in a manner at once weird and reassuring. It would have been a wholly habitable refuge if only there hadn't been, in each of the mirrors, the self-reproach of her own image.

Lord knows, she tried. How many weeks of her life had she wasted trying to subdue and civilize this other Boadicea, dressing her in overpriced designer clothes that ceased to be *soigné* the moment she removed them from their splendid boxes, dieting to the verge of anorexia, and fussing with creams, lotions, lashes, pots of rouge, copying on the oval canvas of her face the faces of Rubens, of Modigliani, of Reni and Ingres. But always behind these viscid masks was

97

the same too full, too lively face, framed by the same abundant, intractable mid-brown hair, which was her mother's hair. Indeed, she was her mother's daughter through and through, except her mind, which was her own. But who is solaced by a sense of having perspicuous intellectual gifts? No one, certainly, who is drunk and surrounded by mirrors and wants, more than anything else in the world, to be loved by the likes of Grandison Whiting, a man who has declared that the first duty of an aristocrat is to his own wardrobe.

Wealth, Grandison Whiting had told his children, is the foundation of a good character, and though he might say some things, like the remark about the wardrobe, only for effect, he was sincere about this. Wealth was also, he would allow, the root of evil, but that was just the reverse of the coin, a logical necessity. Money was freedom, as simple as that, and people who had none, or little, could not be judged by the same standards as those who had some, or much, for they were not free agents. Virtue, therefore, was an aristocratic prerogative, and vice as well.

This was just the beginning of Grandison Whiting's system of political economy which went, in all its corollaries and workings-out, much farther and deeper than Boadicea had ever been allowed to follow, for at certain crucial moments in the unfolding of his system she had been required to go off to bed, or the gentlemen would remove themselves from the table to have their ideas and their cigars in masculine seclusion. Always, it seemed, that moment would come just when she thought she had begun to see him as he truly was—not the kindly, careless Santa Claus of a father indulging her in her girlish adorations, but the *real* Grandison Whiting whose renaissance energies seemed a more potent argument for the existence of God than any of the feeble notions of apologetics that she'd been required to learn by heart at Ste Ursule. Ste Ursule itself had been the most drastic of these exiles from his presence. Though she had come to understand the need for it (with her analyst's help), though she had even wrung a consent from her own heart at the last, the two years' exile from her father had been bitter bread indeed—all the more bitter because she had so clearly brought it on herself.

It had begun, as all her sorrows did, with an enthusiasm. She'd received a video camera for her fourteenth birthday, the latest model Editronic. Within three weeks she had so completely mastered the programs of which the camera was capable, and their various combinations, that she was able to construct a documentary about the operations and daily life of Worry (as the Whiting estate, and the film, was called) that was at once so smooth, so lively, and so professionally innocuous that it was shown in prime time on the state educational channel. This, in addition to what she called her "real movies", which, if less suited to public broadcast, were no less prodigious. Her father gave his approval and encouragement—what else could he have done?—and Boadicea, exalted, exultant, was swept up by a passion of creativity as by a tsunami.

In the three months following her freshman year of high school she mastered a range of equipment and programming techniques that would have required as many years of study at a technical college. Only when, with her father's help, she had obtained her mail order diploma and a union license did she put forth the proposal that she had all along been working toward. Would he, she asked, let her make an in-depth study of his own life? It would be a companion piece to *Worry*, but on a much loftier scale both as to length and to intensity.

At first he refused. She pleaded. She promised it would be a tribute, a monument, an apotheosis. He temporized, declaring that while he believed in her genius, he also believed in the sanctity of private life. Why should he spend a million dollars on the security of his house and grounds and then allow his own Bobo to expose that dear-bought privacy to the common gaze? She promised that no sanctums would be violated, that her film would do for him what Eisenstein had done for Stalin, what Riefenstahl had done for Hitler. *She* adored him, and she wanted the world to kneel beside her. It would, she knew it would, if only he would let her have the chance. At last—what else could he have done?—he consented, with the proviso that if he did not approve the finished product, it would be shown to no one else.

She went to work at once, with that fresh and resistless energy that only adolescence can command, and a skill very nearly equal to her energy. The first rushes were in the promised hieratic manner and made Grandison Whiting seem even more Grandisonian than he did off-screen. He moved through the scenerios of his life with the ponderous, hypnotic grace of a Sun-King, his bright red hair forming a kind of aureole about his pale perfect Celtic face. As for his clothes, they testified in every stitch and pleat to the wearer's inner, unfailing *aretê*. No prime minister, no movie star, no gangster had ever possessed so fine a wardrobe.

The film's fascination for Grandison himself must have been as irresistible as it was embarrassing. It was so patently an act of worship. But it might, for all that, have its use. The resources of art are not often devoted this unstintingly, after all, to celebrating the *values* of the very rich or when they were, there is liable to be a perceptible sense of a commodity being bought and paid for, a smell, as of banks of cut flowers, that is sweet but not wholly natural. Boadicea's film had none of the high gloss of captive art, and yet it was, possibly, in its headlong way, a real achievement.

The work went on. Boadicea was allowed to resume her school attendance at the Amesville High School on a reduced schedule so as to have advantage of the daylight hours. As she felt more secure in the possession of her skills, she permitted herself liberties, little lyric departures from the early grand manner of the film. She caught her father, quite unawares, rough-housing with Dow Jones, his spaniel bitch. She recorded minutes, and soon whole cassettes, of his authentic, and delectable, table-talk, and one of these occasions was when her uncle Charles was on hand. Uncle Charles was the head of the House Ways and Means Committee. She followed her father about on a business trip to Omaha and Dallas, and there was some satisfactory footage of what *seemed* bonafide wheeling and dealing.

She knew, though, that it was not, and she became obsessed (both as artist and as daughter) with penetrating to those shadowed recesses of his life where (she believed) he was most fully himself. She knew that what he ventured to say before her cameras differed essentially from what he would have said in candor among friends; differed still more from what, in his soul, he held to be truth. Or rather she suspected this, for with his children Grandison Whiting would only throw out the most equivocal hints as to his own opinions on any matters more serious than questions of taste and comportment. Instead, he had a donnish knack for showing how, on the one hand, one might think *this*, or, on the other hand, *that*, leaving it quite up in the air which of the twain, if either, represented the convictions of Grandison Whiting.

As the film progressed, and then, as it did not progress, Boadicea found herself running up against this equivocalness in everything her father said, in his very smiles. The more she considered, the less she understood, though she continued, still, to adore. It could not be that her father simply lacked a coherent view of the world and his place in it, that he did whatever had to be done to advance his interests on the basis of mere everyday expedience. This may have been the case with her Uncle Charles (who was, in the way of much younger brothers, as devoted to Grandison as Boadicea herself); it may be the case with many men who inhabit the corridors of power by birthright rather than by conquest, but it was not the case with *him*, not conceivably.

She began to pry. Left alone in his office, she would read the papers laying on his desk, she searched the drawers. She eavesdropped on phonecalls, on his conversations with the staff and operations personnel, on their conversations about him. She learned nothing. She began to spy. With the equipment and competence she'd acquired in order to make her films she was able to bug his office, his private sitting room, and the smoking room. Grandison knew this, for his million-dollar security system was proof against much more formidable assaults than this, but he allowed it to go on. He simply refrained from saying anything in these rooms that he would not have said before a delegation from the Iowa Council of Churches. Indeed, Boadicea was audience to just such a delegation who had come to enlist her father's support (and through him, her uncle's) for legislation that would withhold federal funds from all states and cities that directly or indirectly allowed tax dollars to be spent on cheap Argentine grain. Grandison was never more eloquent but the delegation received no more, in the end, than his signature—and not on a check at that, but on a petition.

She could not turn back. It was no longer for the movie's

sake, or for the sake of any rational need. She surrendered, as to a long-resisted vice. With shame and with a trembling foreboding that there must be bitter consequences to so unseemly an act, yet with a maenad, reckless pleasure in the very enormity of the risk, she placed a microphone behind the headboard of the bed in their best guest room. His father's mistress, Mrs Reade, was expected to be visiting Worry soon. She was also a friend of long-standing, and the wife of the director of an Iowa insurance company in which Grandison held a controlling interest. Surely in these circumstances her father would reveal *something*.

Her father did not go to Mrs Reade's room till late in the evening, and Boadicea had to sit in the sweaty embrace of her earphones, listening to the interminable sound track of *Toora-Loora Turandot*, a weary old Irish musical that Mrs Reade had taken upstairs from the library. The minutes crept by, and the music poked along, and then at last Grandison knocked, and could be heard to enter, and to say: "Enough is enough, Bobo, and this, surely, is too much."

"Darling?" said the voice of Mrs Reade.

"A moment, my love. I have one thing more to say to my daughter, who is eavesdropping on us at this moment, while pretending to study her French. *You* are to be finished, Bobo. In Switzerland, at a very highly recommended finishing school in Villars. I've already informed the principal at Amesville that you'll be going abroad. To learn, I sincerely hope, better manners than you've evidenced these last few months. You're to leave at six in the morning, so let me say now, by way of parting, shame on you, Bobo, and *bon voyage*!"

"Good-bye, Miss Whiting," said Mrs Reade. "When you're in Switzerland you must look up my niece Patricia. I'll send you her address." At that point the microphone was disconnected.

All during the drive from Des Moines—and they were now, a sign announced, only twenty-two miles from Amesville— Boadicea had been too upset to talk. She hadn't meant to be rude to Carl Mueller, though it must have seemed like rudeness. It was anger, raw white anger, that would return in surges of never-diminishing intensity and then, for a while, recede, leaving behind, like the wastes of oil and tar on a seaport's beach, the blackest of black depressions, a horror-stricken sorrow during which she would be assaulted by images of violent self-immolation—of the Saab crashing into a power pylon and bursting into flames, of opened veins, shotgun blasts, and other spectacular annihilations, images she rather entertained than resisted, since to have such monstrous thoughts was in itself a kind of revenge. And then, suddenly, irresistibly, the anger would return, so that she would have to press her eyes closed and clench her fists to keep from being overcome.

Yet she knew all the while that such transports were ridiculous and uncalled-for and that she was, in some sense, indulging herself. Her father, in sending Carl Mueller to the airport, had meant no slight, still less a chastisement. He had planned to come for her himself, his note had said, until this very morning when a business crisis had required him to go to Chicago. Similar crises had brought similar disappointments before, though never so passionate nor so unremitting as this. She really must calm down. If she returned to Worry in this state, she was certain to betray herself before Serjeant or Alethea. Just the thought of them, the mention of their names in her mind, could start her off again. Two years she'd been away, and they had sent a stranger to welcome her home. It was not to be believed, it could never be forgiven.

"Carl?"

"Miss Whiting?" He did not take his eyes from the road.

"I expect you'll think this is silly, but I wonder if you could take me anywhere else but to Worry. The nearer we get, and we're *so* near now, the more I feel unable to cope."

"I'll go where you like, Miss Whiting, but there aren't all that many places to go."

"A restaurant, somewhere *away* from Amesville? You haven't had dinner, have you?"

"No, Miss Whiting. But your folks will be expecting you."

"My father's in Chicago, and as to my brother and sister, I doubt that either of them has gone to any *personal* expense of energy on account of my arrival. I'll simply phone and say that I stopped in Des Moines to do some shopping—

it's what Alethea would do—and that I'm not equal to driving on to Amesville till I've had dinner. Do you mind?"

"Whatever you say, Miss Whiting. I could do with a bite to eat, I guess."

She studied his blunt profile in silence, marveling at his impassivity, the quiet fixity of his driving, which could not, on these monotonous roads, require such unwavering attention.

As they were approaching a cloverleaf, he slowed and asked, still without looking at her: "Somewhere quiet? There's a pretty good Vietnamese restaurant over in Bewley. At least, that's what they say."

"I think, actually, I'd prefer somewhere noisy. And a steak. I'm starved for the taste of rare midwestern beef."

He did, then, turn to look at her. His cheek dimpled with the inception of a smile, but whether it was a friendly smile, or only ironic, she couldn't tell, for his sunglasses masked his eyes. In any case, they were not, she would have supposed, especially candid eyes.

"Aren't there places people go," she insisted, "up by the border? Especially on Saturday nights. This *is* Saturday night."

"You'd need ID," he said.

She took out a plastic packet of cards and handed them to Carl Mueller. There was a Social Security card, a driver's license, a *Reader's Digest* Subscription Library card, an Iowa Women's Defense League Registration card, a card declaring her to be a tithing member of the Holy Blood Pentecostal Mission Church (with a laminated photo), and assorted charge cards, all of them identifying her as Beverley Whittaker, age twenty-two, of 512 Willow Street, Mason City, Iowa.

The Elmore Roller-Rink Roadhouse combined wholesomeness and elegance in a manner archetypally midwestern. Under a glowing greenhouse ceiling lattices of pipes supported an aerial meadow of herbs and houseplants in hanging pots and tiers of terracotta planters. Beneath the greenery a great many antique kitchen tables of oak and pine (all tagged for sale, as were the plants) were grouped about an implausibly large dance floor. It really had been, long ago, a roller rink. Two couples were out on the floor dancing, with lively unspectacular competence, to the 'Chocolate Doughnut Polka'. It was only seven o'clock: everyone else was eating dinner.

The food was wonderful. Boadicea had explained the exact nature of its superiority to anything they might have eaten in Switzerland, had explained it into the ground. Now, with dessert still to be chosen, she had to think of something else for them to talk about, since Carl seemed perfectly prepared to sit there and say nothing. Even with his sunglasses off his face was unreadable, though handsome enough, considered simply as sculpture: the broad brow and blunt nose, the massive muscles of the neck tapering into the simple geometries of his crew-cut, the emphatic carving of the lips, nostrils, and eyes, which yet, for all their distinctness, yielded no meanings of a psychological order. If he smiled, it was that mechanical sort of smile that suggested gears and pulleys. Clank, screek, snik, and then a little card emerges from the metal slot with the word SMILE on it. Sitting there, facing him across the little spray of bachelor buttons and petunias, she tried it herself—tightening the corner of her lips, and lifting them, notch by notch. But then, before he'd noticed, the pendulum swung back and she felt the sting of guilt. What right had she to expect Carl Mueller to be forthcoming with her? She was nothing to him but the boss's daughter, and she'd taken every mean advantage of that position, commandeering his company as though he had no life or feelings of his own. And then *blaming* him!

"I'm sorry," she said, with an utter sincerity of contrition. Carl crinkled his brow. "For what?"

"For dragging you off like this. For taking up your time. I mean—" She pressed her fingers to the sides of her head just above the cheekbones, where the flux of various miseries was beginning to take the form of a monster headache. "I mean, I didn't *ask*, did I, whether you had other plans for this evening?"

He produced one of his clockwork smiles. "That's okay, Miss Whiting. I didn't exactly plan on coming here to Elmore tonight, but what the hell. Like you say, the food's great. You worried about your folks?"

"My feelings are pretty much the opposite of worry. I'm thoroughly pissed off with *all* of them."

"That's what I'd gathered. Of course, it's none of my business, but I can say for a fact that your father didn't have much choice, whether or not to go to Chicago."

"Oh yes, I learned long ago that business is business. And I don't—I *can't*—blame him. But Serjeant could have come. He *is* my brother."

"I didn't mention it before, Miss Whiting—"

"Beverley," she corrected. Earlier she'd made a game of making him call her by the name on her false ID.

"I didn't mention it before, Miss Whiting, because it didn't seem my place to, but the reason your brother couldn't come for you is that two weeks ago he got his license suspended for drunk driving. He was driving home from Elmore, as a matter of fact."

"He could have come along with you then. So could Alethea."

"Maybe they could. But I don't think either of them cares that much for my company. Not that they've got any kind of grudge against me. But after all, I'm just one of the operations managers, not a friend of the family." With which—and with, it seemed, no sense at all of its being a questionable act—he poured the last of the wine in the carafe into his own glass.

"If you want to take me home now, that's all right."

"Just relax, Miss Whiting."

"Beverley."

"Okay, Beverley."

"There actually is a real Beverley Whittaker. She was in Switzerland, hiking. We met in a hospice about halfway up Mont Blanc. There was the most *incredible* lightning storm. Once you've seen lightning in the mountains you can understand why the Greeks put their most important god in charge of it."

Carl nodded gloomily.

She had to stop chattering, but the long silences, when they developed, panicked her equally.

Another couple had gone out on the dance floor, but just as they started dancing the music stopped. The silence enlarged.

She had a rule of thumb for such situations, and it was to take an interest in other people, since that was what *they* were interested in.

"And, uh, what are *you* in charge of?" she asked.

"Pardon?" But his eyes connected just long enough to let her see that he'd understood—and resented—the question.

Which, nevertheless, she must repeat. "You said you were an operations manager. Which operation do you manage?"

"Whatever has to do with the work crews. Recruitment and housing primarily. Transport, payroll, supervision."

"Oh."

"It's a job that has to be done."

"Of course. My father says it's the most important operation on the farm."

"That's a way of saying it's the dirtiest. Which it is."

"Well, it's not what I meant. In fact, I *wouldn't* say that."

"You would if you had to deal with some of the types we end up with. In another month or so, at the height of it, we'll have something like twelve hundred on the payroll, and of that twelve hundred I'd say a good half of them are no better than animals."

"I'm sorry, Carl, but I just can't accept that."

"Well, there's no reason you should have to, Miss Whiting." He smiled. "Beverley, that is. Anyway, it's a good job, and a hell of a lot of responsibility for someone my age, so it would be crazy to complain, if that's what it seems like I'm doing. It's not."

They were rescued by the waitress who came and asked them what they wanted for dessert. Carl asked for bavarian cream. Boadicea, because it was her first meal back in America, ordered apple pie.

A new polka had started up, and Boadicea, admitting defeat, turned her chair sideways to watch the dancers. There was a couple out on the floor now who actually could dance, whose bodies moved with the motions of life. They made the other dancers look like the simulacra you paid to see inside a tent at a county fair. The girl was especially good. She wore a wide, whirling, gypsyish skirt with a flounce at the hem, and the sway and flare and swirl of the skirt seemed to infuse the bland music with energies of an altogether higher order. The boy danced with equal energy but less panache. His limbs moved too abruptly, while his torso seemed never quite to unlock from its innate crouch. It was the body of a Breughel peasant. Even so, the delight in his face was so lively, and it was such a handsome face (not in the least a Breughel), that you couldn't keep from feeling an answering delight. The girl (Boadicea was sure) wouldn't have danced nearly so well with someone else, would not have been so set-on-fire. Together, for as long as the polka lasted, they brought time to a stop at the Elmore Roller-Rink Roadhouse.

6

AMONG THE TRADITIONS and institutions of Amesville High School Mrs Norberg of Room 113 was one of the most awful—in, as Boadicea liked to say, the original sense of the word. Some years before, in a tight three-way contest, she had been elected to the House of Representatives on the ticket of the American Spiritual Renewal Party. In its heyday the A.S.R.P. had been the rallying point of the Farm Belt's most diehard Undergoders, but as their first fine vision of a spiritually awakened America faded, and especially when the party's leaders were proven to be as venal as run-of-the-mill Republicans and Democrats, its members returned to the G.O.P. or became, like Mrs Norberg, lone voices crying in wildernesses of political error.

Mrs Norberg had taught American History and Senior Social Studies at the time of her election, and when she returned to Iowa after her single term in Washington she taught the same subjects, and was teaching them still, though recently she had added to the stature of her legend by having spent a two years' so-called sabbatical in a rest home in Dubuque, where she was taken (much against her will) after having been inspired one day to cut off a student's hair in the school lunchroom. Her students referred to this as the Iceberg's second term of office. They knew she was crazy, but no one seemed to mind all that much. Since Dubuque her frenzies against gum-chewers and note-passers were much abated, and she limited herself to a teacher's conventional weapon, the report card. On an average, twenty per cent of each year's graduating class failed Social Studies and had to take a make-up class to get their diplomas. All her known enemies were failed, of course, but so might be, it seemed, anyone else. Her Fs fell, like the rain, on the just and unjust alike. Some even claimed that Mrs Norberg drew names out of a hat.

This would have been alarming enough with regard only

to its gross injustice, but Boadicea had a special reason to dread the Iceberg's class, in that it had been her Uncle Charles who had taken away Mrs Norberg's seat in the House. When she had expressed her misgivings to her father, he was dismissive. A majority of the people one had to deal with, Grandison declared, were lunatics. One of the chief reasons for Boadicea's attending a public high school was precisely that she might come to terms with this unpleasant truth. As to the possibility of failing, she need not worry: Grandison had already arranged with the principal to correct any grade she received that was less than a B. All she had to do, therefore, was go to Room 113 for one hour every day and sit. She might be as reticent or as outspoken as she chose—it wouldn't matter. But as to getting rid of Mrs Norberg, that was not to be thought of. Incompetent she might be, or even bananas, but she was also the last certified Undergoder on the high school's faculty, and any attempt to dislodge her would have raised a major stink throughout the county and possibly across the state. In three years she would retire: till then she had to be endured.

Given such guarantees—a virtual suit of armor—Boadicea soon became the official gadfly of her Social Studies class. Mrs Norberg seemed rather more grateful than not to be supplied with a combatant who could be relied on to hold—and express—opinions that she would otherwise have been obliged to set forth herself before she could trounce them, never a very satisfactory arrangement for someone who delights in controversy. That these aberrant ideas possessed much more force and cogency as expressed by Boadicea than by the Iceberg's usual straw-men seemed not to trouble her. Like most people of strong convictions, any contradiction registered on her consciousness as so much nonsense. Faith is a selective kind of blindness.

So it was that whenever Boadicea would be holding forth on any subject, from the reasonableness of a graduated income tax to the unreasonableness of her Uncle Charles's recent demagogic vendetta against the A.C.L.U. a fixed smile would settle on the Iceberg's colorless lips, her eyes would glaze, and she would knit her fingers together in a thorny little clump of self-restraint, as who would say: "Though my duty be painful, I shall perform it to the last drop of my blood."

When Boadicea wound down, Mrs Norberg would unclasp her hands, give a little sigh, and thank Boadicea ironically for what she was sure was a "very interesting" or "very unusual" point-of-view. If this seemed insufficiently withering, she would ask others in the class what their thoughts on the matter were, calling first on anyone she suspected to be a fellow-traveller. Most students, prudently, refused to be trapped into any opinion, pro or con, but there was a small contingent, eight of the thirty-two, who could be relied on to parrot Mrs Norberg's established prejudices, however silly, however blatantly contrary to fact. It was always one of these who was allowed to have the last word, a strategy that had the desired effect of making Boadicea seem, even to herself, a minority of one. Also, it tended to diffuse her animosity and deflect it toward the eight reliables, whose names became a kind of baleful litany for her: Cheryl and Mitch and Reuben and Sloan, and Sandra and Susan and Judy and Joan. All the girls, except Sandra Wolf, were cheerleaders, and all, without exception, were mindless. Three of the eight—Joan Small and Cheryl and Mitch Severson—came from the wealthier farm families of the area. The Seversons and Smalls were scarcely comparable to the Whitings, but they did qualify as 'gentry' and were invited as a matter of course to all the larger functions at Worry. It distressed Boadicea to find herself at odds with three of the people with whom she was expected to be on friendly, or at least neighborly, terms, but she couldn't help herself. There was no *need* for them to suck up to Mrs Norberg so egregiously. Their parents weren't Undergoders, not in the benighted way *they* were. Fanaticism on the scale of the A.S.R.P. was a relic of the past. So why did they do it? Assuming they weren't just boot-licking. And for that matter, how did you explain someone like the Iceberg herself? Why were people like that so bent on patrolling people's most private *thoughts*? For that's all the old Undergoder dread of music (etc.) amounted to. They couldn't bear for others to have experiences *they* were incapable of. Resentment. Resentment and jealousy—it was as simple as that, though no one (not even Boadicea) dared to come right out and say so. Things were a little looser lately, but not as loose as all that.

Like most well-seasoned teachers, Mrs Norberg was a confirmed monologuist, and so Boadicea was not called upon every day to speak up for reason and sanity; penance enough to have to be an audience to the Iceberg's rambling reminiscences of her term in Congress (it was her special pride and unique distinction to have been present at every vote taken in those two years). These would shift, by the freest of associations, into (for instance) a cutesy-poo anecdote about the dear sweet squirrels in her back yard—Silverface, Tom-Boy, and Mittens, each of them a little philosopher-in-the-rough—and these whimseys would metamorphose, by imperceptible degrees, into diatribes against the F.D.A., the *bête noir* of the Farm Belt. All this—the memorabilia, the whimseys, the denunciations—would be set forth with an air of winking complicity, for it was the Iceberg's underlying assumption that her students were sensible to their good fortune in having been assigned to her Social Studies class and not that of the wishy-washy liberal Mr Cox.

Listening to these monologues and battering her wits against the woman's impassive, impervious authority, Boadicea came to hate Mrs Norberg with a hatred that would leave her, by the hour's end, trembling with impotent fury. Literally trembling. Sheerly from a sense of self-preservation, she took to cutting classes, although there was no way, with the bus drivers posted at the doors, to leave the building. She would lock herself inside a toilet and sit cross-legged on the stool, working calculus problems. She became openly sarcastic in class, and sneered when she was sneered at. She made a point, whenever a soliloquy commenced, of turning away from the Iceberg and staring out the window, though there was nothing to be seen but sky and clouds and the slow curve of three suspended wires. Mrs Norberg made no other response to these provocations than to move Boadicea to the front row where, if Boadicea chose to divert her gaze, she would simply interpose herself between the viewer and the view.

It was there, in the front row seat next to his, that Boadicea recognized Daniel Weinreb. They had been together in the class for two months without her making the connection. Not that the back of his head (which was mostly all she'd seen of him till the move to the front) was so very distinctive. Also, he'd changed his appearance since she'd fallen, briefly and platonically, in love with him at the El-more Roller-Rink Roadhouse: shorter hair, the moustache gone, the high spirits folded away, and an inert, affectless fortitude in their place. Except to answer the roll-call or shuffle his feet at a question directly addressed to him, he never spoke in class; just as his speech never betrayed his thoughts, his face never betrayed his feelings.

Boadicea was certain, however, that they were not greatly unlike her own. He hated the Iceberg as fervently as she did; he must—or how could he dance so well? Perhaps as a syllogism this left something to be desired, and Boadicea didn't rest content with an *a priori* conviction. She began to collect evidences—glints and flashes of the suspected smoldering fires.

The first thing she discovered was that she was not alone in studying Daniel so closely. Mrs Norberg herself demonstrated a curiosity altogether out of proportion to Daniel's classroom contributions. Often when another student would be speaking her eyes would turn to Daniel, and at the militant moment when she would cut loose from classroom protocols and really *testify* for the gospel of the A.S.R.P., it was toward Daniel these goads were directed, despite that it would be Boadicea, if anyone, who would rise to the bait and argue.

At last, however, toward the end of the second six-week period, Mrs Norberg threw out a challenge that Daniel did not turn away from. There had been a story in the news, recently, that had very much exercised the indignation of Undergoders. Bud Scully, a manager for a Northrup Corp. farm outside LuVerne, had undertaken, on his own initiative, to do what it was no longer permitted the State of Iowa to do: he'd been jamming radio broadcasts originating in Minnesota. The stations had brought suit against him, and he was enjoined to desist. When he refused, on grounds of conscience, and continued his private crusade, he was sent to prison. Undergoders were up in arms. Mrs Norberg, to do her credit, tried to resist the passions of the passing hour (she never, for instance, went beyond Watergate in her American History class), but this time the provocation was too great. She devoted a week of the class's time to an in-depth consideration of John Brown. She read aloud Thoreau's essay on civil disobedience. She played a recording of the hymn of 'John Brown's Body', standing over the tape recorder warily and jerking her head up and down in time to the music. When the hymn was over, with tears in her eyes (a quite inadvertent testimony to the power of music), she told how she had visited the park right here in Iowa where John Brown had drilled his volunteer army for the attack on Harper's Ferry. Then, shouldering her blackboard pointer like a rifle, she showed the class how the soldiers in that army would have drilled, marching back and forth across the shining maple floorboards—right face, left face, Ten-*shun*! to the rear *march*, a perfect spectacle. At such moments, truly, you'd have had to have a heart of stone not to be grateful to be in the Iceberg's class.

All this while she had resisted mentioning Bud Scully by name, though none of them could have been unaware of the intended parallel. Now, after a formal salute to the flag in the corner, Mrs Norberg abandoned all pretense of objectivity. She went to the blackboard and wrote out, in gigantic letters, the martyr's name. BUD SCULLY. Then she went to her desk, secured herself behind her folded hands, and, glowering, defied the world to do its worst.

Boadicea raised her hand.

Mrs Norberg called on her.

"Do you mean," Boadicea asked, with a disingenuous smile, "that Bud Scully is another John Brown? And that what he did was right?"

"Did I *say* that?" the Iceberg demanded. "Let me ask *you*, Miss Whiting: is that your opinion? *Is* Bud Scully's case analogous to that of John Brown?"

"In the sense that he's gone to jail for his convictions you might say so. But otherwise? One man tried to stop slavery, and the other is trying to jam a popular music radio station. At least that's what I understand from the newspaper."

"Which newspaper would that be? I ask, you see, because I gave up reading the papers some time ago. My experiences (especially when I was on the Hill) have shown me that they're not at all reliable."

"It was the *Star-Tribune*."

"The *Star-Tribune*," the Iceberg repeated, turning to Daniel with a knowing look.

"And what it said," Boadicea continued, "in its editorial, was that everyone must obey the law just because it *is* the law, and the only way we're ever going to live together peacefully is to respect the law. Even when it grates against us."

"That seems quite sound on the face of it. The question John Brown poses, though, remains to be answered. Are we required to obey an unjust law?" The Iceberg threw back her head, glittering with righteousness.

Boadicea persisted. "According to the polls, *most* people thought the *old* law was unjust, the law that kept them from reading out-of-state newspapers and from listening to out-of-state broadcasts."

"According," Mrs Norberg said scornfully "to the polls in those same newspapers."

"Well, the Supreme Court felt it was unjust too, or they wouldn't have overturned it. And as I understand it, short of a constitutional amendment, the Supreme Court has the last word on the rightness or the wrongness of laws."

Mrs Norberg's views on the Supreme Court were well known, and accordingly there was a tacit understanding among her students to steer clear of the reefs of this subject. But Boadicea was beyond compassion or prudence. She wanted to demolish the woman's mind and send her back to Dubuque in a straitjacket. She deserved nothing else.

It wasn't going to be that easy, however. Mrs Norberg had a paranoid's instinct for knowing when she was being persecuted. She stepped aside and Boadicea's missile passed by harmlessly.

"It is a knotty question, I agree. And highly complex. Everyone will be affected by it in a different way, and that is bound to color our attitudes. Right here in this room we have someone whose life was touched very directly by the decision Miss Whiting speaks of. Daniel, what is *your* opinion?"

"About what?" Daniel asked.

"Does the State of Iowa have the right, the sovereign right, to bar potentially harmful and disruptive material from being publicly available, or does that represent an interference with our constitutional guarantee of freedom of speech?"

"I can't say I ever thought much about it."

"Surely, Daniel, having gone to prison for breaking the state's law. . . ." She paused for the benefit of anyone in the class who might not have known this. Of course there was no one who hadn't heard Daniel's legend by now. It was nearly of the magnitude of Mrs Norberg's, which probably, more than the principles involved, accounted for her relentless, attentive dislike. "Surely, when you're then released because the Supreme Court—" She lifted her eyebrows sardonically. "—rules, that, after all, the law is *not* the law and never has been . . . *surely*, you must have some opinion on such a subject."

"I guess my opinion is that it doesn't make much difference one way or the other."

"Not make much difference! A change that big?"

"I got out two weeks earlier, and that's about it."

"Really, Daniel, I don't know what you can mean."

"I mean I still don't think it's safe to express an honest opinion anywhere in the state of Iowa. And so far as I know, there's no law that says I *have* to. *And* I'm not about to."

First there was a silence. Then, led by Boadicea, a smattering of applause. Even with that unprecedented provocation, Mrs Norberg did not take her eyes from Daniel. You could almost see the calculations going on behind that fixed stare: was his insolence defensible, in theory, as candor? Or might he be made to pay for it? Nothing less than expulsion would be worth a head-on contest, and at last, with evident reluctance, she decided not to risk it. There would always be another time.

After the class Boadicea lay in wait for Daniel at the entrance to the lunchroom.

"That was terrific," she told him in a stage-whisper, as she slipped into place behind him in the cafeteria line. "A regular adventure movie."

"It was a mistake."

"Oh no! You were completely, universally right. The

only way to deal with the Iceberg is silence. Let her talk to her eight echoes."

He just smiled. Not the fleshly, unforgettable smile of the Elmore Roller-Rink Roadhouse, but a smile that was all mind and meaning. She felt abashed, as though, by making no reply to her, he meant to show that he considered her one of the people it wasn't safe to talk to. The smile faltered.

"Hey," he said, "this is a dumb argument—you telling me I'm right, and me saying I'm wrong."

"Well, you *are* right."

"Maybe, but what's right for me isn't necessarily what's right for you. If you stop sniping at her, what'll there be for the rest of us to listen to?"

"You mean I can afford to be brave because I'm safe."

"And I can't afford it. Which wasn't something I should have spelled out. *That's* the mistake. One of the first things you learn in prison is that the guards like to think that you *like* them. Norberg's no different."

Boadicea wanted to wrap her arms around him, to leap up and cheer for him like some silly cheerleader, to buy him something terrifically expensive and appropriate, such was the enormity of her agreement and of her gratitude at having anyone to agree with.

"School *is* a prison," she agreed earnestly. "You know, I used to think I was the only person in the world who understood that. I was in Switzerland at this awful so-called finishing school, and I wrote a letter home, to my father, explaining all the ways it was a prison, and *he* wrote back saying, 'Of course, my dear Bobo—school is a prison for the very good reason that all children are criminals.' "

"Uh-huh."

They'd reached the food. Daniel took a dish of coleslaw onto his tray and pointed at the fishsticks.

"Actually," she went on, "that isn't exactly what he said. What he said was that teenagers aren't fully civilized yet, and so they're dangerous. Not here in Iowa, perhaps, but in the cities certainly. But one of the differences between here and the cities . . . oh, just soup for me, please . . . is the degree to which people here *do* live by the official code. That's what my father says anyhow."

Daniel gave his school credit card to the check-out girl. The machine fizzed with the prices of his lunch, and the girl handed him back his card. He picked up his tray.

"Daniel?"

He stopped and she asked, with her eyes, for him to wait till they were out of earshot of the check-out girl. When they were, she asked him, "Are you having lunch with anyone else today?"

"No."

"Why not have lunch with me then? I know it's not for me to ask, and you probably prefer to have the time to yourself, to think." She paused to allow him to contradict her, but he just stood there with his devastating superior smile. His handsomeness was so dark, so exotic, almost as though he belonged to another race. "But me," she persisted, "I'm different. I like to talk before I think."

He laughed. "Say, I've got an idea," he said. "Why don't *you* have lunch with *me*?"

"Why how nice of you to ask, Daniel," she minced, her parody of pert insouciance. Or possibly it was the genuine article, pert insouciance itself. "Or should I call you Mr Weinreb?"

"Maybe something in between."

"Very funny." Making her voice comically deep.

"That's what Susan McCarthy always says when she's at a loss for words."

"I know. I'm a close observer. Too." But for all that it had stung—to be compared (and accurately) with the likes of a Susan McCarthy.

They'd found bench-space at a relatively quiet table. Instead of starting to eat, he just looked at her. Started to say something, and stopped. She felt tingly with excitement. She had caught his attention. It stopped short of liking or even, in any committed way, of interest, but the worst was over, and suddenly, incredibly, she couldn't think of anything else to say. She blushed. She smiled. And shook her head, with pert insouciance.

7

AFTER THE ARGUMENT with her hateful—literally
hateful—sister, Boadicea wrapped herself in her old school
cape of green loden and went up to the roof, where the
wind whipped her hair and walloped the cape with satisfying emphasis. The twit, she thought, concerning Alethea,
the prig, the bitch, the sneak, the spy, the snob; the sly,
mindless, soulless, self-regarding slut. The worst of it was
that Boadicea could never, when it came to a showdown,
translate her scorn into language that Alethea would admit
to understanding, whereas Alethea had a monolithic confidence in her snobberies that gave even her most banal jibes
a kind of authority.

Even the roof wasn't far enough. With grim elation Boadicea mounted the west wind pylon, pausing in the lee of
the first vane to marvel, dispassionately, that there could be
enough heat left in these wintry blasts to be converted into
the steady whirling of the metal blades. *Was* it heat? Or
just the momentum of the molecules of gas? Or was there
any difference? In any case, science was wonderful.

So forget Alethea, she told herself. Rise over her. Consider the clouds, and determine the actual colors incor-
porated in their mottled, luminous, numinous gray. Arrange
the world so that *her* intolerable sneering profile was not in
the foreground, and then it would become, perhaps, a
satisfactory sort of world, large and bright and full of ad-
mirable processes that a clear mind could learn to deal with,
the way the pylons dealt with the wind, the way her father
dealt with people, even such otherwise intractable people
as Alethea and, occasionally, herself.

Higher she mounted, above the highest vanes, to the
small eyrie of steel hoops at the top of the pylon. The
winds buffeted. The platform swayed. But she felt no verti-
go, only the steadying satisfaction of seeing the world spread
out in so orderly a way. The great jumble of Worry be-

came, from this height, as comprehensible as a set of blueprints: the fallow flowerbeds and quincunxes of small trees in the Whitings' private gardens on the roof below; then, stepwise in terraces below these, on the more extensive rooftops of the wings, were the pools and playgrounds of the other residents of the complex; farthest down, bounded by a broad defensive crescent of garages, stables, and siloes, were the kitchen gardens, poultry yards, and tennis courts. The few people in sight all seemed to be engaged in emblematic tasks, like figures in a Breughel: children skating, a woman scattering corn for chickens, two blue-jacketed mechanics bent over the idling engine of a limousine, a man walking a dog toward the trees that screened the western gatehouse. To one who stood on the roof those trees would mark the limit of the horizon, but from this higher vantage one could see over them as far as the blue-gray zigzag of housetops that had once been—and not so long ago that Boadicea couldn't remember it herself—the village of Unity. Most of the village's former residents lived in Worry now. Their clapboard houses stood empty through most of the year, as many as still stood at all. It was saddening to think that a whole way of life, a century of traditions, had to come to an end for the new way to begin. But what was the alternative? To keep it going artificially, an instant Williamsburg? In effect that was what the summer people were doing now, at least with the better homes. The rest had been scavenged for their meat—siding, plumbing, curious bits of carpentry—and the bones left to weather into a more picturesque condition, at which point, doubtless, they would go to the auction block too. It was sad to see, but it was necessary—the result of forces too large to be withstood, though they might be channeled and shaped with more or less love and imagination. Worry, with its neo-Norman castellations, its outlying parks and commons, and its innovative social engineering, surely represented the process of feudalization at its most humane and, so to speak, democratic. A utopia of sorts. Whether, finally, it was a utopia for the likes of Boadicea she could never decide. Ownership of so much land and wealth was problematical enough, but beyond this was the moral question of one's relationship with one's tenants. There were over five hundred at the last count. Though *they* would all have denied it—and could in fact be seen denying it in the movie Boadicea had made way back when—their condition was uncomfortably close to serf-dom. But uncomfortable, it seemed, only for Boadicea, since the waiting list of qualified applicants who wanted to sign on and move in was ridiculously in excess of the foreseeable openings. Kids at school were always sounding her out about their chances of being moved to the top of the list; some had offered outright bribes if she would put in a word with her father. Once poor Serjeant had got into hot water for accepting such a bribe.

But to suppose that Daniel Weinreb had so venal a purpose in cultivating her acquaintance was a patent absurdity. The accusation revealed the limits of Alethea's imagination, for it couldn't begin to do justice to the scale of Daniel's ambitions. Daniel meant to be an artist, as great an artist as he could become. Boadicea doubted whether he'd given so much as a moment's thought to the long-term possibilities of their friendship. Aside from the opportunity (which he was finally to take up today) of paying a visit to Worry and trying his hand at the Whitings' various instruments, it was unlikely that he considered the acquaintance especially advantageous. Except for the chance (the glorious chance) to talk with someone else who also meant to become a great artist. So really he didn't seem to have, in a word, designs.

Boadicea, by contrast, lived most of her life in an endless design. Every moment she wasn't entirely focused on the task in hand she was planning, rehearsing, imagining, day-dreaming. What she had planned, vis-à-vis Daniel, was that they would be lovers. She had not drawn up a detailed scenario of how it would come about. She wasn't even entirely sure of the details of their love's consummation, since such pornography as she'd looked into had seemed rather ishy, but she was certain that once they'd actually got involved erotically it would be very nice, not to say ecstatic. Daniel, she'd heard tell from various independent sources, had been 'intimate' with a number of women (one of them six years older than him and engaged to another man), though no one was prepared to say whether he'd definitely gone all the way. Sex, therefore, could be trusted to take care of itself (at least in her daydreams), and Boadicea was free to elaborate the associated drama: how, quite suddenly, on a whim or a dare or after a fight with her sister, she would run off with Daniel to some sinister, far-away capital—Paris or Rome or Toronto—there to lead a life that would be thrilling, elegant, virtuous, simple, and entirely devoted to art in its highest manifestations. Not, however, till they'd graduated, for even in her wildest dreams Boadicea proceeded with caution.

A mile beyond Unity the road climbed a short rise and you could see, for the first time, the gray ferro-concrete tower of Worry. Then the road dipped and the tower sank back into featureless fields.

He was short of breath and his legs were aching from pedaling too fast, but being so near it was psychologically impossible to slow down. Even the wind, gusting from the west and puffing up his windbreaker before him like a small red sail, seemed to be trying to speed him on his way. He turned right at the unmarked turn-off that everyone knew was the road to Worry, zipped past a man out walking a German shepherd, and arrived out-of-breath at the gate-house.

A metal gate sprang up from the road in front of him, a hooter began hooting, stopped just long enough for a recorded voice to tell him to get out of his car, and started up again. A uniformed guard came out of the gatehouse holding a sub-machine gun. It would have been disconcerting anywhere else, but Daniel, never having been to Worry before, supposed this was the standard reception that unannounced visitors received.

He reached into his jacket pocket for the invitation disc that Boadicea had given him, but the guard shouted that he should put his hands above his head.

He put his hands above his head.

"Where do you think you're going, son?" the guard asked.

"I'm visiting Miss Whiting. At her invitation. The disc she gave me is in my pocket."

The guard reached into Daniel's pocket and took out the disc.

Daniel lowered his hands. The guard seemed to consider whether to take offence. Instead he went into the gatehouse with the disc, and for five minutes Daniel saw no more of him. Finally he set his bike on its kickstand and went to the door of the gatehouse. Through the glass he could see the guard talking on the phone. The guard gestured for him to go back to his bike.

"Is something wrong?" Daniel shouted through the glass.

The guard opened the door and handed the phone to Daniel with a peculiar kind of smile. "Here, he wants to talk to you."

"Hello," Daniel said into the grill of the mouthpiece.

"Hello," replied a pleasant, purring baritone. "There seems to be a problem. I assume this is Daniel Weinreb that I'm speaking to."

"This is Daniel Weinreb, yes."

"The problem is this, Daniel. Our security system insists on identifying you as, probably, an escaped prisoner. The guard is understandably reluctant to admit you. In fact, under the circumstances, he hasn't the authority to do so."

"Well, I'm *not* an escaped prisoner, so that should solve your problem."

"But it doesn't explain why the security system, which is preternaturally sensitive, should continue to declare that you are carrying a Pole-Williams lozenge of the type used by the state's prison system."

"Not the lozenge. Just the housing for it."

"Ah-ha. Our system isn't up to making such nice distinctions, apparently. It's none of my business, of course, but don't you think it would be wiser—or at least more convenient—to have it taken out? Then this sort of confusion wouldn't happen."

"You're right—it is none of your business. Now, would you please buzz me in, or do I have to have surgery first?"

"By all means. Let me speak to the guard again, would you?"

Daniel handed the phone to the guard and went back to his bicycle. As soon as he came nearer the gatehouse, the hooter started in again, but this time it was switched off.

The guard came out of the gatehouse and said, "Okay. Just go down the road. The Whitings' entrance is the one with the wrought iron gates. There's another guard there, but he's expecting you."

Daniel nodded, smug with small triumph.

Alethea, at the base of the wind pylon, signaled with her scarf to Boadicea on the summit. Since their quarrel Alethea had put on a riding habit and looked more than ever the *belle dame sans merci*.

Boadicea waved back. She didn't want to come down, but Alethea must have had some reason for being so persistent, and anyway she *did* want to come down since her face and her fingers were numb with cold. The wind and the view had served the simultaneous purpose of calming her down and lifting her up. She could return to earth and talk to Alethea in a spirit of no more than sisterly combativeness.

"I thought," said Alethea, disdaining to shout but waiting until Boadicea was quite close by, "that your story of having invited that boy here was a complete fabrication. But he's come, on his bicycle, and there seems to be some question whether he's to be allowed through the gate. I thought you should know."

Boadicea was taken aback. Alethea's action too much resembled ordinary courtesy for her to take exception to it. "Thank you," she had to say, and Alethea smiled.

"I *gave* him a disc," Boadicea fretted.

"They must have thought he looked suspicious. He does to me."

Inside the stairwell, on the next landing down, was a phone. Boadicea dialed the gatehouse. The guard said that Daniel had already gone through, on her father's say-so.

Alethea was waiting for her by the elevator. "Seriously, Bobo. . . ."

"Didn't you say, less than an hour ago, that my biggest problem was that I was always *too* serious?"

"Yes, of course, but seriously: what can you see in this Weinreb boy? Is it because he was in prison? Do you think that's *glamorous*?"

"That has precisely nothing to do with it."

"I'll allow he has tolerable good looks—"

Boadicea raised her eyebrows challengingly. Daniel's looks deserved more than a five on anyone's scale of ten.

"—but, after all, he does represent the lower depths, doesn't he?"

"His father's a dentist."

"And from what I've heard not even a particularly good one."

"From whom did you hear that?"

"I forget. In any case, good or bad: a dentist! Isn't that enough? Didn't you learn anything in Switzerland?"

"Indeed I did. I learned to value intelligence, taste, and breeding—the qualities I admire in Daniel."

"Breeding!"

"Yes, breeding. Don't provoke me to comparisons."

The elevator arrived. They had captured one of the maids, who'd been trying to go down to the kitchen on two. They rode down in silence until she got off. Boadicea pressed G.

Alethea sighed. "I think you're being very foolish. And, come the day that you finally do drop him, very cruel."

"Who is to say, Alethea, that that day will ever come?"

She'd said it only to be provoking, but hearing the words spoken, she wondered if they might conceivably be true. Was this the beginning of her real life? (As against the provisional life she'd been leading up to now.)

"Oh, Bobo. *Really*!"

"Why not?" Boadicea demanded, a trifle too emphatically. "If we're in love."

Alethea giggled, with complete sincerity. And shook her head, by way of saying good-bye, and set off down the hall in the other direction, toward the stables.

It was, Boadicea had to admit, an enormous if. She loved talking with Daniel, she loved looking at him, for he had the sort of features that bear contemplation. But love? Love, in the sense commemorated by centuries of books and operas and films?

Once, when she'd followed him about on his paper route, they had sat snuggling together in a broken-down car in a dark garage. It had seemed, for those fifteen minutes, the supreme happiness of her life. To be warm. To relax in that utter anonymity. To savor the silences and smells of a stranger's garage—rust, dry leaves, the ghosts of ancient motor oils. They'd talked in a dreamy way of going back to the golden age of V-8 engines and superhighways and being two totally average teenagers in a movie about growing up. A lovely pastoral moment, certainly, but scarcely proof of their being in love.

She wondered if Daniel ever wondered whether they were in love: or whether they would be, some day. She wondered if she could get up the nerve to ask him, and what he would say if she did, for he could hardly come right out and say no, the thought had never crossed his mind. While she was still in the midst of her wonderings, there he was, with his bicycle, on the raked gravel of the crescent. The first snowflakes of the year were alighting on his beautiful black hair. His nose and forehead, his cheekbones and his chin were straight out of the most arrogantly lovely Ghirlandaio in all the museums of the world.

"Daniel!" she called out, bounding down the steps, and from the way he smiled at her in reply she thought that maybe it was possible that they were already in love. But she understood, as well, that it would be wrong to ask, or even to wonder.

Grandison Whiting was a tall, spare-limbed, thin-faced, pilgrimish man who stood in violent contradiction to his own flamboyantly bushy beard, a beard of the brightest carrot-orange, a beard that any pirate could have gloried in. His suit was puritanically plain, but across the muted check of the waistcoat hung a swag of gold chain so heavy as to seem actually serviceable in conjunction, say, with manacles or fetters. And glinting within the cuffs of his coat were cufflinks blazoned with diamonds larger than any that Daniel had ever seen, even in the windows of the Des Moines branch of Tiffany's, so that he seemed to wear, not his heart, but his checkbook on his sleeve.

His manners and accent were uniquely, unnaturally his own; neither English nor Iowan, but a peculiar hybrid of both that preserved the purr of the former and the twang of the latter. You would have felt almost guilty to say that you liked such a person as Grandison Whiting, but for all that Daniel didn't positively dislike him. His strangeness was fascinating, like the strangeness of some exotic bird illustrated in a book of color plates, a heron or an ibis or a cockatoo.

As to the nest that this rare bird inhabited, Daniel was in no such state of equivocation. All of Worry made Daniel uncomfortable. You couldn't walk on the carpets or sit on the chairs without thinking you'd do them some damage. And of all the rooms that Daniel had been taken through, Grandison Whiting's drawing room, where they'd come at five for 'tea', was, if not the grandest, surely the most elegantly perishable. Not that Daniel, by this time, was still making sharp distinctions among the degrees of bon ton. It was all equally unthinkable, and hours ago he'd closed his mind to any but the simplest sense of having to resist the various intimidations of so much money. If you once allowed yourself to admire any of it—the spoons, the cups, the sugar bowl, the exquisite creamer filled with cream as thick and gloppy as mucilage—where would you stop? So he shut it out: he took his tea without sugar or cream and passed up all the cakes for one dry curl of unbuttered toast.

No one urged him to change his mind.

After they'd been introduced all round and the weather had been deplored, Grandison Whiting asked Daniel what he had thought of the harpsichord. Daniel (who'd been expecting a genuine antique, not a modern reconstruction built in Boston forty years ago) replied, guardedly, that it was nothing like a piano, that the touch, and the two manuals, would take some getting used to. What he'd said at the time, to Boa, was "Weird"; what he hadn't said, even to her, was that the Steinway grand was as far beyond his ken as the harpsichord (or as the harp, for that matter), just as weird, in the sense of being wholly and unsettlingly beautiful.

Then Boa's sister Alethea (in a white dress as stiff and resplendent as the table napkins) asked him how, in the wilderness of Amesville, he had managed to take piano lessons. He said he was self-taught, which she must have suspected was less than the whole truth, for she insisted: "Entirely?" He nodded, but with a smile meant to be teasing. She was already, at fifteen, a fanatic in the cause of her own all-conquering good looks. Daniel wondered if she weren't actually the more interesting of the two sisters: interesting as an object, like some dainty cup with flowers painted on it in microscopic detail, or like an armchair with golden legs carved into watery shapes, with that same eggshell elegance, the same intrinsic, unhesitating disdain for boors, bears, clods, and paupers like himself, which Daniel found (somewhat guiltily) arousing. Boa, by contrast, seemed just another person, a contender in the sweepstakes of growth and change, who sometimes would pull ahead of him, sometimes fall behind. No doubt the family money was in her blood as much as it was in Alethea's, but its effect on her was problematical, whereas with Alethea it was as though the money had blotted out everything else: as though she were the *form* that money took translated into flesh and blood—no longer a problem, just a fact.

Alethea went on, with wonderful aplomb considering that no one seemed interested, about horses and riding. Her father listened abstractedly, his manicured fingers patting the tangles of his fantastic beard.

Alethea fell silent.

No one took the initiative.

"Mr Whiting," said Daniel, "was it you I spoke to earlier, when I was at the gatehouse?"

"I'm sorry to have to say it was. Candidly, Daniel, I hoped I might just wriggle out of that one. Did you recognize my voice? Everyone does, it seems."

"I only meant to apologize."

"Apologize? Nonsense! I was in the wrong, and you called me down for it quite properly. Indeed, it was then, hanging up the phone and blushing for my sins, that I decided I must have you come to tea. Wasn't it, Alethea? She was with me, you see, when the alarm went off."

"The alarms go off a dozen times a day," Boa said. "And they're always false alarms. Father says it's the price we have to pay."

"Does it seem an excess of caution?" Grandison Whiting asked rhetorically. "No doubt it is. But it's probably best to err on that side, don't you think? In future when you visit you must let us know in advance, so that we may shut off the scanner, or whatever they call it. And I sincerely hope you *will* return, if only for Bobo's sake. I'm afraid she's been feeling rather . . . cut-off? . . . since she came back from the greater world beyond Iowa." He raised his hand, as though to forestall Boa's protests. "I know it's not for me to say that. But one of the few advantages of being a parent is that one may take liberties with one's children."

"Or so he claims," said Boa. "But in fact he takes all the liberties he can, with whoever allows it."

"It's nice of you to say so, Bobo, since that gives me leave to ask Daniel—you will allow me to call you Daniel, won't you? And you must call me Grandison."

Serjeant snickered.

Grandison Whiting nodded toward his son, by way of acknowledgement, and continued: "To ask you, Daniel (as I know I have no right to): why have you never had that terrible apparatus removed from your stomach? You're quite entitled to, aren't you? As I understand it—and I've had to give the matter some consideration, since officially I'm on the governing board of the state prison system—only convicts who are paroled, or who've committed much more . . . heinous crimes than yours—"

"Which isn't," Boa hastened to remind her father, "any crime at all, since the court's decision."

"Thank you, dear—that's exactly my point. Why, Daniel, having been wholly exonerated, do you submit to the inconvenience and, I daresay, the embarrassment of the sort of thing that happened today?"

"Oh, you learn where the alarms are. And you don't go back."

"Pardon me, um, Daniel," said Serjeant, with vague good will, "but I'm not quite following. How is it that you go about setting off alarms?"

"When I was in prison," Daniel explained, "I had a P-W lozenge embedded in my stomach. The lozenge is gone, so there's no chance of my blowing us all up accidentally, but the housing for it is still there, and that, or the traces of metal in it, is what sets off alarms."

"But why is it still there?"

"I could have it taken out if I wanted, but I'm squeamish about surgery. If they could get it out as easily as they got it in, I'd have no objections."

"Is it a big operation?" Alethea asked, wrinkling her nose in pretty revulsion.

"Not according to the doctors. But—" He lifted his shoulders: "One man's meat. . . ."

Alethea laughed.

He was feeling more and more sure of himself, even cocky. This was a routine he'd often gone through, and it always made him feel like Joan of Arc or Galileo, a modern martyr of the Inquisition. He also felt something of a hypocrite, since the reason he'd kept the P-W housing in his stomach (as anyone who thought about it would have known) was that so long as he was still wired for prison he couldn't be drafted into the National Guard. Not that he minded being or feeling hypocritical. Hadn't he read, in Reverend Van Dyke's book, that we're all hypocrites and liars in the eyes of God? To deny that was only to be self-deluded besides.

However, some molecular switch inside must have responded to this tremor of guilt, for much to his own surprise Daniel started to tell Grandison Whiting of the corruption and abuses he'd witnessed at Spirit Lake. This, on the grounds that Whiting, being on the governing board of the state's prisons, might be able to do something. He developed quite a head of steam about the system of food vouchers you had to buy just to keep alive, but even at the height of it he could see he was making a tactical error. Grandison Whiting listened to the exposé with a glistening attentiveness behind which Daniel could sense not indignation but the meshing of various cogs and gears of a logical rebuttal. Clearly, Whiting had known already of the evils Daniel was denouncing.

Boa, at the close of Daniel's tale, expressed a hearty sense of the wrong being done, which would have been more gratifying if he hadn't seen her through so many other tirades in the Iceberg's classroom. More surprising was Serjeant's response. Though it amounted to no more than his saying that it didn't seem fair, he must have known that he would be flying in the face of his father's as-yet-unexpressed opinion.

After a long and dour look at his son, Grandison Whiting brightened to a formal smile, and said, quietly: "Justice *isn't* always fair."

"You must excuse me," said Alethea, putting aside her cup and rising, "but I see that Father means to have a serious discussion, and that is a pastime, like bridge, that I've never learned how to enjoy."

"As you please, my dear," said her father. "And indeed, if the rest of you would prefer . . . ?"

"Nonsense," said Boa. "We're just beginning to enjoy ourselves." She took hold of Daniel's hand and squeezed. "Aren't we?"

Daniel went, "Mm."

Serjeant took another pastry from the plate, his fourth.

"Let us say, for the sake of argument," said Boa, pouring tea, and then cream, into Daniel's cup, "that justice *is* always fair."

Grandison Whiting folded his hands across his waistcoat, just above his watchchain. "Justice is always just, certainly. But fairness is to justice as common sense is to logic. That is to say, justice may (and often does) transcend fairness. Fairness usually boils down to a simple, heartfelt conviction that the world should be ordered with one's own convenience in mind. Fairness is a child's view of justice. Or a bum's."

"Oh, Father, don't go off on bums." She turned to Daniel. "I don't know how many times we've had the same argument. Always about bums. It's Father's hobbyhorse."

"Bums," he went on imperturbably, "as opposed to beggars. Men who have chosen abjection as a way of life, without the extenuating circumstances of blindness, amputation, or imbecility."

"Men," Boa contradicted, "who simply can't take responsibility for themselves. Men who are helpless before a world that is, after all, a pretty rough place."

"Helpless? So they would have us believe. But all men are responsible for themselves, by definition. All adults, that is. Bums, however, insist on remaining children, in a state of absolute dependency. Think of the most incorrigible such wretch you've seen, and imagine him at the age of five instead of five-and-fifty. What change might you observe? There he is, smaller no doubt, but in moral terms the same spoiled child, whining over his miseries, wheedling to have his way, with no plans except for the next immediate gratification, which he will either bully *us* into giving him or, failing that, will attempt to seduce from us by the grandeur and mystery of his abasement."

"As you may have gathered, Daniel, we're not speaking of a completely hypothetical bum. There was a real man, one summer when we were in Minneapolis, with a shoe missing and a cut over one eye, and this man had the temerity to ask Father for a quarter. Father told him: 'There's the gutter. Be my guest.' "

"She misquotes me, Daniel. I said: 'I would prefer, really, to contribute directly.' And dropped what change I had in my pocket down the nearest drain."

"Jesus," said Daniel, despite himself.

"Perhaps the moral was too astringent to be improving. I confess to having had more than my sufficiency of brandy after dinner. But was it an *unjust* observation? It was he who had chosen to go down the drain, and he'd achieved his desire. Why should I be called on to subsidize his more extensive self-destruction? There are better causes."

"You may be just, Father, but you aren't at all fair. That poor man had simply been defeated by life. Is he to be *blamed* for that?"

"Who but the defeated are to be blamed for a defeat?" Grandison Whiting asked in turn.

"The victors?" Daniel suggested.

Grandison Whiting laughed, somewhat in the manner of his beard. Even so, it didn't register as wholly genuine: its warmth was the warmth of an electric coil, not of a flame. "That was very good, Daniel. I quite liked that."

"Though you'll note he doesn't go so far as to say that you're right," Boa pointed out. "Nor has he said anything about all the horrors you've told us about Spirit Lake."

"Oh, I'm slippery."

"But really, Father, something ought to be done. What Daniel described is more than unfair—it's illegal."

"In fact, my dear, the question of its legality has been argued before several courts, and it's always been decided that prisoners have a *right* to buy such food as they can to supplement what the prison provides. As to its fairness, or justice, I believe myself that the voucher system performs a valuable social function: it reinforces that most precious and tenuous of ties, which connects the prisoner to the outside world, to which he must one day return. It's much better than getting letters from home. Anyone can understand a hamburger; not everyone can read."

Daniel's indignation had escalated from being politely scandalized to full rankling outrage. "Mr Whiting, that is a sinful thing to say! That is brutal!"

"As you said yourself, Daniel—one man's meat. . . ."

He gathered his wits. "Aside from the fact that it creates a situation where guards profit from the prisoners' misery, which you have to admit is not a healthy situation. . . ."

"*Prison* is not a healthy situation, Daniel."

"Aside from that, what about the people who just don't *have* any ties to be 'reinforced'? And no money. There were lots of those. And they were slowly starving to death. I *saw* them."

"That's *why* they were there, Daniel—for you to see. They were an example, for any who might suppose, mistakenly, that it is possible to get through life alone, without what the sociologists call 'primary ties'. Such an example is a powerful socializing influence. You might say it's a cure for alienation."

"You can't be serious."

"Ah, but I am. I'll admit that I wouldn't put the matter quite so plainly in a public forum, but I do believe what I've been saying. It is not, as Boa would have it, 'just for effect'. Indeed, as to whether the system works, recidivism rates show that it does. If prisons are to act as a deterrent to crime, then they must be significantly more unpleasant than the environments available outside of prison. The so-called humane prisons bred career criminals by the millions. Since we began, some twenty years ago, to make the prisons in Iowa distinctly less congenial places to pass the time, the number of released convicts who return on a second offence has been enormously reduced."

"They don't return to prison because they leave Iowa the minute they're released."

"Splendid. Their behavior outside Iowa is not our concern as members of the state board. If they've reformed, so much the better. If not, we're well rid of them."

Daniel felt stymied. He considered further objections, but he began to see how each of them might be stood on its head. He found himself admiring Whiting, in a sneaky way. Perhaps 'admire' was too strong. There was a fascination, certainly.

But did it (this fascination) derive from the man's ideas (which were not, after all, so original as to be beyond comparison) or rather from knowing that this was the actual and unique Grandison Whiting, celebrated and vilified in newspapers and on tv? A man, therefore, more real than other men, more vivid, composed of some lordlier substance so that even his hair seemed more red than all other red hair, the lines of his face more crisply expressive, and the inflections of his speech full of larger significances.

There was more talk, along less divisive lines, and even some laughter. Serjeant so far overcame his shyness (not of Daniel but of his father) as to tell a droll and fairly scathing story about his analyst's extra-marital difficulties. Boa insisted on telling about Daniel's moment of glory in Mrs Norberg's class, and made it sound a much larger moment than it had been. Then, as the talk began noticeably to flag, a servant came in to tell Mr Whiting that he was wanted on the telephone, urgently, by Miss Marspan.

Grandison Whiting excused himself.

A moment later Serjeant took his leave.

"Well," said Boa eagerly, "what do you think?"

"About your father?"

"He's incredible, isn't he?"

"Yes. He is incredible." That was all he said, nor did she seem to require more.

The snow had continued steadily through the afternoon. It was arranged that Daniel would ride home in the next car going in to town. He had only a twenty-minute wait at the gatehouse (with a different and much friendlier guard on duty), and there was the further good luck that his ride was in a pick-up in the back of which he could put his bicycle.

At first Daniel couldn't understand why the driver of the truck was glaring at him with such a degree of unprovoked ill will. Then he recognized him: Carl Mueller, Eugene's brother, but more to the point, Roy Mueller's oldest son. It was common knowledge that Carl worked at Worry, but in all his daydreams since he'd started being a friend of Boa Whiting Daniel had never indulged in this one.

"Carl!" he said, slipping off a mitten, holding out his hand.

Carl glowered and kept both gloved hands on the steering wheel.

"Carl," Daniel insisted. "Hey, it's been a long time."

The guard was standing by the open gate, above which a lighted sign commanded them still to WAIT. He seemed to be watching them, though against the dazzle of the truck's headlights this small contest must have passed unwitnessed. Even so, Carl appeared to have been unnerved, for he conceded Daniel the acknowledgement of a grimace.

WAIT changed to PASS.

"Christ, this is some snowstorm, isn't it?" Daniel said, as they moved ahead in second gear along the path that Worry's own plows had cleared not long before.

Carl said nothing.

"The first real blizzard of the year," he went on, twisting sideways in his seat so as to look directly at Carl's stony profile. "Will you look at it come down."

Carl said nothing.

"He's incredible, isn't he?"

Carl said nothing. He shifted to third. The truck's rear end swayed on the packed snow.

"That Whiting is incredible. A real character."

With a slow unsymmetrical rhythm the wipers pushed the wet snow off to the sides of the windshield.

"Friendly, though, once he puts aside his company manners. Not that he ever lets it *all* hang out, I suppose. You'd know that better than I. But he does like to talk. And theories? More theories than a physics textbook. And one or two of them would set a few people I know back on their fat asses. I mean, he's not your average run-of-the mill fiscal conservative. Not a Republican in the grand old tradition of Iowa's own Herbert Hoover."

"I don't know what you're fucking talking about, Weinreb, and I'm not interested. So why not just shut the fuck up, unless you want to ride that bicycle the rest of the way to town."

"Oh, I don't think you'd do that, Carl. Risk a swell *managerial* position like yours? Risk your exemption?"

135

"Listen, you god-damn draft-dodger, don't talk to me about exemptions."

"Draft-dodger?"

"And you fucking well know it."

"As I see it, Carl, I performed *my* service to God and country at Spirit Lake. And while I'll admit I'm not exactly anxious to go off to Detroit and protect the good people of Iowa from dangerous teenagers, the government knows where I am. If they want me, all they have to do is write and ask."

"Yeah. Well, they probably know what they're up to, not drafting shits like you. You're a fucking murderer, Weinreb. And you know it."

"Up yours, Carl. And up your fucking father's too."

Carl stepped, too suddenly, on the brake. The truck's back wheels sloughed to the right. For a moment it looked like they'd do a complete spin, but Carl managed to ease them back on course.

"You put me out here," Daniel said shrilly, "and you'll lose that fat job tomorrow. You do *anything* but take me to my front door, and I'll have your ass for it. And if you think I can't, just wait. Just wait *anyhow*."

"Chickenshit," Carl replied softly. "Chickenshit Jewish cocksucker." But he took his foot off the brake.

Neither said any more till the truck pulled up in front of the Weinreb house on Chickasaw Avenue.

Before getting out of the cab Daniel said, "Don't pull away till I've got my bike out of the back. Right?"

Carl nodded, avoiding Daniel's eyes.

"Well, then, good-night, and thanks for the lift." Once more he held out his hand.

Carl took the offered hand and grasped it firmly. "So long, murderer."

His eyes locked with Daniel's and it became a contest. There was something implacable in Carl's face, a force of belief beyond anything that Daniel could ever have mustered.

He looked away.

And yet it wasn't true. Daniel was not a murderer, although he knew there were people who thought he was, or who

136

said they thought it. In a way Daniel rather liked the idea, and would make little jokes to encourage it, offering his services (in jest) as a hit man. There has always been a kind of glamor in the mark of Cain.

The murder had taken place shortly after Daniel's release from prison. The father and older brother of his friend Bob Lundgren had been forced off the road on their way back from a co-op meeting, made to lie flat in a ditch, and shot. Both bodies had been mutilated. The stolen car was found the same day in a parking lot in Council Bluffs. The assumption was that the two murders were the work of terrorists. There had been a rash of similar killings all through that winter and spring, and indeed for many years. Farmers, especially Undergod farmers, had many enemies. This was the main reason behind the proliferation of fort-ress-villages like Worry, for despite their sponsors' claims they were not provably more efficient. Only safer.

The murders had taken place in April, three weeks before Bob Lundgren was scheduled to be paroled from Spirit Lake. Considering the repeated threats he'd made against both victims, it had been fortunate for Bob that the murders had preceded his release. As it was, people assumed that he'd hired someone to do the work for him—some fellow prisoner who'd been let out ahead of him.

The reason that Daniel in particular had come under suspicion was that the following summer he'd gone to work for Bob, supervising large work-crews of convicts from Spirit Lake. It was a fantastic summer—fraught with tension, filled with pleasure, and highly profitable. He'd lived in the main farmhouse with Bob and what was left of his family. His mother stayed upstairs, locked in her bedroom, except for sporadic forays into the other rooms, late at night, when she would break up the furniture and call down the wrath of God. Bob finally had her sent off to a rest-home in Dubuque (the same one Mrs Norberg had gone to). That left his brother's widow and her twelve-year-old daughter to take care of household matters, which they did with a kind of zombie-like zeal.

Every weekend Bob and Daniel would drive up to Elmore or one of the other border towns and get thoroughly sloshed. Daniel got laid for the first time in his life, and for many times besides. As an ex-convict (and possibly a killer) he was generally left to himself by men who would otherwise have gladly kicked shit out of him.

He enjoyed himself (and earned a lot of money), but at the same time he didn't believe in what was happening. A part of him was always backing off from these events and thinking that all these people were insane—Bob, the Lundgren women, the farmers and whores boozing in Elmore. No one in his right mind would want to live a life like this.

Even so, when Bob asked him to come back the next summer, he'd gone back. The money was irresistible, as was the chance for three months to be a grown-up instead of a high school student, than which no form of life is more downtrodden, disenfranchised, and depressed.

Bob was married now, to a girl he'd met in Elmore, and his brother's widow and her daughter had moved out. Now instead of boozing only on the weekends they were boozing every night. The house had never quite recovered from the elder Mrs Lundgren's jihad, and Julie, Bob's twenty-two-year-old bride, did not exert herself in its rehabilitation beyond the point of getting almost all of one bedroom wallpapered. She spent most of the daylight hours in a daze of boredom in front of the tv.

Once, sitting on the back porch on a rainy August night and reminiscing about the good old days at Spirit Lake, Daniel said, "I wonder what ever happened to old Gus."

"Who?" Bob asked. The tone of his voice had altered strangely. Daniel looked up to see an expression on his friend's face that hadn't been there since those times in prison when the subject of his family would get into his bloodstream and bring out the Mr Hyde in him. There it was again, that same occluded gleam of malice.

"Gus," Daniel said carefully. "Don't you remember him? The guy who sang that song the night Barbara Steiner let go."

"I know who you mean. What made you think of him just now."

"What makes a person think of anything. I was daydreaming, thinking about music, I guess—and that started me thinking about him."

Bob seemed to consider the adequacy of this explanation.

The look on his face slowly faded to a mild irritation. "What about him?"

"Nothing. I was just wondering what ever became of him. Wondering if I'd ever see him again."

"I didn't think he was a particular friend of yours."

"He wasn't. But the way he sang made a big impression on me."

"Yeah, he was an all-right singer." Bob uncapped another Grain Belt and took a long gurgling swallow.

They both fell silent and listened to the rain.

Daniel understood from this exchange that it was Gus who must have murdered Bob's father and brother. He was amazed how little difference the knowledge seemed to make in the way he felt about either Bob or Gus. His only concern was to defuse Bob's suspicions.

"I'd like to be able to sing like that," he said. "You know?"

"Yeah, you've told me on the average of I would estimate once a day. So what I'd like to know, Dan, is why *don't* you ever sing? All you have to do is open your mouth and yell."

"I will. When I'm ready."

"Dan, you're a nice guy, but you're as bad as I am for putting things off to tomorrow. You're worse—you're as bad as Julie."

Daniel grinned, uncapped another Grain Belt, and held it up in a salute. "Here's to tomorrow."

"Tomorrow," Bob agreed, "and may it take its own sweet time in coming."

The subject of Gus had never re-arisen.

When Daniel had left Worry it was six-thirty, but already it had seemed the dead of night. By the time he was home, after the slow drive through the snowstorm, he had expected no more than left-overs heated up. But in fact his mother had waited dinner. The table was set and everyone was watching a panel discussion about the new fertilizers in the living room. They had not waited, the twins in particular, with much good grace, and before Daniel was out of his windbreaker and had given his hands a symbolic splash in the wash basin (saving the water for the toilet tank), they were all of them sitting down and his mother was spooning out servings of tuna fish casserole. Aurelia passed the plate of sliced bread with a look of malevolence. Cecelia giggled.

"You didn't have to wait dinner for me, you know. I said I'd be home late."

"Fifteen after seven is not an unthinkable hour for dinner," Milly said, more for the sake of the twins than for him. "In New York City, for instance, people often don't have anything to eat before nine, even ten o'clock."

"Uh-huh," said Cecelia sarcastically.

"Did you have a nice time?" his father asked. It was rare nowadays that his father asked even so much as that, for Daniel had become protective of his privacy.

Daniel tapped a finger to his mouth, full of the tuna and noodles. The casserole had cooked too long, and the noodles were dry and hard to swallow. "Terrific," he finally brought out. "You wouldn't *believe* their piano. It's as big as a ping-pong table practically."

"That's all you did, all afternoon?" Cecelia asked. "Played a piano?"

"And a harpsichord. And an electric organ. There was even a cello, but I couldn't really do anything with that. Except touch it."

"Didn't you even *look* at the horses?" Aurelia asked. She turned to Milly plaintively. "The horses out there are so *famous*."

"Perhaps Daniel isn't interested in horses," Milly suggested.

"I didn't see the horses, but I did see Grandison Whiting."

"Did you," said Milly.

Daniel took a meditative sip of milky tea.

"Well?" said Cecelia.

"Was he nice to you?" Aurelia asked, coming right to the point.

"I wouldn't say nice exactly. He was friendly. He has a big bushy red beard, and a ring on his finger with a diamond on it as big as a strawberry." He measured the approximate size of the strawberry between finger and thumb. "A small strawberry," he conceded.

"I *knew* he had a beard," said Cecelia. "I saw *that* on tv."

"What did you say to him?" Aurelia asked.

"Oh, we talked about a lot of things. Mostly politics, I guess you'd say."

Milly set down her fork judgmentally. "Oh, Daniel— don't you have a grain of sense?"

"It was an interesting conversation," he said defensively. "I think he *enjoyed* it. Anyhow *he* did most of the talking, and Boa got her licks in, as usual. I was what you're always saying I should be—an intelligent listener."

"I'd like to know what's wrong with talking about politics," his father demanded. It was Mr Weinreb's stated conviction that Daniel's friendship with the daughter of the richest man in Iowa was not to be regarded as an exceptional occurrence and did not require special handling.

"Nothing," said Milly, "nothing at all." She didn't agree with her husband about this but wasn't prepared, yet, to make an issue of it. "Cecelia, you eat the peas too."

"Peas have vitamins," said Aurelia smugly. She was already on her second helping.

"How'd you get home?" his father asked.

"There was a pick-up coming in to town. They stopped it at the gate. If that hadn't come along, they were going to send me back in a limousine."

"Are you going back next Saturday?" Aurelia asked.

"Probably."

"You shouldn't overdo it, Daniel," Milly said.

"She's my girlfriend, Mom. She can come here. I can go there. It's that simple. Right?"

"Nothing's that simple."

"Why don't you ask her to dinner with us?" Aurelia suggested.

"Don't be silly, Aurelia," Milly scolded. "You're all acting like Daniel's never been out of the house before. And by the way, Daniel, there was a phonecall for you."

"I answered," said Cecelia. "It was a girl." She turned Daniel's own ploy against him and waited to be asked.

"So? Who?"

"She wouldn't say what her name was. But it sounded like Old Wiremouth to me."

"Don't make fun of people with braces," said her father sharply. "Someday you'll probably have them too."

"And eat your peas," Milly added.

"They're burnt."

"They're not burnt. Eat them."

"They'll make me throw up."

"I don't care. Eat them."

"What did she want, the girl who called?"

Cecelia stared balefully at a teaspoon-size mound of peas sticky with white sauce. "She wanted to know where you were. I said you were out, but I didn't know where. Now I wish I'd *told* her."

Daniel reached over with his spoon and scooped up all but three of the peas. Before Milly could say a word he'd eaten them.

Cecelia gave him a grateful smile.

Down in his own room he had to decide whether his futzing around with the instruments at Worry counted as practice and whether, therefore, he was at liberty to omit his hour of Hanon's *Virtuoso Pianist*. He decided it didn't count and he wasn't at liberty.

With the first fifteen exercises behind him, which was as much as he could get through in an hour, the next decision was easier. He *wouldn't* do his homework for chemistry, and he *wouldn't* read the Willa Cather novel for Eng. Lit. He would read the paperback that Boa had given him. It was really more of a pamphlet than a paperback, printed on pulp so recycled it was a wonder that it had got through the presses intact.

The white letters of the title shone through a ground of ink, so:

HOW TO BEHAVE

IN ORDER TO

DEVELOP

THE PERSONALITY

YOU WANT

No author's name appeared on the cover or the title page.

The publisher was the Develop-Mental Corporation of Portland, Oregon.

Boa had got the book from her brother Serjeant, who had got it in turn from a college roommate. The book had convinced Serjeant to drop out of college and take (briefly) boxing lessons. It had convinced Boa to have her hair cut short (it had since grown out again) and to get up every morning at six to study Italian (which to her own and everyone's amazement she was still doing). Daniel thought that he was already doing approximately his utmost by way of advancing slowly and steadily toward his major life goals, but he wasn't so sure that his personality couldn't bear improvement. In any case Boa had been insistent that he should read it.

Daniel was a naturally fast reader. He'd finished the book by ten o'clock. Generally he didn't think that much of it. It was self-help at a pretty simple-minded level, with lots of mottoes you were supposed to whisper to yourself in order to get motivated. But he understood why Boa had wanted him to read it. It was for the sake of the Second Law of Develop-Mental Mechanics, which appeared first on page twelve (where it was heavily underscored by a ballpoint pen) and then repeated many times throughout.

The Second Law of Develop-Mental Mechanics is as follows: 'If you want something you've got to take it. If you want it bady enough you will.'

8

THE SECOND LAW of Develop-Mental Mechanics notwithstanding, it was some time before this tacit promise was
to be fulfilled. Boa herself was not at once persuaded that
her virginity should be numbered among the somethings
that get taken by those who want them badly enough. Then,
by the time she'd been brought round, early in April,
Daniel found himself unaccustomedly beset by technical
difficulties. But a way was found, and they became, just as
Boa had imagined they would, and just as Daniel had
imagined too, lovers.

In June Daniel was faced with an awkward choice, which
is to say, a real one. All through the school year he had
been confidently expecting to fail Mrs Norberg's Social
Studies class, but when the grades were posted he came off
with an almost miraculous B (the same grade Boa got). All
at once it became possible to take up Bob Lundgren's standing offer to work again that summer at his farm. Eighteen
weeks at $230 a week meant more than four thousand
dollars. Even taking into account the expense of weekend
carousals in Elmore and a further outlay for some sort of
motorbike in order to keep on visiting Worry, the job would
still have meant a bigger chunk of money that he could
hope to put aside by any other means. The fact remained,
however, that he didn't really need so much money. In his
overweening pride he had only applied to one college,
Boston Conservatory. He hadn't expected to get in (except
in the idiot way he half-expected all his wishes to come
true), and he hadn't. His tapes were returned with a letter
saying very bluntly that his playing in no way measured up
to the Conservatory's minimum requirements.

Boa, meanwhile, had been accepted at all but one of the
eight schools she'd applied to. Accordingly, their plan for
next year was for Daniel to find a room and a job of some
sort near the college of Boa's choice. Harvard seemed the

likeliest, since maybe Daniel would get into the Conservatory on his next try, and meanwhile he'd be able to start taking voice lessons, Boston being so musical.

As to the summer just ahead, Daniel had been expecting to stay in Amesville to repair his inevitable F in Social Studies, the bright side of which was that he'd have been able to see Boa just about any day he liked. Also, Boa's favorite aunt from London was going to pay a long visit to Worry, and this aunt, Miss Harriet Marspan, was a musical amateur in the old sense of doing and caring for nothing else, and for its own sake only, thinking not of where it might lead, nor of what profit it might yield. Boa thought she performed with unusual capability and immense good taste. The three of them would form the Marspan Iowa Consort to which end Boa had already sewn together a sort of banner of welcome and hung it across the whole width of the music room.

However if Daniel went off to work for Bob Lundgren, the Marspan Iowa Consort would amount to no more than an old pink sheet with assorted scraps of cotton stitched to it. Yet if he stayed, what would he be accomplishing? For all her excellences Miss Harriet Marspan didn't sound like a natural ally. Even her devotion to music made him uneasy when he thought about it, for how was Daniel to measure up to standards of accomplishment formed in one of the musical capitals of the world? She would flay him, like another Marsyas.

But then again, some time or other he'd have to take the plunge; he'd have to leave the audience and join the chorus on the stage. However; and yet; but then again—the questions and qualifications multiplied endlessly. And yet it ought to have been a simple choice. But then again.

On the night before he had to give a final yes or no to Bob Lundgren, Milly came down to his room with a pot of coffee and two cups. With a minimum of beating around the bush (without even pouring the coffee) she asked what he was going to do.

"I wish I knew," he said.

"You'll have to make up your mind soon."

"I know. And that's about all I know."

"I'd be the last person in the world to tell you to pass up a chance to earn the kind of money you earned last summer. It's twice what you're worth."

"And then some," he agreed.

"Besides which, there's the experience."

"For sure, it's a good experience."

"I mean it could lead to more of the same, numskull. If you want to do that kind of work for a living, and God knows, in this day and age it's about the only kind of work that has a guaranteed future."

"Mm. But it isn't what I want. Not for ever."

"I didn't suppose it was. So what it boils down to—pardon me for putting it so bluntly—is whether you want to take that big a gamble."

"Gamble?"

"Don't make me spell it out, Danny. I am not a fool. I wasn't born yesterday."

"I still don't know what you mean."

"For heaven's sake, I know that you and Miss Whiting aren't performing duets down here *all* the time. You can hear that piano all over the house—when someone's playing it."

"Are you complaining?"

"Would it do any good? No, in fact, I think it's *wonderful* that you two young people should have strong interests in common." She grinned accusingly. "And what you choose to do down here is none of my business."

"Thanks."

"So I'll say only this: nothing ventured, nothing gained."

"You think I should stay in town this summer."

"Let's say I won't reproach you for enjoying yourself a bit, if that's what you want to do. And I'll see that Abe doesn't either."

He shook his head. "It's not what you think, Mom. I mean, I *like* Boa and all, but we neither of us believe in . . . um. . . ."

"Matrimony?"

"You said it, I didn't."

"Well, candidly, neither did I at your age. But anyone who crosses the street can be hit by a truck."

Daniel laughed. "Really, Mom, you've got it all turned

round backwards. The way I see it, the real choice is whether I can afford to turn down the money Bob is offering for the sake of having a bit of fun."

"Money is a consideration, that's so. No matter how nice they are, or how considerate, rich people *will* involve you in spending more than you can possibly afford. I sometimes think it's their way of weeding the rest of us out. I say that from bitter experience."

"Mom, that's not the case. I mean, there's no way to spend that kind of money in Amesville, much less at Worry."

"Well, well. I'd love to be proven wrong. But if you should need a few dollars sometime, to tide you over, I'll see what I can do."

"That's very sweet of you. I think."

Milly looked pleased. "One more word of advice, and I'll leave you to the horns of your dilemma. Which is—I trust that one of you is taking suitable precautions."

"Um, yes. Usually."

"Always. With the rich, you know, things don't work the same. If a girl finds herself pregnant, she can go off for a holiday and get rid of her embarrassment."

"Jesus, Mom, I hope you don't think I've been *planning* to get Boa knocked up. I'm not *stupid*."

"A word to the wise. But if my back should ever be turned, you'll find what you need in the upper left drawer of the chest-of-drawers. Lately, though this is strictly between us, *I* haven't had much use for them."

"Mom, you're too much."

"I do what I can." She held up the coffee pot. "You want any?"

He shook his head, then reconsidered and nodded, and finally decided against it and said no.

Though she had been three times married, Miss Harriet Marspan seemed, at the age of thirty-seven, the incarnation of Spinsterhood, its deity or patron saint, but at the huntress rather than the virgin-martyr end of the scale. She was a tall, sturdy-looking woman with prematurely gray hair and sharp, appraising gray eyes. She knew all her own good points and the basic skills of enhancing them, but nothing she could do could counteract the basic chill emanating from her as from the entrance to a food locker. Miss Marspan was oblivious to this, and acted on the assumption that she was rather a lot of fun. She had a silvery, if not contagious, laugh, a shrewd wit, perfect pitch, and unremitting powers of concentration.

Boa had become her favorite niece during the term of her exile to Villars, to which Miss Marspan, though not a skier, had made several visits at the height of the season. Additionally, Boa had twice spent the holidays with Miss Marspan at her Chelsea flat, being taken about to operas, concerts, and private musicales every night of her visit. At the dinner table of Lord and Lady Bromley (Bromley was an important television producer) Boa had sat between the composer Lucia Johnstone and the great castrato Ernesto Rey. And through it all they had pursued with endless patience, with infinite caution, with delectable subtlety, the one subject in which Miss Marspan chose to interest herself —musical taste.

As to music *per se*, Boa thought that for a woman of such definite opinions Miss Marspan was oddly lacking in preferences. She could (for instance) make the finest discriminations among the various interpretations of a Duparc song but seemed to have little interest in the song itself, except as an arrangement of vowels and consonants to be produced in accordance with the rules of French phonetics. "Music," she liked to say, "doesn't *mean* a thing." Yet the music she enjoyed the most was Wagner's, and she was a mine of information about the associated stage business she'd witnessed during different performances of *The Ring*. Daniel found this more disconcerting than Boa, who was used to similar equivocations from her father. Boa insisted that it must be simply a matter of age: after a while one took the basic amazement of art for granted, much as one might take for granted the rising of the sun in the morning, its setting in the evening. As a theory Daniel couldn't fault this, but he wasn't convinced either. He disliked and distrusted Miss Marspan, all the while he strained to make a good impression on her. In her presence he behaved as he would have behaved in a church, moving slowly, speaking deliberately, saying nothing that might contradict her established doctrines.

Never, for instance, did he declare his deep-felt conviction that Raynor Taylor's music was dust from the tomb; he deferred as well in the matter of Moravian hymns of Colonial America. He even started enjoying the hymns after a while. The Marspan Iowa Consort never did undertake anything Daniel thought of as serious music, which was both a disappointment and a relief. For all his practice and preparations in the past two years (more than two years now!) he knew he wasn't ready for much more than the catches, ditties, jingles, and rounds that Miss Marspan, with the help of the library's data-links, was so ingenious in unearthing from assorted music libraries around the country.

Though he didn't say so to Boa, not even after Miss Marspan had left, Daniel felt ashamed of himself. He knew that somehow he had cooperated in the subversion of his own principles. The excuse he'd offered himself at the time —that the hours of chit-chat with Miss Marspan had been so vacuous as to amount to no more than the silence he'd maintained in Mrs Norberg's classroom—was a crock of shit. What he'd done, plain and simply, was to suck up to her. It was true, then, about money: if you so much as rubbed shoulders with it, it began to corrupt you.

One night, in disgust with himself, and wanting nothing more than to go back to being the person he'd been a year ago, he phoned Bob Lundgren to see if he could get his old job back, but of course it had long since been taken. Bob was drunk, as usual these days, and insisted on hanging on talking even though Daniel told him he couldn't afford it. Bob made some digs, first about Daniel's supposed deficits, then about Boa directly. You were supposed to suppose that he was trying to be good-humored in a locker-room way, but his jokes got more and more overtly malicious. Daniel didn't know what to say. He just sat there, on the edge of his parents' bed (that was where the phone was), holding the sweaty receiver, feeling worse and worse. A resentful silence grew between them, as Daniel finally refused to pretend to be amused.

"Well, Dan old boy, we'll be seeing you," Bob said at last.
"Right."
"Don't do anything I wouldn't do."

"Oh, for sure," said Daniel, in a tone intended to be wounding.

"And what the hell is that supposed to mean?"

"It was supposed to mean that that would give me lots of latitude. It was a joke. I laughed at all your jokes. You should laugh at some of mine."

"I didn't think it was a very funny joke."

"Then we're even."

"Fuck off, Weinreb!"

"Have you heard the one about the nympho who married an alcoholic?"

Before Bob could answer that one he hung up. Which was the end, pretty definitely, of that friendship. Such as it had been.

One day, during the most ruthless part of August, and just after the twins had been packed off with a dozen other Brownies for their first taste of summer camp, Milly announced that she was being taken to Minneapolis for a full week of movies, shopping, and sybaritic sloth. "I'm tired," she declared, "of swatting mosquitoes in a rented cabin while Abe goes off to stare at the ripples in the pond. It's not my idea of a vacation; it never has been." Daniel's father, who had in fact been planning another fishing trip, gave in without even trying to negotiate a compromise. Unless, as seemed likely, the negotiations had already been handled off-stage and the official supper-time capitulation had been put on entirely for Daniel's benefit. The upshot of his parents' departure was that Daniel, who had often been a guest for lunch and dinner, was asked to stay at Worry for the whole week they were to be gone.

He'd thought that by now he couldn't be phased, that he'd confronted enough of the place's pomps and splendors, had touched and tasted them often enough that a more steady view would have no power over him. But he was phased, and it did have considerable power. He was given the room next to Boa's, which was still provided, from the era of Miss Marspan's visit, with a prodigious sound system, including a horseshoe organ he could play (using earphones) at any hour of the day or night. The height of the ceiling as he sprawled in his bed, the more formidable height of the windows that rose to within inches of the moldings, the view from these windows across a small forest of unblighted elms (the largest concentration of elm trees left in Iowa), the waxed glow of rosewood and cherry furnishings, the hypnotic intricacies of the carpets (there were three), the silence, the coolness, the sense of wishes endlessly, effortlessly gratified: it was hard to keep any psychological distance from such things, hard not to desire and (therefore) covet them. You were always being stroked, caressed, seduced—by the scent and slither of the soap, by the sheets on the bed, by the colors of the paintings on the walls, the same enamel-like colors that appeared, fizzing in his head, when he squeezed his eyes closed during orgasm: pinks that deepened to a dusky rose, deliquescent blues, mauves and lavenders, celadon greens and lemon yellows. Like courtesans pretending to be no more than matrons of a certain elegance, these paintings, in their carved and gilded frames, hung on damask walls quite as though they were, as they declared, mere innocent bowls of fruit and sworls of paint. In fact, they were all incitements to rape.

Everywhere you looked: sex. He could think of nothing else. He'd sit at the dinner table, talking about whatever (or, more likely, listening), and the taste of the sauce on his tongue became one with the taste of Boa an hour before when they'd made love, a taste that might be overwhelmed, all at once, by a spasm of total pleasure right there at the dinner table that would stiffen his spine and immobilize his mind. He would look at Boa (or, just as often, at Alethea) and his imagination would begin to rev until it had gone out of control, until there was nothing in his head but the image, immense and undifferentiated, of their copulation. Not even theirs, really, but a cosmic abstraction, a disembodied, blissful rhythm that even the flames of the candles obeyed.

It was the same when they would listen to music. He had read, in some book of advice lent him by Mrs Boismortier, that it was a bad idea to listen to too many records. The way to discover what any piece of music was about was to perform it yourself, or lacking that, to hear it performed live. The habit of listening to records was a form of self-abuse. But, ah, there is something to be said for the habit.

Lord God, such music as they listened to that week! Such pleasures as they shared! Such flurries of fingers, such cadences and cadenzas, such amazing transitions to the minor key, such sighs and smiles and secret sympathies suddenly made plain as in the most brilliant and luminous of mirrors!

It dawned on him that this is what being in love was all about. This was why people made such a fuss over it. Why they said it made the world go round. It did! He stood with Boa on the roof of Worry's tower and watched the sun rise above the green body of the earth and felt himself to be, with her, ineffably, part of a single process that began in that faraway furnace that burned atoms into energy. He could not have explained how this was so, nor could he hold on for more than a moment to his highest sense of that enveloping Love, the moment when he had felt needles of light piercing his and Boa's separate flesh, knitting their bodies like two threads into the intricate skein of that summer's profusions. It was only a single moment, and it went.

But every time they made love it was as though they were moving toward that moment again, slowly at first, then suddenly it would be there again in its immense, arisen majesty within them, and still the delirium swelled as they moved from height to effortless height, exalted, exulting, exiles from earth, set free from gravity and the laws of motion. It was heaven, and they had the keys. How could they have kept themselves from returning, even supposing they had wanted to?

9

LATE ON THE last night of his sojourn at Worry, returning from Boa's room to his own, Daniel was met in the hallway by Roberts, Mr Whiting's valet. In a confidential whisper Roberts said that Mr Whiting would like to have a word with Daniel in his office. Would he come this way? It seemed useless to plead that he wasn't properly dressed to visit Mr Whiting, so off he went, in his bathrobe and slippers, to the drawing room in which he'd first taken tea with the family, then through a kind of lock connecting that room to the inner keep, a sealed corridor of whirling motors, winking lights, and eccentric clockwork contraptions. He wondered, walking through this fairy-trap, if it had ever actually served the purpose for which it had been built. Were there, lost in the perpetual rotary motion of these various whirligigs, or caught in the repeating decimal of some data-bank underfoot, snared souls for ever unable to return to their flesh? To which question there could be no answer for anyone who entered, as he did now, corporeally.

Grandison Whiting's office was not like other rooms at Worry. It did not astonish. It was furnished with only ordinary office furniture of the better sort: glass bookcases, two wooden desks, some leather chairs. Papers littered every surface. A swivel lamp, the only one burning, was aimed at the door by which he'd come in (Roberts had not followed him through the fairy-trap), but even with the light in his eyes he knew that the man who sat behind the desk could not be Grandison Whiting.

"Good evening, Daniel," the man said, in what was unmistakably Grandison Whiting's voice.

"You've shaved off your beard!"

Grandison Whiting smiled. His teeth, agleam in the subdued light, seemed the exposed roots of his skeleton. His entire face, without his beard, had the stark character of a memento mori.

"No, Daniel, you see me now as I am. My beard, like Santa's, is assumed. When I'm here quite by myself, it is a great relief to be able to take it off."

"It isn't real?"

"It's quite real. See for yourself. It's there in the corner, by the globe."

"I mean. . . ." He blushed. He felt he was making a complete fool of himself, but he couldn't help it. "I mean— *why?*"

"That's what I so much admire in you, Daniel—your directness. Do sit down—over here, out of the glare—and I'll tell you the story of my beard. That is, if you're interested."

"Of course," Daniel said, taking the proffered chair cautiously, so that his bathrobe wouldn't part.

"When I was a young man, a little older than yourself, and about to leave Oxford and return to the States, I had the good fortune to come across a novel in which the hero changes his character by buying and wearing a false beard. I knew that I would have to change *my* character shortly, for I would never be a credit to my position, as they say, until I'd learned to assert myself much more strenuously than I was accustomed to doing. I had tended to be reclusive in my college days, and while I'd learned a good deal concerning economic history, mostly forgotten since, I'd failed utterly to master the essential lesson that my father had sent me to Oxford to learn (and which *he* had learned there); namely, how to be a gentleman.

"You smile, and you do well to smile. Most people here suppose that one becomes a gentleman by adopting what is called 'good manners'. Good manners, as you must know (for you've picked them up very quickly), are mainly an encumbrance. In fact, a gentleman is something else entirely. To be a gentleman is to get what you want with only an implicit threat of violence. America, by and large, has no gentlemen—only managers and criminals. Managers never assert themselves sufficiently, and are content to surrender their autonomy and most of the money they help to generate to us. In return they're allowed the illusion of a guiltless life. Criminals, on the other hand, assert themselves too much and are killed by other criminals, or by us. As always, the middle way is best." Whiting folded his hands with a consciousness of completion.

"Pardon me, Mr Whiting, but I still don't quite see how wearing a, uh. . . ."

"How a false beard helped me to be a gentleman? Quite simply. I had to act as though I weren't embarrassed by my appearance. That meant, at first, I had to overact. I had to become, somehow, the sort of person who would actually have such a big bushy red beard. When I did act in that manner I found that people behaved much differently toward me. They listened more closely, laughed louder at my jokes, and in general deferred to my authority."

Daniel nodded. In effect, Grandison Whiting was stating the Third Law of Develop-Mental Mechanics, which is 'Always pretend that you're your favorite movie star—and you will be.'

"Have I satisfied your curiosity?"

Daniel was flustered. "I didn't mean to give the impression that, uh. . . ."

"Please, Daniel." Whiting held up his hand, which glowed with a pale roseate translucence in the beam of the lamp. "No false protests. Of course you're curious. I should be dismayed if you were not. I'm curious about you, as well. In fact, the reason I called you from your bed—or rather, from Boa's—was to say that I've taken the liberty of gratifying my curiosity. And also to ask you if your intentions are honest."

"My intentions?"

"Concerning my daughter, with whom you were having, not half an hour ago, intimate relations. Of, if I may say so, the highest quality."

"You were watching us!"

"I was returning a compliment, so to speak. Or has Bobo never mentioned the incident that sent her packing to Villars?"

"She did but. . . . Jesus, Mr Whiting."

"It isn't like you to flounder, Daniel."

"It's hard not to, Mr Whiting. All I can think to say, once again, is why? We supposed you knew what was going on pretty much. Boa even got the impression that you approved. More or less."

"I suppose I do approve. Whether more or less is what I'm trying to determine now. As to why, it was not (I hope) merely the gratification of a father's natural curiosity. It was so that I'd have the goods on you. It's all down on video-tape, you see."

"All?" He was aghast.

"Not all, possibly, but enough."

"Enough for what?"

"To prosecute you, if need be. Bobo is still a minor. You're guilty of statutory rape."

"Oh Jesus *Christ*, Mr Whiting, you wouldn't!"

"No, I don't expect it will be necessary. For one thing, that might force Bobo to marry you against her own wishes, or against yours, for that matter. Since, my lawyer tells me, you could not, in that event, be prosecuted. No, my intention is much simpler: I want to force the issue before you've wasted each other's time in hesitations. Time is too precious for that."

"You're asking *me* if I'll marry your daughter?"

"Well, you didn't seem about to ask *me*. And I can understand that. People generally wait for me to take the initiative. It's the beard, I suppose."

"Have you asked Boa about this?"

"As I see it, Daniel, my daughter's made her choice, and declared it. Rather openly, I should say."

"Not to me."

"The surrender of virginity is unequivocal. It needs no codicil."

"I'm not sure Boa sees it that way."

"She would, I've no doubt, if you asked her to. No one with any sensitivity wants to appear to be haggling over matters of the heart. But in our civilization (as you may have read) certain things go without saying."

"That was my impression too, Mr Whiting. Until to-night."

Whiting laughed. His new, beardless face modified the usual Falstaffian impression of his laughter.

"If I have forced the issue, Daniel, it was in the hope of preventing your making a needless mistake. This plan of

156

yours to precede Boa to Boston is almost certain to lead to unhappiness for both of you. Here the inequality in your circumstances only lends a piquancy to your relations; there it will become your nemesis. Believe me—I speak as one who has been through it, albeit on the other side of the fence. You may have your pastoral fantasies now, but the good life cannot be led for less than ten thousand a year, and that requires both the right connections and a monastic frugality. Boa, of course, has never known the pinch of poverty. But you have, briefly. Though long enough to have learned, surely, that it is to be avoided at all costs."

"I'm not planning to go back to prison, Mr Whiting, if that's your meaning."

"God forbid you should, Daniel. And please, don't we know each other well enough for you to dispense with 'Mister Whiting'?"

"Then how about 'Your Lordship'? Or 'Excellency'? That wouldn't seem quite as formal as Grandison."

Whiting hesitated, then seemed to decide to be amused. His laugh, if abrupt, had the ring of sincerity.

"Good for you. No one's ever said that to my face. And of course it's perfectly true. Would you like to call me 'Father' then? To return to the original question."

"I still don't see what's so terrible about our going to Boston. What simpler way of finding out if it works?"

"Not terrible, only foolish. Because it won't work. And Boa will have wasted a year of her life trying to make it work. Meanwhile she'll have failed to meet the people she's going to college to meet (for that's the reason one goes to college; one can study far better in solitude). Worse than that, she may have done irreparable harm to her reputation. Sadly, not everyone shares *our* enlightened attitude toward these arrangements."

"You don't think she'd be even more compromised by *marrying* me?"

"If I did, I would scarcely go out of my way to suggest it, would I? You're bright, resilient, ambitious, and—allowing for the fact that you're a lovesick teenager—quite level-headed. From my point of view, an ideal son-in-law. Bobo doubtless sees you in a different light, but I think, all in all, that she's made a wise, even a prudent, choice."

"What about the, quote, inequality of our circumstances, unquote? Isn't that even more a consideration in the case of getting married?"

"No, for you'd be equals. My son-in-law could never be other than well-to-do. The marriage might not work, of course, but that risk exists in all marriages. And the odds for its working are, I should think, much better than the odds for the Boston trial balloon. You can't dip your toes into marriage: you must plunge. What do you say?"

"What can I say? I'm flabbergasted."

Whiting opened a silver cigarette case standing on his desk and turned it round to Daniel with a gesture of invitation.

"No thank you, I don't smoke."

"Nor do I, but this is grass. I always find that a bit of a buzz makes the decision-making process more interesting. Almost any process, really." By way of further endorsement he took one of the cigarettes from the case, lit it, inhaled, and, still holding his breath, offered it to Daniel.

He shook his head, not believing it was marijuana.

Whiting shrugged, let out his breath, and sagged back in his leather chair.

"Let me tell you about pleasure, Daniel. It's something young people have no understanding of."

He took another toke, held it in, and offered the cigarette (coming from Grandison Whiting, you could not think of it as a joint) again to Daniel. Who, this time, accepted it.

Daniel had been stoned only three times in his life—once at Bob Lundgren's farm with some of the work-crew from Spirit Lake, and twice with Boa. It wasn't that he disapproved, or didn't enjoy it, or that the stuff was so impossible to get hold of. He was afraid, simply that. Afraid he'd be busted and sent back to Spirit Lake.

"Pleasure," said Grandison Whiting, lighting another cigarette for himself, "is the great good. It requires no explanations, no apologies. It is what is—the reason for continuing. One must arrange one's life so that all pleasures are available. Not that there's time to *have* them all. Everyone's budget is limited in the end. But at your age, Daniel, you should be sampling the major varieties. In moderation. Sex, above all. Sex (perhaps after mystic transports, which come without our choosing) is always the most considerable, and cloys the least. But there is also something to be said for drugs, so long as you can hold on to your sanity, your health, and your own considered purpose in life. I gather, from the efforts you're making to learn to be a musician, despite an evident inaptitude, that you wish to fly."

"I . . . uh. . . ."

Whiting waved away Daniel's stillborn denial with the hand that held the cigarette. Its smoke, in the beam of the lamp, formed a delta of delicate curves.

"I do not fly myself. I've tried, but lack the gift, and have small patience with effort in that direction. But I have many good friends who do fly, even here in Iowa. One of them did not return, but every delight has its martyrs. I say this because it's clear to me that you've made it your purpose in life to fly. I think, in your circumstances, that has been both ambitious and brave. But there are larger purposes, as I think you have begun to discover."

"What is your purpose, Mr Whiting? If you care to say."

"I believe it is what you would call power. Not in the crude sense that one experiences power at Spirit Lake, not as brute coercion—but in a larger (and, I would hope, finer) sense. How to explain? Perhaps if I told you of my own mystical experience, the single such I've been gifted to have. If, that is, you can tolerate so long a detour from the business in hand?"

"So long as it's scenic," said Daniel, in a burst of what seemed to him show-stopping repartee. It was very direct grass.

"It happened when I was thirty-eight. I had just arrived in London. The euphoria of arrival was still in my blood. I had been meaning to go to an auction of carpets, but had spent the afternoon, instead, wandering eastward to the City, stopping in at various churches of Wren's. But it was not in any of those that the lightning struck. It was as I was returning to my hotel room. I had placed the key in the lock, and turned it. I could feel, in the mechanical movement of the tumblers, the movements, it seemed, of the entire solar system: the earth turning on its axis, moving in its orbit, the forces exerted on its oceans, and on its body too, by the sun and moon. I've said 'it seemed', but it was no seeming. I felt it, as God must feel it. I'd never believed in God before that moment, nor ever doubted Him since."

"Power is turning a key in a lock?" Daniel asked, fuddled and fascinated in equal measure.

"It is to feel the consequences of one's actions spread through the world. There is a picture downstairs—you may have noted it: *Napoleon Musing at St Helena* by Benjamin Haydon. He stands on a cliff, facing a garish sunset, and his shadow is thrown behind him, a huge shadow. Two seabirds circle in the void before him. And that is all. But it says everything, to me." He fell into a considering silence, and then resumed: "It is an illusion, I suppose. All pleasures are, in the end, and all visions too. But it's a powerful illusion, and it is what I offer you."

"Thank you," said Daniel.

Grandison Whiting lifted a questioning eyebrow.

Daniel smiled, by way of explanation. "Thank you. I can't see any reason to go on being coy. I'm grateful: I accept. That is, if Boa will have me."

"Done," said Whiting, and held out his hand.

"Assuming," he was careful to add, even as they shook on it, "that there are no strings attached."

"I can't promise that. But where there is agreement as to principle, a contract can always be negotiated. Shall we invite Bobo to join us now?"

"Sure. Though she can be a bit grouchy when she just wakes up."

"Oh, I doubt she would have gone to sleep. After he'd accompanied you here, Roberts brought Bobo to my secretary's office, where she has been able to observe our entire tête-à-tête over the closed circuit tv." He looked over his shoulder and addressed the hidden camera (which must have been trained on Daniel all this while): "Your ordeal is over now, Bobo dear, so why don't you join us?"

Daniel thought back over what he'd said to Whiting and decided that none of it was incriminating.

"I hope you don't mind?" Whiting added, turning back to Daniel.

"Mind? It's Boa who'll mind. Me, I'm past being shocked. After all I've lived at Spirit Lake. The walls have ears there too. You haven't bugged my room at home, have you?"

"No. Though my security officer advised me to."

"I don't suppose you'd tell me if you had."

"Of course not." He smiled, and there were those bony teeth again. "But you can take my word for it."

When Boa arrived upon the scene, she was, as Daniel had predicted, in a temper over her father's meddling (over, at least, the manner of it), but she was also pleased to be all at once engaged with a whole new set of destinies and decisions. Planning was Boa's forte. Even as the champagne bubbled in her glass, she'd begun to consider the question of a date, and before the bottle was empty they'd settled on October 31. They both loved Halloween, and a Halloween wedding it was to be, with jack-o-lanterns everywhere, and the bride and groom in black and orange, and the wedding cake itself an orange cake, which was her favorite kind anyhow. Also (this was Grandison's contribution) the wedding guests would be able to stay on for a fox hunt. It had been years since there had been a proper hunt at Worry, and nothing was so sure to bring Alethea round to a cheerful sense of the occasion.

"And then, after the wedding?" Grandison Whiting asked, as he untwisted the wire fixed to the cork of the second bottle.

"After the wedding Daniel shall carry me off whithersoever he will for our honeymoon. Isn't that lovely: whithersoever?"

"And then?" he insisted, thumbing the cork.

"Then, after a suitable interval, we shall be fruitful and multiply. Starting off this early, we should be able to produce litters and litters of little Weinrebs. But you mean, don't you, what will we *do*?"

The cork popped, and Whiting refilled the three glasses.

"It does occur to me that you'll have rather a gap to fill before the next academic year begins."

"That assumes, Father, that your years will continue to be of the academic variety."

"Oh, you must both get your degrees. That goes without saying. You've already settled on Harvard—wisely—and I'm

161

sure room can be found there for Daniel too. So you needn't alter your plans in that respect. Only defer them."

"Have you asked Daniel if he *wants* to go to Harvard?"

"Daniel, do you want to go to Harvard?"

"I know I ought to. But where I really did want to go was the Boston Conservatory of Music. But they turned me down."

"Fairly, do you think?"

"Sure, but that doesn't make it hurt any less. I just wasn't 'accomplished' enough."

"Yes, that was my sister-in-law's opinion, too. She said you'd done wonders for the short time you'd studied, and in view of the fact that you evidenced no innate talent for music."

"Oof," said Daniel.

"Did you think we never spoke of you?"

"No. But that's a pretty deflating opinion. The more so because it's very close to what someone else once said, someone who was also . . . knowledgeable."

"On the whole, Harriet thought very highly of you. But she didn't think you were cut out for a career in music. Not a very satisfying career at any rate."

"She never said that to me," Boa objected.

"Surely because she knew you'd have passed it on to Daniel. She had no wish to wound his feelings gratuitously."

"Then why are *you* telling him, Father?"

"To persuade him to make other plans. Don't suppose, Daniel, that I'd have you give up music. You couldn't, I'm sure. It is a passion, perhaps a ruling passion. But you needn't become a professional musician to be serious about music. Witness Miss Marspan. Or if she seems too dessicated to serve as a model to you, consider Moussorgsky, who was a civil servant, or Charles Ives, an insurance executive. The music of the nineteenth century, which remains our greatest music, was written for the discerning delectation of a vast audience of musical amateurs."

"Mr Whiting, you don't need to go on. I've said the same thing to myself many times. I wasn't suggesting that it's the Boston Conservatory or nothing. Or that I have to go to a music school at all. I would like to take some private lessons with someone good—"

"Naturally," said Whiting.

"As for the rest of what I ought to do, you seem to have it all laid out. Why not just say what you have in mind, and I'll tell you how it strikes me?"

"Fair enough. To begin with the immediate future, I'd like you to go to work for me here at Worry. At a salary, shall we say, of forty thousand a year, paid quarterly, in advance. That should be enough to set you up. You'll have to spend it, you know, as fast as it comes in. It will be expected that you flaunt your conquest. To do less would show a lack of appreciation. You'll become, for a time, the hero of Amesville."

"Our picture will be in all the papers," Boa put in. "And the wedding will probably be on the tv news."

"Necessarily," Whiting agreed. "We can't afford to neglect such an opportunity for public relations. Daniel will be another Horatio Alger."

"Tell me more." Daniel was grinning. "What do I have to do to earn my preposterous salary?"

"You'll work for it, believe me. Essentially it will be the same job you did for Robert Lundgren. You'll manage the crews of seasonal workers."

"That's Carl Mueller's job."

"Carl Mueller is getting the sack. That is another aspect of your triumph. I hope you have nothing against revenge?"

"Sweet Jesus."

"Well, *I* have something against revenge, Father, though I won't enter into an argument on theoretical grounds. But won't other people whom Daniel has to work with resent him if he takes Carl's job away?"

"They'll resent him in any case. But they'll know (they already do know, I'm sure) that there are objective reasons for firing Carl. He's rather systematically taken kickbacks from the hiring agencies he works through. His predecessor did as well, and it may almost be thought to be one of the fringe benefits of his job. But I hope that you, Daniel, will resist the temptation. For one thing, you'll be earning something over double Carl's salary."

"You realize," Daniel said in as neutral a tone as he could manage, "that Carl will lose his draft classification along with his job."

"That's Carl's lookout, isn't it? By the same token, you stand to inherit his exemption. So I suggest that you do have that P-W housing removed from your stomach. Harvard's security network is probably a few degrees tighter than mine. You wouldn't want to be setting off alarms every time you went to class."

"I'll be only too happy to be rid of it. As soon as I start the job. When would you like me to report?"

"Tomorrow. Drama requires despatch. The more sudden your rise, the more complete your triumph."

"Mr Whiting—"

"Still not 'Father'?"

"Father." But it did seem to stick in his mouth. He shook his head, and said it again. "Father, the one thing I still don't understand is why. Why are you doing all this for me?"

"I've never tried to resist what I regarded as inevitable. That is the secret of any very prolonged success. Then too, I like you, which sweetens the pill considerably. But it wasn't my decision, ultimately. It was Bobo's. And it was, I think, the right one." He exchanged a nod of acknowledgement with his daughter. "Old families need an infusion of new blood from time to time. Any other questions?"

"Mm. Yes, one."

"Which is?"

"No, I realize now it's something I shouldn't ask. Sorry."

Grandison Whiting didn't press the point, and the conversation moved back towards the laying of plans, which (since they were not to be carried out) need not be reported here.

The question Daniel didn't ask was why Whiting had never grown his own beard. It would have been so much easier in the long run, and he'd never have run the risk of being accidentally unmasked. But since the answer was probably that he'd tried to grow one and it hadn't come in to his liking, it hadn't seemed diplomatic to ask.

Daniel decided (among the many other plans that were formed that night) to grow a beard himself. His own was naturally thick and wiry. But after the wedding, not before.

He wondered if this were the fate he'd foreseen for himself so long ago, when he was pedaling along the road to Unity. Every time he'd gone to Worry, he'd had to pass the

same spot on the road where he'd stopped and had his revelation. He could remember little of that vision now, only a
general sense that something terrific was in store for him.
This was certainly terrific. But it wasn't (he finally decided)
the particular benediction that his vision had foretold. That
was still up ahead, lost in the glare of all his other glories.

10

IT SEEMED IRONIC to Daniel, and a bit of a defeat, that he should be having his first flight in an airplane. He had sworn to himself, in the not-so-long-ago heyday of his idealistic youth, that he would never fly except on his own two transubstantial wings. Now look at him—strapped into his seat, his nose pressed against the postage-stamp of a window, with four hundred pounds of excess baggage, and a track record of absolute zero. For all his brave talk and big ambitions, he never tried—never tried trying—once Grandison Whiting had laid down the law. It was Daniel's own fault for mentioning that he meant to smuggle in a flight apparatus from out-of-state, his fault for believing Whiting's stories about friends of his right here in Iowa who flew. Pure bullshit, all of it. Not that it mattered, awfully. It only meant he'd had to postpone the big day for a while longer, but he knew that time would fly even if he didn't.

Now the waiting was behind him, all but a few hours. He and Boa were on their way. To New York first, where they would change for a jet to Rome. Then Athens, Cairo, Tehran, and the Seychelles for a winter tan. Economy was the official reason for changing at Kennedy rather than going direct from Des Moines, since everything, including travel bookings, was cheaper in New York. Daniel, despite his every extravagance, had established a reputation as a pennypincher. In Des Moines he'd wasted one whole day fleeing from one tailor to another, horrified by their prices. He understood, in theory, that he was supposed to be above such things now that he was *nouveau riche*, that the difference between the prices of two equivalent commodities was supposed to be invisible to him. He ought not to itemize bills, nor count his change, nor remember the amounts, or even the existence, of sums that old friends asked to borrow. But it was amazing, and dismaying, what the smell of money did to otherwise reasonable people, the way they came sniffing and snuffling around you, and he couldn't stop resenting them for it. His character rejected the aristocratic attitude that money, at least on the level of 'friendly' transactions, was no more to be taken account of than the water you showered with, much as his body would have rejected a transfusion of the wrong blood-type.

But economy was only an excuse for booking the honeymoon through New York. The real reason was what they'd be able to do during the twelve hours between planes. That, however, was a secret. Not a very dark secret, since Boa had managed for a week now not to guess despite the broadest hints. Surely she knew and wasn't letting on from sheer love of feigning surprise. (No one could equal Boa at the art of unwrapping presents.) What could it be, after all, but a visit to First National Flightpaths? At last, sweet Jesus: at long, sweet last!

The plane took off, and the stewardesses performed a kind of pantomime with the oxygen masks, then brought round trays of drinks and generally made an agreeable fuss. Clouds rolled by, revealing checkerboards of farmland, squiggles of river, plumblines of highway. All very disappointing compared to the way he'd imagined it. But after all, *this* wasn't the real thing.

First National Flightpaths was the real thing. First National Flightpaths specialized in getting beginning flyers off the ground. "All you need," the brochure had said, "is a sincere feeling for the song you sing. We just provide the atmosphere—and leave the flying to you."

He had been drinking steadily all day during the wedding and the reception, without (he was pretty certain) letting it show, even to Boa. He continued drinking on the plane. He lit a cigar, which the stewardess immediately made him put out. Left feeling abashed and cantankerous, he started—or rather, restarted—an argument he'd had earlier that day with Boa. About her Uncle Charles, the Representative. He had given them a sterling service for twelve as a wedding present, which Boa had insisted on cooing over privately, as they were driving to the airport. Finally he'd exploded and said what he thought about Charles Whiting—*and* his brother Grandison. What he thought was that Grandison had arranged their marriage for the benefit of Charles, and of the family name, knowing that Charles was shortly to be involved in something approaching a scandal. Or so it had been presented in some of the more outspoken newspapers on the East Coast. The scandal concerned a lawyer hired by a sub-committee of Ways and Means (the committee that Charles chaired) who had caused a stink—no one knew precisely what about since the government had managed to clamp the lid on before the actual details became public. Somehow it concerned the American Civil Liberties Union, an organization about which Charles had made several intemperate and highly publicized remarks. Now the sub-committee lawyer had vanished, and Uncle Charles was spending all his time telling reporters he had no comments. From the first inklings in the *Star-Tribune* it was obvious to Daniel that the wedding had been arranged as a kind of media counterweight to the scandal—weddings being irreproachable P.R. It was not obvious to Boa. Neither of them knew more about it than could be gleaned from papers, since Grandison Whiting refused, categorically, to discuss it. When, only days before the wedding, he realized the depth of Daniel's suspicions he became quite incensed, though Boa had managed to smooth both their tempers. Daniel had apologized, but his doubts remained. From these entanglements had issued their quarrel in the Whiting limousine (a quarrel further complicated by Boa's panicky concern that the chauffeur should not overhear them); this was again the subject of their quarrel en route to Kennedy; it promised to be their quarrel for ever, since Boa would not allow any doubts about her father to go unchallenged. She became Jesuitical in his defense, and then strident. Other passengers made reproving glances at them. Daniel wouldn't give up. Soon he'd driven Boa to making excuses for Uncle Charles. Daniel reacted by upping the level of his sarcasm (a form of combat he'd learned from his mother, who could be scathing). Only after Boa had burst into tears, would he lay off.

The plane landed in Cleveland, and took off again. The stewardess brought more drinks. Though he'd managed to stop arguing, he felt rotten. Balked. Resentful. His anger turned everything good that had happened into something equally bad. He felt cheated, corrupted, betrayed. All the glamor of the past nine weeks evaporated. All his posturings before his friends were wormwood now—for he knew they'd be making the same calculations and seeing his marriage in this new, less rosy light.

And yet, wasn't it possible that Boa was right in a way? If her father hadn't dealt with him in a manner wholly truthful, he may at least have limited himself to half-truths. Then too, whatever motives Grandison Whiting may have concealed, the result was still this happy ending here and now. He should, as Boa suggested, put the rest out of mind, relax, lie back and enjoy the beginning of what looked to be the endless banquet ahead.

Besides, it wouldn't do to arrive at First National Flightpaths feeling any otherwise than mellow.

So, by way of thinking of something else, he read, in the airline's own magazine, an article about trout fishing written by one of the country's top novelists. When he'd finished it, he was convinced that trout fishing would be a delightful pastime to take up. Would there be trout, he wondered, in the Seychelles? Probably not.

The nicest thing about New York, Daniel decided, after being there five minutes, was that you were invisible. Nobody noticed anyone else. In fact, it was Daniel who wasn't noticing, as he found out when someone almost got away with his carryon suitcase, which Boa rescued by a last-minute grab. So much for patriotic feelings about his old home town. (For he was, as he'd many times pointed out to Boa, a New Yorker by birth.)

The taxi ride from the airport to First National Flightpaths took a maddening forty minutes. (The brochure had promised: "Just ten minutes from Kennedy.") It took another fifteen minutes to register as Ben and Beverley Bosola (the brochure had also pointed out that New York law did not hold it criminal to adopt or use an alias, so long as fraud was not involved) and to be shown to their suite on the twenty-fourth floor. There were three rooms: a regular hotel room (with double-bed, kitchenette, and a sound system to equal the best at Worry) and two small studios adjoining. When the attendant asked Daniel if he knew how to work the apparatus, he took a deep breath and admitted that he didn't. The explanation, together with a demonstration, took another five minutes. You smeared a little stickum on your forehead and over that snugged on a headband to which the wires connected. Then you had to lay back in what Daniel would have sworn was a dentist's chair. And sing. Daniel tipped the attendant ten dollars, and finally they were alone.

"We've got eleven hours," he said. "Ten, really, if we don't want to miss the plane. Though it's silly, isn't it, talking about planes when here we are, ready to take off ourselves. Jesus, I'm so nervous."

Boa threw back her head and whirled one small whirl on the mustard yellow carpet, making the pumpkin-orange of her wedding dress billow out about her. "So am I," she said quietly. "But in the nicest way."

"Do you want to make love first? They say that helps sometimes. To put you in the right frame of mind."

"I'd rather do that afterwards, I think. It may seem terribly presumptuous to say so, but I feel the most complete confidence. I don't know why."

"I do too. But, you know, for all that, it might not work. You can never tell in advance. They say only about thirty per cent make it the first time."

"Well, if not tonight, another time."

"But *if* tonight, oh boy!" He grinned.

"Oh boy," she agreed.

They kissed and then each of them went into a separate sound studio. Daniel, following the attendant's advice, sang through his song once before wiring himself in. He had chosen Mahler's 'Ich bin der Welt abhanden gekommen'. From the first moment he'd heard the song on a recording, a year ago, he'd known that *that* was the song for his first flight. Its three short stanzas read like an instruction manual for takeoff, and the music. . . . Nothing could be said about such music: it was perfection.

He sang, wired in, to his own accompaniment, recorded on a cassette, and at the end of the second stanza—"For really, I am dead to the world"—he thought he had lifted off. But he hadn't. A second time, as the song went on— "Lost in death to the world's riot, I rest in a realm of perfect quiet"—he felt the music propelling his mind right out of his flesh.

But at the end of the song he was still there, in that pink padded chair, in his starched shirt and black tux, in his own obdurate flesh.

He sang the song again, but without the same conviction, and without results.

Not to panic. The brochure said that very often the most effective song, in terms of reaching escape velocity, isn't one for which we have the highest regard or greatest love. Probably his problem with the Mahler song was technical, despite the trouble he'd taken to transpose it down to his own range. All the authorities agreed that it was useless to tackle music beyond your capabilities.

His next offering was 'I am the Captain of the Pinafore', to which he gave all the extra faith and oomph he could muster. That was the way he still remembered it, almost like a hymn, from the dream he'd dreamt the night before he got out of Spirit Lake. But he couldn't stop feeling silly about it and worrying what someone listening would have thought. Never mind that the studio was sound-proof. Naturally, with that kind of self-consciousness, his score was another big zero.

He sang his two favorite songs from *Die Winterreise*, to which he could usually bring a sincere, droopy *Weltschmerz*. But in the middle of the second song he broke off. There was no use even trying, feeling the way he felt.

It was less an emotion than a physical sensation. As though some huge black hand had gripped his chest and squeezed. A steady pressure on his heart and lungs, and a taste of metal on his tongue.

He got down on the mustard carpet and did pushups rapidly, till he was out of breath. That helped some. Then he went out into the bedroom to pour himself a drink.

A red light glowed above the door to Boa's studio: she was flying.

His instant reaction was to be happy for her. Then came the envy. He was glad, thinking about it, that it hadn't happened the other way round. He wanted to go in and look at her, but that seemed somehow like admitting defeat:

you look at people do the things you'd like to do yourself—and can't.

The only booze in the icebox was three bottles of champagne. He'd been drinking it all day long and was sick of it, but he didn't want to phone room service for beer, so he guzzled a bottle of it as quickly as he could.

He kept looking up at the light above the door, wondering if she'd taken off on her first try, and what song she'd used, and where she was now. She might have been anywhere in the city, since all the First National's studios had direct access to the outside. Finally, unable to stand it any more, he went in and looked at her. Or rather, at the body she'd left behind.

Her arm had fallen from the armrest and hung limply in a filmy envelope of orange *crêpe de chine*. He lifted it, so limp, and placed it on the padded rest.

Her eyes were open, but blank. A bead of saliva drooled down from her parted lips. He closed her eyes and wiped away the spittle. She seemed colder than a living body ought to be; she seemed dead.

He went back to his own room and tried again. Doggedly, he went through everything twice. He sang songs by Elgar and Ives: they weren't as great as Mahler's but they were in Daniel's own language, and that was a consideration. He sang arias from Bach cantatas, choruses from Verdi operas. He sang songs he'd never heard before (the studio was well-equipped with both scores and accompaniment cassettes) and old love songs he remembered from the radio, years and years before. Three hours he sang, until there was nothing left of his voice but a rasp and an ache deep in his throat.

When he returned to the outer room, the light was still on over Boa's door.

He went to bed and stared at that baleful red eye glowing in the darkness. For a while he cried, but he made himself stop. He couldn't believe that she could just go off like this, knowing (as she surely must) that he'd been left behind. It was their wedding night, after all. Their honeymoon. Was she still angry with him for what he'd said about her father? Or didn't anything else matter, once you could fly?

But the worst of it wasn't that she had gone: the worst of it was that he was here. And might be, for ever.

He started crying again, a slow steady drip of tears, and this time he let them come, for he remembered the brochure's advice not to let your feelings get bottled up inside. Eventually, with a bottle of tears and of champagne both emptied, he managed to fall asleep.

He woke an hour after the plane had departed for Rome. The light was still burning above the studio door.

Once, when he was learning to drive, he'd backed Bob Lundgren's pick-up off the side of a dirt road and couldn't get the back wheels up out of the ditch. The bed of the truck was full of bags of seed, so he couldn't just go off to look for help, since Bob had few neighbors who would have been above helping themselves. He'd honked the horn and blinked the lights till the battery was dead—to no avail. Eventually he'd exhausted his impatience and started to see the situation as a joke. By the time Bob found him, at two a.m., he was completely unruffled and calm.

He'd reached that point again. If he had to wait for Boa, then he'd wait. Waiting was something he was good at.

He phoned down to the desk to say he'd be keeping the suite for another day and to order breakfast. Then he turned on the tv, which was showing what must have been the oldest cowboy movie ever made. Gratefully he let his mind sink into the story. The heroine explained to the hero that her parents had been killed in the massacre on Superstition Mountain, which seemed a truth as inexplicable as it was universal. His breakfast came, a gargantuan breakfast fit for the last hours of a man condemned to the gallows. Only after he'd finished his fourth fried egg did he realize that it was meant to be breakfast for two. Feeling replete, he went up to the roof and swam, all by himself, in the heated pool. He did slow weightless somersaults in the water, parodies of flight. When he returned to the room, Boa's light was still glowing. She was spread out on the reclining seat exactly as he'd left her the night before. With half a thought that she might, if she were in the room and watching him, decide to be a dutiful wife and return to her body (and her husband), he bent down to kiss her forehead. In doing so, he knocked her arm from the armrest. It dangled from her shoulder like a puppet's limb. He left it so, and returned to the outer room, where someone had used his few minutes away to make the bed and take away the tray of dishes.

Still feeling oddly lucid and *dégagé*, he looked through a catalogue of cassettes available (at ridiculous prices, but what the hell) from the shop in the lobby. He phoned down an order, more or less at random, for Haydn's *The Seasons*.

At first he followed the text, hastening back and forth between the German and the English, but that required a more focused attention than he could muster. He didn't want to assimilate but just, lazily, to enjoy. He went on listening with half an ear. The drapes were drawn and the lights turned off. Every so often the music would take hold, and he'd start being able to see little explosions of color in the darkness of the room, quick arabesques of light that echoed the emphatic patterns of the music. It was something he remembered doing ages ago, before his mother had run away, when they had all lived here in New York. He would lie in his bed and listen to the radio playing in the next room and see, on the ceiling, as on a black movie screen, movies of his mind's own making, lovely semi-abstract flickerings and long zooming swoops through space, compared to which these little bips and flashes were weak tea indeed.

From the first, it would seem, music had been a visual art for him. Or rather, a spatial art. Just as it must be for dancers. (And confess it: didn't he enjoy himself more when he danced than when he sang? And didn't he do it better?) Or for a conductor even, when he stands at the core of the music's possibility and calls it into being by the motions of his baton. Perhaps that explained why Daniel couldn't fly— because in some essential way that he would never understand music was for ever alien to him, a foreign language that he must always be translating, word by word, into the language he knew. But how could that be, when music could mean so much to him? Even now, at a moment like this!

For Spring and Summer were fled, and the bass was singing of Autumn and the hunt, and Daniel was lifted outside himself by the music's gathering momentum. Then, with a ferocity unmatched by anything else in Haydn, the hunt itself began. Horns sounded. A double chorus replied. The fanfare swelled, and formed . . . a landscape. Indeed, the tones that rolled and rollicked from the bells of the horns *were* that landscape, a broad expanse of wooded hills through which the hunters careened, resistless as the wind. Each "Tally-ho!" they cried was a declaration of possessing pride, a human signature slashed across the rolling fields, the very ecstasy of ownership. He'd never understood before the fascination of hunting, not on the scale it was conducted at Worry. He'd supposed it was something rich people felt obliged to do, as they were obliged to use silver and china and crystal. For what intrinsic interest could there be in killing one small fox? But the fox, he saw now, was only a pretext, an excuse for the hunters to go galloping off across their demesne, leaping walls and hedges, indifferent to boundaries of every kind, because the land belonged to them so far as they could ride and sing out "Tally-ho!"

It was splendid, undeniably—splendid as music and as idea. Grandison Whiting would have been gratified to hear it set forth so plainly. But the fox takes a different view of the hunt, necessarily. And Daniel knew, from the look he had seen so often in his father-in-law's eyes, that *he* was the fox. He, Daniel Weinreb. He knew, what's more, that the whole of wisdom, for any fox, may be written in a single word. Fear.

Once they put you in prison, you're never entirely out of it again. It enters you and builds its walls within your heart. And once the hunt begins it doesn't stop till the fox has been run to earth, till the hounds have torn it and the huntsman has held it up, a bleeding proof that the rulers and owners of the world will have no pity on the likes of a fox.

Even then, even in the grip of this fear, things might have happened otherwise, for it was a pellucid, not a panicky, fear. But then, in the afternoon (Boa had yet to return), it was anounced, as the third item on the tv news, that a plane on its way to Rome had exploded over the Atlantic, and that among the passengers (all of whom had perished) was the daughter of Grandison Whiting and her newlywed husband. There was a picture, from the wedding, of the official kiss. Daniel, in, his tux, had his back turned to the camera.

The explosion was said to be the work of unidentified terrorists. No mention was made of the A.C.L.U. but the implication was there.

Daniel was sure that he knew better.

PART III

II

THIRTY IS A bad birthday when you've got nothing to show for it. By then the old excuses are wearing pretty thin. A failure at thirty is likely to be a failure the rest of his life, and he knows it. But the worst of it isn't the embarrassment, which may even do you some good in small dosages; the worst of it is the way it works its way into the cells of your body, like asbestos. You live in the constant stink of your own fear, waiting for the next major catastrophe: pyorrhoea, an eviction notice, whatever. It's as though you'd been bound, face to face, to some maggoty corpse as an object lesson in mortality. Which had happened once to someone in a movie he'd seen, or maybe it was only a book. In any case, the life Daniel saw laid out before him that morning, the morning of his thirtieth birthday, seemed bad news at almost the same scuzzy level, the only difference being the body he was tied to was his own.

The things he'd hoped to do he hadn't done. He'd tried to fly, and failed. He was a nothing musician. His education had been a farce. He was broke. And none of these conditions seemed amenable to change. By any system of bookkeeping this had to be accounted failure. He would admit as much, cheerfully or morosely according to his mood and state of sobriety. Indeed, to have admitted to anything else among the people he called his friends would have been a breach of etiquette, for they were failures too. Few, admittedly, had touched rock bottom yet, and one or two were only honorary failures who, though they'd fallen short of their dreams, would never be entirely destitute. Daniel, though, had already been there, though only in the summer, and never for more than a week at a time, so perhaps it hadn't amounted to more than playacting—dress rehearsals for the worst that was yet to come. For the time being though, he was too good-looking to have to sleep on the street, except by choice.

Indeed, if blessings were to be counted, then looks would have to top the list, despite this morning's taste of ashes. There it was in the speckled bathroom mirror, as (with borrowed razor and lather from a sliver of yellow laundry soap) he crisped the borders of his beard: the face that had saved him at so many eleventh hours, the feckless friendly face that seemed his only by the luckiest accident, so little did it ever reveal his own chagrined sense of who he was. Not Daniel Weinreb any more, Dan of the glittering promise, but Ben Bosola, Ben of the dead end.

The name he'd taken to register at First National Flight-paths had been his ever since. Bosola, after the family who'd rented the basement room on Chickasaw Avenue that became his bedroom. Ben, for no particular reason except that it was an Old Testament name. Ben Bosola : schmuck, hustler, lump of shit. Oh, he had a whole litany of maledictions, but somehow, much as he knew he deserved every epithet, he could never quite believe he was really as bad as all that. He *liked* the face in the mirror, and was always a little surprised, pleasantly, to find it there, smiling away, the same as ever.

Someone tapped on the bathroom door, and he started. He'd been alone in the apartment five minutes ago.

"Jack, is that you?" said a woman's voice.

"No. It's Ben."

"Who?"

"Ben Bosola. I don't think you know me. Who are you?"

"His wife."

"Oh. Do you need to use the toilet?"

"Not really. I just heard someone in there, and wondered who. Would you like a cup of coffee? I'm making one for myself."

"Sure. Whatever."

He rinsed his face in the toilet bowl, and dabbled the shaven underside of his chin with Jack's (or would it be his wife's?) cologne.

"Hi," he said, emerging from the bathroom with his brightest smile. You'd never have known from those bright incisors the rot that was happening further back in his mouth, where three molars were already gone. How dismayed his father would have been to see his teeth like this.

Jack's wife nodded, and placed a demitasse of coffee on the white formica dining ledge. She was a short, tubby woman with red, rheumatic hands and red, rheumy eyes. She wore a muumuu patched together from old toweling, with long harlequin sleeves that seemed anxious to conceal her hands' misfortunes. A single thick blond braid issued from a mound of upswept hair and swung, tail-wise, behind her.

"I didn't know Jack was married," Daniel said, with amiable incredulity.

"Oh, he isn't, really. I mean, legally we're man and wife, of course." She made a self-deprecating snort, more like a sneeze than a laugh. "But we don't *live* together. It's just an arrangement."

"Mm." Daniel sipped the tepid coffee, which was last night's heated over.

"He lets me use the place mornings that he goes to work. In return I do his laundry. Etcetera."

"Uh-huh."

"I'm from Miami, you see. So this is really the only way I can qualify as a resident. And I don't think I could *bear* to live anywhere else now. New York is so. . . ." She flapped her terrycloth sleeves, at a loss for words.

"You don't have to explain."

"I *like* to explain," she protested. "Anyhow, you must have wondered who I was, just barging in this way."

"What I meant was, I'm a temp myself."

"You are? I would never have thought so. You seem like a native somehow."

"In fact I am. But I'm also a temp. It would take too long to explain."

"What did you say your name was?"

"Ben."

"Ben—that's a lovely name. Mine's Marcella. Horrible name. You know what you should do, Ben: *you* should get married. It doesn't necessarily have to cost a fortune. Certainly not for someone like you."

"Mm."

"I'm sorry, it's none of my business. But it is worth it, in the long run. Marriage, I mean. Of course, for me, at this point, it doesn't make that much practical difference.

181

I'm still living in a dorm, though they *call* it a residence hotel. That's why I like to come here when I can, for the privacy. But I do have a registered job now, waitressing, so in another couple of years, when I've qualified as a resident in my own right, we'll get a divorce and I can find my own apartment. There's still a lot of them, if you're qualified. Though, realistically, I suppose I'll have to share. But it will be a damn sight better than a dorm. I hate dorms. Don't you?"

"I've usually managed to avoid them."

"Really? That's amazing. I wish I knew your secret."

He smiled an uncomfortable smile, put down the cup of silty coffee, and stood. "Well, Marcella, you'll have to guess my secret. 'Cause it's time I was off."

"Like that?"

Daniel was wearing rubber sandals and a pair of gym shorts.

"This is how I arrived."

"You wouldn't like to fuck, would you?" Marcella asked. "To be blunt."

"Sorry, no."

"That's all right. I didn't suppose you would." She smiled wanly. "But that's the secret, isn't it—the secret of your success?"

"Sure enough, Marcella. You guessed."

There was no point in escalating the conflict. In any case, the harm was done, from Marcella's point of view. Nothing so rankles as a refused invitation. So, meek as a mouse, he said bye-bye and left.

Down on the sidewalk it was a blowy, overcast day, much too cold for this late in April and *much* too cold to be going around shirtless. People, naturally, noticed, but in either a humorous or an approving way. As usual he felt cheered up by the attention. At 12th Street he stopped in at what the painted sign over the window still faintly declared to be a book store and had his morning shit. For a long while after, he sat in the stall reading the graffiti on the metal partition and trying to come up with his own original contribution. The first four lines of the limerick came to him ratatat-tat, but he was baffled for an ending

until, having decided to leave it blank, as a kind of competition, lo and behold, it was there:

> There once was a temp whose despair
> Was a cock by the name of Pierre,
>   For it lived in his crotch
>   And made daily debauch
> By (Fill in the blank if you dare)!

Mentally he tipped his hat to his Muse, wiped Arab-style
with his left hand, and sniffed his fingers.

Five years before, when there were still a few smoldering embers of the old chutzpah left in him, Daniel had developed a passion for poetry. 'Passion' is probably too warm
a term for an enthusiasm so systematic and willed as that
had been. His vocal coach-cum-Reichian therapist at the
time, Renata Semple, had had the not uncommon theory
that the best way to fly, if you seem to be permanently
grounded, was to take the bull by the horns and write your
own songs. What song, after all, is more likely to be heartfelt than one original to the heart that feels it? Daniel, who
tended to take for granted the lyrics of the songs he so
lucklessly sang (who in fact preferred them to be in a
foreign language, so as not to be distracted from the music),
had had a whole new continent to explore, and one which
proved more welcoming and accessible than music *per se*
had ever been. At first, maybe, his lyrics were too jingly or
too sugary, but he very soon got the hang of it and was
turning out entire little musicals of his own. There must
have been something wrong with the theory, however, for
the songs Daniel wrote—at least the best of them—though
they never got *him* off the ground, had worked quite well
for several other singers, including Dr Semple, who usually
didn't have an easy time of it. If his songs weren't at fault,
it would seem the fault must lie in Daniel himself, some
knot in the wood of his soul that no expense of energy
could smooth away. So, with a sense almost of gratitude for
the relief that followed, he had stopped trying. He wrote
one last song, a valedictory to Erato, the Muse of lyric
poetry, and didn't even bother trying it out on an apparatus.
He no longer sang at all, except when he was alone and felt

spontaneously like singing (which was seldom), and all that remained of his poetic career was a habit of making up limericks, as evidenced today in the toilet.

Actually, notwithstanding his grand renunciation of all *beaux artes* and *belles lettres*, Daniel was rather proud of his graffiti, some of which were good enough to have been remembered and copied out, by other hands, in public conveniences all about the city. Each time he found one thus perpetuated, it was like finding a bust of himself in Central Park, or his name in the *Times*—proof that he'd made his own small but characteristic dent on the bumpers of Western Civilization.

On 11th Street, halfway to Seventh Avenue, Daniel's antennae picked up signals that said to stop and reconnoiter. A few housefronts away, on the other side of the street, three black teenage girls were pretending to be inconspicuous in the recessed doorway of a small apartment building. A nuisance, but Daniel had lived long enough in New York to know better than ignore his own radar, so he turned round and took his usual route to the gym, which was shorter anyhow, along Christopher Street.

At Sheridan Square he stopped in for his traditional free breakfast of a glop-filled doughnut and milk at the Dodge 'Em Doughnut Shop. In exchange Daniel let the counterman use the gym on nights that he was in charge. Larry (the counterman) complained about his boss, the customers, and the plumbing, and just as Daniel was leaving he remembered that there'd been a call for him the day before, which was a bit strange since Daniel hadn't used the doughnut shop phone as an answering service for over a year. Larry gave him the number he was supposed to call back: Mr Ormund, extension twelve, 580–8960. Maybe there'd be money in it, you never can tell.

Adonis, Inc., across Seventh Avenue from the doughnut shop and upstairs above a branch of Citibank, was the nearest thing Daniel had to a permanent address. In exchange for handling the desk at different times and locking up three nights a week, Daniel was allowed to sleep in the locker-room (or, on the coldest nights, inside the sauna) whenever he cared to. He kept a sleeping bag and one change of clothes rolled up in a wire basket, and had his own cup with his name on it—BENNY—on a shelf in the bathroom. Two other temps also had cups on the shelf and sleeping bags in their lockers, and when all three of them slept over it could get pretty claustrophobic. Fortunately, they seldom all three coincided on the same night, since there were usually other, less spartan possibilities. At irregular but cherished intervals Daniel would be asked to act as watchdog for someone's vacant apartment. More often he'd spend the night with a known quantity from the gym, such as, last night, Jack Levine. Once or twice a week he'd take pot luck from the street. But there were nights when he didn't care to pay the price for such extra comfort, and on those nights it was good to have the gym to fall back on.

There were basically two classes of people who worked out at Adonis, Inc. The first were show biz types—actors, dancers, singers; the second were policemen. It could be argued that there was a third class as well, larger than either of the others and the most faithful in attendance—the unemployed. But almost all of these were either unemployed show biz types or unemployed cops. It was a standing joke at the gym that these were the only two professions left in the city. Or, which was nearer the case, the only three.

Actually, New York was in much better shape than most of the other collapsing East Coast cities, since it had managed over the last fifty years to export a fair share of its problems by encouraging the more energetic of these problems to lay waste the slums they lived in and loathed. The Bronx and most of Brooklyn were rubble now. No new housing was built to replace the housing burned down. As the city shrank, its traditional light industries followed the Stock Exchange to the southwest, leaving behind the arts, the media, and the luxury trade (all three, paradoxically, in thriving condition). Unless you could get on the welfare rolls (or were an actor, singer, or policeman), life was difficult verging on desperate. Getting on welfare wasn't easy, since the city had slowly but systematically tightened the requirements. Only legal residents qualified for welfare, and you only got to be a legal resident if you could prove you'd been profitably employed and paying taxes for five years or (alternately) that you were a graduate of a city high school. Even the latter proviso wasn't without a tooth or two, for the high schools no longer acted simply as part-time penetentiaries, but actually required students to master a few rudimentary skills, such as programming and English grammar. By these means New York had reduced its (legal) population to two and a half million. All the rest (another two and a half million? If the authorities knew, they weren't telling) were temps, and lived, like Daniel, as best they could—in church basement dormitories, in the shells of abandoned midtown offices and warehouses, or (those with some cash to spare) in Federally subsidized 'hotels' that provided such amenities as heat, water, and electricity. In his first years in New York, before money became the overriding consideration (for Boa, providentially, had brought along in her hand luggage what had seemed a lifetime's supply of pawnable jewelry—until it had all been pawned), Daniel had lived at such a hotel, sharing a semi-private room with a temp who worked nights and slept days. The Sheldonian, on Broadway at West 78th. He'd hated the Sheldonian while he was there, but those days were far enough behind him now to look like the Golden Age.

It was still relatively early when he arrived at the gym, and the manager, Ned Collins, was setting up a routine for a new customer, a fellow Daniel's own age but badly gone to seed. Ned bullied, exhorted, and flattered in exquisite proportion. He would have made—he did make—a first-rate psychotherapist. No one was better at flogging someone through a crisis of morale or at goosing them out of the doldrums. Ned, and the feeling he generated of basic psychological comfort, was the main reason Daniel had made Adonis, Inc., his home.

After he'd swept the hallway and the stairs, he started to work on his own routine, and after a hundred incline sit-ups, he had shifted down to first gear—a mood, or mode, of slow, thoughtless strength, such as derricks must feel when they're most happy. Ned hectored the new customer. The wind rattled the windows. The radio played its small repertory of tunes for the brain-damaged and then delivered a guileless, Pollyanna version of the news. Daniel was too self-involved to be bothered. The news floated by like noise from the street, like faces drifting by outside a restaurant: signs of the city's teeming life, welcome as such, but all homogenized and indistinct.

After an hour and a half he laid off and took over the desk from Ned, who left for lunch. When he was sure no one on the floor of the gym was watching, Daniel took the key-ring from the drawer and went into the locker-room where he opened the coin box of the pay-phone. With a quarter from the box, he dialed the number Larry had given him.

A woman answered: "Teatro Metastasio. May I help you?"

The name set off all his alarm bells, but he answered, calmly enough: "Yes. I have a message to call Mr Ormund, on extension twelve."

"This is extension twelve, and this is Mr Ormund speaking."

"Oh." He skated past his double-take without skipping a beat. "This is Ben Bosola. My answering service said I was to phone you."

"Ah yes. There is a position open here at the Teatro that a mutual friend said you would be qualified to fill."

It had to be a practical joke. The Metastasio was, more than La Fenice, more than the Parnasse in London, the source, mainstay, and central glory of the bel canto revival. Which made it, in many purists' eyes, the most important opera house in the world. To be asked to sing at the Teatro Metastasio was like receiving a formal invitation to heaven.

"Me?" Daniel said.

"At the moment, of course, Ben, I can't answer *that* question. But if you would like to come in, and let us have a look at you. . . ."

"Certainly."

"Our mutual friend has assured me that you're a perfect diamond in the rough. His very words. What we must consider is, how rough, and what sort of polishing will be required."

"When would you want me to come by?"

"Is now too soon?"

"Um, actually, a bit later would be better."

"I'll be here till five. You know where the Teatro is?"

"Of course."

"Just tell the man in the box office you want to see Mr Ormund. He'll show you the way. Bye-bye."

"Bye-bye," said Daniel.

"And," he added, when he could hear the dial-tone, "amen, amen, amen."

The Metastasio!

Realistically, he just wasn't that good. Unless it was a place in the chorus. That must be it. But even so.

The Metastasio!

Mr Ormund had said something about his *looks*, or *looking* at him. That was probably what was behind it. What he must do then, surely, was to look his best—and not his grotty best but his posh best, since this was, after all (and praise God), a *job* interview! That meant getting hold, somehow, of Claude Durkin, in one of whose closets Daniel kept the last suit remaining to him from his pre-honeymoon shopping spree in Des Moines. It had survived only because he'd been wearing it the night everything else was stolen from his room at the Sheldonian. The jacket was tight across the shoulders now, thanks to Adonis, Inc., but the basic cut was conservative and didn't too much give away its antiquity. In any case, it was all he had so it would have to do.

Daniel took another quarter out of the coin box, and phoned Claude Durkin. He got an answering device, which could mean either that Claude was out or that he wasn't feeling sociable. Claude periodically came down with crushing depressions that kept him incommunicado for weeks at a time. Daniel explained to the answering device the urgency of his situation, and then, when Ned got back from lunch, trotted off to Wall Street where Claude lived, wearing the jeans and turtleneck from his locker—if worst came to worst, he'd have to see Ormund in those.

The whole Wall Street area was a high security zone, but Daniel was registered as a visitor at the William Street checkpoint and was able to breeze right through. Claude, however, still wasn't home when Daniel arrived at his building, or he couldn't be bothered, so Daniel plunked down on the concrete ledge of an ornamental pool and waited. Daniel was good at waiting. In fact, he made his living as a waiter, waiting in ticket lines. He would go to a box office early on the morning that seats became available (sometimes, a day or two in advance) in order to buy tickets for people who weren't free to stand in the line themselves, or just didn't want to. Working at the gym provided him with a roof over his head; waiting paid for his groceries, at least from September through May, when there was something worth waiting in line for. In summer, he had to find other means of survival.

Claude Durkin was one of Daniel's best customers. Also, gingerly, a friend. They'd met in Daniel's palmier days when he was taking a course at the Manhattan League of Amateurs. The M.L.A. was less a music school than an introduction service. You went there to meet other musicians at your own level of taste, zeal, and incompetence. Claude had been going there, off and on, for years and had taken most of the courses in the catalogue. He was forty when they met, a bachelor, and a fairy, though of uneven capability. In his youth he'd flown fairly regularly, though always with great effort. Now he got aloft at most two or three times a year, with ever greater effort. Daniel always wondered, though he was too polite to ask, why Claude didn't just take off permanently, the way (it would seem) that Boa had, the way he meant to if he ever reached escape velocity, which (it would also seem) he was never going to. Alas.

He waited, and he waited, fantasizing all the while about the Metastasio, though he knew he shouldn't since he might not get the job. Gradually, the weather seemed to warm up. The fountain choked and gurgled at the center of the pool. A lost poodle ran around in circles, yapping, and finally was found. A policeman asked to see his ID—and then recognized him. It was a policeman from the gym.

At last, the third time he asked the doorman to buzz, he got in. Claude had been home all along, it turned out—asleep. He was in one of his bluer moods, which he nevertheless tried to conceal out of deference to Daniel's euphoria. Daniel told the brief tale of Ormund's call, and Claude made an effort to seem impressed, though he was still half-asleep.

Daniel refused Claude's first offer of a bath in his tub, and accepted the second. While Daniel soaked, and then while he scrubbed, Claude, in full-lotus position on the carpet, described the dream he'd just awakened from. It involved flying through, around and over various churches in Rome, imaginary churches that Claude was able to describe in wearisome detail. Though he'd long since ceased to be a practising Catholic, or even a practising architect, churches were Claude's thing. He knew everything there was to be known about the ecclesiastical architecture of Renaissance Italy. He'd even taught a course in it at N.Y.U. until his father had died and left him a large hunk of secular architecture, the rents from which had made it possible to lead his present liberated, disgruntled life. He was always at loose ends, taking up interests and setting them aside like bibelots in an antique shop. His most abiding preoccupation was the decoration of his apartment, which changed every few months in accordance with his most recent acquisitions. The walls of all his rooms were one endless sideboard displaying bits and pieces of poor old demolished Europe: Ionic capitals, little ivory madonnas, big walnut madonnas, details of stucco-work, samples of moldings, fragments of statues in every degree of dismemberment, pewter dishes, silver dishes, swords, gilded letters from the fronts of shops, all of it stacked up higgledy-piggledy on the custom-made shelves. Each piece of junk, each precious jewel had its own story concerning the shop where he'd bought it or the ruin he'd dug it out of. To do Claude credit, most of his acquisitions he'd scouted out himself. Whenever he flew, his destination was some bomb site in France or Italy where he would flit about the rubble like some disembodied magpie, giddy with plundering. Then, when he'd flown back to his nest on Wall Street, he'd send off instructions to various agents who specialized in scavenging for American collectors. All in all, it seemed to Daniel a great waste of flight-time, not to mention money. He'd even said as much to Claude one Christmas in the tactful (he hoped) form of a limerick written in the flyleaf of the book he'd given him as a present (the book was a nineteenth-century guidebook to Italy that he'd found in a box of garbage). It stood now, the limerick, carved on a granite tombstone, below Claude's name and the date of his birth, an accepted component of the *mise-en-scène*:

There once was a fairy named Claude
Who loved to go visiting God;
    If God wasn't home
    He would seek Him in Rome
On Maria Minerva's façade.

Having told his dream and worried a portent or two out
of it, Claude approved of Daniel's turnout, with the exception of his tie, which he insisted on his replacing with one
of his own in last year's latest design of giant waterdrops
running down clear green glass. Then, with a kiss on the
cheek and a pat on the rump, he saw Daniel to the elevator
and wished him the best of luck.

Poor Claude, he looked *so* woebegone.

"Cheer up," Daniel urged, just before the doors chomped
shut between them. "That was a *happy* dream." And
Claude, complying, bent his lips into the shape of a smile.

The waiting room to Mr Ormund's office, where Daniel
waited half an hour, was decorated with so many chromo-
lithoes of the Metastasio's stars that you almost couldn't
see the raw silk wall-covering behind them. All the stars
were represented bewigged and bedizened in the costumes
of their most celebrated roles. All were inscribed, with
heaps of love and barrels of kisses, to (variously): "Caris-
simo Johnny", "Notre très cher maître", "Darling Sambo",
"Sweetest Fatty", and (by stars of a lesser magnitude) "Dear
Mr Ormund".

Dear Mr Ormund, in person, was a frightfully fat, professionally jolly, foppishly dressed businessman, a Falstaff
and a phoney of the deepest dye, that darkest brown that
hints of darker purples. Phoneys (from the French, *faux
noirs*) were almost exclusively an Eastern phenomenon. Indeed, in Iowa and throughout the Farm Belt whites who
dyed their skin black or even used any of the more drastic
tanning agents, such as Jamaica Lily, were liable to pay heavy
fines, if discovered. It was not a law frequently enforced,
and perhaps not frequently broken. Only in cities where
blacks had begun to reap some of the political and social
advantages of their majority status did phoneys at all
abound. Most left some conspicuous part of their anatomy

undyed (in Mr Ormund's case it was the little finger of his right hand), as a testimony that their negritude was a choice and not a fatality. Some went beyond dyes and frizzing, and opted for cosmetic surgery, but if Mr Ormund's slightly *retroussé* nose weren't naturally come by, then he had been discreet in selecting a model, for there were still centimeters to spare before it would be a full-fledged King Kong. If he were ever to let his skin slip back to its natural pallor, you'd never have known what he'd been. Which made him, of course, less than a hundred-per-cent, gung-ho, complete and irreversible phoney, but phoney enough, for all that, for Daniel, shaking hands with him and noticing the tell-tale pinky, to feel distinctly off balance psychologically. In some ways he was an Iowan still. He couldn't help it: he disapproved of phoneys.

"So you're Ben Bosola!"

"Mr Ormund."

Mr Ormund, instead of releasing Daniel's hand, kept it enclosed in both his own. "My informants did not exaggerate. You *are* a perfect Ganymede." He spoke in a lavish, lilting contralto that might or might not have been real. Could he be a castrato as well as a phoney? Or did he only affect a falsetto, as did so many other partisans of bel canto, in emulation of the singers they idolized?

Let him be what he would, as odd or as odious, Daniel couldn't afford to seem flummoxed. He rallied his wits, and replied, in a voice perhaps a little fuller and chestier than usual: "Not quite Ganymede, Mr Ormund. If I remember the story, Ganymede was about half my age."

"Are you twenty-five then? I'd never have thought so. But do sit down. Would you like a sweet?" He waved the hand with its one pink finger at a bowl of hard candies on his desk, then sank down into the sighing vinyl cushions of a low sofa. Reclining, propped on one elbow, he regarded Daniel with a fixity of interest that seemed at once shrewd and idle. "Tell me about yourself, my boy—your hopes, your dreams, your secret torments, your smoldering passions—everything! But no, those matters are always best left to the imagination. Let me read only the memoirs of those dark eyes."

Daniel sat stiffly, his shoulders touching but not resting against the back of a spindly imitation-antique chair, and offered his eyes up for inspection. He reflected that this was what other people must experience, going to a dentist.

"You've known tragedy, I can see. And heartbreak. But you've come through it smiling. In fact, you always bounce back. Am I right?"

"Right as rain, Mr Ormund," said Daniel, smiling.

"I've known heartbreak, too, *cara mio*, and some day I will tell you of it, but we have a saying in the Theater— first things first. I mustn't go on tormenting you with my inane chatter when, naturally, it is the *position* you wish to hear of."

Daniel nodded.

"I'll begin with the worst: it pays a mere pittance. You probably knew that."

"I just want a chance to prove myself, Mr Ormund."

"But there *are* gratuities. For some of the boys here, I believe, they have been not inconsiderable, not inconsiderable at all. It depends, finally, on you. It's possible just to coast along with the zephyrs, but it's equally possible, with a bit of spunk, to make yourself a bundle. You wouldn't believe it to look at me now, Ben, but I began, thirty years ago, when this was still the Majestic, as you're beginning now: an ordinary usher."

"An usher?" Daniel repeated, in candid dismay.

"Why, what did you suppose?"

"You didn't say what the position was. I guess I thought. . . ."

"Oh dear. Dear, dear, dear. I'm very sorry. Are you a singer, then?"

Daniel nodded.

"Our mutual friend has played a *most* unkind joke, I fear. On both of us. I have no connection with that side of the house—none at all. I'm *so* sorry."

Mr Ormund rose from the sofa, making the cushions sigh anew, and went to stand beside the door to the waiting room. Was his distress genuine or feigned? Had the misunderstanding been mutual, or had he been leading Daniel down the garden path for his own amusement? With the door being shown him so literally, Daniel didn't have time to sort through such fine points. He had to make a decision. He'd made it.

"There's nothing for you to be sorry for, Mr Ormund. Or for me either. That is, if you'll still let me have the job."

"But if it would interfere with your career. . . ?"

Daniel gave a theatrical laugh. "Don't worry about that. My career can't be interfered with, because it doesn't exist. I haven't studied, in a serious way, for years. I should have known better than suppose the Metastasio would be calling me up for a place in the chorus. I'm not good enough, it's simple as that."

"My dear," said Mr Ormund, placing his hand gently on Daniel's knee, "you're *superb*. You're ravishing. And if this were a rational world, which it is not, there's not an opera house in this hemisphere that wouldn't be delighted to have you. You *mustn't* give up!"

"Mr Ormund, I'm a punk singer."

Mr Ormund sighed, and removed his hand.

"But I think I'd be a terrific usher. What do you say?"

"You wouldn't be . . . ashamed?"

"If I stood to earn money from it, I'd be delighted. Not to mention the chance I'd have to see your productions."

"Yes, it does help if you like the stuff. So many of the boys don't have an educated ear, I'm afraid. It *is* a special taste. Are you familiar, then, with the Metastasio?"

"Only by reputation."

"You've *never* been inside?"

Daniel lifted up his hands in a gesture of admission.

"Oh dear. Dear, dear, dear."

"Another difficulty?"

"Well, Ben. You see. . . ." He raised his hand to his lips and coughed delicately. "There *is* a grooming code our ushers must observe. A rather strict code. You've not *seen* one of our ushers here, I gather?"

"No."

They both stood silent for a time. Mr Ormund, standing behind his desk, struck a business-like attitude, clasping his hands behind his back and thrusting his wine-barrel belly forward aggressively.

"Do you mean," Daniel asked cautiously, "that I'd have

to . . . uh . . . darken my complexion?"

Mr Ormund burst into silvery laughter, lifting his arms in minstrel merriment. "Dear me, no! Nothing so drastic. Though, to be sure, I'd be the last person to prevent any of the boys from exercising the *option*. No, we couldn't *require* anyone to convert against his *will*. (Though it would be false to deny that I find it an appealing *idea*.) But there is a uniform that must be worn, and though it's essentially a modest sort of uniform, it is rather, how shall I say, jaunty? Maybe blatant comes closer."

Daniel, who had walked all over the city in nothing but gym shorts, said that he didn't think that would phase him.

"Also, I'm sorry to say we can't allow beards."

"Oh."

"That is a pity, isn't it? Yours is so full and emphatic, if I may say so. But you see, the Metastasio is noted for its authenticity. We do the operas the way they first were done, so far as that's possible. And liveried servants did not have beards in the age of Louis Quinze. One may find precedent for mustachioes, if that's any consolation, even rather swaggering ones. But no beards. *Ahimé*, as our Spanish friends say."

"*Ahimé*," Daniel agreed sincerely. He bit his lip and looked down at his shoes. His beard had been with him twelve years now. It was as essential a part of his face as his nose. Further, he felt safe behind it. No one, in those twelve years, had ever recognized him behind his mask of dense black hair. The risk was small, admittedly, but it couldn't be denied.

"Forgive my impertinence, Ben, but does your beard conceal some personal *defect*? A weak chin, perhaps, or scar tissue? I wouldn't want to have you make the sacrifice only to discover that we couldn't, after all, hire you."

"No," said Daniel, with his smile back in place. "I'm not the Phantom of the Opera."

"I do so hope you'll decide to take the job. I *like* a boy with wit."

"I'll have to think about it, Mr Ormund."

"Of course. Whatever you decide, do let me hear from you tomorrow morning. In the meantime, if you'd like to see the performance tonight, and get some idea of what exactly is expected, I can offer you a seat in the house's own box that's going begging tonight. We're doing *Demofoönte*."

"I've read the reviews. And yes, of course, I'd love to."

"Good. Just ask Leo in the box office as you go out. He has an envelope in your name. Ah: one last thing before you go, Ben. Am I right in assuming that you've had some instruction in the use of small arms? Enough to load, and aim, and such."

"In fact I have—but it seems a strange thing to assume."

"It's your accent. Not that it's at all pronounced, but I have a rather good ear. There's just the faintest echo of the Midwest in your r's and your vowels. Like an off-stage oboe. May I assume, further, that you've had some training in self-defense?"

"Only what I got in the regular phys. ed. program. Anyhow, I thought you wanted an usher, not a bodyguard."

"Oh, you'll rarely, if ever, be called on to *shoot* anyone. It hasn't come to that yet in *this* theater. (Knock on wood.) On the other hand, I don't suppose a week goes by without our having to give the heave-ho to *some* asshole. Opera still does have the power to excite passions. Then too, there are the claques. You shall surely have a chance to see *them* this evening, for they're bound to be out in force. Geoffrey Bladebridge is making his première in the role. Till now only Rey has sung the part. The house will undoubtedly be packed with the partisans of both men."

"Fighting?"

"Let us hope not. Generally they just scream at each other. That can be nuisance enough, when most of the audience has come here to listen." Mr Ormund once again offered his hand. "But enough idle chatter. Duty calls, ta-ra, ta-ra! I hope you enjoy the performance this evening, and I'll expect to hear from you tomorrow."

"Tomorrow," Daniel promised, as he was shown the door.

Daniel clapped dutifully when the curtain came down at the end of Act One of *Demofoönte*, the single wet blanket in an audience berserk with approval. Whatever had stirred them to these raptures he couldn't work out. Musically the

production was professional but uninspired: mere archae-
ology pretending to be art. Bladebridge, whom most of this
commotion was about, had sung neither wisely nor too well.
His stage-manner was one of polite, disdainful boredom,
which he varied, when he wished to call attention to a particularly strenuous embellishment, by a gesture (always the
same) of the most schematic bravado. At these moments, as
he extended his meaty, jeweled hands, tilted back his head
(but carefully, so as not to dislodge his towering wig), and
let loose a blood-curdling trill or a long, loud, meandering
roulade, he seemed the apotheosis of unnaturalness. The
music itself, though a pastiche of four composers' settings
of the same Metastasio libretto, was uniformly monotonous,
the slimmest of excuses for the endless flowerings the singers
foisted on it. As to drama, or poetry, forget it. The whole
unwieldy operation—scenery, costume, staging—seemed
quite defiantly pointless, unless the mere expenditure of so
much money, energy, and applause was, in itself, a kind of
point.

He felt almost the same befuddlement as when, so many
years ago, in the alternate world of his childhood, he had sat
in Mrs Boismortier's living room and listened to a Mozart
string quartet. With this difference—that he had lost the
humility that had allowed him, as a child, to go on believing,
provisionally, in the worth of what befuddled him. He decided, therefore when the house-lights finally went up, that
he would not return for the second act. Never mind that
he probably wouldn't have the chance to see anything at
the Metastasio again. (He'd already made up his mind to
that.) He had too high a respect for his own opinion to go
on watching what he'd decided was complete claptrap.

Even so, once he was out in the lobby he couldn't resist
the opportunity of circulating among the Metastasio's regular patrons, who were (despite their dominoes, which were,
as in old Venice, *de rigueur*) not at all so glittering an assembly as might be found, between the acts, at either the
Metropolitan or the State Theater. There were, to be sure,
more phoneys. Most castrati of celebrity rank were blacks,
just as in the heyday of bel canto they had been, mainly,
Calabrians or Neapolitans, the poorest of the poor. Wherever blacks were offered for public worship, whether in the

ring or on the stage, there were certain to be phoneys on hand worshipping. But this lot were an uncommonly discreet sort of phoney; the men tended to dress, like Daniel, in conservative and slightly *démodé* business suits, the women in dresses of well-nigh conventual plainness. Some of the genuine blacks allowed themselves a higher level of luminescence, with feathers or a bit of lace livening their masks, but the general tone, even among them, was decidedly muted. Possibly, even probably, a different tone was set downstairs in the Metastasio's casino, but only members with a key were admitted there.

Daniel propped himself against a pillar of fake marble and watched the parade, such as it was. Just as he'd made up his mind, for the second time, to leave, he was suddenly latched on to by the girl he'd met that morning, Jack Levine's official wife, who saluted him loudly with "Ben! Ben Bosola! What a pleasant surprise." For the life of him he couldn't remember her first name. She lifted her domino.

"Mrs Levine," he murmered. "Hello."

"Marcella," she reminded him, and then, to show that in the face of *Demofoönte* personal slights were of no account: "Isn't it the most beautiful . . . the most wonderful . . . the dreamiest, creamiest. . . ."

"Incredible," he agreed, with just enough conviction to get by.

"Bladebridge is going to be our next *great* singer," she declared in a passion of prophecy. "A true *soprano assoluto*. Not that Ernesto is in any way *less* important. I'd be the last person to speak *against* him. But he's old, and his top notes are already gone—*that* can't be denied." She shook her head with vigorous melancholy, wagging her long blond braid.

"How old is he?"

"Fifty? Fifty-five? Past his prime, anyhow. But *such* an artist, even now. No one has ever equalled his *Casta diva*. Isn't it amazing, our meeting again so soon? Jack didn't mention your being a buff. Naturally, I made him tell me all about you as soon as he got home."

"I'm not what you'd call a real buff. I'd say that I'm at least six or seven levels from the top on anyone's scale of buffdom."

Her hollow, hooting laugh was as inane as his remark.

Even with the terrycloth muumuu removed and repackaged in brown velvetine, Marcella was intensely the sort of person you didn't want to be seen with in public. Not that it mattered, since he wouldn't be returning to the Metastasio.

So, as penance for his condescension, he forced himself to be nicer than the circumstance strictly required.

"Do you get here often?" he asked.

"Once a week, on my night off. I've got a subscription seat way in the last row of the Family Circle."

"Lucky you."

"Don't think I don't know it. At the start of this last season they raised the prices again, and I honestly didn't think I'd be able to renew. But Jack was an angel and lent me the money. Where are you sitting?"

"Uh, in a box."

"A box," she repeated reverently. "Are you *with* someone?"

"Don't I just wish! In fact, I'm all alone in the box."

A wrinkle of doubt creased her forehead. Since he couldn't see any reason not to, and since it was something to talk about, he told her the story of Ormund's phone call and their cross-purposed interview that afternoon. She listened like a child hearing the story of the Nativity, or of Cinderella for the very first time. Her large eyes, framed by the slits of her mask, grew moist with unshed tears. The first of the intermission bells rang just as the tale was completed.

"Would you like to share the box with me?" he offered, in a burst of generosity (which, admittedly, cost him nothing).

She wagged her braid. "It's sweet of you to ask, but I couldn't."

"I don't see why not."

"The ushers?"

"As long as you're not taking someone else's seat, they won't know."

She looked anxiously at the people filing up the stairs, then at Daniel, then back at the stairs.

"There are four seats in the box," he urged. "I can only fill one of them."

"I wouldn't want to be responsible for your losing your job before you'd even started."

"If they're going to be pissy about a thing like that, they're not the kind of people I should be working for." Since he wasn't going to take the job, it was easy to be high-minded.

"Oh, Ben—don't *say* that! To work here—at the Metastasio—there's nothing *anyone* wouldn't give for the opportunity. To see every performance, every night!" The tears finally reached saturation point and trickled into her mask. The sensation must have been uncomfortable, for she pushed the domino up into her hair, and with a wadded-up hankie from the sleeve of her dress, dabbed at her smudged cheeks.

The second bell rang. The lobby was almost empty.

"You'd better come along," Daniel urged.

She nodded, and followed him to the door of the box. There she stopped to give one last swipe at her tears. Then she tucked away the hankie and gave him a big, brave smile.

"I'm sorry. I really don't know what came over me. It's just that the Teatro is the center of my whole *existence*. It's the only reason I go on living in this stupid city and working at my lousy job. And to hear you being, I don't know, so *cavalier* about it. . . . I can't explain. It upset me."

"I didn't mean to."

"Of course not. I'm being an old silly. Is this your box? We'd better go in before they spot us."

Daniel opened the door and stepped back to allow Marcella to go before him. Halfway across the small antechamber she stood stock-still. At the same moment the house-lights dimmed, and the audience applauded the entrance of the conductor into the pit.

"Ben," Marcella whispered, "there *is* someone else."

"I see her. But there's no need to panic. Just take the seat beside her, as though you belong there. She probably snuck in the same as you. Anyhow, she won't bite."

Marcella did as she was bidden, and the woman paid her no heed. Daniel took the chair behind Marcella.

As the strings commenced a jittering introduction to the duet between Adrasto and Timante the intruder lowered her opera glasses and turned round to regard Daniel over her shoulder. Even before he'd recognized her, Daniel felt a premonitory malaise just watching the slow torsion of her spine.

Before he could rise, she had caught him by the sleeve. Then, deftly, without putting down her opera glasses, she plucked off his mask.

"I knew it. Despite the beard—despite the mask—I knew it!"

Marcella, though only a bystander to this drama, began once more, and quite audibly, to weep.

Miss Marspan released Daniel to deal, in summary fashion, with Marcella. "Hush!" she insisted, and Marcella hushed.

"As for you," (to Daniel), "we'll speak later. But now, for goodness' sake, be quiet and pay attention to the music."

Daniel bowed his head by way of submission to Miss Marspan's command, and she fixed her falcon gaze upon the mild Adrasto, the merciless Timante, nor did she ever, in the whole course of the second act, turn round again. She was that certain of her grip.

As they rode, with the curtains of the taxi drawn, zigzagging along the potholed streets, Daniel tried to formulate a plan. The only solution he could think of, which might restore his shattered status quo and keep his whereabouts unknown to Grandison Whiting, was for him to murder Miss Marspan. And that was no solution. Even if he'd had the gumption to try, which he didn't, he'd be more likely to wind up her victim, since Miss Marspan had let it be known (by way of assuring the taxi driver that it was safe to take them through Queens) that she carried a licensed pistol and was trained in its use. He could foresee the tenuous fabric of his incognito unraveling inexorably, twelve years of shifts and dodges undone in a moment by this woman's whim, and he could do nothing but come along for the ride. She wouldn't even listen to explanations until she'd seen for herself that Boa was alive.

"Is it all right if I ask you a question?" he ventured.

"All in good time, Daniel. If you please."

"Have you been looking for me? Because otherwise I don't see. . . ."

"Our crossing paths was chance. I was seated in the box

opposite to yours, and a tier above. While I waited for a friend to join me, I studied the crowd through my glasses. There is usually someone else one knows on hand for such an evening. You seemed familiar, but I couldn't place you at once. Naturally enough. You didn't have a beard, or wear a domino, when I knew you. *And* I supposed you to be dead. At the intermission I watched you in the lobby, and even contrived, standing on the other side of the pillar, to hear some of your conversation with that girl. It was you. It is you. And you tell me that my niece is alive. I cannot, I confess, imagine your motive in having kept these matters secret, but I'm not really interested in your motives. I'm interested in my niece, in her well-being."

"It's not pretty where we're headed," he cautioned. "But it keeps her going."

Miss Marspan made no reply.

Daniel parted the curtain to see how far they'd come. What he could see looked like any part of Queens he'd ever been to: there was the wide, untrafficked highway lined on either side by junked out cars and overturned trucks, a few of which gave signs of being inhabited. Farther back from the road were the blackened shells of single-dwelling houses. It was hard to believe that away from the highway there were still large areas of Queens that had been left un-blighted. He let the curtain fall closed. The taxi swerved, avoiding something in the road.

He could make a break for it now, he supposed. He could go and live among those ruins, there to be ruined himself. But that would have meant surrendering Boa to her father, an act he could not, would not, be driven to. It had been his whole pride, the source of all his self-respect, that he had, by privations great and small, by the daily indignities of these twelve years, been responsible for Boa's maintenance ("well-being" would be stretching it). Other men have families. Daniel had his wife's corpse (for such she was now, legally) to sustain him. But it served the same purpose: it kept him from believing, despite every other evidence, that his defeat was final, whole, and entire.

Once, he'd known why he was doing this, and why he must persevere. Fear moved him. But that fear had come, in time, to seem unfounded. Grandison Whiting might be a selfish man, but he was not insane. He might have judged Boa in error in taking Daniel as her spouse, he might have wished Daniel dead, he might even have arranged that to happen, other persuasions failing—but he wouldn't have murdered his daughter. However, as the specific fear had diminished there had come in its stead a distaste for Whiting, and all his works and wiles, that mounted finally to horror.

He had no rationale for his aversion. In part it was simple class feeling. Whiting was an arch-reactionary, a Machiavelli, a Metternich, and if his reasons for it were more intellectual than most such sons-of-bitches' reasons, even (Daniel had to admit) more persuasive, that only made him a more dangerous son-of-a-bitch than most. There was a religious side to it too, though Daniel resisted the idea of his having any connection whatever with religion. He was a no-nonsense, cut-and-dried, self-justified atheist. Relgion, in the words of his friend Claude Durkin, was something you had to learn about in order fully to appreciate the Old Masters. But the book he'd read way back when in Spirit Lake had got a hold on Daniel, and the Reverend Jack Van Dyke's blithe paradoxes had wormed their way into his mind, or will, or whatever corner of the soul it is that has faith in things unseen. There, in the darkness where no rational contradiction could touch it, the idea grew, and ramified, that Grandison Whiting was one of those Caesars whom Van Dyke had written of, who rule the world and unto whom there must be renderings, despite that they are savage, corrupt, and conscienceless.

In short, distance had turned Grandison Whiting into an idea—an idea that Daniel was determined to resist in the one way given him to do so: by refusing him the possession of his daughter's twelve-years-comatose body.

Ward 17, where the corpse (as it was, in the eyes of the Law) of Boadicea Weinreb was to be found, occupied only a small part of the third sub-basement of the annex of First National Flightpaths. After Daniel had signed in at the desk in the lobby, and after Miss Marspan had, under protest, checked her pistol with the guard outside the elevator, they were allowed to go down to the ward unescorted, for

Daniel's was a familiar face at the Annex. They walked down a long reverberating tunnel lighted, now harshly, now dimly, by irregularly spaced tubes of neon mounted on the broad low arch of the ceiling. On either side of them, spaced with the tight, terrible regularity of markers in a cemetery, lay the inert and weakly respiring bodies of those who had never returned from their flights into the spaces beyond their flesh. Only a few of the hundreds in this one ward would ever resume a corporeal life, but the husks lingered on, ageing, withering, until some vital organ finally failed, or until the accounting office sent down the order to disconnect the life-supporting machineries, whichever came sooner.

They stopped before Boa's cot, a kind of rubber sling suspended from a tubular frame.

"The name. . . ." Miss Marspan observed, stooping to read the chart fixed to the foot of the bed. The sights of the ward had robbed her of her usual decisiveness. "Bosola? There's some mistake."

"It was the name we registered under, when we came here."

Miss Marspan closed her eyes and laid her gloved hand lightly over them. As little as he liked the woman, Daniel could not but feel some sympathy for her. It must have been hard to accept this shriveled chrysalis as the niece she'd known and loved, so far as love was in her nature. Boa's skin was the color of grimed lightbulbs of frosted glass and seemed, stretched tight across each prominence of bone, as brittle. All fullness was wasted, even her lips were thin, and the warmth you could detect in her hollow cheeks seemed borrowed from the humid airs of the tunnel and not her own. Nothing spoke of life or process except the plasma oozing through translucent tubes into the slow-revolving treadmill of her arteries and veins.

Miss Marspan squared her shoulders and made herself approach more closely. Her heavy skirts of pigeon-gray silk snagged on the frame of the cot adjacent to Boa's. She knelt to loosen it, and remained a long while on one knee looking into the void of Boa's face. Then she rose, shaking her head. "I can't kiss her."

"She wouldn't know if you did."

She backed away from Boa's cot, and stood in the central aisle, looking about her nervously, but anywhere she turned the same sight was endlessly multiplied, row on row, body on body. At last she looked up, squinting, into the neon light.

"How long have you kept her here?" she asked.

"In this ward, five years. The wards on the upper floors are a bit cheerier, supposedly, but a lot more expensive. This is all I can afford."

"It is a hell."

"Boa's not here, Miss Marspan. Only her body. When she wants to come back, *if* she wants to come back, she will. But if that isn't what she wants, do you think a vase of flowers by the bed is going to make any difference?"

But Miss Marspan wasn't listening to him. "Look, up there! Do you see? A moth."

"Oh, there's no harm in insects," Daniel said, unable to repress his resentment. "People eat cockroaches, you know. All the time. I used to work in a factory that mashed them up."

Miss Marspan regarded Daniel with a level gaze; then, with the deliberated strength of a seasoned athlete, struck his face with the back of her gloved hand. Though he'd seen it coming and had braced himself, it was a blow to bring tears to the eyes.

When the echo had died out, he spoke out, not in anger but in pride. "I've kept her alive, Miss Marspan, think of that. Not Grandison Whiting, with his millions. Me, with nothing—*I* kept her alive."

"I'm sorry, Daniel. I . . . appreciate what you've done." She touched her hair to see that it was in place, and Daniel, in sarcastic mimicry, did the same. "But I don't see why you don't keep her with you, at home. Surely that would be cheaper than this . . . mausoleum."

"I'm a temp, I don't have a home. Even when I had a room at a hotel, it wouldn't have been safe to leave her there alone. Rooms get broken into, and what would happen to anyone in Boa's condition then—"

"Yes, of course. That didn't occur to me."

She flexed her fingers within their sheath of kid, flexed them and bent them backward, as if to defy the helplessness

205

she felt. She had come here ready to step in and take charge, but there was nothing to take charge of.

"Grandison, I take it, has never learned of this? He doesn't know that either of you is alive?"

"No. And I don't want him to, ever."

"Why? If I may ask."

"That's my business."

Miss Marspan considered this. "Fair enough," she decided at last, to Daniel's disconcertion.

"You mean you'll agree to that? You won't tell him?"

"I would have thought this was too soon to begin bargaining," she answered coolly. "There's still much I want to know. But, if it will ease your mind, I can tell you that there's little love lost between Grandison and myself. My sister, Boa's mother, finally succeeded in killing herself a year ago."

"I'm sorry."

"Nonsense. You didn't know her, and if you had I'm sure you'd have despised her. She was a foolish, vain hysteric with a modicum of redeeming virtues, but she was my sister and Grandison Whiting destroyed her."

"And he'd destroy Boa too, if you let him." He said it without melodrama, in the calm accents of faith.

Miss Marspan smiled. "Oh, I doubt that. She was the brightest of his children, the one of whom he had the highest hope. When she died, as he believed, his mourning was as real, I daresay, as yours or mine."

"Maybe it was. But I don't give a shit about his feelings."

Miss Marspan's glance let it be known that even in these circumstances she did not like such language.

"Let's get out of here."

"Gladly. Let me say this first, though, while it's clear to me. The paramount question, the question I've been considering since we set off in the taxi, is whether Boadicea would be more . . . inclined . . . to return here, to you, or to her father."

"Here, to me."

"I think I have to agree."

"Then you won't tell him!"

"On one condition. That you allow me to have Boa taken from this place. If she's ever to come back, I can't

206

believe she'd find this prospect at all inviting. It might even act to change her mind."

"There've been studies. After a certain time it doesn't seem to make any difference where they are, physically. The return rate is the same down here as anywhere."

"Possibly, but I've never trusted studies. You have no objection, I hope, to my helping you if I can?"

"I guess that depends on the form that it would take."

"Oh, I'm not about to lavish money on you. I have little enough myself. But I do have connections, which are the better part of anyone's wealth, and I'm fairly sure I can find a home in which Boa would be safe and you'd be comfortable. I'll talk to Alicia about it tonight, for she was at the opera with me, and she's certain to have stayed up to find out what I've been so mysteriously up to. Is there somewhere I can get in touch with you in the morning?"

He couldn't answer all at once. It had been years since he'd trusted anyone, except in passing or in bed, and Miss Marspan wasn't someone he wanted to trust. But he did! At last, amazed at the turn his life had taken, all in a single day, he gave her the number of Adonis, Inc., and even let her, when they drove back to the city, drop him off outside the door before she returned to her friend's apartment.

Lying alone in the sauna and listening to Lorenzo's indefatigable exertions in the locker-room, Daniel had difficulty getting to sleep. He came very close to going out and joining in and getting his rocks off just as a sedative, but though ordinarily that's what he would have done, tonight was different. Tonight he would have felt a hypocrite if he'd mixed in with the others. Now that he could see a way out, the faintest glimmer of escape, he was aware just how much he wanted to put Adonis, Inc. behind him. Not that he hadn't been having a wonderful time once he'd left off struggling and striving and just laid back and floated with the current. Sex is the one luxury for which money isn't a qualification. So long live sex. But tonight he'd decided, or remembered, that he could, with a bit of effort, do better.

For openers, he'd take the job at the Metastasio. His only reason for having decided, earlier, not to was the fear of being recognized. But Miss Marspan had recognized him, even with his beard, and so the moral of the story seemed to be that maybe he ought to take more risks. Hadn't that been Gus's advice, when they'd said good-bye? Something like that.

Moments before he fell asleep he remembered it was his birthday. "Happy birthday, dear Daniel," he whispered into the rolled-up towels that served him as a pillow. "Happy birthday to you."

He dreamed.

But when he woke, shivering, in the middle of the night, most of the dream had already slipped away. He knew, though, that it had been a dream of flight. His first. All the details of his flight eluded him—where it had been, to what height, how it had felt. He remembered only being in a foreign country, where there was an old tumbledown mosque. In the courtyard of this mosque there was a fountain, and all about the fountain were pairs of shoes with pointy toes, lined up in rows. They'd been left there by worshippers who'd gone into the mosque.

The wonder of this courtyard was the fountain at its center, a fountain comprised of three stone basins. The upper basins seemed to be supported, so abundantly did the water flow, by the jets of white water spouting up from the basins below. From the topmost basin, rising to inconceivable heights, was the final fiercest flowering of all. It rose, and rose, until the sun turned it to spray.

And that was all. He didn't know what to make of it. A fountain in a courtyard with old shoes around it. What sort of omen was that?

12

Mrs Alicia Schiff, with whom Daniel was now to live, was, in the considered and by no means unreproving opinion of her friend Harriet Marspan, "the nearest thing to a genius I've ever known." She was also, very nearly, a hunchback, though it seemed so natural and necessary a part of her character that you could almost believe she'd come by it the way she'd come by her squint—by dint of years scrunched up over a desk copying music—the way that pines at high altitudes are shaped by titanic winds. All in all, the sorriest wreck of human flesh Daniel had ever become acquainted with, and custom could never quite reconcile him to the facts: the crepey, flaking skin of her hands; the face all mottled pink and lemon and olive like a spoiled Rubens; the knobby head with its strands of sparse white hair, which she sometimes was inspired to cover with a scruffy red parody of a wig. Except when she left the apartment, which was seldom now that she had Daniel to run interference with the outside world, she dressed like the vilest and most lunatic vagrant. The apartment was filled with heaps, little and big, of cast-off clothes—blue jeans, bathrobes, dresses, sweaters, stockings, blouses, scarves, and underwear—which she changed into and out of at any hour of the day or night, with no apparent method or motive; it was sheer nervous habit.

At first he feared he'd be expected to excavate and order the apartment's debris. The clothes were the least of it. Interleaved with these were layers and layers of alluvial deposits, a Christmas morning desolation of wrappings, boxes, books and papers, of crockery and rattling tins, of puzzles, toys, and counters from a dozen never-to-be reassembled games. There was also, though mostly on the shelves, a collection of dolls, each with its own name and personality. But Mrs Schiff assured Daniel that he wouldn't be expected to act as chambermaid, that on the contrary she'd be grateful if he left things where they were. "Where," she had actually said, "they belong."

He *was* expected to do her shopping, to deliver letters and scores, and to take her elderly, ginger-colored spaniel Incubus for his morning and his evening walk. Incubus, like his mistress, was an eccentric. He had a consuming interest in strangers (and none at all in other dogs), but it was an interest he did not wish to see reciprocated. He preferred people who would let him snuffle about on his own, investigating their shoes and other salient smells. However, if you ventured to talk to him, much less to pet him, he became edgy and took the first opportunity to escape from such attentions. He was neither mean nor friendly, neither frisky nor wholly torpid, and was very regular in his habits. Unless Daniel had some shopping to accomplish at the same time, the course of their walk never varied: due west to Lincoln Center, twice round the fountain, then (after Daniel had dutifully scooped up that morning's or evening's turd and disposed of it down a drain) home again to West 65th, just round the corner from the park, where Mrs Schiff, no less predictable in her habits, would be hovering, anxious and undemonstrative, somewhere in the hallway of the apartment. She never condescended to Incubus, but spoke to him on the assumption that he was a precocious child, enchanted (by his own preference) into the shape of a dog. She treated Daniel no differently.

Daniel, in exchange for these services, and for providing a masculine, protective presence, received the largest of the apartment's many rooms. The others were so many closets and cubbyholes, the legacy of the apartment's previous existence as a residence hotel. When Mrs Schiff had inherited the building, twenty years ago, she had never bothered to take down the plasterboard partitions, and indeed had added her own distinctive wrinkle to the maze in the form of folding screens and freestanding bookshelves (all of her own carpentering). Daniel felt awkward, at first, occupying the only humanly proportioned room in the apartment, and even when he was convinced, from her reluctance to enter his room, that Mrs Schiff really preferred her own cozy warrens, he never stopped being grateful. It was a grand room, and with a coat of fresh paint on the walls and the floor sanded and waxed it became magnificent.

Mrs Schiff did like to *be* visited, and it was soon their settled custom, when her day's work was over and he had returned from the Metastasio and taken Incubus twice round the fountain and back home, to sit in her bedroom, with a pot of gunpowder tea between them and a packet of cookies (Daniel had never known Mrs Schiff to eat anything but sweets), and to talk. Sometimes they might listen to a record (she had hundreds, all horribly scratched,) but only by way of intermission. Daniel had known many good talkers in his time, but none of them could hold a candle to Mrs Schiff. Wherever her fancy lighted, ideas formed, and grew, and became systems. Whatever she spoke seemed illumined, sometimes in only a whimsical way, but often seriously and even rather intensely. Or so it seemed, till, with a turn of a phrase, she'd veer off on some new tangent. Most of it, in the way of much supposed 'great conversation', was mere mermaid enchantment and fool's gold, but some of it did stick to the ribs of the mind, especially those ideas that derived from her ruling passion, which was opera.

She had a theory, for instance, that the Victorian Age had been a time of massive and systematic repression on a scale more awful than was ever to be achieved again on the stage of history, even at Auschwitz, that all of Europe, from Waterloo to World War Two, was one colossal police state, and that it was the function of Romantic Art, but especially of opera, to train and inspire the rising younger generation of robber barons and aristocrats to be heroes in the Byronic mold; that is, to be intelligent, bold, and murderous enough to be able to defend their wealth and privilege against all comers. How she'd come to this theory was by listening to Verdi's *I Masnadieri*, which was based on a play of Schiller about an idealistic young man whom circumstance requires to become the head of a band of outlaws and who ends up killing his fiancée sheerly on principle. Daniel thought the whole thing ridiculous until Mrs Schiff, peeved at his obstinacy, got down her copy of Schiller and read *The Robbers* aloud, and then, the next evening, made him listen to the opera. Daniel admitted there might be something to it.

"I'm *right*. Say it—say that I'm right."

"Okay, you're right."

"Not only am I right, Daniel, but what's true of Schiller's apprentice mafioso is true of all the heroic criminals from that day to this, all the cowboys and gangsters and rebels without causes. They're all businessmen in disguise. Indeed, the gangsters even dispensed with the disguise. I should know—my father was one."

"Your father was a gangster?"

"He was one of the city's leading labor racketeers in his day. I was an heiress in my gilded youth, no less."

"Then what happened?"

"A bigger fish gobbled him up. He had a number of so-called residence hotels like this one. The government decided to eliminate the middleman. Just when he thought he'd become respectable."

She said it without rancor. Indeed, he'd never known her to be phased at anything. She seemed content to understand the hell she lived in (for such she insisted it was) with her best clarity of apprehension, and then to pass on to the next apprehensible horror, as though all existence were a museum of more or less malefic exhibits: instruments of torture and the bones of martyrs side by side with jeweled chalices and the portraits of merciless children in beautiful clothes.

Not that she was callous herself, but rather that she had no hope. The world dismayed her, and she turned from it to her own snug burrow, which the wolves and foxes had somehow not yet discovered. There she lived in the inviolate privacy of her work and her contemplations, seldom venturing out except to the opera or to one or another of her favorite restaurants, where she would hold forth to other musician-friends and dine on a succession of desserts. She had surrendered long since to the traditional vices of a recluse: she didn't bathe, or cook meals, or wash dishes; she kept strange hours, preferring night to day; she never let sunlight or fresh air into her own rooms, which came to smell, most intensely, of Incubus. She talked to herself constantly, or rather to Incubus and the dolls, inventing long wandering whimsical tales for them about the Honeybunny twins, Bunny Honeybunny and his sister Honey Honeybunny, tales from which all possibility of pain or conflict was debarred. Daniel suspected that she slept with Incubus as well, but what of that? Was anyone harmed by her dirtiness or dottiness? If there was such a thing as the life of the mind then Mrs Schiff was one of its champions, and Daniel's hat was off to her.

So, for that matter, was hers, for she was beset, like so many who live apart from the world, with a naïve self-conceit that was at once ludicrous and deserved. Indeed, she was aware of this, and prone to discussing it with Daniel, who had rapidly been elevated to the status of confessor.

"My problem has always been," she confided one evening, a month after he'd moved in "that I have a hyperkinetic intelligence. But it's also been my salvation. When I was a girl, they wouldn't keep me in any of the schools my father bundled me off to, as part of his program of redeeming the family name. My problem was I took my education seriously, which would have been forgivable in itself, except that I tended to be evangelical in my enthusiasms. I was labeled a disruptive influence, and treated as such, which I resented. Soon I made it my business to *be* a disruptive influence, and found ways to make my teachers look like fools. Lord, how I hated school! My daydream has always been to go back, as a celebrity, and give a speech at the graduation exercises, a speech denouncing them all. Which is perfectly unfair of me, I know. Did *you* like school?"

"Well enough, up to the point where I was sent off to prison. I did well, and kids seemed to like me. What are the alternatives at that age?"

"You weren't just deathly bored?"

"Sometimes. Sometimes I still am. It's the human condition."

"If I thought that were the case, I'd kill myself. Truly."

"You mean to say you're never bored?"

"Not since I've been able to help it. I don't *believe* in boredom. It's a euphemism for laziness. People do nothing, and then complain they're bored. Harriet does, and it drives me up the wall. She actually supposes it would betray a lack of breeding to take an active interest in her own life. But, poor dear, it's not her fault, is it?"

This question seemed to be addressed less to Daniel than to

Incubus, where he lay in his mistress's rumpled sheets. The spaniel, sensing this, lifted his head from its dozing position to one of alert consideration.

"No," Mrs Schiff went on, answering her own question, "it's the way she was brought up. We none of us can help the way our twigs are bent."

The question having been answered, Incubus lowered his head back to the pillow.

She knew the Metastasio's operas by heart and would cross-examine him minutely about every performance he worked at: who had sung, how well or poorly, whether a tricky piece of stage business had come off. She knew them so well not from having seen them that often but because, in many cases, she'd written them herself. Officially she was no more than the Metastasio's chief copyist, though sometimes, when a text was well-known to be so corrupt as scarcely to exist, the program would include a small credit: 'Edited and arranged by A. Schiff.' Even then, she got no royalties. She worked, she declared, for love and the greater glory of Art, but that, Daniel decided, was only half the truth. She also worked, like other people, for money. If the fees she received were small, they were frequent and, when you added them to the rents from the buildings, enough to keep her supplied with such essential luxuries as dogfood, books, rare records, and her monthly chits at *Lieto Fino* and *La Didone*, where, rather than at home, she chose to entertain.

That side of her life Daniel was not privy to in these first months, and it was only gradually, from hints dropped by Mr Ormund and yellowed clippings discovered among the debris of the apartment, that he learned that Mrs Schiff had once been a celebrity of no small degree in the beau monde of bel canto, having fallen in love, eloped with, and married the greatest of modern-day castrati, Ernesto Rey. The marriage had subsequently been annulled, but Rey had continued to be faithful in his fashion. He was the only one of her friends she allowed to visit her at home, and so Daniel developed a nodding acquaintance with the man who was generally considered the greatest singer of his day (albeit that day was waning).

Offstage the great Ernesto was the least likely candidate

for prima donna that ever was—a thin, twitchy wisp of a man whose smooth pale face seemed frozen in an expression of wide-eyed alarm, the consequence (it was said) of too many face-lifts. He was untypical of other castrati in being white (he was born in Naples), diffident (he assumed, among strangers, a flat, nasal monotone an octave below his natural voice), and guilt-ridden (he attended Mass every Sunday), and untypical of anyone else in being a castrato. He had recorded *Norma* five times, and each recording was better than the last. Of the first recording, a critic old enough to have heard her in performance said that Rey's *Norma* was superior to Rosa Ponselle's.

Mrs Schiff was as much in love with him now as on the day they'd eloped, and Rey (by her account, and everyone else's) still took that love as painfully for granted. She flattered him; he drank it in. She worked like a troupe of acrobats to keep him amused; he tolerated her efforts but made none himself, though he was not otherwise a witless lump. In all matters concerning interpretation and general aesthetic strategy she acted as his coach, and served as spokesman with those conductors and recording engineers who would not at once bend to his will. She devised, and continually revised, all his supposedly *ad libitum* passages of fioratura, keeping them safely within his ever-diminishing range without apparent loss of brilliance. She even vetted his contracts and wrote press releases—or rather, rewrote the tasteless tosh produced by his own salaried agent, Irwin Tauber. For all these services she received no fee and small thanks. She wasn't insensible to such slights and seemed, indeed, to take a bittersweet satisfaction in complaining of them to Daniel, who could be counted on to respond with sympathetic indignation.

"But why do you keep putting up with it?" he asked at last. "If you *know* he's like that and he's not going to change?"

"The answer is obvious: I must."

"That's not an answer. *Why* must you?"

"Because Ernesto is a great artist."

"Great artist or not, no one's got the right to shit on you."

"Ah, but there's where you're wrong, Daniel. In saying

215

that you show you don't understand the nature of great artistry."

This was a direct assault on Daniel's sore point, as Mrs Schiff well knew. The matter was dropped.

She soon knew everything about him, the whole story of his messed-up life. With Boa installed in Daniel's room there was no point in reticence, and not much possibility of it. In any case, after twelve years of living under an alias the opportunity to tell all was too tempting to resist. There were times, as when she'd delivered the low blow just mentioned, that he thought she took unfair advantage of his revelations, but even then her home truths had no sting of malice. Her skin was just very thick, and she expected yours to be too. All in all, as a mother confessor she beat Renata Semple hollow. Renata, for all her Reichian jargon and weekly plumbing of the depths, had handled Daniel's ego with too tender a regard. Small wonder if his therapy had never done him any good.

In short, Daniel was once again a member of a family. Viewed from without they were a strange enough family: a rattling, hunchbacked old woman, a spoiled senile cocker spaniel, and a eunuch with a punctured career (for though Rey didn't live with them, his off-stage presence was as abiding and palpable as that of any paterfamilias away every day at the office). And Daniel himself. But better to be strange together than strange apart. He was glad to have found such a haven at last, and he hoped that most familial and doomed of hopes, that nothing would change.

But already there was news on the radio: a freak cold spell had done extensive damage to crops in Minnesota and the Dakotas, and a calamitous blight was attacking the roots of wheat plants throughout the Farm Belt. It was rumored that this blight had been laboratory-produced and was being propagated by terrorists, though none of the known organizations had come forward to claim credit. The commodities market was already in turmoil, and the new Secretary of Agriculture had made a public announcement that strict rationing might become necessary in the fall. For the present though, food prices were holding steady for the good reason that they were already higher than most people could afford. All through that spring and summer there were food riots in such usual trouble spots as Detroit and Philadelphia. Mrs Schiff, whose imagination was always excited by headlines, began stockpiling bags of dry dogfood. In the last such crisis, four years before, petfood had been the first thing to disappear from the shelves, and she had had to feed Incubus from her own limited ration. Soon an entire closet was packed solid with ten-pound bags of Pet Bricquettes, Incubus's brand of choice. For themselves they did not worry: the Government would provide, somehow.

13

IN SEPTEMBER WHEN the Metastasio opened for the new season, Daniel reported back to work with a gratitude that verged on servility. It had been a lean summer, though better by far than previous summers, thanks to his having a roof over his head. He hadn't been at the job long enough when the Teatro had closed early in June to have put aside more than a few dollars, and he was determined not to have recourse to Miss Marspan, who had already assumed the financial costs involved in keeping Boa functionally alive. Nor did he feel quite right, any longer, panhandling, for if he were to be seen, and word of it got back to Mr Ormund, he was pretty sure it would have cost him his job. For lack of other resources he did what he'd vowed never to do: he dipped into the capital whose scant interest had paid Boa's bills during her long sojourn at First National Flightpaths. That money had come from the sale of her jewelry, and till now he'd been able to avoid applying it to his own needs. Now, however, Boa was provided for by other and better means, and so Daniel could square it with his conscience by considering it a loan: once he was back at work, he'd return the money to the account.

Back at work it didn't work that way, for he rediscovered the joy of being flush. It was like having his paper route again. There was change in his pocket, bills in his wallet, and all New York to entice him. He got himself some decent clothes, which he'd have had to in any case, since Mr Ormund had made it clear that he didn't want his boys to come in looking like ragamuffins. He started going to a ten-dollar barber, which was likewise pretty *comme il faut*. And now that he wasn't helping out at Adonis, Inc., he had to pay a regular membership fee, which took a $350 bite out of the bank account. But the dividends were out of all proportion to the investment, since once he was back at work Mr Ormund had assigned him to the Dress Circle, where the tips were many times in excess of what he'd got, starting out, up in the Balcony (though still not so considerable as the pickings in the Grand Tier).

Tips were only, as Mr Ormund had explained, the tip of the iceberg. The real payoff came in the form of courtship, with all its immemorial perks—dinners, parties, weekends on Long Island, and attentions even costlier and kinder, depending on one's luck, ambition, and ability to hold out for more. At first Daniel had resisted such temptations from a sense, which twelve years in the big city had not yet wiped out, of what the world at large would have called him if he did not resist. Nor was Mr Ormund in any haste to thrust him into the limelight. But increasingly he wondered whether his actions made any difference to the world at large. When, as the new season got under way, he continued, reluctantly, to decline any and all invitations, even one so little compromising as to accept a drink and stop to chat with a boxholder during one of the duller ensembles, when drinks and chat were the order of the day, Mr Ormund decided that there must be a fuller understanding between them, and called Daniel to his office.

"Now I don't want you to think, mignon," (that, or 'mignard', was his pet name for his current favorites) "that I am some vile procurer. No boy has ever been asked to leave the Teatro for failing to put out, and all our patrons understand that. But you *shouldn't* be so entirely standoffish, so arcticly cold."

"Did old Carshalton complain?" Daniel asked, in a grieved tone.

"Mr Carshalton is a very obliging, amiable gentleman, with no other wish, bless him, than to be talked to. He realizes that age and corpulence—" Mr Ormund heaved a sympathizing sigh. "—make any larger expectation unlikely of fulfillment. And in point of fact he did not complain. It was one of your own colleagues—I shall not name him—who called the matter to my notice."

"God damn."

Then, as an afterthought: "That was directed at the unnamed colleague, not at you, sir. And I say it again—God damn . . . him."

"I see your point, of course. But you must expect, at

this stage, to attract a certain amount of jealous attention. In addition to your natural advantages, you've got, as they say, carriage. Then too, some of the boys may feel—though it's perfectly unfair, I know—that your reserve and shyness reflects on their too easy acquiescence."

"Mr Ormund, I need the job. I like the job. I don't want to argue. What do I have to do?"

"Just be friendly. When someone asks you into their box, comply. There's no danger of rape: you're a capable lad. When someone in the casino offers you a flutter on the wheel, flutter. That's simply sound business practice. And who knows, your number might come up! If you're asked to dinner after the show, and if you're free, at least consider the possibility, and if it seems you might enjoy yourself then do the world a favor and say yes. And, though it's not for me to suggest such a thing—and, in fact, I don't at all approve of it, though the world will keep turning for all I say—it is not unheard-of for an arrangement to be worked out."

"An arrangement? I'm sorry, but you'll have to spell that one out a little more."

"My dear, dear country mouse! An arrangement with the restaurant, of course. Good as the fare is at *L'Engouement Noir*, for instance, you don't suppose there isn't a certain latitude in the prices on the menu?"

"You mean they give rebates?"

"More often they'll let you take it out in custom. If you bring them someone for dinner, they'll let you take someone to lunch."

"That's news to me."

"I daresay the boys will all be friendlier when they see you're not entirely above temptation. But don't think, mignon, that I'm asking you to peddle your ass. Only your smile."

Daniel smiled.

Mr Ormund lifted his finger to pantomime that he had remembered something forgotten. He wrote down a name and address on a memo pad, tore the paper loose with a flourish, and handed it to Daniel.

"Who is 'Dr Rivera'?" he asked.

"A good and not overly expensive dentist. You simply

must get those molars looked after. If you don't have the money now, Dr Rivera will work something out with you. He's a great lover of all things connected with the arts. Take care now. It's almost intermission."

The dental work ended up costing almost a thousand dollars. He had to withdraw a larger sum from the bank than the total of all his previous borrowings, but it seemed so wonderful to have his teeth restored to their primal innocence that he didn't care. He would have spent the whole sum that remained in the account for the pleasure of chewing his food once again.

And such food it was! For he had taken Mr Ormund's advice to heart and was soon a familiar figure at all the relevant restaurants: at *Lieto Fino*, at *L'Engouement Noir*, at *Evviva il Coltello*, at *La Didone Abbandonata*. Nor did he pay for these banquetings with his virtue, such as it was. He only had to flirt, which he did anyhow, without trying.

His expanded social life meant, necessarily, that he had fewer evenings to spend at home with Mrs Schiff, but they saw nearly as much of each other now in company as they had in private, for Mrs Schiff was an old *habituée* of *La Didone* and *Lieto Fino*. To be seen at her table (which was also, often, the table of Ernesto Rey) was no small distinction, and Daniel's stock rose higher among those patrons who paid heed to such things (and who would go there, *except* to pay heed to such things?), while in the ushers' changing room Daniel—or rather, Ben Bosola—had become the star of the moment, without an intervening stage of having been just one of the boys.

No one was more instrumental in Daniel's winning to such pre-eminence than the person who had so little time ago tattled on him to Mr Ormund. Lee Rappacini had been working at the Metastasio almost as long as Mr Ormund, though to look at them side by side you wouldn't have believed it. Lee's classic face and figure seemed as ageless as Greek marble, though not, certainly, as white for he, like his superior in this one respect, was a phoney. Not, however, by preference, but to gratify the whim of his latest sponsor, none other than that latest luminary, Geoffrey Bladebridge. Further to gratify his sponsor's whims Lee wore (its molded plastic bulging from the white tights of his livery) what was known in the trade as an insanity belt, the purpose of which was to ensure that no one else should enjoy, gratis, what Bladebridge was paying for. As to what benefits the castrato did enjoy, and his rate of payment, mum was the word, though naturally speculation was rife.

Lee's mobile captivity was a source of much drama. Even to go to the toilet he had to have resort to Mr Ormund, who was entrusted with one of the keys. Every night there were remarks, pleasantries, and playful attempts to see if the device might be circumvented without actually being removed. It couldn't. Daniel, as laureate of the changing room, wrote the following limerick celebrating this situation:

> A tawny young usher named Lee
> Wore a garment with this guarantee:
> His bowels would burst
> Or would turn into wurst
> If ever he lost the last key.

To which Lee's ostensible and probably heartfelt response was simply gratitude for the attention. His enforced retirement was having the effect it usually does: people had stopped being actively interested. To be made the butt of a joke was still to be, for the nonce, a kind of cynosure.

This was a frail enough basis for friendship, but it developed that he and Daniel had something in common. Lee loved music, and though that love had been, like Daniel's, unrequited, it smoldered on. He continued to take voice lessons and sang, Sunday mornings, in a church choir. Every night, no matter what the opera or its cast, he listened to what the Metastasio was offering and could claim, as a result, to have seen over two hundred performances each of *Orfeo ed Eurydice* and of *Norma*, the two most enduringly popular of the company's repertory. Whatever he heard seemed to register with a vividness and singularity that confounded Daniel, for whom all music, however much it might move him at the moment, went in one ear and out the other, a great liability during the endless after-hours post-mortems. By comparison, Lee was a veritable tape recorder.

It soon developed that they shared not only a love of

music for its own sake but a lust for flight as well. For Lee as for Daniel this had always been a balked desire and (therefore) a subject better to be avoided. Indeed, there was no one who worked at or frequented the Metastasio who had much to say about flying. The castrati who reigned supreme on its stage seemed as little capable of flight as of sex. Some claimed that though they were able to fly, they had no wish to, that song itself was glory enough, but this was generally thought to be a face-saving imposture. They didn't fly because they couldn't, and the happy result (for their audience) was that they did not, like most other great singers, simply vanish into the ether at the height of their careers. By comparison to the Metropolitan, which devoted its flagging energies to the Romantic repertory, the Meta-stasio offered incomparably better singing as such, and if their productions didn't stir the imagination in quite the same way, if they couldn't offer the vicarious thrills of a *Carmen* or a *Rosenkavalier*, there were (as even Daniel would finally come to see) compensations. As the audiences of Naples had so long ago proclaimed: *Evviva il coltello!* Long live the knife—the knife by whose actions such voices were made.

Daniel had thought himself cured of his old longings, thought he'd achieved a realistic, grown-up renunciation. Life had denied him any number of supreme pleasures and ultimate fulfillments, despite which it was still worth living. But now, talking with Lee and worrying the meatless bone of why and wherefore *they* were set apart, he felt the familiar anguish return, that immense and exquisite self-pity that seemed tantamount to a martyrdom.

By now, of course, Daniel knew all there was to be known about the theory, if not the practice, of flight, and he took a kind of donnish satisfaction in disabusing Lee of many fond misconceptions. Lee believed, for instance, that the basic trigger that released the singer's spirit from his body was emotion, so that if you could just put enough *con amore* into what you sang, you'd lift off. But Daniel explained, citing the best authorities, that emotion was quite literally only the half of it, and the other half was transcendence. You had to move, with the music, to a condition above the ego, beyond your emotion, but without losing track of its shape or its size. Lee believed (this being the first article of the bel canto faith) that words were more or less irrelevant and music was paramount. *Primo la musica.* In evidence of this he could adduce some awesomely ridiculous lyrics that had nevertheless been the occasion for one or another proven flight. But on this point too Daniel could give chapter and verse. Flight, or the release to flight, took place at the moment when the two discrete hemispheres of the brain stood in perfect equipoise, stood and were sustained. For the brain was a natural gnostic, split into those very dichotomies of semantic sense and linguistically unmediated perception, of words and music, that were the dichotomies of song. This was why, though the attempt had been made so often, no other musicians, but only singers, could strike that delicate balance in their art that mirrored an answering, arcane balance in the tissues of the mind. One might come by one's artistry along other paths, of course; all artists, whatever their art, must acquire the knack of transcendence, and once it had been acquired in one discipline, some of the skill was transferable. But the only way to fly was to sing a song that you understood, and meant, down to the soles of your shoes.

Daniel and Lee did not limit themselves to theory. Lee was the proud, if powerless, possessor of a Grundig 1300 Amphion *Fluchtpunktapparat*, the finest and most expensive flight apparatus available. No one else, until Daniel, had ever been allowed to try and use it. It stood in the center of a bare, white chapel of a room in Geoffrey Bladebridge's penthouse apartment on West End Avenue where, on the afternoons when Bladebridge was not about, they would hammer at the doors of heaven, begging to be let in. As well might they have tried flapping their arms in order to fly. They soldiered on, regardless, through aria after aria, song after weary song, never saying die and getting nowhere.

Sometimes Bladebridge returned home before they'd given up and would insist on joining them in the capacity of vocal coach, offering advice and even, damnably, his own shining example. He assured Daniel that he had a very pretty baritone voice, too light for most of the things he attempted, but perfect for bel canto. It was sheer meanness.

He probably thought Daniel and Lee had a thing for each other, which the insanity belt was baffling, and though Daniel was of the mature opinion that theoretically all things were possible and all men polymorphously perverse, he knew that Bladebridge's opinion was in this case unfounded. He had only to look at Lee and see the pink tip of his nose in the middle of his teak-brown face, like a mushroom on a log, to be turned off entirely.

In December, just before Christmas, Lee showed up at the Metastasio without the tell-tale bulge of the insanity belt spoiling the line of his trousers. His romance with Blade-bridge was over, and so, pretty much (and not coincidentally) was his friendship with Daniel.

Life, to be fair, was not all striving and yearning and certain defeat. In fact, barring those frustrating sessions hooked up with the *Fluchtpunktapparat*, Daniel had never been happier, or if he had it was so long ago he couldn't remember what it had been like. Now that he had a registered job, he could take out books from the public library, though with Mrs Schiff's enormous stock of books at his disposal that dream-come-true was almost a superfluous luxury. He read, and listened to records, and sometimes just lazed about without a care. The whirl of his social life only accounted for two or three evenings a week, and he worked out at the gym with about the same regularity.

Living out of the way of nightly temptation, he found his appetite for sex much reduced, though his life-style was still a long way from strict celibacy. When he did feel like mixing in, he went downtown to his old haunts and so preserved his reputation at the Metastasio for friendly inaccessibility. As a result, there was a decided falling-off of active interest among those patrons of the opera who, quite understandably, hoped for a better quid pro quo than Daniel was prepared to offer. What with the rationing that had gone into effect in January, it was beginning to be a buyer's market for good-looking boys. His life grew still quieter, which suited him just fine.

Strangely (for he'd feared it would be a source of upset, or at any rate of depression), Daniel found he liked living with

Boa and looking after her. There was a set of exercises he went through each morning, moving her limbs so as to keep the muscles in a minimally functional condition. While he worked her balsa-light arms in the prescribed semaphores, he would talk to her, in somewhat the half-conscious, half-serious way that Mrs Schiff would talk to Incubus.

Did Daniel think she was listening? It wasn't out of the question. Unless she'd left the earth utterly, it stood to reason that she might sometimes come back to see how her abandoned vehicle was getting on—whether it might, conceivably, be driven again. And if she did, it didn't seem unreasonable to suppose that she would also take an interest in Daniel, and stop for a while to hear what he had to say. He knew now that they'd never truly been husband and wife and that he had, therefore, no legitimate grievance at being left in the lurch. What he'd thought had been love for Boa was just being in love. Or so he would tell her while he manipulated her light, lifeless limbs. But was it really so? It was hard to remember the exact feelings of twelve, no, thirteen years ago. As well try to recall the vanished weathers of those few months they'd been together, or the life he'd led in some previous incarnation.

So it did seem strange to find himself actually feeling a kind of fondness for this bag of bones that lay in the corner of his room, breathing so quietly that she never could be heard, even from close by. Strange to suppose that she might be with him, nevertheless, at any moment of the night or day, observing, and judging, like a bonafide guardian angel.

14

MARCELLA, BEING A season subscriber, continued to turn up at the Metastasio every Tuesday. Finding that Daniel had after all become an usher, she couldn't resist seeking him out at intermission or (after he'd been transferred to the Dress Circle) lingering out on 44th Street to waylay him after the show. "Just to say hello." What she wanted was gossip about the singers. Any little scrap she accepted with the reverence of one being initiated into solemn mysteries. Daniel thought her a fool, but he enjoyed the role of high priest and so continued to supply her with crumbs and titbits about her demigods. After a while he took to sneaking her into a good seat that he knew to be standing empty. These attentions did not go unnoticed by his colleagues, who affected to believe him smitten with Marcella's very deniable charms. Daniel went along with the joke, praising her in the gross hyperboles of libretto verse. He knew that despite their banter the friendship did him credit among his fellow-ushers, all of whom had a friend, or set of friends, whose adulation and envy was a principal source of their own self-importance. That Daniel had his Marcella showed that for all his airs he wasn't above such quotidian transactions. Indeed, his involvement went beyond merely basking in the false glory of an unmerited esteem; Marcella insisted on expressing her gratitude to Daniel by bringing him five-pound canisters of Hyprotine Nutritional Supplement, which she 'shoplifted' from a deli where she had established an understanding with the clerk at the check-out counter. What a world of mutuality it was!

One evening (this was back in November), after Daniel, with the collusion of Lee Rappacini, had managed to get her into the orchestra to see the last two acts of what was billed as Sarro's *Achille in Sciro* (though, in fact, the score was Mrs Schiff's creation from first to last, and one of her best), Marcella accosted him at the corner of 44th and 8th with more than her usual urgency. Daniel, who was wearing only his uniform and freezing his shapely ass off, explained that tonight was out of the question, since he was on his way to a dinner at *La Didone* (with, once again, the constant Mr Carshalton, whom nothing, it seemed, could discourage).

Marcella, insisting she needed only a minute, reached into her duffle-sized handbag and took out a box of Fanny Farmer chocolates with a big red bow around it.

"Really, Marcella, that's going too far."

"Oh, it isn't for you, Ben," she said apologetically. "It's a Thanksgiving present for Ernesto Rey."

"Then why don't you give it to *him*? He'll be singing tomorrow night."

"But I'll be working then, you see. And anyhow I couldn't. I really just couldn't. And if I did get up the nerve, *he* probably wouldn't take it, and if he did take it, he'd probably throw it away as soon as my back was turned. That's what I've heard, anyhow."

"That's because there might be poison in it. Or something unseemly. It's been known to happen."

Marcella's eyes began to glisten. "You don't think because I've said a word or two in praise of Geoffrey Bladebridge, that I'm part of some claque, do you?"

"I don't think it, no, but Rey doesn't know you from Adam. Or Eve, for that matter."

Marcella wiped her tears away and smiled to show that her heartbreak was of no account. "That's why—" She snuffled. "—if it came from someone he *knows*, it wouldn't be so futile. You could tell him the chocolates are from someone *you* know. And trust. And that they're just my way of thanking him for the pleasure of so many beautiful performances. Would you do that for me?"

Daniel shrugged. "Sure, why not?"

If he'd stopped to think he might have answered that himself and been spared what was to come. The wise thing to have done would have been, as Marcella suggested, to dispose of the box of chocolates as soon as she was out of sight, or to eat them himself, if he dared. Instead he did as he'd promised and gave the chocolates that same evening to Rey, who was also dining at *La Didone*, with his agent Irwin Tauber. Daniel explained the situation, and Rey accepted the gift with a nod, not even bothering to ask him to thank his benefactress. Daniel returned to his *escargots* and Mr Carshalton's descriptions of the Vermont wilderness, and he thought no more about it.

The next evening a stage-hand delivered to Daniel a handwritten note from Rey, who was singing in *Norma*. The note read: "Do thank your friend on my behalf for her box of sweets and her so friendly letter. She seems entirely charming. I don't understand why she is so shy as not to approach me directly. I'm sure we'd have got on!" Daniel was miffed at Marcella's smuggling a letter into her box of chocolates, but as Rey's reaction was so cordial, what did it matter?

He genuinely forgot the whole thing—and so never connected it with Rey's altered manner towards him, which didn't amount to much more, at first, than common courtesy. When he called on Mrs Schiff and found Daniel at home, he remembered his name—for the first time since they'd been officially introduced seven months ago. Once, at *Lieto Fino*, when Daniel, having come with another party, stayed on to have coffee at Mrs Schiff's table, Rey, who was maudlin drunk, insisted on hearing the story of Ben Bosola's life, a sad and unlikely tale that Daniel felt embarrassed to be telling in front of Mrs Schiff, who knew the sad and unlikely truth. At Christmas, Rey gave Daniel a sweater, saying it had been a gift from one of his fans and didn't fit him. When Rey asked, during one of his coaching sessions, if Daniel could act as his accompanist (Mrs Schiff having burnt her hand making tea), Daniel accepted this as a tribute to his musicianship, and even when Rey praised his playing, which had been one long fumble, he attributed this to good manners. He wasn't being disingenuous or willfully blind; he believed, even now, that the world was his shepherd, with a natural instinct for providing green pastures and attending to his wants.

In February Rey asked Daniel to dinner at *Evviva il Coltello*, an invitation he delivered in such caressing tones that Daniel could no longer evade his meaning. He said no, he'd rather not, Rey, still purring, demanded a reason. He couldn't think of any except the true one—that if Rey should demand that instant capitulation that all stars seem to think was their due, his refusal might well prompt Rey to retaliate by putting Daniel on his blacklist. His job would be in jeopardy, and his arrangement with Mrs Schiff as well. At last to avoid explanations he consented to be taken out: "But only this once."

All through dinner Rey talked about himself—his roles, his reviews, his triumphs over enemies. Daniel had never before been witness to the full sweep of the man's vanity and hunger for praise and still more praise. It was at once an awesome spectacle and a deadly bore. At the conclusion of the dinner Rey declared, flatly and matter-of-factly, that he was in love with Daniel. It was such an absurd non sequitur to the past two hours of self-aggrandizing soliloquy that Daniel nearly got the giggles. It might have been better if he had, since Rey seemed determined to regard his polite demurs as shyness.

"Come, come," Rey protested, still in good humor, "let's have no more pretences." He laid his many-ringed hand on the handkerchief peeking out of the breast pocket of his suit.

"Who's pretending?"

"Have it your way, *idolo mio*. But there *was* that letter—that can't be denied—and I shall continue to keep it—" He patted the pocket of his suit. "—here, next to my heart."

"Mr Rey, that letter wasn't from me. And I have no idea what it said."

With a coquettish glance Rey reached into the inner pocket of his suit, and removed a folded and much-frayed paper, which he placed beside Daniel's coffee cup. "In that case, perhaps you'd like to *read* what it says."

He hesitated.

"Or do you know it by heart?"

"I'll read it, I'll read it."

Marcella's letter was written on scented, floral-bordered notepaper in a schoolgirlish script embellished with a few cautious curlicues meant for calligraphy. Its message aspired to the grand manner in much the same way. "To my most dear Ernesto," it began. "I love you! What more can I say? I realize that love is not possible between two beings so different as you and I. I am but a plain, homely girl, and even if I were as beautiful in reality as I am in my daydreams I don't suppose that would make much difference. There would still be a Gulf between us. Why do I write, if it is useless to declare my love? To thank you for the priceless gift of your music! Listening to your godlike voice has given me the most important, the sublimest moments of my life. I live for music, and what music is there that can equal yours? I love you—it always comes back to those three little words, which mean so much. I . . . love . . . you!" It was signed, "A worshipper from afar."

"You think I wrote this glop?" Daniel asked, having read it through.

"Can you look me in the eye and deny it?"

"Of course I deny it! I *didn't* write it! It was written by Marcella Levine, who is just what she says, a plain homely girl with a thing for opera singers."

"A plain homely girl," Rey repeated with a knowing smile.

"It's the truth."

"Oh, I appreciate that. It's my truth too, the truth of my *Norma*. But it's rare for a young man of *your* nature to understand such riddles so clearly. I think you really may have the makings of an artist in you."

"Oh for Christ's sake. What would I be doing—" He stopped short, on the verge of an irretrievable slight. It wouldn't do to declare that no one in his right mind would write mash notes to a eunuch, when Rey evidently took such attentions for granted.

"Yes?" Rey folded the note and replaced it, next to his heart.

"Listen, what if I introduced you to the girl who wrote the note? Would that satisfy you?"

"I am curious, certainly."

"She has a Tuesday subscription, and you're singing next Tuesday, aren't you?"

"*Sono Eurydice*," he said, in melting tones.

"Then if you like, I'll take you to her between the acts."

"But you mustn't prepare her!"

"It's a promise. If I did, she might get cold feet and not show up."

"Tuesday, then. And shall we come here again after, for a bite?"

"Sure. The *three* of us."

"That assumes, caro, that there *are* three of us."

"Just wait. You'll see."

On Tuesday, at the intermission, Rey appeared in the lower lobby of the Metastasio, already decked out in the costume of Eurydice and seeming, even close up and without the lights assisting, a very sylph, all tulle and moonlight—albeit a sylph of the court rather more than of the country, with enough paste jewels to have equipped a small chandelier and enough powder on his face and wig to have sunk a thousand ships. Being so majestical, he moved with the freedom of a queen, parting the crowds before him as effectively as a cordon of police. He commandeered Daniel from his post at the orange juice stand, and together they mounted the grand staircase to the Grand Tier level, and then (to everyone's wonder) went up the much less grand staircase to the Balcony, where, as Daniel had been certain they would, they found Marcella at the edge of a group of the faithful. Seeing Daniel and Rey advancing upon her, she stiffened into a defensive posture, shoulders braced and neck retracted.

They stopped before her. The group at whose edge Marcella had been standing now reformed with her and her visitors at its center.

"Marcella," Daniel said, in a manner meant to assuage, "I'd like you to meet Ernesto Rey. Ernesto, may I present Marcella Levine."

Marcella dipped her head slowly in acknowledgement.

Rey offered his slender hand, dazzling with false diamonds. Marcella, who was sensitive on the subject of hands, backed away, pressing knotted fists into the brown velvetine folds of her dress.

"Daniel tells me, my dear, that it is to you that I am beholden for a *letter* I lately received." You could almost hear the clavier underlining his *recitativo*, so ripe was his delivery.

"Pardon me?" It was all she could manage.

"Daniel tells me, my dear, that it is to you that I am beholden for a *letter* I lately received." His reading of the line did not vary in any particular, nor could you tell, from his regal inflections, whether this statement portended thanks or reproof.

"A letter? I don't understand."

"Did you, or did you not, give this charming young man a *letter* for me, enclosed in a box of chocolates?"

"No," she shook her head emphatically, "I never."

"Because," Rey went on, addressing the entire crowd that had gathered about them, "if it *was* your letter—"

The long blond braid wagged wildly in denial.

"—I only wanted to say what a very kind and warm and wonderful letter it was, and to thank you for it, *personally*. But you tell me that you *didn't* send it!"

"No! No, the usher must have . . . confused me with someone else."

"Yes, that's what he must have done. Well, my dear, it was a pleasure to make your acquaintance."

Marcella bowed her head, as though to the block.

"I hope you enjoy the second act."

There was an approving murmur from all the onlookers.

"And now you must all excuse me. I have my entrance to make! Ben, my little trickster, I shall see *you* at eleven." With which he spun round in a billow of tulle and made his way, royally, down the stairs.

Daniel had changed out of his uniform into a ragtag sweater and a pair of jeans and would not have been allowed into *Evviva il Coltello* if he hadn't been accompanying the great Ernesto. Then, to compound the offense, he told the waiter he wasn't hungry and wanted nothing more than a glass of mineral water.

"You really should take better care of yourself, caro," Rey insisted, while the waiter still hovered in the background.

"You *know* it was her," Daniel said, in a furious whisper, resuming their conversation from the street.

"In fact, I know it wasn't."

"You terrified her. That's why she denied it."

"Ah, but you see I was looking at her eyes. A person's eyes always tell the truth. It's as good as a lie detector test."

"Then look at mine and tell me if I'm lying."

"I've been looking for weeks now—and they are, all the time."

Daniel replied with a subdued Bronx cheer.

They sat in silence, Daniel glowering, Rey complacently amused, until the waiter came with wine and mineral water. Rey tasted, and approved, the wine.

When the waiter was out of earshot, Daniel asked: "*Why?* If you think I wrote that letter, why would I go on denying it?"

"As Zerlina says: '*Vorrei e non vorrei.*' She'd like to, but she also wouldn't like to. Or as someone else says, I forget who exactly: '*T'amo e tremo.*' And I can understand that. Indeed, with the baleful example of your friend before you, Bladebridge's inamorata, I can sympathize with your hesitations, even now."

"Mr Rey, I'm not hesitating. I'm refusing."

"As you like. But you should consider that the longer you put it off, the harder the terms of surrender. It's true of all sieges."

"Can I go now?"

"You will leave when I do. I don't intend to be made a public mockery. You will dine with me whenever I ask you to, and you will display your usual high spirits when you do so." As an object lesson Rey splashed wine into Daniel's glass until it had brimmed over onto the tablecloth. "Because," he went on, in his throatiest contralto, "if you do not, I shall see to it that you have no job and no apartment."

Daniel lifted the glass in a toast, spilling still more of the wine. "Cheers, Ernesto!"

Rey clinked his glass with Daniel's. "Cheers, Ben. Oh, and one last thing—I don't care how else you choose to pass your time, but I don't want to hear that you've been seen in public with Geoffrey Bladebridge, whether alone or in a group."

"What's *he* got to do with anything?"

"My sentiments exactly."

The waiter appeared with a new tablecloth, which he spread deftly over the one stained by the spilled wine. Rey informed him that Daniel had regained his appetite, and Daniel was presented with the menu. Without needing to look he ordered the most expensive hors d'oeuvre and entrée that the restaurant offered.

Rey seemed delighted. He lit a cigarette and began to discuss his performance.

15

MARCH WAS A month of judgements. The annual disaster of winter seemed to have rent asunder all the rotted threads of the social fabric in a single weekend. Social organization collapsed beneath successive shocks of power failures, shortages, blizzards, floods, and ever more audacious acts of terrorism. Units of the National Guard sent out to arrest this avalanche defected en masse. Armies of crazed urban refugees spilled out of the ghettoes and swarmed over the fallow countryside, only to suffer the fate of Napoleon's troops in their retreat from Moscow. That was in Illinois, but every state had a tale of similar *terribilitá*. After a while you didn't bother to keep track, and after a while longer you couldn't anyhow, since the media stopped reporting the latest disasters, on the hopeful theory that the avalanche might stop misbehaving if it weren't spoiled by so much attention.

Meanwhile life went on pretty much as usual in New York, where disaster was a way of life. The Metastasio advanced curtain time an hour so that people could be home before the twelve-thirty curfew, and one by one the restaurants catering to the bel canto trade closed for the duration, all but *Evviva*, which doubled its prices, halved its portions, and carried on. The general feeling in the city was one of jittery exhilaration, camaraderie, and black paranoia. You never knew whether the person ahead of you in a breadline might not be the next thread to snap and—Ping!—shoot you down in your tracks, or whether you might not, instead, fall head over heels in love. Mostly people stayed indoors, grateful for each hour that they could go on gliding gently down the stream. Home was a lifeboat, and life was but a dream.

Such was Daniel's *Weltanschauung*, and such pretty much was Mrs Schiff's as well, though her stoic calm was modified by a melancholy concern for Incubus, who, despite the bags of Pet Bricquettes stockpiled in the closet, was having a bad time of it. Early that year he'd developed an ear infection, which got steadily worse until he couldn't bear to be stroked anywhere about the head. His balance was affected. Then, either from resentment at being kept indoors or because he'd truly lost control, he stopped using his box in the bathroom and began pissing and shitting at random throughout the apartment. The smell of sick spaniel had always been a presence in these rooms, but now, as undiscovered turds fermented in the mounds of cast-off clothes, as dribbles and pools of urine soaked down through the layers of detritus, the stench became a reality even for Mrs Schiff—and unbearable to anyone else. Finally Rey presented an ultimatum—either she had the apartment cleared out and scrubbed down to the floorboards, or he would stop calling on her. Mrs Schiff submitted to necessity, and she and Daniel spent two days cleaning up. Four large bags of clothes were sent off to be cleaned, and four times that amount went into the garbage. Of the many discoveries made in the course of these excavations the most notable was that of the entire score of an opera she'd written eight years ago to the da Ponte libretto for *Axur, re d'Ormus*. After an airing, this was despatched to the Metastasio and accepted for production the following year. She gave a quarter of her fee to Daniel for finding the score, and the remainder just covered her dry cleaning bill. A silver lining, though clouds continued to gather.

The first major intrusion of the world's disorders on their private lives occurred when the pharmacist at First National Flightpaths informed Daniel that the Annex could no longer supply him with the liquid nutrient by which Boa was kept alive. The legal fiction of her death meant that no rationing card could be issued in her name. Daniel's panicky protests elicited the address of a dealer in black market medical supplies, an elderly, out-of-work pharmacist in Brooklyn Heights, who pretended, when Daniel went to him, to have given up such traffickings. Such were the protocols of the black market. Daniel waited two days for his need to be verified. Finally a boy who couldn't have been more than ten or eleven called at the apartment while Daniel was at the Teatro, and Mrs Schiff showed him to Daniel's room, where Boa lay in her endless enchanted sleep. The need being verified, Daniel was allowed to buy a two weeks' supply, no more, at a price formidably higher than the going rate at First National. He was advised that the price was likely to continue to rise so long as rationing was in force.

Transatlantic phone lines had been one of the first victims of the crisis. You couldn't even send a cable now without government authorization. The mail was the only way he could get an S.O.S. through to Miss Marspan. A Special Delivery letter might take two days, or a month, or might not arrive at all. Daniel sent off four letters from four different post offices; all arrived at Miss Marspan's flat in Chelsea the same morning. If she had any suspicions that Daniel was inventing difficulties to line his own pocket she kept them to herself. She increased her banker's order to five hundred dollars a month, twice the sum he'd asked for, and sent him a rather valedictory letter full of news about the decline and fall. Food wasn't London's problem any longer. Years ago every park and flower box in the city had been converted to growing vegetables, while in the countryside much pastureland had been restored to tillage, reversing the process of centuries. London's weak link was its water supply. The Thames was low, its waters too rank to be treated. Miss Marspan went on for two closely-written pages about the exigencies of life on two pints of water a day. "One doesn't dare drink even that," she wrote, "though it serves for cooking. We are drunk night and day, all of us who've had the wisdom and wherewithall to stock their cellars. I'd never considered becoming an alcoholic, but I find it surprisingly congenial. I begin at breakfast with a Beaujolais, graduate to claret sometime in the afternoon, and turn to brandy in the evening. Lucia and I seldom get so far afield as the South Bank these days, since there is no public transport, but the local churches keep us supplied with music. The performers are usually as drunk as their audience, but that is not without its interest, and even relevance, musically. A Monteverdi madrigal becomes so poignant, bleared with wine, and as for Mahler. . . . Words fail. It is quite generally agreed, even by our leading M.P.s, that this is, definitely, *le fin du monde*. I gather it is the same in

New York. My love to Alicia. I shall bend every effort to be at the première of the rediscovered *Axur*, assuming that the final collapse is postponed for at least another year, as it has been traditionally. Thank you for continuing to care for our dearest Boadicea. Yours, etc."

Harry Molzer was one of the most serious bodybuilders at Adonis, Inc. No one nowadays had the heroic physiques of the gods of the Golden Age half a century ago, but by contemporary standards Harry did well—a 48-inch chest, 16½-inch biceps. What he lacked in sheer bulk he made up in articulate detail. Having that body was Harry's whole life. When he wasn't at work patrolling the 12th precinct, he was in the gym perfecting his Michelangelesque proportions. All his earnings went into the upkeep of his hungry muscles. As an economy he shared a small studio apartment near the gym with two other unmarried cops, whom he despised, though he was never anything less than cordial with them— or, really, with anyone. He was, in the opinion of the manager, Ned Collins, the next-best thing to a saint, and Daniel pretty much had to agree. If purity of heart was to will one thing, Harry Molzer was right up there with Ivory Snow.

Rationing hit Harry hard. The Rationing Board was supposed to allow for individual somatic differences, but Harry was carrying around as much muscle as three or four average men. Even with the supplementary coupons police were entitled to, there was no way that Harry could have kept going at 195 pounds without resorting to the black market. Naturally, he resorted, but even on the black market the powdered protein he needed was not obtainable. Such concentrates were the first things hoarders had gone for. He switched to dry beans as the next-best source of protein, becoming notorious for his farts in the process, but by March even beans cost more, at black market prices, than Harry could afford. His muscles diminished and at the same time, because of the starch in the beans, he began to put on a thin cushion of flab.

Harry would never resign himself to the inevitable. He was always at the gym—staring morosely into the mirrors that lined the inner walls, or grimacing in private combat with the weights; standing at a window between sets and watching the traffic down in the square, or twisting in fast, furious torsion on the inclined sit-up board. But will power alone was not enough. Despite his unremitting effort, Harry's body was saying good-bye. Without a steady supply of protein the hard exercise only hastened the self-destruction of his tissues. Ned Collins tried to get him to cut back his schedule, but Harry was beyond being reasoned with. He kept to exactly the same routine he'd followed in the days of his glory.

Harry had never been notably gregarious. For some like Daniel the gym served as a social club. For Harry it was a religion, and he wasn't the sort to talk in church. Yet he had been liked, and even reverenced, by those who shared his faith but lacked his zeal. Now, in proportion as he had been liked, he was pitied—and avoided. Whatever corner of the gym he worked in would gradually be deserted, as though there might be a kind of contagion in Harry's agony. In any case there were fewer people showing up these days. No one had that much surplus energy. And no one liked to be around Harry.

There were, inevitably, those who lacked the compassion or the moral imagination to understand what was happening to Harry, and it was one of this small number who, early one April afternoon, pushed him over the edge. Harry was doing bench presses and using, as he always did now, much more weight than he could handle. On the last rep of his second set his left arm began to buckle but he managed to straighten his arm and lock his elbow. His face was flushed a violent red. The straining cords of his neck formed a delta with his grimacing teeth at its apex. The barbell swayed alarmingly, and Ned jumped up from the desk, where he'd been talking with Daniel, and raced across the floor of the gym to get to Harry in time. It was then that the moral imbecile in question called out, from his perch on the parallel bars. "Okay, Hercules, one more rep!"

The bar crashed down into the stanchions and Harry sprang up from the bench with a scream. Daniel thought the bar had crushed his hand, but it was rage, not pain, that spilled from his lungs. Months and years of swallowed angers exploded in an instant. He swept up an eighty-pound dumbbell lying by the bench and hurled it at his tormentor. It missed him shattering an expanse of mirror and passing through a wall of plaster and lathe into the changing room behind. "Harry!" Ned pleaded, but Harry was out of control, beyond appeal, berserk. One by one, in a systematic ecstacy of destruction, he smashed every mirror in the gym, using the heaviest barbells in the rack. He sailed a twenty-pound plate, discus-like, into the soft-drink dispenser. He overturned a rack of dumbbells onto the floor. It felt like a bomb had hit the building. Through it all no one dared try and stop him.

When the last mirror was gone, and much of the supporting wall, Harry turned to face the three windows that looked down at Sheridan Square. They were still intact. He walked over to one of them, dumbbell in hand, and regarded the crowd that had gathered on the sidewalk and in the street.

"Harry, please," Ned said softly.

"Fuck it," said Harry in a mournful, tired voice. He turned away from the windows and went into the changing room, closing the door behind him. Daniel watched him, through a rent in the plaster wall, go to his locker. For a long while he fumbled patiently with the combination lock. When he had got it open at last, he took his police-issue revolver from its holster, walked over to the single surviving mirror that hung above the sink, and struck his last, unconscious, classic pose as he pointed the barrel of the pistol at his temple. Then he blew out his brains.

Adonis, Inc. never did reopen.

Food had become everyone's problem. According to the media's steady buzz of placatory bulletins, there was enough to go round for many months to come. The difficulty was distribution. Supermarkets and grocery stores throughout the city had been pressed into service by the Rationing Board, but black market prices were now so inflated that it was worth your life to be seen leaving a distribution center with an armload (or pocketful) of groceries. Even convoys of five or six men might be set upon. As for the police, they were mainly concentrated in the parks or outside the parking lots where the black markets operated.

241

Despite this protective presence not a week went by without another, and more violent, mob-assault upon these last tawdry bastions of privilege. By the end of March there was no longer a black market in the physical sense—only a network of individuals united by an invisible hierarchy. The economic system was being simplified to its atomic components: every man was his own armed camp.

Thanks to the closet stocked with Pet Bricquettes, Daniel and Mrs Schiff were never reduced to direst need. Daniel, a passable though seldom inspired cook, concocted a kind of bread pudding from crumbled Bricquettes, Hyprotine powder, and an artificial sweetener, which Mrs Schiff claimed actually to prefer to her usual fare. He also organized groups of the building's residents to make trips to their distribution center, a former Red Owl Supermarket on Broadway. And, in general, he coped.

As the weather warmed it began to look as though he would scrape through the crisis without having to ask for Ernesto Rey's help. He would have, if worst had come to worst (if, for instance, Miss Marspan had balked at the rising cost of charity). Living with Boa's body had confirmed Daniel in his sense of duty, had made it seem less abstract. He would do anything he had to in order to keep her alive—and in his own possession. What could Rey demand of him, after all, that he hadn't done already, either by preference or out of curiosity? This was a question he tended to dwell on rather more than was quite healthy. He would lie there alone in his room going over the possibilities with a glazed, insomniac persistence. Some of those possibilities were pretty terrible, but fortunately none of his imaginings, even the mildest, would come to pass.

It had become clear that Incubus was dying, though neither the dog nor his mistress were prepared to face the fact. He kept pretending he wanted to be taken out for a walk, moping about the hallway and whining and scratching at the outside door. Even if he'd had the strength to make it as far as the corner lamppost, there was no question of giving in to him, since a dog on the street these days was just meat on the hoof and an incitement to riot.

Mrs Schiff was devoted to the dying spaniel, and Incubus took every unfair advantage of her sympathy. He was everlastingly querulous, begging for food which he then refused to eat. He wouldn't let Mrs Schiff read or write or even talk to anyone but himself. If she tried to get round these prohibitions by disguising a conversation with Daniel as a tête-à-tête with Incubus, he would sense it and punish her by staggering off to the darkest part of the apartment and flopping down in inert despair. A few moments later Mrs Schiff would be there beside him, petting him and apologizing, for she could never hold out very long against his sulks.

One night, not long after the closing of the gym, Incubus came into Mrs Schiff's room and insisted on being helped up onto her bed, though until now he'd accepted the new prohibition against this. His incontinence and the ensuing drastic overhaul of the apartment had inspired Incubus with an almost human sense of guilt, which each new spontaneous defecation served to keep alive.

Daniel, passing the room and seeing Incubus sprawled on the bed, set in to scolding him, but both dog and mistress gave him such pitiable looks that he didn't have the heart to insist. He came in the room and sat in the armchair by the bed. Incubus lifted his tail a scant inch off the sheets and let it drop. Daniel patted him on the rump. He began to whine: he wanted a story.

"I think he wants you to tell him a story," said Daniel.

Mrs Schiff nodded wearily. She had developed a kind of subdued horror of her own whimsies from having had to recite them so many times when she was feeling the opposite of whimsical herself. Her Scheherazade complex, she called it. It was useless, at these times, to try and abridge the tale being told, for Incubus could always sense when she'd departed from the established format and formulae and would whine and worry her until the straying story-line had been brought back to the narrow paths of orthodoxy. At last she'd learned, like a good sheep, not to stray.

"This is the story," Mrs Schiff began, as she'd begun so many times before, "of Bunny Honeybunny and his sister Honey Honeybunny and of the beautiful Christmas they spent in Bethlehem, the very first Christmas of all. One night, at just about bedtime, when Bunny Honeybunny was about to turn in for a well-deserved rest, for he had had, as usual, a *very* busy day, his dear little sister Honey Honeybunny came hopping, hippity-hop, into their cozy little burrow deep in the roots of a gnarly old oak tree, and she said to her brother—'Bunny! Bunny! You must come out and look at the sky!' Bunny had seldom seen his sister so excited, so, sleepy as he was (and he was very sleepy)—"

Incubus knew better than to succumb to such hints. *He* was wide-awake and intent upon the story.

"—he hopped, hippity-hop, out of their dear little burrow, and what do you think he saw, shining up there in the sky?"

Incubus looked at Daniel.

"What did he see?" Daniel asked.

"He saw a star! And he said to his sister Honey Honeybunny, 'What a beautiful and truly amazing star! Let us follow it.' So they followed the star. They followed it over the meadows where the cows had settled down to sleep, and across the broad highways, and over the lakes as well, for it was winter and the lakes were all covered with ice, until at last they arrived in Bethlehem, which is in Judea. By this time, naturally, they were both quite tired from their journey and wanted nothing so much as to go to bed. So they went to the biggest hotel in town, the Bethlehem Hotel, but the night-clerk was very rude and said there was no room at the hotel, because of the census the government was taking, and that even if there had been room he wouldn't have let rabbits into his hotel. Poor Honey Honeybunny thought she would cry, but as she didn't want to make her brother unhappy on *her* account she decided to be brave. So, with a merry twitch of her long furry ears, she turned to Bunny and said, 'We don't need to stay at any silly old hotel. Let's go find a manger and stay there. Mangers are more fun anyhow!' So they went to look for a manger, which was no problem at all, for lo and behold, there was a cheery little manger just behind the Bethlehem Hotel with oxen and asses and cows and sheep . . . and something else besides! Something so wonderful and soft and warm and precious they couldn't believe their bunny-rabbit eyes."

"What did they see in the manger?" asked Daniel.

"They saw Baby Jesus!"

"No kidding."

"Yes, there he was, the little Lord God, and Mary and Joseph too, kneeling beside him, and any number of shepherds and angels and wise men, all kneeling down and offering Baby Jesus presents. Poor Bunny Honeybunny and Honey Honeybunny felt just terrible, of course, because they didn't have any presents for Baby Jesus. So, to cut a long story short—"

Incubus looked up vigilantly.

"—the two darling rabbits hopped off into the night, hippity-hop, all the way to the North Pole, which represents a lot of hopping, but there was never a word of complaint from *them*. And when they got to the North Pole, what do you suppose they found?"

"What did they find there?"

"Santa's workshop is what they found. It was still early in the evening, so Santa was still there, and Mrs Santa Claus as well, and all the little elves, millions of them, who help Santa make his toys, and the reindeer who help Santa deliver them, but I'm *not* going to name all the reindeer."

"Why not?"

"Because I'm tired and I have a headache."

Incubus began to whine.

"Comet and Cupid and Donner and Blitzen. And Dasher and Prancer and . . . and. . . . Help me."

"Rudolph?"

"With his nose so bright, of course. How could I forget Rudolph? Well, after everyone had sat down in front of the blazing fire and warmed their little paws and enjoyed a nice slice of Mrs Santa's carrot cake, the two Honeybunnies explained why they'd had to come to the North Pole. They told Santa about Baby Jesus and how they'd wanted to give him a present for Christmas but didn't have any. 'So what we were hoping,' said Honey Honeybunny, 'was that we could give him ours. Santa Claus, naturally, was deeply touched by this, and Mrs Santa had to turn away to dry her tears. Tears of happiness, you understand."

"Is there any other kind?" Daniel asked.

Incubus shifted his head uneasily.

"Well," said Mrs Schiff, folding her hands purposefully

in her lap, "Santa told the Honeybunnies that *of course* they could give their presents to Baby Jesus, if they would help him load them into his great bag and put it into his sleigh."

"And what were the presents they put in the bag?" Daniel asked.

"There were rooty-toot-toots and rummy-tum-tums and dolls and frisbees and doctor kits with candy pills and tiny little thermometers for pretending to take a temperature. Oh, and a hundred other lovely things: games and candy and myrrh and frankincense and opera records and the Complete Works of Sir Walter Scott."

Incubus laid down his head, content.

"And he loaded the bag of presents into his sleigh, and helped the two Honeybunnies in behind him, and gave a crack of his whip and—"

"Since when does Santa have a whip?"

"Santa's had a whip time out of mind. But he rarely if ever has to use it. Reindeer know instinctively where they should fly. So—away they all flew, instinctively, like the down of a thistle, straight to the manger in Bethlehem where Jesus and Mary and Joseph and the shepherds and angels and wise men, and even the night-clerk at the hotel, who'd experienced a change of heart, were waiting for Santa and the Honeybunnies, and when they saw them up there in the sky, which was lit up, you'll remember, by that beautiful star, they all let out a great hurrah. 'Hurrah!' they shouted. 'Hurrah for the Honeybunnies! Hurrah! Hurrah! Hurrah!'"

"Is that the end of the story?"

"That's the end of the story."

"Do you know what, Mrs Schiff?"

"What?"

"Incubus just went wee-wee in your bed. I can see it on the sheets."

Mrs Schiff sighed, and nudged Incubus, who was dead.

16

THERE SEEMED TO be general agreement among the commentators, many of them not given to expressions of easy optimism, that a new day was dawning, that a corner had been turned, that life would go on. Those for whom the word was not a bugaboo said there had been a revolution, while those less millennially-minded called it a time of reconciliation. The weather was nicer, of course, as it invariably is in May and June. No one was quite sure what marked the commencement of this brighter era, much less whether the forces of darkness were in full retreat or had only stopped to catch their breath, but when the country woke up from the nightmare of its long collapse, a lot of problems had disappeared from the headlines along with a number of people.

The most amazing change, from Daniel's point of view, was that flight had been decriminalized in four of the Farm Belt states (though not yet in Iowa). Further, the government had dropped its prosecution of the publishers of the anonymous under-the-counter shocker, *Tales of Terror*, which purported to be the confessions of the man who'd blown up the Alaska pipeline nineteen years ago, single-handed, and who now regretted this and subsequent crimes, all the while plainly glorying in their depiction. The government, by ceasing to require the publishers to divulge the author's identity, was saying, in effect, that bygones were bygones. The result was that people could afford to buy the book at its lower (over-the-counter) price, and were, by the millions, Daniel among them.

Along another axis of reconciliation, the Reverend Jack Van Dyke was back in the news as the first big-shot liberal to support the Puritan Renewal League, the latest splinter-group of Undergoders to try and make it in the big time. *Time* magazine had a cover photo showing Van Dyke and

Goodman Halifax rigged out in the black Stetsons, stiff white collars, red rayon bow-ties, and insignia-blazoned denim jackets that were the P.R.L.'s cheerfully anachronistic uniform. The two men were shown pledging allegiance to a flag in Arlington Cemetery. It wasn't Daniel's idea of the dawn of a new era, but Halifax had been behind the move to decriminalize flight, which was certainly to be counted to his favor, however involuted and Van Dykean the motives ascribed to him by *Time*.

Daniel would have taken a larger and more affirming interest in these developments, but sad to say the vector of his own life refused to follow this general upward trend. Worst, in fact, had come to worst, for Miss Marspan had discontinued her assistance in the most definitive way. She was dead, one of a multitude to perish in London's ongoing, multiple epidemic. Daniel was informed of her death in a telex from her bank. The bank regretted any inconvenience that might issue from the sudden interruption of its monthly drafts but as the deceased had made no provision in her will for such payments to be maintained, it could not act otherwise.

Daniel was similarly limited in his course of action. Until the spirit of the new era reached the Rationing Board and moved them to reconsider the plight of such as Boa, it would not be possible to return her to the dismal wards of the First National Flightpaths Annex. In any case, he no longer had cash sufficient to secure her stay at the Annex for more than a few months. Telling himself he had no choice, he went to Ernesto Rey.

The terms set for his capitulation were not generous. He was to have his skin dyed a deep teak-brown, all but a broad circle on each cheek that would be left its natural color, so as (Rey explained) to reveal his blushes. His hair, being jet-black, need not be dyed, but would be frizzed, fluffed, and shaped, topiary-wise, as fashion should dictate. He would accompany Rey whenever required to, wearing the livery of the Metastasio, or something equally gay and gaudy, and he would perform small services symbolic of his subjection, such as opening doors, page-turning, and shining shoes. Further, he would engage, actively and unstintingly, in whatever carnal pursuits Rey should direct him towards, provided only (this was the one concession Daniel was able to obtain) such pursuits were legal and within the natural range of his competence. He would not otherwise be permitted to have sex, to which end he was to be fitted with an insanity belt. He would affect, both in public and private, to be infatuated with his benefactor, and to all inquiries as to why he acted in these ways he was to reply that he followed the promptings of a loving heart. In return Rey undertook to provide for Boa's well-being for such time as he should require these services of Daniel and for a year thereafter.

The articles of this contract were sworn to at a special dinner at *Evviva il Coltello* in the presence of Mrs Schiff and Mr Ormund, both of whom seemed to regard the occasion as auspicious. Mr Ormund, indeed, was a proper mother of the bride, alternating between outbursts of ebullience and tears. He undertook to deliver Daniel that very evening into the hands of his own cosmetician and to supervise his entire transformation. This was, he declared, the very thing he'd hoped for when first he'd laid eyes on Ben and recognized him as a latent brother. Mrs Schiff was less effusive in her congratulations. She obviously regarded his physical remodeling as so much folderol, but she approved the relationship as being calculated to promote Ernesto's peace of mind and thereby to enhance his art.

Daniel had never before known humiliation. He'd experienced fleeting embarrassments. He'd regretted ill-considered actions. But through all his tribulations, in Spirit Lake and during his long years as a temp in New York, he had never felt any deep or lasting shame. Now, though he tried as before to retreat to the sanctuary of an inner, uncoercible freedom, he knew humiliation. He did not believe, any longer, in his innocence or righteousness. He accepted the judgement of the world—the sneers, the smiles, the wisecracks, the averted eyes. All this was his due. He could wear the livery of the Metastasio without injury to his pride—even, at his better moments, with a kind of moral panache, like those pages in Renaissance paintings who seem, by virtue of youth and beauty, the rivals of the princes whom they serve, but he could not wear the livery of prostitution with so cavalier a grace: it pinched, it tickled, it itched, it burned, it abraded his soul.

He tried to tell himself that his condition had not been essentially altered, that, though he might give his neck to the yoke, his spirit remained free. He remembered Barbara Steiner, and the prostitute (her name forgotten) who'd inaugurated his own sexual career in Elmore, and the countless professionals here in New York with whom, in their free moments, he'd sported, both hustlers and whores. But there was no comfort in such comparisons. If he had not judged them so harshly as he judged himself, it was because just by being prostitutes they had placed themselves outside the pale. Whatever other qualities of worth they might boast—wit, imagination, generosity, exuberance—they remained, in Daniel's eyes, honorless. As now he was himself. For didn't they—didn't he?—say, in effect, that love was a lie, or rather, a skill? Not, as he'd believed, the soul's testing ground; not, somehow, a sacrament.

Sex, if it was not the soul's avenue into this world, and the flesh's out of it, was simply another means by which people gained advantage over each other. It was of the world, worldly. But what was left then that wasn't worldly, that didn't belong to Caesar? Flight, perhaps, though it seemed that dimension of grace would always be denied him. And (logic demanded) death. He doubted, from his earlier failure in this direction back at Spirit Lake, whether he'd ever have the gumption to kill himself, but Mrs Schiff knew nothing of that, and he found a definite relief in throwing out dark hints to her. Scarcely a night went by without Daniel indulging in a rumble of off-stage thunder, until at last Mrs Schiff lost all patience with him and called him to task.

"So you wish you were dead—is that what you're muttering?" she demanded one night during the second week of his captivity, when he'd come home half-drunk and bathetic. "Such stuff and nonsense, Daniel, such tiresome drivel! Really, you surprise me, carrying on in this catastrophic way. It isn't like you. I hope you're not like this in front of Ernesto. It wouldn't be fair to him, you know."

"All you ever fucking think of is Ernesto! What about me?"

"Oh, I *think* of you constantly. How should I not, with our being thrown together every day? But I do worry about Ernesto, that's true. And I *don't* worry about you. You're much too capable and sturdy."

"You can say that when I'm sitting here in this pelvic straitjacket so that I can't even take a piss by myself?"

"You want the key? Is *that* all!"

"Oh fuck it, Mrs Schiff, you're *trying* to misunderstand."

"Has he made you do something so awful, then, that it can't be spoken of?"

"He hasn't made me do fucking anything!"

"Ah ha!"

"Ah ha yourself."

"It's not humiliation that's bothering you at all. It's anxiety. Or are you, perhaps, a bit disappointed?"

"As far as I'm concerned he can keep me in wraps till I'm ninety-five: I won't complain."

"I must say, Daniel—you *seem* to be complaining. It's quite possible, you know, that Ernesto will go on being satisfied with the status quo. Our marriage stopped, in effect, with the slicing of the cake."

"So, why does he do it?"

"*Bella figura*. It's good form to have a glamorous young person in one's private possession. Admittedly, *I* couldn't have been called glamorous, even in my youth, but in those days my father was still a prominent racketeer, so there was a social cachet. In your case, I think he is determined to one-up Bladebridge. The man does worry him—quite needlessly, I think. But among the people whose good opinion he covets your conquest has been taken note of, at least as much as if you were a Rolls-Royce that he'd bought and then had customized."

"Oh, I know all that. But *he* talks about how much he loves me. He's always going on about his *passion*. It's like living inside an opera libretto."

"I could think of nowhere *I'd* rather live. And I do think it ungenerous of you not to lead him on somewhat."

"You mean to say I'm not a good whore."

"Let your conscience be your guide, Daniel."

251

"What do you suggest I do?"

"Chiefly, take an interest. Ernesto is a singer, and singers want more than anything else to be listened to. Ask to be allowed to go to his rehearsals, to sit in on his master classes. Praise his singing. Effuse. Act as though you meant every word in the letter you wrote to him."

"Damn it, Mrs Schiff—I didn't write that letter!"

"More's the pity. If you had, then you might be ready to learn to sing yourself. As you are, you never shall."

"No need to rub my nose in it. I guess I've learned that fact of life."

"Ah, there's that whine in your voice again. The bleat of the guiltless lamb. But it isn't some implacable predestining Force that keeps you from being the singer you might be. It's your *choice*."

"Oh fuck off. I'm going to bed. Do you have the key? I need to take a piss."

Mrs Schiff examined the various pockets of the clothes she was wearing, and then of the clothes she'd discarded in the course of the day. Her rooms were gradually reacquiring their former clutter now that Incubus was gone. At last she found her key-ring on her worktable. She followed Daniel to the bathroom, and, after releasing him from the insanity belt, stood in the doorway while he went to the toilet. A precaution against his whacking off. She was a very conscientious jailer.

"Your problem, Daniel," she continued, after his first sigh of relief, "is that you have spiritual ambition but no faith." She considered that a while and changed her mind. "No, that sounds more like *my* problem. Your problem is that you have a Faustian soul. It is a larger soul, perhaps, than belongs to many who, for all that, can fly with the greatest of ease. Who ever supposed size was a mark of quality, eh?"

Daniel wished he'd never started this discussion. All he'd wanted was a shoulder to cry on, not new insights into his inadequacy. All he wanted was a chance to piss and turn the lights out and sleep.

"Merely to be striving, ever and always, is no distinction. That's what's wrong with German music. It's all development, all *sehnsucht* and impatience. The highest art is happy to inhabit *this* moment, here and now. A great singer sings the way a bird warbles. One doesn't need a large soul to warble, only a throat."

"I'm sure you're right. Now would you leave me alone?"

"I *am* right. And so is Ernesto, and it galls me, Daniel that you will not do him justice. Ernesto has a spirit no *larger* than a diamond, but no less perfect. He can do what you only dream of."

"He sings beautifully, I'll grant you that. But he can't fly any more than I can."

"He can. He chooses not to."

"Bullshit. Everyone knows castrati can't fly. Their balls and their wings come off with the same slice of the knife."

"I've looked after Ernesto for days at a time while his spirit was winging about thither and yon. You may believe, if you need to, that he faked that for my benefit, but I know what I know. Now I wish you'd wipe yourself and let me go back to work."

Since Incubus's death Mrs Schiff had been in spate, writing a new opera, which was to be her own and no one else's. She wouldn't discuss her work in progress, but she became impatient with anything that didn't directly relate to it. As a result, she was generally mysterious or irritable, and hell to live with either way.

Daniel took the opportunity, before he was locked up again, to wash in the sink. He bathed incessantly these days, and would have bathed still more if Mrs Schiff had allowed it.

"As to what you were saying earlier," Mrs Schiff noted, while he dried himself, "I think you'll soon come to enjoy your humiliations, the way people do in Russian novels."

Daniel could see himself blushing in the bathroom mirror.

Blushes are like tulips. In the spring there is a profusion of them, and then as the year gets rolling they become fewer and fewer. For a while it was enough that he be noticed by a stranger for Daniel to be afflicted by a spasm of shame, but inevitably there were times when, his mind being fixed

253

on other matters, he was oblivious to the attention he received. As a natural consequence, he received less attention. For those moments when the world insisted on goggling, pointing fingers, and calling names, Daniel developed a small arsenal of defense mechanisms, from the pre-emptive sniping of "You're another!" (best delivered to bonafide blacks who limited their hostility to ironic glances) to maniac self-parody, as when he would pretend to strum a banjo and start to sing a brain-damaged medley of minstrel-show tunes (a ploy that could strike terror to the hearts even of potential muggers). Reluctantly, he came to understand the secret phoneys shared with freaks of all descriptions— that people feared him as they might fear to see their own idiot ids capering about before them and proclaiming their secret desires to every passer-by. If only they knew, he would wistfully reflect, that they're not even *my* secret desires; that they're probably not anyone's. So long as he bore that in mind he could even enjoy grossing people out— some people more than others, naturally. In short, just as Mrs Schiff had prophesied, he was learning to savor his abasement. And why not? If there is something you've got to do and there's a way to enjoy it, you'd be a fool to do it any other way.

Toward his benefactor, too, Daniel took a more accommodating line. Though he never relented so far as to disguise the fact of an enforced compliance, he did try to act the part he'd been engaged to play, albeit woodenly. He resisted the impulse to wince when Rey would pet and pinch and otherwise feign a lubricious interest, which he only did when they were in public, never when they were alone. Then, in a way because there was an equivocal kind of cruelty in it, he began to reciprocate these attentions— but only when they were alone, never in company. He would call him "Sugar Daddy", "Dear Heart", "Lotus Blossom", and any of a hundred other endearments borrowed from Italian and French libretti. Under the pretext of "wanting to look his best" for Rey, he squandered quantities of hard cash on overpriced and tasteless clothes. He ran up huge bills with Mr Ormund's cosmetician. He coquetted, strutted, posed, and preened. He became a wife.

None of these abominations seemed to register. Perhaps

Rey, as a eunuch, accepted Daniel's outrages as a fair representation of human sexuality. Daniel himself began to wonder how much of his posturing was parody and how much a compulsive letting-off of steam. The celibate life was beginning to get to him. He began having wet dreams for the first time since puberty, and dreams of every sort in much greater abundance. One afternoon he found himself sneaking off to a double bill of the sleaziest porn—not just ducking into a theater on impulse but actually forming and following a plan. Most of the porn he'd seen had struck him as silly or stupid, and even the best of it couldn't live up to his own unassisted fantasies, much less to the real throbbing thing. So what was he doing there in the dark, staring up the blurred gigantic images of genitalia and feeling sweet indescribable confusions? Cracking up?

His dream-life posed much the same question. During his stint with Renata Semple his dreams had been Grade B, or lower—short, simple, guileless dreams a computer could have put together from the data of his daily life. No longer. The most vivid of his new dreams, and the scariest for what it seemed to suggest about his mental health, concerned his old friend and betrayer, Eugene Mueller. At an early point in the dream Daniel was dining at *La Didone* with Rey and Mrs Schiff. Then he was out on the street. A mugger had come up behind him and asked, in a conversational tone, whether he'd like to be raped. The voice sounded uncannily familiar, and yet not to belong to anyone he knew. A voice from his past, before New York, before Spirit Lake. "Eugene?" he guessed, and turned around to face him and to fall, instantly, in love. Eugene spread his arms, Gene-Kelly-style, and smiled. "None other! Back from the bathroom—" he did a buck-and-wing and went down on one knee, "—and ready for love!"

Eugene wanted to fly to Europe immediately, for a honeymoon. He explained that it was he who'd been responsible for the plane crash in which Daniel and Boa had died. Daniel began crying, from (he explained) sheer surfeit of joy. They began to have sex. Eugene was very assertive, not to say rough. Daniel cut his hand, and there was some confusion as to the nature of the pain he was experiencing. He told Eugene to stop, he pleaded, but Eugene went right on. Nails were being driven into his hands and feet, to secure (Eugene explained) his wings.

Then he was standing on a chair, and Eugene was on a chair on the far side of the room, encouraging him to fly. Daniel was afraid even to lift his arms. Blood dribbled down over the feathers. Instead of flying, which didn't seem possible, he started to sing. It was a song he'd written himself, called 'Flying'.

The moment he started to sing he woke up. He couldn't believe it had been, he didn't *want* it to be, no more than a dream. Awful as it had been, he wanted it to be real. He wanted to make love to Eugene again, to sing, to fly. But here he was in his room, with the moonlight coming in at the half-parted curtain and making a ghost of Boa under her single sheet. His cock was erect and the glans was pressed painfully against the unyielding plastic of the insanity belt. He started crying and then, without stopping crying, stumbled across the room to get pencil and paper. On the hardwood floor, by moonlight, he wrote down everything he could remember of his dream.

For hours he would read over that transcript and wonder what it had meant. Did it mean that he might, after all, be able some day to sing? To fly? Or simply that his insanity belt was living up to its name?

Whatever it might mean, he felt a lot better all the next day, a day of high summer and bright speedy clouds. He walked through Central Park relishing everything, the flashings of light on the leaves of the trees, the corrugations of bark, the russet stains of iron bleeding across mammoth facets of a rock, swoopings of kites, women with strollers, the nobility of the towering apartment buildings that formed a grand horseshoe round the southern end of the park. And throngs of sexy people, all of them, whether they knew it or not, cruising, sending out signals, asking to be laid. The park was a vast dance floor of shuffling loins and appraising glances, of swinging limbs and shifting possibilities. The odd thing was that Daniel, despite his supercharged alertness to this clandestine bacchanal, didn't mind, this once, being relegated to the status of observer. He could, of course, if he'd wished to, have offered some lucky wight

the still available delights of lips, tongue, and teeth, but
Daniel had never been an altruist to that degree. Without
requiring a strict teeter-totter equivalence of orgasm for
orgasm, he did believe in some kind of quid pro quo. So he
walked, loveless and at liberty, wherever the paths would
take him—around the reservoir and through a series of mini-
wildernesses, past the impromptu cabarets of street performers, past rows of sad bronze businessmen, drinking it
all in or just gazing up into the cloudlands and trying to
recapture the fading dream, that feeling of being poised right
on the edge of flight (albeit on the seat of a chair). What had
it meant? What *did* it mean?

Then, out of the blue, as he loped down a long flight of
steps leading to an ornamental pond, a statue answered that
question. An angel rather—the angel who stood, wings un-
furled, atop a tall fountain in the center of the pool. The
dream the angel chose to interpret was not last night's but
the dream he'd dreamt in the sauna of Adonis, Inc., on the
night of his thirtieth birthday, the dream about the fountain
in the courtyard of the mosque that had seemed so obscure
then and was so clear now as he stood at the edge of the
pool and was drenched in the wind-borne spray of the
veritable fountain.

The fountain was the fountain of art; of song; of singing;
of a process that renews itself moment by moment; that is
timeless and yet inhabits the rush and tumble of time, just as
the fountain's trumpeting waters are endlessly conquering
the same slim splendid space. It was what Mrs Schiff had
said about music, that it must be a warbling and willing to
inhabit *this* instant, and then *this* instant, and always *this*
instant, and not just willing, and not even desirous, but
delighted: an endless, seamless inebriation of song. *That* was
what bel canto was all about, and that was the way to
fly.

Shortly after ten that night Daniel, in his latest Arabian gear,
appeared on Rey's East 55th Street doorstep with a bowl of
his special bread pudding. The doorman, as ever, looked
askance, not to say daggers, but Daniel borne along by winds
of inspiration, just whistled a few bars of 'I Whistle a Happy
Tune' and sailed into the elevator.

Rey, naturally, was surprised to be visited so late and without warning. He'd already changed from his daytime drabs to the night's relative splendor, a shot-silk kimono with a few choice panels of embroidery.

Daniel held out the still-warm bowl. "Here, *amorino*, I made you a pudding."

"Why, thank you." Rey received the pudding in both hands and lifted it up to sniff at it. "I didn't realize you were such a homebody."

"I'm not, usually, but Mrs Schiff swears by my bread pudding. It's my own recipe, and very low in calories. I call it humble pie."

"Would you care to come in and enjoy it with me?"

"Do you have any cream?"

"I'll look. But I doubt it. Where would one get cream nowadays?"

Daniel took a stoppered jug of cream from within his burnoose. "On the black market."

"You think of everything, *mon ange*."

In the kitchen, Rey, ever careful of his figure, spooned out a small portion of the pudding for himself, and a larger one for Daniel.

When they were settled before the fireplace, under a fauvish pastel portrait of Rey in the role of *Semiramide*, Daniel asked Rey if he would do him a favor.

"It depends on the favor, surely. This is delicious pudding."

"I'm glad you like it. Would you sing a song for me?"

"What song?"

"Any at all."

"That's the favor you ask?"

Daniel nodded. "I just suddenly had to hear you sing. With the Teatro closed for the summer. . . . Records are wonderful, but they're not the same thing."

Rey rifled through the sheet music on the piano. He handed Daniel the score of Schubert's 'Vedi quanto t'adoro', and asked if he could handle the accompaniment.

"I'll do my best."

They went through the opening bars several times, Rey humming the vocal line, until he was satisfied with the tempo. Then he sang, without ornament or embellishment, the words Metastasio had written, the notes Schubert, a hundred years later, had set:

> *Vedi quanto t'adoro ancora, ingrato!*
> *Con un tuo sguardo solo*
> *Mi togli ogni difesa e mi disarmi.*
> *Ed hai cor di tradirmi? E puoi lasciarmi?*

It dawned on Daniel, even as his fingers fumbled along in the loveliness, that Rey was not so much singing as setting forth a literal truth. Though he'd never heard the aria before, the Italian seemed to translate itself with spontaneous, pentecostal clarity, vowel by golden, anguished vowel: *"See! ingrate, how I still adore you! A look from you is still enough to shatter my defenses and to strip me bare. Have you the heart to betray such love? And then to leave me?"*

Rey broke off at this point, Daniel having altogether lost track of the accompaniment from the marvel of Rey's singing. They started out from the beginning again, and this time Rey introduced to the bare skeleton of Schubert's written score a tremolo that mounted by imperceptible degrees to utmost extravagance at *"E puoi lasciarmi?"* Then, abruptly, at *"Ah! non lasciarmi, no"* the heightened color was gone, as though a veil had fallen from the face of the music. He sang in a silvery, slightly hollow tone that suggested that he (or rather, Dido, whom he'd become) had been abandoned at the very instant she implored not to be. It was heartbreaking, heroic, and thoroughly exquisite, a sorrow and a sunset condensed into a single string of pearls.

"How was that?" Rey asked, when they'd finished the last repetition of the opening stanza.

"Stupendous! What can I say?"

"I mean, in particular, the '*E puoi lasciarmi?*' which Alicia has objected to?"

"It was like being slapped in the face by Death."

"Ah, you should be a reviewer, *bell' idol mio.*"

"Thanks a lot."

"Oh, I'm quite sincere."

"I don't doubt that."

"I *might* even be able to arrange it for you."

Daniel looked down at his brown hands resting on the

closed keyboard and expelled a short, self-defeated snort of laughter.

"You wouldn't want that?" Rey asked with, it would seem, honest incomprehension.

"Ernesto—I wouldn't want to review it, if I couldn't *do* it."

"Then you've never given up the wish to be a singer?"

"Does anyone ever give up his wishes? Do you?"

"That is an unanswerable question, I'm afraid." Rey went to the divan and sat down, his arms spread wide across the cushions. "All *my* wishes have come true."

Ordinarily Daniel would have found such complacence infuriating, but the song had modified his perceptions, and what he felt, instead, was a rather generalized tristesse and a wonder at the immense gulf between Rey's inner and his outer man, between the hidden angel and the wounded beast. He went and sat down at a confidential, but not amorous, distance from him and leaned back his head so that it rested on Rey's forearm. He closed his eyes and tried to summon up the exact curve and sweep and nuance of that "*E puoi lasciarmi?*"

"Let me ask you more directly then," Rey said, in a tone of cautious speculation. "*Do* you want to be a singer?"

"Yes, of course. Isn't that what I said in my letter to you?"

"You've always denied that was your letter."

Daniel shrugged. "I've stopped denying it." His eyes were still closed, but he could tell by the shifting of the cushions that Rey had moved closer. A fingertip traced the circle of pallor on each of his cheeks.

"Would you—" Rey faltered.

"Probably," said Daniel.

"—kiss me?"

Daniel arched his neck upward till his lips had touched Rey's, a very little distance.

"The way you would kiss a woman," Rey insisted in a hushed voice.

"Oh, I'll do better than that," Daniel assured him. "I'll love you!"

Rey sighed a sigh of gentle disbelief.

"Or at least," Daniel said, trying for a bit of tremolo of his own, "I'll see what I can do. Fair enough?"

Rey kissed one cheek. "And I—" Then the other. "—will teach you to sing. At least—"

Daniel opened his eyes at the same moment that Rey, with a look of pain and the hint of a tear, closed his.

"—I'll see what I can do."

As he was leaving the lobby with the empty pudding bowl, the doorman could be heard to mutter something subliminally derogatory. Daniel, still aglow with a sense of his victory, and proofed thereby against all injury, turned round and said, "I beg your pardon? I didn't catch that."

"I said," the doorman repeated murderously, "phoney, fucking whore."

Daniel considered this, and considered himself in the lobby's mirrored wall, while he ran a comb through his frizzy hair. "Yes, that may be," he concluded judiciously (tucking away the comb and taking up the bowl again). "But a *good* whore. As was my mother before me. And you can take our word, it's not easy."

He winked at the doorman and was out the door before the old fart could think of a comeback to that one.

But the distinction Daniel was making had not sunk very deep into the doorman's consciousness, for when Daniel was out of sight, he adjusted his visored and braided cap to a significant, steadfast angle and repeated his earlier, irrevocable judgement. "Phoney, fucking whore."

17

THOUGH IT HAD begun at four in the afternoon and no
one of any consequence had arrived till well after six, this
was officially a fellowship breakfast. Their host, Cardinal
Rockefeller, the Archbishop of New York, moved democratically from group to group, amazing one and all by
knowing who they were and why they'd been invited. Daniel was certain someone was prompting him via his hearing
aid, in the manner of carnival psychics, but perhaps that
was sour grapes, since the Cardinal, when he'd offered his
ring for Daniel to kiss, had affected to believe that he was
a missionary from Mozambique. Rather than contradict him
Daniel said that everything was swell in Mozambique, except that the missions were in desperate need of money, to
which the Cardinal equably replied that Daniel must speak
to his secretary, Monsignor Dubery.

Monsignor Dubery, a man of affairs, knew quite well
that Daniel was of Rey's party and would later be helping
to provide entertainment for the Cardinal's inner circle. He
tried his best to partner Daniel with other social pariahs
present, but all in vain. A black Carmelite nun from Cleveland snubbed Daniel soundly the moment the Monsignor's
back was turned. Then he was matched with Father Flynn,
the actual missionary from Mozambique, who regarded his
introduction to Daniel as a deliberate affront on the part of
Monsignor Dubery, and said so, though not to Dubery's
face. When Daniel, for want of other common grounds, told
of Cardinal Rockefeller's earlier confusion, Father Flynn lost
his bearings utterly and began, in a fury of indiscretion, to
denounce the entire archdiocese of Sodom, meaning New
York. Daniel, fearing to be blamed for deliberately provoking the man to these ecstasies, soothed and placated, with
no success. Finally he just came right out and warned Father
Flynn that he couldn't hope to advance the interests of his

mission by behaving so, and that seemed to serve. They parted quietly.

Hoping to avoid Monsignor Dubery's further attentions, Daniel strayed among the public rooms of the archiepiscopal residence. He watched a high-power game of snooker until he was given, politely, to understand that he was in the way. He studied the titles of books locked within their glass book-shelves. He had a second glass of orange juice but prevented the well-meaning bartender from slipping in any vodka, for he didn't dare tamper with what was so far, knock on wood, a completely level head.

Which he needed. For tonight he was making his debut. After fully a year of study with Rey, Daniel was going to sing in public. He would have preferred a debut uncompli-cated by social maneuverings with those who were shortly to provide his audience, but Mrs Schiff had explained what it had been too self-evident to Rey for him to attempt to discuss—the importance of starting at the top.

In all New York there could not have been a more select audience than that which attended Cardinal Rocke-feller's musicales. The Cardinal himself was a devotee of bel canto and was regularly to be seen in his box at the Meta-stasio. In return for his very visible patronage and the sparing use of his name in fund-raising brochures, the Meta-stasio supplied St Patrick's with a roster of soloists that no church in Christendom could have hoped to rival. It also supplied talent for more secular occasions, such as the pre-sent fellowship breakfast. Rey, though scarcely subject himself to such impressments, was a devout Catholic and quite content to grace the Cardinal's salon with his art so long as a certain reciprocity was maintained; so long, that is, as he was received as a guest and given access to the latest ecclesiastic scuttlebutt, which he followed with much the same fascination that the Cardinal gave to opera.

Daniel found an empty room, the merest closet with two chairs and a television, and sat down to nurse his drink and his anxiety. He thought, in principle, that he should have been at least nervous and possibly upset, but before he could begin to generate even a tremor in this direction, his intro-spections were derailed by a stranger in the uniform of the Puritan Renewal League. (Cardinal Rockefeller was notoriously ecumenical.) "Howdy," said the stranger, tipping his Stetson back to reveal a small freckled cross in the middle of his black forehead. "Mind if I just collapse in that other chair?"

"Be my guest," said Daniel.

"The name's Shelly," he said, collapsing. "Shelly Gaines. Isn't it awful the way, even when you're a phoney yourself, it's the first thing you notice in someone else? Other people, I could care less, but when I see one of my own, boom!" He tossed his Stetson on top of the tv. "Paranoia time. Do you suppose Hester Prynne ever came up against another lady with a scarlet letter embroidered on *her* blouse? And if so, was she friendly? Not likely, I think."

"Who was Hester Prynne?" Daniel asked.

"Foiled again," said Shelly Gaines. He found, on the floor beside his chair, a beermug with a third of the beer left in it and emptied it in one long chug-a-lug. "Cheers," he said, wiping his lips on the cuff of his denim jacket.

"Cheers," Daniel agreed, and finished his orange juice. He smiled at Shelly, for whom he'd felt an instant, patronizing friendliness. He was one of those people who should leave fashion well enough alone. A nondescript, round-faced, soft-bodied sort who would have been typecast as Everyman. Not the right kind of material for a phoney, or (Daniel would have supposed) for the P.R.L. And yet he tried so hard. Whose heart wouldn't have gone out to him?

"You're a Christian, aren't you?" Shelly asked, following his own dark trains of thought.

"Mm."

"I can always tell. Of course, people in our scrape don't have much choice in the matter. Are you here *with* someone? If I may be so bold."

Daniel nodded.

"R.C.?"

"Beg pardon?"

"You'll have to excuse me." He rolled his eyes, pressed his hand to his stomach, and brought forth a miniscule burp, "I've been drinking since four o'clock, and I've spent the last half-hour trying to talk with a missionary from somewhere in Africa who is quite insane. Understand, I have the greatest admiration for our brothers and sisters out there among the heathens, but good Lord, shouldn't *we* have our own folk-ways? Another rhetorical question. R.C. means Roman Catholic. Did you really not know?"

"No."

"And Hester Prynne is the heroine of *The Scarlet Letter*."

"I did know that."

"Guess who's with us tonight?" said Shelly, veering in a new direction.

"Who?"

"The mysterious Mr X. The guy who wrote *Tales of Terror*. Have you read it?"

"Bits."

"He was pointed out to me by dear old Dubery, who can be relied on, usually, to know about people's sins. But I must say the fellow seemed inoffensive to *me*. Now if he'd pointed you out as Mr X I'd have believed him implicitly."

"Because I do seem offensive?"

"Oh no. Because you're so good-looking."

"Even in blackface?" Poor Daniel. He could never keep from flirting. He dug for compliments as instinctively as a bird for worms.

"Even? Especially!" Then, after a pause meant to be pregnant with eye-contact: "Do you know, I could swear I know you from somewhere. Do you ever go to Marble Collegiate?"

"Van Dyke's church on Fifth Avenue?"

"And mine. I'm one of the great man's curates."

"No, I've never been there. Though I've thought of going lots of times. His book made a big impression on me when I was a teenager."

"On all of us. Are you in holy orders?"

Daniel shook his head.

"That was a stupid question. But I thought, because you're wearing that thing. . . ." He nodded at Daniel's crotch. "I was celibate myself once. Three and one-half years. But finally it was just too much for my weak flesh. I do admire those who have the strength. Are you staying for the *singspiel?*"

He nodded.

"And do you know what it's to be?"

"Ernesto Rey is here, and he's brought someone else. His protégé."

"Really! Then I suppose I'll have to linger on. Do you want another of whatever you're having?"

"Just orange juice, and no thank you, I don't."

"You don't drink? Pelion on Ossa!" Shelly Gaines levered himself up from his chair and turned to leave, then turned again to whisper to Daniel: "There he is. Just coming into the next room. Now who would suppose that *that* was Mr X?"

"The guy with the tie with the raindrops on it?"

"Raindrops? Good grief, what eyesight! It seems a plain blurry green to me, but yes, that's the man."

"No," said Daniel, "I certainly wouldn't have believed it."

When Shelly Gaines had gone to the bar, Daniel approached his old friend Claude Durkin, who was having a conversation with one of the more imposing priests at the party, a falcon-eyed man with an iron-gray crewcut and a loud, likeable laugh.

"Hi," said Daniel.

Claude nodded to him and went on talking, eyes averted from this unexpected embarrassment. Daniel stood his ground. The priest looked at him with amused interest, until Claude finally did a double-take.

"Oh my God," he said. "Ben!"

Daniel held out his hand, and Claude, with just the slightest hesitation, took it. In (as an afterthought) both of his.

"Claude, if you'll excuse me," said the priest, according Daniel a neutral but somehow still friendly smile, which Daniel returned with one of his best.

"I didn't recognize you," Claude said lamely, when they were left to themselves.

"I'm not recognizable."

"No. You're not. It *is* nice to. . . . For God's sake."

"I wasn't expecting to see you here either."

"It's my last night in town."

"Not on my account, I hope."

Claude laughed. "No, of course not. But it is startling, your warpaint. How long has it been since I last saw you? Not since you retrieved your suit from my closet, I think."

266

"Thank you for the loan of your tie, by the way. I see you got it back all right."

Claude looked down at his tie, as though he'd spilled something on it. "I did try to phone. They said *they* didn't know what had become of you either. Then when I called again, a while later, the number was disconnected."

"Yeah. The doughnut shop went out of business a long time ago. How have you been? And where are you going?"

"I've been fine. In fact, I'm a changed man. And I'm going to Anagni, south of Rome. Tomorrow."

Daniel looked at Claude and tried to rethink him as the author of *Tales of Terror* and the destroyer of the Alaska pipeline. He couldn't. "And what will you do in Anagni?"

"Build a cathedral?"

"You're asking me?"

"It sounds ridiculous, even to me, even now, but it's the God's truth. There was a cathedral there, one of the best Romanesque cathedrals. Frederick Barbarossa was excommunicated there. It was bombed, and I'm going there to help rebuild it. As one of the stone masons. I've joined the Franciscans, you see. Though I haven't taken my final vows. It's a long story."

"Congratulations."

"It's what I've always wanted. We'll be using almost the original technology, though we do cheat a little as to actually lifting the stones. But it will be a step up from just scrabbling about in the rubble for souvenirs. Don't you think?"

"I do. That's what I meant—congratulations."

"And you, Ben—what are you doing?"

"The same, pretty much. I'm doing what I've always wanted. You'll see, if you stay for the whole evening."

"You know, I don't think you've changed an iota."

"Does anyone, ever?"

"I hope so. I sincerely do hope so."

A bell rang, the signal for Daniel to change.

"Gotta go now. But can I ask you a question first? Strictly between ourselves."

"So long as you won't be offended if I don't answer it."

"On second thought, I'll just go on wondering. Anyhow,

you'd pretty well have to say no, even if the answer was yes."

"Those are always good questions to avoid, I agree. What a pity there's so little time left. It would be nice to get together for a more formal good-bye. Anyhow—good luck with your cathedral."

"Thanks, Claude. The same to you."

He offered his hand again, but Claude went him one better. He grasped him by the shoulders and solemnly and unpassionately, as though he were awarding the Legion of Honor, kissed each of his cheeks.

For the first time that evening, Daniel blushed.

While Rey sang his own brief offering, a Carissimi cantata abridged and ornamented by the trusty hand of Mrs Schiff, Daniel changed into his costume, an old tux from the back of Rey's closet, which he had, with the help of Mrs Galamian, the Metastasio's wardrobe mistress, meticulously tattered and torn. He *still* wasn't feeling more than agreeably nervous. Maybe he was one of those fortunate few who just weren't phased by performing. Maybe he'd actually enjoy it. He tried to concentrate on Rey's roulades, but for all the brilliance of the singing the music was almost impossible to fix one's attention on. Carissimi had had his off days, no doubt about it. He was, however, one of the Cardinal's particular favorites, so the propriety of Rey's choice could not be called into question. If Rey's impeccable pyrotechnics nevertheless left the audience (pared down now to a bare fifty or so) somewhat restive and willing to be cajoled into simply enjoying themselves, who could complain, except possibly Carissimi?

Rey finished and was applauded. He joined Daniel briefly in the green room, went out to take a second bow, and returned. "I shall go sit beside the Cardinal now," he advised Daniel. "Don't enter for another couple minutes."

Daniel watched the two minutes disappear on his wristwatch, then put on his ever-so-dented top hat, and made his entrance, smiling. Aside from the mildest tingling in his legs and lower back he had no symptoms of stagefright. The Cardinal was sitting in the third row of chairs with Rey, benignly impassive, beside him. Claude was in the first row next to the nun from Cleveland. Many of the Cardinal's other guests were familiar to Daniel from the Metastasio. One or two had taken him to dinner.

He lifted his hands, fingers spread wide, to frame his face. He let his eyes roll, slowly, to the back of his head. He began to sing. "Mammy!" he sang. "How I love ya, how I love ya! My dear old Mammy." He kept very close, vocally, to the authorized Jolson version, while exaggerating the body language. It was a polite version of the fractured minstrel-show he would perform to freak out selected strangers. He finished suddenly and, before there could be applause, moved right in to the next number, 'Nun wandre Maria' from Wolf's *Spanisches Liederbuch*. Daniel accompanied its tortured and rather schizzy pieties with the same overwrought gestures he'd used for 'Mammy'. They seemed, in this context, more like kabuki than schmaltz.

"The next song I'd like to sing for you," Daniel announced, removing his top hat and reaching into his pocket for a pair of rabbit ears, "needs a bit of introduction, but only a little bit. The lyrics are my own, though the idea behind them originates with the woman who wrote the music, Alicia Schiff. It's Bunny Honeybunny's opening number from a little musical we're putting together called *Honeybunny Time*." He fixed the rabbit ears in place. "There's nothing much you need to know about honeybunnies that the song doesn't pretty well explain, except that they're very lovable." He smiled. "So without more ado—" He nodded to the pianist. The rabbit ears wobbled on their wire stems and went on wobbling to the end of the song.

Goodness gracious sakes alive,
The bees are buzzing in their hive,
Making honey strangely sweet
Such as bunnies love to eat.

He sang as if transfigured by delight, negotiating the various vocal hurdles with room to spare. The music was ravishing, a chocolate box of a song that managed to make his dopey lyrics seem not only sincere but even, in a disturbing way, devotional. Where it really came alive was at the refrain, a long, looping chain of alleluias and la-la-las that soared and swooped and skittered around the steady swirling compulsions of the piano. Wonderful music, and here he was, standing in front of Cardinal Rockefeller and all his guests and singing it. He was aware, all the while he sang, of faces beginning to break into smiles, and aware, as he took in their reactions, of the music, and there was no disjunction between these two awarenesses.

> Eenie meenie meinie mo,
> Aren't those bees the limit though!
> They love me so, they'd never sting,
> And all I do for them is—sing!

Off he went on another roller-coaster ride of la-la-la's. This time, knowing that he'd brought it off once and could therefore bring it off again, he began, diffidently, to camp it up in proper honeybunny style. The people in the audience—that's what the faces had become: an audience; *his* audience—were grinning now, were eating out of his hand, were loving him.

Suddenly a switch flipped inside him, and a light came on, one bright flash of everlasting glory, and there was no way to explain it but he knew that if he'd been wired into a flight apparatus at just that moment (and the moment was gone already) he would have taken off. He knew it, and it made no difference, because he was flying already—up to the ceiling, around the chandelier, over the housetops, and across the wide blue sea.

He sang the last verse at full tilt, with weird, bemused exuberance.

> La di da and la di dee,
> This is living, yessiree!
> Eating honey from a comb
> In my honeybunny home!

For the third chorus he did, impromptu, what he'd never dreamed of doing during the weeks of rehearsal: he danced. It was unabashedly naïve, the merest hop and shuffle, but just right (he guessed) for a honeybunny. Anyhow it felt right, if also risky. Once, concentrating on his footwork, he almost lost hold of the vocal line, but if he'd fallen on his face it wouldn't have made any difference.

He had become a singer. Which nobody could deny.

"And will there be more honeybunny songs?" Cardinal Rockefeller inquired, after Daniel had returned from the green room in his own human character.

"I hope so, your Grace. We're working on it."

"When there are, I shall try to persuade you to exert your fascination over us again. Such charm and, if I may call it so, innocence are all too rare. You, and your distinguished teacher, are both to be commended."

Daniel murmured thanks, and Rey, by way of advertising this accolade to the company at large, knelt to kiss the Cardinal's ring. The Cardinal then led Rey off to an adjoining room and Daniel was left to receive various metaphorical posies of praise and a single matter-of-fact posy, from Monsignor Dubery, of six rather washed-up lilies. The nun from Cleveland apologized for her snub and gave him the address of her convent so he might send her the sheet music of this and all future honeybunny songs. Old acquaintances from the Metastasio offered prophecies of greatness.

When the circle of well-wishers had dwindled to a few garrulous shoulder-rubbers, Shelly Gaines, asserting the privilege of prior acquaintance, came forward with a drink in each hand—beer for himself, a screwdriver for Daniel— and commandeered the newborn star for, as he said, "some man-talk."

"Your own song is, of course, beyond all praise, and entirely anomalous, if that isn't the same thing. It isn't pop, though it is in a way, and it isn't bel canto, though it requires a voice of bel canto elasticity, and it's nothing at all like operetta, though I suppose that's what it must be nearest to. Really quite amazing—and in that I speak only of the song, nothing of the singer, who was—" Shelly rolled his eyes in imitation of Daniel's own neo-darktown-strutters style. "—the prophet of an entire new form of madness."

"Thank you."

"But beyond compliments, Ben. . . . May I call you Ben?" Daniel nodded.

"Beyond mere rapturous applause, Ben, I would like to

make you an offer." He raised a finger as though to fore-stall Daniel's objections. "A professional offer. I gather, from the second song on the program, that your goals aren't entirely limited to the, how shall I say, commercial side of show biz."

"Really, I don't have *any* goals."

"Now, now, no false modesty."

"I mean, I'm still a student. A student's goal is just to learn."

"Well then, my offer should interest you precisely as a student. How would you like to sing at Marble Collegiate? As one of our soloists."

"No fooling?" Daniel said, lighting up. And then, "No, that wouldn't be possible."

"Ah, the Cardinal has already taken you to *his* bosom, has he? One just can't be quick enough."

"No, not at all. And I'm sure he has no intention of doing so. He's got the whole Metastasio to take his pick from. I'm simply not up to that level."

"You'd certainly be up to ours, Ben. And then some. We're not especially notable for our music program. A Bach cantata is about our farthest stretch, and that only once or twice a year. On the other hand, we try for more than a sing-along. From your point of view it would represent experience, which is a commodity you won't be lacking for long, but do you, at the moment have any other plans? Rehearsals are on Wednesday evenings. And I think I could get a hundred a week out of the budget. What do you say?"

"What can I say? I'm flattered, but—"

"Mr Rey would object—is that it?"

"He might. More likely, he'd haggle over the fee."

"What else then?"

"Where would I be? In a loft at the back, or up front where people would be watching me?"

"Surely, Ben, after what I saw tonight, you're not going to tell me that you're the shy type! I've never seen such sang-froid. And in front of *this* audience!"

Daniel bit his lip. There was no way to explain. He'd known he'd come up against this problem as soon as he became, in any degree, successful, but despite the steady progress he'd made studying under Rey, success hadn't seemed an immediate danger. Hope had sprung eternal, of course, in his all-too-human breast, but the rational half of him, which was in charge of major decisions, had considered such hopes to be pipe-dreams, and so he'd let himself drift with the current from week to week till he arrived at the inevitable moment of decision, here at last.

How long, once he became, even in the smallest way, a public figure, could he hope to preserve his incognito? And more to the point: was that what he wanted, forever and always?

"Shelly," he temporized, "I'm grateful for your offer, believe me. And I'd like to say yes right now, but there's someone I have to talk it over with first. Okay?"

"You know where you can find me. Meantime, yours sincerely, and all that." Shelly, a little sad and rebuffed, departed, bumping into the music room's disordered chairs. No one else came forward.

Daniel looked for Claude through all the other rooms, but he must have left at the end of the concert. A small desolation settled over Daniel's spirit. He wanted to deposit his six lilies in a waste basket (he was certain they'd done duty at a week of funerals) and go home and crash.

But that would never do. It was important now to circulate, and so he circulated. But as far as he personally was concerned the party was over.

Claude had not forgotten him, however. The next morning a delivery truck appeared on West 65th with a peculiar and very precious cargo, consisting of (1) a Sony flight apparatus, (2) a tombstone with a limerick on it, and (3) a tie representing raindrops. There was also a telegraphically short letter from Claude saying good-bye, explaining that Franciscans weren't allowed to fly, and wishing him good luck as a honeybunny.

When the delivery men were gone and his room had been rearranged to accommodate the two new items of furniture, Daniel sat down before the flight apparatus and let temptation have its way with him. But he knew he wasn't ready, and he knew that he'd know when he was, and he didn't succumb.

That night, as though in recompense, he had his first

(actually his second) real flying dream. He dreamed he was flying over an imaginary Iowa, an Iowa of marble mountains and blithe valleys, of golden, unreal cities and fabulous farms dazzling the eye with fields of Fabergé wheat. He woke unwilling to believe it had been only a dream. But grateful, nevertheless, to have been given so unmistakable a sign.

18

EARLIER ON THE evening of that dream, in the taxi returning from Cardinal Rockefeller's, Rey had hinted at the possibility, then announced the fact, of Daniel's manumission. Daniel expressed an honest surprise and a not dishonest regret; prudently, he did not by so much as one hurrah express his jubilation.

It was not to be an absolute sundering. Daniel would continue to study with the great Ernesto, but on the more customary footing of offering him, in lieu of immediate payment, a third of his professional income over the next seven years. Daniel signed a contract to this effect, witnessed by Mrs Schiff and Irwin Tauber, who, as Daniel's agent, was to receive a further fifteen per cent. If this were exploitation, Daniel was delighted to be considered prospectively exploitable. Could there be any sincerer testimony to their faith in his future than their wanting to secure a piece of it for themselves?

His delight was soon to be tempered by the reality of his first paycheck. His wage from Marble Collegiate was an even hundred dollars; after deductions for Federal, State, and City taxes and for Social Security, and after Rey's and Tauber's percentages, Daniel was left with $19.14. So, when fall arrived, it was back to the Metastasio. Mr Ormund kindly allowed him to take off early on Wednesdays to attend his choir's rehearsals. Further, he was promoted to the position (alternating with Lee Rappacini) of croupier on the casino's roulette wheel, a post which, even after the Metastasio's and Mr Ormund's rake-offs, was an undeniably juicy plum.

Not that Daniel was given to fretting about money. He was still predominantly of the grasshopper persuasion and unable to take alarm at remote contingencies. By the terms of his agreement with Rey, Boa would be looked after for another year. Congress, meanwhile, was drawing up a uniform code of laws concerning flight, a code that would certainly see to it that no one would be put in the impossible position Daniel had been in, of being able to keep Boa alive only by resorting to the black market. In a year's time, when Daniel would have to reassume the burden of her support, it should not, therefore, be quite so crushing and unfair a burden. If he saved, he might even be able to put her back in First National Flightpaths. Such are a grasshopper's sanguine, summertime thoughts.

Having had, on the whole, a rather easy time of it during his year of concubinage, Daniel did not find freedom going to his head. In any case, these terms are relative. In a practical sense his life wasn't much changed, except that now he could, when the urge came over him, go out and get laid. Mostly, however, except for a three-day binge right after the belt came off, the urge didn't come over him, not in the old overmastering and time-consuming way. This diminution of his erstwhile perpetual motion may have had something to do with sublimation, but he doubted it. Renata Semple had always maintained that sublimation was a load of Freudian bullshit, that the best lays also transmitted the largest zaps of creative energy. Maybe he was just getting old and wearing out. Maybe his present sex-life represented the optimum level for his metabolism and previously he'd been overdoing it. In any case he was happy, wasn't he, so why worry?

For two months he'd been letting his skin fade back to its natural color when an incident at the Natural History Museum made him think again. He was wandering lonely as a cloud among cases of curious rocks and mineral specimens, letting his mind get lost in the twists and turns, the dazzle and glitter of Nature's own chinoiseries, when out of the dim past stepped Larry, the counterman of the now defunct Dodge 'Em Doughnut Shop. Larry, with more directness than grace, dropped a metaphorical handkerchief at Daniel's feet, waited to see if it would be picked up, and when it wasn't, moved on to some ore-bearing boulders with a wistful, hard-boiled, "All right, Sambo, whatever you say." And never a glimmer of recognition. There was a time, and rather a long one, when Daniel had seen Larry on the average of twice a day to pick up his phone messages and generally to coze. Larry, admittedly, had a partiality for phoneys, but even so! Is love as blind as that?

Daniel knew that every time he sang at Marble Collegiate he was taking a calculated risk of being recognized by someone from the still dimmer past. Because of Van Dyke's association with the P.R.L. there was a constant influx of church groups and convention delegates dropping in for the Sunday services, and among these visitors there was bound, some time, to be someone from Amesville or environs who'd known the old, unreconstructed Daniel Weinreb. His fears hadn't finally stood in the way of his taking the job, but it might be just as well to continue to wear a mask that had proven so effective. Everyone would suppose he remained a phoney by preference, but that couldn't be helped. Besides, admit it, it had its moments.

He determined, at least, to change his markings. On his next visit to the cosmetician he had a small, mandorla-shaped spot bleached out high on his forehead, a process as painful as it was expensive. Then, to his great and immediate relief, the circles on his cheeks were filled in and his frizzed hair was straightened and cut to form a bang of oily ringlets obscuring the upright almond of whiteness on his brow. The new mask, being less flaunting, was even more effective as a disguise. His own mother, as the saying goes, wouldn't have known him now.

A year passed: a year immense with events, prodigies of history and of his own changed heart (if the heart it is, indeed, that registers the sense of vocation, of being summoned to a destined task, and not the eyes, or hands, or spine); a year of blessed tumult; a happy year too quickly gone by. What he did in that year could be quickly told. With Mrs Schiff he finished a draft of a full-scale two-act version of *Honeybunny Time*, which Tauber immediately began showing to producers (all of them thought it was a put-on), and he wrote, or re-wrote, some seven or eight songs of his own. But what he learned would require a fairly epic catalogue. Insights blossomed into fugitive visions, branched into viable propositions, interlocked into systems, and the systems themselves seemed to resonate mysteriously with all manner of things, great and small, with his hugest, haziest intuitions as with the curves and colors of a gladiolus in a plastic pot. It was as though he'd been offered an interlinear translation to the whole span of his life. Old chunks of unsorted awareness fell together in patterns as lucid as a Mozart melody. Once, home alone and scaling the heights of *Don Giovanni*, the shape of the day's epiphany was just that: a mere seven notes that seemed, from the height at which he heard them, to say more of justice, judgement and tragic fate than all of Aeschylus and Shakespeare rolled into one. It didn't have to be music that got him going, though it was usually a work of art and not the raw materials of Nature. New York doesn't have that much unmodified Nature to offer, except its skies and what could be made to grow in the park, but it was chock-full of artifice and booming day and night with music. Daniel didn't want for stimuli.

How long could one go on summing things up like this? Mrs Schiff said forever, so long as one remained on friendly terms with one's Muse. But who was the Muse and what did she require? There Mrs Schiff could offer no oracles.

The question was important to Daniel, for he'd come in a rather superstitious way to believe that possibly Boa was his Muse. Hadn't his awakening coincided with the time that he'd brought her here to live with him? But how ridiculous, to speak at all of 'living' with her, when she was nothing but an empty shell. It was with Mrs Schiff, it was with Rey, that he'd *lived* for these three years. Yet he didn't for a moment suppose them to be Muses. They'd been his teachers; or, if that didn't do them sufficient honor or express the size of the debt, his Masters. The Muse was something, or some One, else.

The Muse, first of all, was a woman, a woman to whom one remained faithful, and Daniel had, in his fashion, remained faithful to Boa. This might or might not be significant, might or might not connect to some fundamental bedrock of truth beneath the unexplored murk of the subconscious. When it wasn't shining in the clear sunlight of joy, sex could be infinitely mysterious. But Daniel's conception of Boa as his Muse was more literal than that. He thought of her as an active presence, a benign will-o'-wisp, touching his spirit and lighting his way with unseen, subliminal glimmerings. In much the same way he had, in his earliest youth, imagined his mother flying to him from far away, hovering over him, whispering to him, regarding him with a mournful, secret love that had been, nevertheless, the force that had sustained him through the desolations of the first loneliest years in Amesville. He had been wrong then; his mother had not been with him, had never known how to fly. But did that mean he was wrong now? Boa *was* a fairy; she might be with him; he believed she was, and, believing it, he spoke to her, prayed to her, beseeched her to let him off the hook.

For the free ride was over. Rey, though he'd regarded it as an unqualified waste of money, had fulfilled the terms of their agreement. Now, with that debt satisfied, it was up to Daniel. Boa's minimum weekly requirement cost a whopping $163, and there was no let-up in sight, as this wasn't the black market price. Rationing was over, and Daniel was able to buy her supplies directly from the First National Flightpaths' pharmacy. $163 represented the basic cost of one week's vacation outside your body as fixed by the new Federal guidelines. By this means the government hoped to discourage fairies from permanently abandoning their vehicles by the roadside. Logically Daniel had to approve the new uniform code Congress had come up with—even in this particular. Alackaday, who would have supposed that such a wonder's coming to pass would have been nothing but a new source of grief for Daniel, who had marched in so many parades and sung at so many rallies in this very cause? But such was the case, and though there had been a few woeful outcries in the press from parents and spouses (and even a granddaughter) who were in the same costly fix as Daniel, there really wasn't much hope of this law being changed, for it represented a genuine consensus.

$163 stood at the borderline of what was possible and left a very scant residue from which to supply his own necessities. It was painful, it was downright cruel, to be earning a good living for the first time in years and still to have no security, no comfort, no fun. He let Boa know it in no uncertain terms (assuming she was listening in). Enough was enough. He wanted to be rid of her. It wasn't fair of her to expect him to go on like this. Fifteen years! He threatened to phone her father, and set deadlines for doing so, but since these threats weren't carried out, he had to assume either that she wasn't listening, or didn't believe his threats, or didn't care. Upping the ante, he menaced her with being disconnected from the umbilicus of tubes that sustained her vegetable life, but this was the merest huffing and puffing. Kill Boa? She was, God knows, an albatross around his neck; she was a constant memento mori (more so than ever, now that Claude Durkin's tombstone nestled at the foot of her bed); but she was his wife, and she might be his Muse, and to fail in his obligation to her would just be asking for trouble.

Aside from these notions about his Muse, Daniel was not, in general, a superstitious sort, but he was fast becoming a Christian, at least in the latter-day sense of the word as set forth in the teachings of Reverend Jack Van Dyke. According to Van Dyke, all Christians got to be that way by suspending their disbelief in a preposterous but highly improving fairy tale. This presented no difficulties to Daniel, who took naturally to pretending. His whole life these days was a game of make-believe. He pretended to be black. He had pretended, for one whole year, to be passionately in love with a eunuch. Sometimes he and Mrs Schiff would pretend for hours at a time to be honeybunnies. Why not pretend to be a Christian? (Especially if it brought in, theoretically, a hundred bucks a week and, more to the point, a chance to perform in physical and social dimensions that suited the size of his voice and his art, which Marble Collegiate did to a T.) Why not *say* he was saved, if it might make someone else happy and did him no harm? Wasn't that all most priests and ministers do? He'd never been the type, when people asked how he was feeling and he was feeling rotten, to *say* he felt rotten. He said he felt swell, and smiled, and he expected others to do the same. That was simply civilization, and so far as he could see, Christianity was just the logical outcome of such principles, the most devious and effective way ever discovered of being polite.

Mrs Schiff, an old-fashioned atheist, didn't approve of his conversion, as he styled it, and they had some of their most enjoyable arguments on this topic. She said it wasn't intellectually self-respecting to say you believed (for instance) that someone could die and then return to life, which was what Christianity boiled down to. It was all right for people who really did believe such nonsense to say so; it was even good that they did, since it gave one fair warning as to the limits of their rationality. But in Daniel it was charlatanry pure and simple. Daniel replied that nothing was pure and simple, least of all himself.

Once, when Mrs Schiff had been dead-certain about a fact of music history (had Schumann written a violin concerto?), he made a wager with her, the forfeit being that she must accompany him to Marble Collegiate on a Sunday of his choosing. She was wrong. He chose a Sunday when Van Dyke was to preach on the immortality of the soul, and Daniel would be singing in Bach's *Actus Tragicus*. It was not, as it turned out, one of Van Dyke's best efforts, and the choir as well (including, alas, Daniel) had bitten off rather more than they could chew. Mrs Schiff was commiserating, but otherwise unmoved.

"Of course," she conceded, "one must be grateful to churches for providing free concerts this way, but it does smack a little of the soup kitchen, doesn't it? One has to sit there for the sermon and the rest of it for the sake of a very little music."

"But that isn't the point," Daniel insisted, somewhat testily, for he was still smarting from the mess he'd made of *'Bestellet dein Haus'*. "People don't go to church for the sake of the music. They go there to be with the other people who go there. Being physically present, that's the crucial thing."

"Do you mean that it's a kind of proof that there is a community and they're part of it? I should think a concert would do that just as well, or better, since one can talk in the intervals. And the music, if you'll forgive my saying so, would probably be a touch more professional."

"I stank, I know that, but my singing, good or bad, is irrelevant."

"Oh, you weren't the worst offender. Far from it. You're learning to fake the notes you can't reach very ably. But what *is* the point, Daniel? In a word."

"In a word, hope."

"Well then, in a few words."

"What was the cantata about? Death. The fact that that is what's in store for all of us, and that there's no way round it, and we all *know* there's no way round it."

"Your Mr Van Dyke maintains differently."

"And so did you, just by being there. That's the point. Everyone has doubts. Everyone despairs. But when you're there in church, surrounded by all those other people, it's hard not to believe that some of them don't believe *something*. And by our being there we're helping them believe it."

"But what if all of them are thinking the same as us? What if none of them are bamboozled and are just offering their moral support to others, who similarly aren't bamboozled?"

"It's a matter of degree. Even I'm bamboozled, as you say, a little. Even you are—if not in church, then when you're listening to music, and even more when you're writing your own. What's the difference, ultimately, between Bunny Honeybunny's song and Bach's saying, 'Come, sweet hour of death, for my soul is fed with honey from the mouth of the lion'?"

"The chief difference is that Bach's is immeasurably greater music. But I should say another difference is that my tongue is firmly in my cheek concerning the philosophic views of honeybunnies."

"Your tongue isn't entirely in your cheek, though, and perhaps Bach's isn't completely out of his. He has his ambiguous moments."

"But he knows, he says, that his Redeemer liveth. And *I* know that mine doesn't."

"So you say."

"And what do you say, Daniel Weinreb?"

"More or less the same as you, I suppose. But I *sing* something else."

It was the night before Christmas, and the night before the night before Daniel was to appear in the Off-Broadway première of *Honeybunny Time*. Dreams, it seems, really do come true. But he was not happy, and it was hard to explain to Boa, who was the underlying cause of this unhappiness, why this should be so. There she sat, propped up in her little cot, a Christmas angel complete with a halo and a pair of wings from Mrs Galamian's stock of costumes for the first-act dream-ballet that had been scrapped during the last week of rehearsals. Yet the problem was easily stated. He was broke, and while his prospects had never been brighter, his income had rarely been less. He'd had to leave the Metastasio two months ago, time enough to exhaust the little money he'd put away to tide him through an emergency. But this was the one emergency he hadn't reckoned with—success. Rey and Tauber were both adamant as to receiving their full cuts. Daniel had done the arithmetic, and even if *Honeybunny Time* didn't just fizzle right out, Daniel's net earnings from it would still fall short of what was required at the heady rate of some three hundred dollars a month. And if the show were a smash, he wouldn't do any better, since he'd had to sign over his interest in the book for the chance to play Bunny. That, as Irwin Tauber had explained, was show business. But try and explain that to a corpse.

"Boa," he said, touching one of the nylon wings. But he didn't know where to go from there. To talk to her at all was an admission of faith, and he didn't want to believe, any more, that she might be alive, and listening, and biding her time. If she were, it was cruel of her not to return. If she weren't, if she'd left this world for ever, as she'd left this husk of herself, this disposable container, then there could be no harm in his ceasing to care for it as well. "Boa, I'm not giving up another fifteen years. And I'm not going to peddle my ass again. I suppose I could ask Freddie Carshalton to loan me something, but I'm not going to. Or Shelly Gaines, who probably doesn't have it to spare. What I am going to do is I'm going to call your father. If that's wrong, then I'll just have to bear the guilt. Okay?"

The halo glinted.

"If you want to come back later, you'll have to come back to him. Maybe that's what you've been waiting for. Am I right?"

He leaned forward, careful not to touch the tube that snaked into her left nostril, and kissed the lips that were legally dead. Then he got up and went out into the hall and down the hall to Mrs Schiff's office, where the telephone was.

In all these years he'd never forgotten the phone number for Worry.

An operator answered at the third ring. He said he wanted to speak to Grandison Whiting. The operator asked his name. He said only that it was a personal call. The operator said she would give him Mr Whiting's secretary.

Then a new voice said, "Miss Weinreb speaking."

Daniel was too taken aback to reply.

"Hello?"

"Hello," he echoed, forgetting to use the deeper voice with which he'd addressed the operator. "Miss Weinreb?"

Which Miss Weinreb? he wondered. His secretary!

"I'm afraid Mr Whiting isn't available at the moment. I'm his secretary. Can I take a message?"

In the other room Daniel could hear the telephone ringing. But it couldn't be the telephone. It must be the doorbell. In which case Mrs Schiff would answer it.

"Which Miss Weinreb would that be?" he asked cautiously. "Cecelia Weinreb?"

"This is Aurelia." She sounded miffed. "Who is *this*, please?"

"It's a personal call. For Mr Whiting. It concerns his daughter."

There was a long silence. Then Aurelia said, "Which daughter?" Hearing her dawning surmise, he became uneasy.

At that moment Mrs Schiff burst into the office. In one hand she held the halo from Boa's head. He knew, just by looking, what she was going to tell him. He replaced the phone in its cradle.

It hadn't been the doorbell.

"It's Boa," he said. "She's come back."

Mrs Schiff nodded.

Boa was alive.

Mrs Schiff put the halo down on top of the desk, where it rocked unsteadily. Her hands were shaking. "You'd better go see her, Daniel. And I'll phone for a doctor."

19

A WEEK AFTER it opened at the Cherry Lane, *Honeybunny Time* was transferred uptown to the St James Theater, right across the street from the Metastasio, and Daniel was a star. His name, his own name, the name of Daniel Weinreb, was spelled out on the marquee in winking lights. His face, dark as molasses, could be seen on posters all over the city. His songs were on the radio day and night. He was rich and he was famous. *Time* featured him on its cover, rabbit ears and all, under a 36-point rainbow-shaped and -hued headline asking, portentously: BEL CANTO—IS THAT ALL THERE IS? Inside, in an exclusive article, Mrs Schiff told something like the story of his life.

It was not his doing. Or perhaps it was. The phonecall to Worry had been automatically recorded and traced by Whiting's security system. At his sister's suggestion, the voice-prints of the call were compared with those of tapes Daniel had made with Boa in days gone by.

The police appeared at the door of Mrs Schiff's apartment at the very moment the curtain was going up on *Honeybunny Time*. Mrs Schiff, presciently indisposed, was on hand to receive them. Boa had already been taken off to a clinic to recuperate from the effects of her fifteen-year-long coma and so was spared the first onslaught. When the police had finally been persuaded that only Daniel could supply them with the name of the clinic and had been despatched to the Cherry Lane, Mrs Schiff, seeing that the cat was, in any case, out of the bag, decided to cash in her chips. With Irwin Tauber's help she got through to the editor-in-chief of *Time*, and before Daniel had sung the closing reprise of 'Honeybunnies go to Heaven', she had struck a deal, giving *Time* exclusive rights to her own 4,000-word version of the romance of Daniel Weinreb. There was no way, after that, that *Honeybunny Time* wasn't going to be a hit.

Daniel was furious, but also, secretly, delighted. Even so, he determined, for form's sake, to be angry with Mrs Schiff for having so profitably violated his confidences. Of course, it had only been a matter of time, once his phonecall to Worry had been traced, before Daniel was apotheosized; a matter of hours, probably, as Mrs Schiff tried, through Irwin, to explain. And, to do her credit, her version of the past three years was as skillful a whitewash as any press agent could have contrived. According to Mrs Schiff Daniel's relationship with Rey had been based on mutual esteem and a shared devotion to the glory of the human voice. Her story dwelt mainly on Daniel's undying love for his wife, his struggles against manifold adversities (she included his recipe for bread pudding), the discovery of his buried talent and (this last being intended, surely, as a private poke in the ribs) his Christian faith. Nowhere did she state anything that wasn't strictly true, but it was scarcely the whole truth; nor—such were her powers as a storyteller—did the whole truth ever make much headway, once it did begin to leak out, via Lee Rappacini and a few other old friends. The media doesn't like to waste its heroes, and that's what Daniel had become.

Boa was preserved from most of this within the heavily guarded portals of the Betti Bailey Memorial Clinic, an upper-crust, Westchester version of First National Flightpaths. At her own orders no one but Daniel and the Clinic's staff were to be allowed into her room. He came there once a day in a rented limousine. While the limousine waited for the gates to be opened, the press would gather round with their cameras and their questions. Daniel would smile at them through the bullet-proof glass, which served the camera's needs. As to the questions—Where had Boa been these many years? Why had she returned? What were her plans?—Daniel was as much in the dark as anyone, for they had yet to speak to each other. Usually she was asleep, or pretending to be asleep, and he would sit by her bed, arranging hecatombs of cut flowers and waiting for her to make the first move. He wondered how much of all he'd said over the last three years she'd been at hand to take in. He didn't want to go through it all again, and in any case little of that was any longer to the point. The Boa who'd come back bore no resemblance to the living Boa he remembered. She was the same gaunt, hollow-eyed object that had lain all those years, inert, on the other side of his room, whom to love was as impossible as if she had been a bundle of sticks. She seemed infinitely old and wasted. Her dark hair was streaked with gray. She did not smile. Her hands lay at her sides as though she had no interest in them, as though they were not hers but only a more cumbersome piece of bed linen. Once in these two weeks of visits she had opened her eyes to look at him, and then had closed them again when she saw that he'd become aware of her attention.

Yet he knew she was capable of speech, for she'd given orders to the staff not to admit any visitors but Daniel. Even this small distinction was scarcely a balm to his heart when he knew, through Dr Ricker, the Director of the Clinic, that no one, aside from the press, had sought to be admitted. Once Boa's miraculous return to life had become a matter of public interest, her father had made himself unavailable for comment. To the rest of the world Daniel and Boa may have been the love story of the century, but to Grandison Whiting they were gall and wormwood. He was not, Daniel supposed, a forgiving sort of person.

Meanwhile, Daniel's bandwagon rolled onwards and upwards, a triumphal chariot, a juggernaut of success. Five of his songs were at the top of the charts. The two most popular, 'Flying' and 'The Song Does Not End', were songs he'd written in the sauna of Adonis, Inc., back before any of this had begun. Except, logically, it must have begun then, or even before. Perhaps it all went back to that spring day on County Road B, when he'd been stopped in his tracks by that devastating inkling of some unknown glory. Sometimes he'd look up at the issue of *Time* that he'd nailed to the wall of his room at the Plaza with four stout nails and wonder if *that* had been the actual, foredestined shape of the vision that had loomed behind the clouds that day— that dark face with its animal ears and the dumb question rainbowed over it. He would have preferred a more inward and transfiguring glory to have been intended, as who would not, but if this was what the moving finger had writ, it would be churlish not to be grateful for benefits received—and received, and received.

The next rung of the ladder, the next plum to fall in his lap, was an hour-and-a-half special on A.B.C. A third of the program was to be numbers from *Honeybunny Time*; another third, a selection of bel canto arias and duets featuring the great Ernesto, with Daniel doing little more than waft, metaphorically, an ostrich-feather fan; then, after a medley of such personal favorites as 'Old Black Joe' and 'Santa Lucia', learned in Mrs Boismortier's classroom, there was to be a re-creation of 'The March of the Businessmen' from *Gold-Diggers of 1984* (with Jackson Florentine making a guest appearance), winding up with the inevitable 'Flying', in which an entire chorus was to be borne aloft on wires. Irwin Tauber, who had volunteered, with a shrewdness equal to his magnanimity, to reduce his commission to a standard ten per cent, sold the package for three-and-a-half million dollars, of which Rey, in return for relinquishing his over-all slice of Daniel's next seven years, was to receive a million and a half outright.

Midas-like, Daniel's success affected everyone within touching distance. Rey, besides his million and a half, booked a tour through the Midwest. Rather, he expanded the tour he'd already been planning, for the whole country was, quite independently of Daniel, in the throes of a passion for all things musical, but especially for bel canto. Rey, a legend in his own right, had become by his association with Daniel exponentially more legendary, and his fees reflected it. Mrs Schiff, too, had her share of these repletions. Besides the royalties rolling in from *Honeybunny Time*, the Metastasio had agreed, against all precedent, to present *Axur, re d'Ormus* as her original work, dispensing with the fiction that it was from the hand of Jommelli. She brought out her own long-playing record of *Stories for Good Dogs*. She opened a pet show at Madison Square Garden. She appeared on a list of the Ten Best-Dressed Women.

Perhaps the strangest consequence of Daniel's celebrity was the cult that sprang up around not just his myth but his image. His younger admirers, not content with mere passive adulation, determined to follow his darkling example and went out, in their thousands and soon their tens of thousands, and had themselves transformed into exact replicas of their idol—to the often considerable dismay of their thousands and tens of thousands of parents. Daniel became, by this means, a *cause célèbre*, a symbol of all that was most to be extolled or most to be abhorred in the new era, a real-life Honeybunny or the Anti-Christ, depending on who you listened to. His face, on a million posters and record-sleeves, was the standard that the era lifted up in defiance of the age gone by. Daniel, at the center of all this commotion, felt as helpless as a statue borne aloft in a procession. His position gave him a wonderful view of the surrounding bedlam, but he had no idea at all where he was being carried. He loved every ridiculous minute, though, and hoped it would never stop. He started making notes for a new musical that he wanted to call *Highlights of Eternity*, or else *Heads in the Clouds*, but then one day he'd read through his notes and realized they didn't make any sense. He had nothing to say. He only had to stand in the spotlight and smile. He had to pretend to be this fabulous creature, Daniel Weinreb. Nothing more was asked.

On an afternoon in February, on a day of bright and numbing cold, Boadicea opened her eyes and drew a deep breath that was partly a sigh and partly a yawn. Daniel didn't dare so much as look toward her for fear of startling her back into the glades of her long silence. He went on staring at the facets of the stone in his ring, waiting for her mind to materialize before him in the form of words. At last the words arrived, faint and colorless. "Dear Daniel." She seemed to be dictating a letter. He looked at her, not knowing how to reply. She didn't look away. Her eyes were like porcelain, shining but depthless. "I must thank you for . . . the many flowers." Her lips closed and tightened to signify a smile. The least movement, the blinking of her eyelids, seemed to require a conscious effort.

"You're welcome," he answered carefully. What does one say to a bird that decides to light on one's finger? Hesitantly, he spoke of crumbs: "If there's anything else I can bring you, Boa, just say the word. Anything that might help to pass the time."

"Oh, it passes without help. But thank you. For so much. For keeping this body of mine alive. It still seems strange." She turned her head to one side, then the other, "like a pair of very stiff shoes. But they're getting broken in. Day by day. I practise. I forge new habits. This morning, for the first time, I practised smiling. It suddenly seemed important. They didn't want me to have a mirror, but I insisted."

"I saw your smile," he noted weakly.

"It's not very authentic yet, is it? But I'll get the hang of it soon enough. Speech is much more difficult, and I already speak very clearly, do I not?"

"Like a native. But don't feel you have to. I mean, if it doesn't feel comfortable yet. There's plenty of time, and I'm a basically very patient person."

"Indeed. The nurses say you have been a saint. They are, all three of them, in love with you."

"Tough luck. I'm already taken." Then, abashed: "That's not to say . . . I mean, I don't expect, after all this time. . . ."

"Why not? Isn't it the best thing to do with bodies when you have them? So I seem to recall." She practised her smile, with no greater success than before. "But I agree, it would be premature. I have been amazed, though, how quickly it all does come back. The words, and the way they try to connect with more meanings than they ever possibly will. As a fairy, one learns to do without them, by and large. But that was the reason I came back."

"I'm afraid I lost track of that. *What* was the reason you came back?"

"To talk to you. To tell you you must learn to fly. To carry you off, so to speak."

He winced, visibly.

She went on in the same evangelical vein. "You can, Daniel. I know there was a long time when you couldn't. But you can now."

"Boa, I've tried. Believe me. Too many times."

"Precisely: too many times. You've lost faith in yourself, and naturally that gets in the way. But before I returned to this body I watched you. For days, I don't know how many, I watched you sing. And it was there, all that you need. It was there in the very words of one of the songs.

290

Honey from the mouth of the lion. If you'd been using a machine, you would have taken off any number of times."

"It's good of you to say so. But I'm sorry that was your reason for having come back. It's a bit of a lost cause, I'm afraid."

Boa blinked. She lifted her right hand and, as she looked at it, the first flicker of distinct expression stirred the muscles of her face. It was an expression of distaste.

"I didn't come back for any other reason, Daniel. Though I have no wish to have to deal with my father, that was a secondary consideration. Your threat possibly made me return a little sooner. But I never thought, and surely had no desire, to begin this . . . circus."

"I'm sorry about the fuss. It hasn't been my doing, though I guess I haven't exactly resisted it either. I enjoy circuses."

"Enjoy what you can, by all means. I've enjoyed myself largely enough, these fifteen years and more. And I shall again."

"Ah! You mean, you already intend . . . when you've got back the strength . . . ?"

"To take off again? Yes, of course—as soon as I can. What other choice can there be, after all? It is, as my father might say, a business proposition. Here one finds, at most, only a little pleasure; there, there is only pleasure. Here, if my body perishes, I must perish with it; when I am there, the body's death will cease to concern me. My care, then, is for my safety. Why should I be trapped in the collapse of a burning building, when all that is required to escape it is that I walk out the door?"

"Ma'am, you preach a powerful sermon."

"You're laughing at me. Why?"

He threw up his hands in a gesture of self-parody that had become as automatic as the inflections of his voice. "Am I? If I am, then it's at myself that I laugh. All you say is true. So true it seems ridiculous that I'm still around, discussing the matter."

"It does seem so strange to me. It isn't just you—it's all these people. Most of them don't even try. But maybe that will change. *You* must try, at least." Her voice seemed oddly out of tune when she spoke with any emphasis. "Perhaps our circus may do some good, after all. You are so much in the public eye. You can set an example."

He snorted in self-derision, then felt ashamed. She didn't know his reasons, he hadn't told her what he'd done just that afternoon.

"I'm sorry," he said, with grudging penitence. "I was laughing at myself again. I did something today I shouldn't have done, that I'm already regretting."

"Was that a laugh, before? It didn't seem so." She didn't ask what he'd done. Her eyes seemed incurious.

But he didn't let that stand in the way of his confession. "You see," he explained, "I said, in an interview this afternoon, that I *could* fly. That I love to fly. That I'm always just zipping off into the ether, which I described in abundant detail."

"So? I see no harm in saying that. You *can* fly."

"But I never have, Boa. I never, never, never have, and despite your glad tidings I've got a feeling that I never will. But after what I said today, I'm going to have to go on pretending for the whole fucking world."

"Why did you say it then?"

"Because my agent has been pressuring me to for weeks. For my image. Because it's what people expect of me, and you've got to give them their money's worth. But I'll tell you where I draw the line. I'm not going to pretend to take off in the middle of a concert. That is just too gross. People wouldn't believe it."

She looked at him as though from the depth of a cold, clear pond. She had not believed what he'd said.

"And because, finally, I *want* people to think that I can. Because, if I can't, then I'm no better than Rey."

"How strange. Your words make less and less sense. I think, perhaps, if you would leave now. . . ? I mean to answer all the questions you've been so kind as not to ask. I know I owe that to you, but it's a long story, and I'm tired now. And confused. Could we put it off till tomorrow?"

He shrugged, and smiled, and felt resentful. "Sure. Why not?" He stood up, and took a step toward her bed, and then thought better of it.

She looked straight at him and asked, tonelessly, "What do you want, Daniel?"

"I was wondering if I should kiss you. As a matter of courtesy."

"I'd rather you didn't, really. It's my body, you see. I don't like it. I'm not, in a sense, quite alive yet. Once I've begun to enjoy food again—perhaps then."

"Fair enough." He lifted his coat from the hook on the back of the door. "I'll see you tomorrow."

"Tomorrow," she agreed.

When he was almost out the door she called him back, but in so weak a voice he wasn't certain, till he'd looked around, that he'd heard her speak his name.

"On second thought, Daniel, *would* you kiss me? I don't like my body. Perhaps I'll like yours."

He sat beside her on the bed. He picked up her limp hand from where it lay on the unruffled sheet and placed it on his neck. Her fingers held to his skin infirmly, with only enough strength to support the weight of her arm.

"Does it turn you off," he asked, "my being a phoney?"

"Your skin? It seems an odd thing for you to have done, but it all seems odd, the way people act. Why did you do it?"

"You don't know?"

"I know very little about you, Daniel."

He put his hands about her head. It seemed insubstantial, the wispy graying hair like ashes. There was no tension, no resistance in her neck—nor, it would seem, anywhere in her body. He inclined his head till their lips were touching. Her eyes were open but unfocused. He moved his lips by fractions of inches, as though he were whispering into her mouth. Then he parted her lips with his tongue, pushed past her teeth. His tongue nudged hers. There was no reply. He continued to move his tongue over and around hers. There began to be a resisting tension in her neck. She closed her eyes. With a parting nip of her lower lip, he disengaged.

"Well?" he asked. "What does it do for you?"

"It was . . . I was going to say frightening. But interesting. It made you seem like an animal. Like something made of meat."

"That's why they're called carnal relations, I guess." He lowered her head to the pillow and replaced her hand at her side. He forebore to say what she put him in mind of: a funeral urn.

"Really? It's not the way I remember it. But that is what 'carnal' means, isn't it? Is that what it's usually like? For you, I mean?"

"There's generally a little more response. There have to be two animals involved, if you want results."

Boa laughed. It was rusty, and she couldn't sustain it, but it was a real laugh.

"I laughed," she said, in her next breath. "And I'm so . . ." She raised both her hands and pressed the fingers together. ". . . inexpressibly relieved!"

"Well, that's anatomy for you."

"Oh, not just physically relieved. Though perhaps that is the more important aspect, at last. But I'd worried so. About having no *feelings*. No earthly feelings. I didn't think I'd be able to sing again, without feelings. But if I can laugh. . . . You see?"

"Good. I'm glad you can laugh. Maybe it was my kiss that did the trick. Just like the fairy tale. Almost like it, anyhow."

She let her hands rest, one atop the other, on her stomach. "I don't feel tired now. I'll tell you about my life in the beyond, if you like."

"So you won't have to wait till tomorrow to leave?"

She smiled, and it was, though faint, a real smile, not the simulation she'd been practising. "Oh, you'll have months of me. How can I sing in this condition? And months are a long time here, aren't they? They're not, in the beyond. Time is quite beside the point."

"Fifteen years just go by in a flash?"

"Thirteen did. That's what I'm trying to explain."

"I'm sorry. Tell your story. I won't interrupt." He put his coat on the hook, pulled the chair a bit closer to her bed, and sat down.

"I was caught in a trap, you see. That first night, after I left my body, I was so . . . delighted." She spoke with a peculiar fervor, with the sudden, illumined lucidity of martyrdom. The present, flesh-encumbered moment vanished in the blaze of a remembered noon. "I flew out of the hotel and up, and the city, beneath me, became a kind of

294

slow, ponderous, magnificent firework display. It was a cloudy night, without stars, so that, very soon, the city became the stars, some still, some moving. The longer I looked, the clearer it became, and vaster too, and more orderly, as though each node of light were laboring to explain itself, to tear itself up out of the darkness and . . . and kiss me. Though not like your kiss, Daniel. Really, I don't think it can be explained. It was such an immensity of beauty." She smiled, and held up her hands to mark off some twelve inches. "Bigger than this."

"And you didn't want to leave it in order to come back to the hotel and nurse my wounded ego. That's natural enough."

"I did though, reluctantly. You were still singing, and I could tell, you wouldn't make it. You weren't even near the edge. You are now. But you weren't then."

"Thanks for the Band-Aid. But do go on. You returned to the starry night. And then?"

"The hotel was near the airport. The planes coming in and out seemed, in a comic way, irresistible. Like elephants dancing in a circus. And the sound they made was like Mahler, pulverized and homogenized. It seemed *objectively* fascinating, though I suppose there was a fascination, underlying that, of a different nature. For what I did that night was follow one of these planes back to Des Moines. It was the same plane we'd come in, as a matter of fact. From Des Moines it was easy to find Worry. I was there by morning. I knew you'd be furious that I wasn't back yet. I knew I'd made us miss our flight to Rome."

"Providentially."

"None of that mattered. I was determined to see my father. To see him as he really was. That had always been my obsession, and that part of me hadn't changed."

"So did you get to see him naked?"

"It was moral nakedness I was after."

"I know that, Boa."

"No, I never did. I saw him get up on the day after our wedding, eat breakfast, talk to Alethea about the stables, and then he went into his office. I tried to follow. And never made it, of course. I was caught in the fairy-trap in the corridor."

"You must have known it was there."

"I didn't believe it could harm me. There didn't seem to be any limit to what I could do. I felt like some giant unstoppable wave. I believed I could have anything I wanted just by wanting it. Flying is like that. The only thing was, when I saw the trap, or heard it, rather, for one's first sense of it is of a kind of siren song played on a tuning fork, far, far away and posing no possible danger . . . when I heard it, *that* was what I wanted, what my soul lusted for. Whoever designed the thing is someone who has flown, who knows the sweetest sensations of flight and how to magnify them and draw them out. The damned machine is irresistible."

"A little rotary engine that spins round and round like a clothes dryer?"

"Oh, it is easy to resist the lure of ordinary machinery. As easy as refusing a piece of candy. But this bore no relation to anything except, possibly, the solar system itself. There were wheels within wheels, and sets of wheels within sets of wheels, in an infinite recession. One moved through them, flew through them, with a kind of mathematical exultation, a steady unfolding of 'Eurekas!', each one pitched, so to speak, an octave higher than the last."

"It sounds better than television, I've got to admit."

"It was like that too: a drama whose plot always became more interesting. Like a game of contract bridge that was, at the same time, a string quartet. Like a test you couldn't fail, though it stretched you to your limit."

"It must have been a great vacation."

"They were the thirteen happiest years of my life."

"And then?"

"The tv was turned off. I can still remember the dismay of that moment, as the thing ground down to a stop, and I became aware of where I was and what I'd done. I wasn't alone, of course. There had been hundreds of us whirling in the same ring-dance, dosie-do, and then ker-plunk. The spell was broken, and there we were, reeling a little still, but beginning to remember. And wishing the dead machine would start up again and sweep us back up into its lovely gears."

"Had your father turned it off then?"

"He? No, never. A mob had broken into Worry. A large

mob by the look of the damage they'd been able to do. I never saw the fighting. By the time I'd mustered some purpose and worked my way out of the trap, the National Guard was in charge, so I know nothing about my rescuers, neither their reasons nor what became of them. Perhaps they'd all been killed."

"It was never in the news."

"My father doesn't like publicity."

"When was that?"

"The spring before last. Before the trees had budded."

Daniel nodded. "Things were pretty desperate in general around then. That was when—" He stopped short.

"When my aunt died, were you going to say? I know about that. In fact, I was there. I was here too, of course. I didn't really think you'd have wanted, or been able, to keep my body alive all that time, but I had to find out. I went to the hotel. There's a kind of cemetery on the roof, with the names of all the missing, and where we must go to find our bodies. Once I'd seen what I'd become, my only wish was to get as far from it as I could. It seemed another kind of trap. I didn't want to become . . . meat. I still felt, in a way, new-born, unfledged. For all its fascinations, one doesn't *grow* inside a trap. My own sense of it was that only a few weeks had gone by, the weeks I'd spent in Amesville after I'd got out of the trap."

"Pursuing your father still?"

"No. He'd changed. He was older, of course, and also, I thought, smaller. No, it wasn't on his account I lingered there. It was the landscape. That was as fine as ever. The skies and fields, they seemed my real parents, my source. I watched the first shoots force their way into the light, and each one was like a parable. I was a bird. In the trap I had rushed from complexity to further complexity. Now I became simpler, slower. Though I would still be overtaken by sudden alarms. One of them brought me to New York, and when I'd found this body, a worse alarm drove me away. I went to London, and after my aunt's death, fled again, this time to Villars, where I'd been sent to school. I fell in love again with the mountains and lived an eagle's life. There were many of us there, and I began to learn, from the others, that there were forces of beauty and of . . .

attraction . . . greater than the earth's. As you leave it; as you mount above the clouds, above the winds, you shrink into a pinpoint of . . . it isn't thought, it isn't sentience . . . of purpose, call it. But a purpose so pure, so . . . unearthly. . . . And then, at a certain height, you cease to be finite at all. There is no distinction of you and them, of here and there, of mind and matter."

"What is there then? Anything?"

"One joins a kind of conscious sphere with the earth at its center, and the sphere revolves. It's what, in a way, the trap had imitated."

"Is it real?"

"Who can say? It seems, at the time, the only reality. But there's something beyond even that. What I describe is the view from the threshold, as it were. I knew that, but I didn't take the next step. If I had, I wouldn't have returned. That's quite certain. Something always held me back. The present delight. But not just that. That other gravity: of the earth and its fields, of my body. This body."

"Jesus." Daniel shook his head in mournful admiration. "I'm sorry. I really am sorry."

"You needn't be. I did what I had to, no more. I wasn't ready to go farther than I did. I hadn't made a proper farewell. Now I have."

"You don't want me to come back here again?"

"Did my words betray me again? Come back again if you feel you need to. But not on my account. I've told you as much as I know how to tell."

Daniel accepted this with the politest of grimaces. Then, smiling at the absurdity of the question that had popped into his head but seeing that it was, by its very irrelevance and triviality, a small revenge for her own Olympian betrayals, he said: "Before I go then, there's one dumb question I'd like to ask you. Can you guess what it is?"

"About your parents?"

"No. *Time* magazine filled me in about them. My father's retired and a bit senile. My mother runs a restaurant, and considers me an ingrate. Aurelia works for your father, and, like him, has nothing to say about me. My other sister is married and has taken over my father's dental practice. My question was dumber than that. What did you sing the night you took off? Did you get off on the first song you sang? Was it as easy as that?"

"I remembered the dream you'd told me about, the dream you had at Spirit Lake. So I sang that song. It was the first thing that came into my head."

"'I am the Captain of the Pinafore'. You sang *that*?"

"And not even all the way through."

Daniel laughed. It seemed splendidly unfair.

"I'm sorry I asked. Well . . . good-bye, then." He took his coat from the hook on the door.

"Good-bye, Daniel. You will fly, won't you?"

He nodded, and closed the door.

He did, of course, return many times to the Clinic, and Boa never failed to be cordial. Daniel felt obliged to give his own account of the intervening years, though he doubted whether his story held any real interest for her. Mostly when they talked it was about music. Day by day she grew stronger, until at last she was strong enough to attempt departure. She offered to let him be present on the day, just as she might have asked him to see her off at a dock. He declined to do so. She had been certain she'd succeed and she did. Two weeks after she had left her body, medical support was withdrawn, according to her written instructions. Her body continued its automatic processes for another few days, and then it stopped.

Early in July her ashes were spread, secretly, from a low-flying plane, over the fields of her father's estate.

EPILOGUE

THE TURKEY WAS half raw, but when Michael, at the head of the table, declared it to be done to a turn, they all assented to the proposition in open defiance of the truth. Poor Cecelia wasn't to blame. She'd had to drive in to Amesville at noon to pick up Milly and Abe, and Milly, who had been threatening to boycott the family reunion along with her other daughter, had taken an hour to be persuaded to get in the car. By the time Cecelia got back to Unity and shoved the turkey in the oven, the dinner was doomed to failure, at least as a culinary event. If it was anyone's fault it was Daniel's, since it was because of his eight o'clock curtain that they couldn't wait till the turkey was done. Family reunions shouldn't have to be run on a timetable.

Daniel loved the house the Hendricks lived in. He wanted to move it, stuffed pike, slapdash sylvan canvas, and all, onto the stage of a theater and use it for the set of *Werther*. Behold, it would say, this is the way you must live! With coasters under drinks and African violets pining on the windowsill and mincing china statuettes and babies growing up and trying to smash the lot of it.

Daniel was entranced, and already half-in-love with his nephew and namesake, and had already begun, in an avuncular manner, to corrupt the boy, building up towers of alphabet blocks for him to knock down and then inciting everyone to clap for this display of wit and skill. Danny understood at once the nature of applause, that it represented the highest degree of adult attention one could command. He wanted more. Daniel built higher towers, spelling out longer words—TOWER, FLOWER, MANIFEST— and Danny knocked them down with the lightning-bolts of his god-like hands, and the adults continued to enjoy themselves and to applaud. Until they did at last grow restive and started talking to each other again, at which point Danny had knocked over his father's drink and had to be taken upstairs to bed.

Of the six other grown-ups at the family reunion, three were complete strangers to Daniel, though Michael, Cecelia's husband, claimed to be able to remember Daniel from the days when they'd been neighbors on Chickasaw Avenue. Daniel, trying to dredge up a reciprocal remembrance, could only produce an account of a slice of apple pie he'd received as a trick-or-treat offering from Michael's parents, the Hendricks, and the difficulty he'd had eating it through the mouth-hole of his mask. Actually, it had been another neighbor who'd given him that slice of pie, and the reason he remembered it so clearly was because it had been so much better than his mother's apple pie. He didn't, however, go into that.

Across the table from Daniel sat Michael's much younger brother, Jerry, and Jerry's girlfriend (his fiancée, until a week ago), Rose. Rose was (if Daniel were excepted) Amesville's first genuine phoney. *Her* color didn't come off in the bathtub. She was also a follower of N.B.C's Dr Silentius and wore a large button that said GOD IS WITHIN. Between them, Rose and Daniel had kept the table-talk limping along in the face of several massive brownouts. It wasn't that his family was being unduly hostile (except for Milly, who was); it was more the natural reticence that anyone feels who's forced to cozy up to a stranger, which after all, was the situation they were in.

Of them all Abe seemed least unstrung. He was his usual gently taciturn self. Daniel thought *Time* had been unfair to say he was senile. The only time his mind seemed distinctly to slip the tracks was when, after his second whiskey sour, he asked Daniel, in a tone of guarded inquiry, what prison had been like. Daniel gave the same evasive answer he'd given the first time his father had asked the question nineteen years ago. Prison was a disgrace and he'd rather not discuss it. To which his father replied, once again, that that was probably the wisest attitude Daniel could take. Time, Abe declared, heals all wounds.

Daniel declined, and then was compelled to accept, a ritual

second helping of the stuffing. Just as his plate was passed back to him the phone rang. Cecelia disappeared into the kitchen and returned looking disappointed.

"That was Mr Tauber," she informed Daniel. "He was making sure you were here. He said your chauffeur will be here in half an hour or so."

"His chauffeur!" Milly echoed, scathingly. "Get that." She spoke—habitually, it seemed—with her mouth full. Daniel couldn't remember her doing that when he'd known her. She seemed, in just about every way, to have become coarser. Perhaps it came of running a restaurant.

"I thought," Cecelia said, frowning (for she'd warned her mother about being sarcastic), "that it might be Aurelia. The least she could do is call up and say hello to Daniel."

"Well, I'm sure she would," said Milly, grinding pepper onto her potatoes, "if she didn't have her job to think of."

"Aurelia works for your old buddy Whiting," Abe volunteered.

"He knows that," Milly said, glaring at her husband.

"But it's about all I know," Daniel said, placatingly. "How did it happen?"

"Very simple," Cecelia answered. "She sucked up to him."

"Cecelia! Really!"

"Oh, not *physically*, Mother. But every other way she could think of. It started, actually, on the day of your wedding, Daniel. My sister isn't one to waste time. She started in on Boadicea, gushing about horses. Boadicea had to promise her that she could come out and ride one of her father's horses."

"It was perfectly *natural* for Aurelia to talk about horses. She had a passion for horses. Even Daniel should be able to remember that." Milly was determined to defend her absent daughter, if only because Aurelia had had the courage to stick to her guns and stay away from the family reunion.

"She had a passion for anything that cost money. Anyhow," Cecelia went on, relieved to have found, at last, a subject for conversation, "when we all next got together, at the memorial service for you and Boa, Aurelia's first concern was to remind Miss Whiting, the one who lives in Brazil now—"

"Alethea lives in Brazil?" Daniel asked.

Cecelia nodded impatiently. "She came right out and told her about Boadicea's promise. Well, what could they do? They invited her out there, and she did one of her numbers, and got invited back. She was out at Worry at least once a week for the rest of that summer."

"You could have gone too, if you'd wanted," Milly argued.

Cecelia disdained to reply.

"And from that she went on to become his secretary?" Daniel asked.

"*One* of his secretaries."

"Cecelia's jealous," Milly explained. "Aurelia earns approximately double what she does. Despite how many years in dental school?"

"A lifetime."

"Aurelia *is* awfully pretty," Rose explained.

"She certainly is," Abe agreed with paternal complaisance. "But so is Cecelia. Every bit as pretty. They're twins, after all."

"I'll drink to that," said Michael, and held out his empty wine glass.

Daniel, sitting next to the bottle, refilled his brother-in-law's glass.

"Let's change the subject, shall we?" suggested Cecelia. "I'm sure Daniel has all kinds of questions he's dying to ask."

"I'm sure I must, but so help me I can't think of one."

"Then I can," said Rose, holding out her glass to him. "Or have you already heard about Eugene Mueller?"

"No." The bottle was empty, so Daniel reached behind him for a fresh bottle from the bucket on the folding table. "Has Eugene returned from the dead too?"

Rose nodded. "Years and years ago. With a wife and two sons and a degree from Harvard Law School."

"No kidding."

"They even say he's going to be the next mayor. He's a real idealist. *I* think."

"If he is elected," Michael said, "he'll be the first Democrat mayor in Amesville in nearly half a century."

"Incredible," said Daniel. "Gee, I wish I could *vote* for him."

"He was a good friend of yours, wasn't he?" Jerry asked. Daniel nodded.

"And his *brother*," Rose went on, ignoring dirty looks from both Milly and Cecelia, "that is to say, his oldest brother, Carl—you knew him too, didn't you?"

Daniel popped the cork from the third bottle and managed to fill Rose's glass without spilling a drop. "We'd met," he allowed.

"Well, he's dead," said Rose with satisfaction. "A sniper got him in Wichita."

"What was he doing in Wichita?"

"He'd been called up for National Guard duty."

"Oh."

"I thought you'd like to know."

"Well, now he knows," said Milly. "I hope you're satisfied."

"That's too bad," said Daniel. He looked round the table. "Anybody else need to be replenished?"

Abe looked at his glass, which was almost empty.

Milly said, "Abe."

"I guess I've had my limit."

"I guess you have," said Milly. "You have some more, if you want, Daniel. You're probably more used to it than we are."

"That's show business, Mother. We drink it for breakfast. But in fact I've reached my limit too. I've got to go on stage in two hours."

"An hour and a half, more nearly," said Cecelia. "Don't worry—I'm keeping track."

The phone rang again just after Cecelia had passed round the dessert, which was home-made raspberry ice cream. It was tremendous ice cream, and she was back at the table before anyone had bothered to start talking again.

"Who was that?" Michael asked.

"Another crank. Best thing is just ignore them."

"You, too?" said Milly.

"Oh, they're all harmless enough, I'm sure."

"You should tell them to stuff it," said Rose militantly. "That's what I do."

"You *all* get crank phone calls?" Daniel asked.

307

"Oh, I don't get them on *your* account," Rose assured him. "It's because I'm a phoney."

"I told her not to," said Jerry morosely, "but she wouldn't listen. She never listens."

"It's a person's own business what color she is." She looked Daniel square in the eye. "Am I right?"

"Don't lay the blame on Daniel's shoulders," Milly snapped. "It was your own damned folly, and you'll just have to live with it till the stuff wears off. How long does that take, by the way?"

"About six months," said Daniel.

"Christ All-Mighty." Jerry turned to his ex-fiancée. "You said six *weeks*."

"Well, I don't intend to *let* it wear off. So there. You all act like it's a crime or something. It's not a crime—it's an affirmation!"

"I thought we'd agreed," said Cecelia, "that Rose's trip to the beauty parlor was something we weren't going to talk about."

"Don't all look at me," said Rose, who was showing some visible signs of distress. "*I* didn't bring it up."

"Yes you did," said Jerry. "You brought it up when you said about the phonecalls you'd been getting."

Rose began to cry. She left the table and went out into the living room, and then (the screen door banged) into the front yard. Jerry followed a moment later, mumbling an apology.

"What kind of phonecalls?" Daniel asked Cecelia.

"Really, it isn't worth discussing."

"There's various kinds," said Milly. "Most are just obscene in an ordinary loudmouth way. A few have been personally threatening, but you can tell they don't really mean it. I've also had a couple who said they were going to burn down the restaurant, and I reported those to the police."

"Mother!"

"And so should you, Cecelia, if you do get that kind."

"It isn't Daniel's fault if a bunch of lunatics have nothing better to do with their time than to. . . . Oh, I don't know."

"I'm not blaming Daniel. I'm answering his question."

"I was going to ask you, Daniel," said his father, with a composure that came from not having paid attention to

308

what had seemed, by the sound of it, just another squabble, "about the book you gave me. What's it called?" He looked under his chair.

"*The Chicken Consubstantial with the Egg*," said Daniel. "I think you left it in the other room."

"That's it. Kind of a strange title, isn't it? What does it mean?"

"It's a sort of popular modern-day account of the Holy Trinity. And about different heresies."

"Oh."

"When I was in prison you brought me a book by the same writer, Jack Van Dyke. This is his latest book, and it's actually rather amusing. I got him to sign it for you."

"Oh. Well, when I read it, I'll write him a letter, if you think he'd like that."

"I'm sure he would."

"I thought perhaps it was something you wrote."

"No. I've never written a book."

"He sings," Milly explained, with ill-controlled resentment. Abe's vagaries brought out her mean streak. " 'La di da and la di dee, this is living, yessiree.' "

This time it was Cecelia who got up from the table in tears, knocking over, as she did so, the folding table on which the overflow of the dinner had been placed, including the carcass of the half-cooked turkey.

Daniel regarded the idyll of the Hendricks' front yard with a wistful, megalopolitan nostalgia. It all seemed so remote and unobtainable—the pull-toy on the sidewalk, the idle water-sprinkler, the modest flower-beds with their parallelograms of pansies, marigolds, petunias, and bachelor buttons.

Milly was perfectly within her rights being pissed off with him. Not just for not having got in touch for all those years, but because he'd violated her first principles, as they were written out in this front yard and up and down all the streets of Amesville: stability, continuity, family life, the orderly handing on of the torch from generation to generation.

In his own way, Grandison Whiting was probably after pretty much the same thing. Except in his version of it, it

309

wasn't just a family he wanted, but a dynasty. At the distance from which Daniel observed it, it looked like six of one, half a dozen of the other. He wondered if it was really the only way it could be done, and thought it probably was.

"Where do you go next?" Michael asked, as though reading his thoughts.

"Des Moines, tomorrow. Then Omaha, St Louis, Dallas, and God only knows. Big cities, mostly. We're starting out in Amesville for symbolic reasons. Obviously."

"Well, I envy you, seeing all those places."

"Then we're even. I was just sitting here envying your front yard."

Michael looked out at his front yard and couldn't see much there besides the fact that the grass was getting brown from lack of rain. It always did in August. Also, the couch out here on the porch smelled of mildew, even in this dry weather. And his car was a heap. In every direction he looked there was something broken down or falling apart.

The year after he'd dropped out of St Olaf's College in Mason City, Michael Hendricks had played rhythm guitar in a country-western band. Now, at twenty-five, he'd had to relinquish that brief golden age for the sake of a steady job (he ran his father's dairy in Amesville) and a family, but the sacrifice still smarted, and the old dreams still thrashed about in his imagination like fish in the bottom of a boat that have outlasted all reasonable expectations. Finding himself, all of a sudden, the brother-in-law of a nationwide celebrity had been unsettling, had set those fish into a proper commotion, but he'd promised his wife not to seem to be looking for a handout from Daniel in the form of a job with his road show. It was hard, though, to think of anything to say to Daniel that didn't seem to lead in that direction.

At last he came up with, "How is your wife?"

Daniel flinched inwardly. Just that morning, on top of his standard argument with Irwin Tauber, he'd had a fight with him on the subject of Boa. Tauber insisted that until the tour was over they should stick to the story that Boa was still convalescing at the Betti Bailey Clinic. Daniel maintained that besides being simply the best policy, honesty would also generate further publicity, but Tauber said that death is always bad P.R. And so, as far as the world knew, the romance of the century was still a going concern.

"Boa's fine," said Daniel.

"Still in the hospital though?"

"Mm."

"It must be strange, her coming back after all that time."

"I can tell you in confidence, Michael. I don't feel that close to her any more. It's a heart-throb of a love story in theory. In practice it's something else."

"Yeah. People can go through a lot of changes in fifteen years. In less time than that."

"And Boa isn't 'people'."

"How do you mean?"

"When you're out of your body that long, you stop being altogether human."

"You fly though, don't you?"

Daniel smiled. "Who's to say I'm altogether human?"

Not Michael, evidently. He chewed on the idea that his brother-in-law was not, in some essential respect, his fellow man. There was something to it.

Far off down County Road B, in the direction of Amesville, you could see the limousine coming for Daniel.

There was a single backdrop for the show as it was being presented tonight in the auditorium of the Amesville High School, an all-purpose Arcadian vista of green hills and blue sky framed by a spatter of foliage on one side and a sprightly, insubstantial colonade on the other. It was utterly bland and unspecific, like a cheese that tastes only of Cheese, not like any particular kind, and as such was very American, even (Daniel liked to think) patriotic.

He loved the set and he loved the moment when the curtains parted, or went up, and the lights of a theater discovered him there on his stool in Arcady, ready to sing yet another song. He loved the lights. The brighter they became, the brighter he wanted them to be. They seemed to concentrate in their tireless gaze the attention of the entire audience. They *were* his audience, and he played to them, and did not, therefore, have to consider the separate faces swimming beneath that sea of light. Most of all he loved his own voice, when it threaded into the delicate tumble of other voices that swelled and subsided in his own twenty-two piece orchestra, the Daniel Weinreb Symphonette. And he was willing, at last, that this should be his life, his only life. If it were small, that was a part of its charm.

So he sang his old favorites, and they looked at him, and listened, and understood, for the force of song is that it must be understood. His mother, with a fixed smile on her face, understood, and his father, sitting beside her and tapping his foot in time to Mrs Schiff's *alla turca* march-tune, understood quite as clearly. Rose, in the next row, hiding her tape recorder under her seat (she had taped the entire family reunion as well), understood, and Jerry, watching little bubbles of colored light behind his closed eyes, understood, although a major part of his understanding was that this sort of thing wasn't for him. Far at the back of the auditorium Eugene Mueller's twelve-year-old son, who had come here in defiance of his father's strict orders, understood with a rapture of understanding, not in gleams and flashes, but as an architect might understand, in a vision of great arching spaces carved by the music from the raw black night; of stately, stated, mathematic intervals; of commodious firm delight. Even Daniel's old nemesis from Home Room 113, even the Iceberg understood, though it was a painful thing for her, like the sight of sunlit clouds beyond the iron grating of a high window. She sat there, stiff as a board in her fifth row seat, with her mind fixed on the words, especially on the words, which seemed at once so sinister and so unbearably sad, but it wasn't the words she understood, it was the song.

At last, when he'd sung all but the last number on the program, Daniel stopped to explain to his audience that though in general this was a practice of which he did not approve, he had been persuaded by his manager, Mr Irwin Tauber, to use a flight apparatus while he sang his last song for them. Perhaps he would not take off, perhaps he would: one never knew in advance. But he felt as though he might, because it felt so great to be back in Amesville among his family and friends. He wished he could explain

312

all that Amesville meant to him, but really he couldn't begin to, except to say that there was still more of Amesville in him than of New York.

The audience dutifully applauded this declaration of loyalty.

Daniel smiled and raised his arms, and the applause stopped.

He thanked them.

He wanted them, he said, to understand the wonder and glory of flight. There was nothing, he declared, so glorious, no ecstasy so sublime. What was it, he asked rhetorically, to fly? What did it mean? It was the act of love and the vision of God; it was the highest exaltation the soul can reach to; it was, therefore, paradise; and it was as *real* as the morning or the evening star. And anyone who wanted to fly could do so at the price of a song.

"The song," he had written in one of his songs, "does not end," and though he had written that song before he'd learned to fly himself, it was true. The moment one leaves one's body by the power of song, the lips fall silent, but the song goes on, and so long as one flies the song continues. He hoped, if he were to leave his own body tonight, they would remember that. The song does not end.

That wasn't the song he meant to sing now, however. The song he was going to sing now was 'Flying'. (The audience applauded.) The Symphonette started its slow ripply introduction. Daniel's assistant wheeled the gimmicked flight apparatus on-stage. Daniel hated the thing. It looked like something from the bargain corner of a mortuary showroom. Irwin Tauber had designed it himself, since he didn't want anyone else but himself and Daniel to know that the wiring was rigged. Tauber might be a whiz at electronics but as a designer he had negative flair.

Daniel was wired into the apparatus. It felt like sitting in a chair that was tipping over. That was so that when he pretended to go limp he wouldn't fall on his face.

He rested his hand lightly on the armrest. With his thumb he felt for the hidden switch under the satin on the armrest. Even now, he didn't *have* to use it. But he probably would.

He sang. "We're dying!" he sang.

We're dying!
We're flying
Up to the ceiling, down to the floor,
Out of the window, and down to the shore.

We're ailing!
We're sailing
Over the ocean, down to the sea,
Into the tempest, across a cup of tea.

We're sowing!
We're flowing
Down through the sewer, out with the tide,
And in at the gate that yawns so wide.

We're dying!
We're flying
Up to the ceiling, down to the floor,
Out of the window, and in at the door.

Like a sudden flood the Symphonette swept him into the chorus. Despite being strapped down to the apparatus, he was singing beautifully.

Flying, sailing, flowing, flying:
While you're alive there's no denying
That flying and sailing and flowing and flying
Are wiser and saner and finer pursuits
Than cheating and lying and selling and buying
And trying to fathom . . . a fathomless truth.

He repeated the chorus. This time, as he came to the last line, at the caesura, he applied the lightest of pressures to the switch on the armrest, and at the same moment closed his eyes and ceased to sing. The Symphonette finished the song by themselves.

The dials of the apparatus showed that Daniel was in flight.

It was the moment Mrs Norberg had been waiting for. She stood up, in her fifth row seat, and took aim with the revolver she had concealed, the evening before, in the upholstery of her seat. A needless precaution, for there had been no security check at the door.

The first bullet lodged in Daniel's brain. The second ruptured his aorta.

Later, when, preliminary to her sentencing, the judge was to ask Mrs Norberg why she had killed Daniel Weinreb, she would reply that she had acted in defense of the system of free enterprise. Then she placed her right hand on her breast, turned to the flag, and recited the Pledge of Allegiance. "I pledge allegiance," she declared, with her voice breaking and tears in her eyes, "to the flag of the United States of America, and to the republic for which it stands, one nation under God, indivisible, with liberty and justice for all."